Praise for Elizabeth Gill

'A wonderful book, full of passion, pain, sweetness, twists and turns. I couldn't put it down'
Sheila Newberry, author of *The Gingerbread Girl*

'Original and evocative – Elizabeth Gill is a born storyteller'
Trisha Ashley

'An enthralling and satisfying novel that will leave you wanting more'
Catherine King

'Drama and intrigue worthy of *Call the Midwife*'
Big Issue

'An enchanting read for all true romantics'
Lancashire Evening Post

'Elizabeth Gill writes with a masterful grasp of conflicts and passions hidden among men and women of the wild North Country'
Leah Fleming

Elizabeth Gill was born in Newcastle upon Tyne and as a child lived in Tow Law, a small mining town on the Durham fells. She has been a published author for more than thirty years and has written more than forty books. She lives in Durham City, likes the awful weather in the northeast and writes best when rain is lashing the windows.

Also by Elizabeth Gill

Available in paperback and ebook

Miss Appleby's Academy

The Fall and Rise of Lucy Charlton

Far From My Father's House

Doctor of the High Fells

Nobody's Child

Snow Angel

The Guardian Angel

Available in ebook only

Shelter from the Storm

The Pit Girl

Under a Cloud-Soft Sky

Paradise Lane

The Foxglove Tree

The Hat Shop Girl

The Landlord's Daughter

. . . and many more!

The Quarryman's Wife

Elizabeth Gill

Quercus

First published in Great Britain in 2018
This edition published in 2018 by

Quercus Editions Ltd
Carmelite House
50 Victoria Embankment
London EC4Y 0DZ

An Hachette UK company

A CIP catalogue record for this book is available from the British Library

PB ISBN 978 1 78648 265 5
EBOOK ISBN 978 1 78648 266 2

10 9 8 7 6 5 4 3 2 1

Typeset by CC Book Production
Cover design by Debbie Clement

Printed and bound in Great Britain by Clays Ltd, Elcograf S.p.A.

For the people of Halifax, Nova Scotia. For Christine Barbour, who not only took me to her favourite restaurants but invited me into her home and introduced me to her friends. For the people who own and run and work at The Waverley Hotel where I stayed and wrote for seventeen nights. They gave me the Oscar Wilde room, complete with exquisite antique desk. For the taxi driver, who had been one of the Vietnamese boat people and lives now in a free land. For those people who were brave enough to leave their homes, many learning a new language, in order to reach this beautiful and blessed place. Thanks to all of you for your many kindnesses to me. I did enjoy myself.

One

Stanhope, Weardale. 1857.

It took Nell Almond a fortnight after her husband died before she burst into tears. She had thought she wasn't going to cry. She was so busy carrying out her husband's last wishes with the help of the new solicitor, Jos Calland, that she made no time for herself.

Harold had been very specific in the things that he wanted her to do. She was to dismiss the two managers from the limestone quarry which was the family's livelihood and the biggest in the dale, because the new manager would be there as soon as he was contacted, the will assured her. She had therefore written to Bernard Lennox the day after the funeral, the man her husband had chosen to take over from him, and was expecting an answer any day now. She did not feel bad about Daniel, her son-in-law, who had served her badly, but she felt guilty about Zeb Bailey, the undermanager. He had been a good manager and the woman he was to marry, Miss Alice Lee, who kept the sweet shop in Stanhope, had been very kind to Nell when she had most needed it.

The trouble was, that two days after the funeral, Miss Lee came to the house and asked if Mrs Almond would see her. Nell was inclined to say no, but when she had needed somebody to take care of her grandchild, Miss Lee had helped, and so she could not turn the woman away without an audience, brief though it must be.

Even before the woman entered the room, Nell was angry. This was the person who had taken in a murderer, to the horror of the village, and now she was going to marry him. He had killed another man on the street just below this house and had served nine years in prison. Alice Lee had ignored what everybody else said and thought, and Nell could not believe that Miss Lee had the audacity to come here and beg for Zeb Bailey's job as undermanager at the quarry.

It was only then that Nell knew the resentment she had always felt for Alice Lee had turned to hate. Alice had taken Arabella's baby when Arabella had died giving birth to it, and at Nell's insistence given the child to Shirley McFadden, a quarryman's wife, to keep and nurse. It had been the right thing to do, but the time had long since arrived for Shirley to give Frederick back to his grandmother, who now had no one. Nell shuddered at the thought and then drew in her breath as Alice Lee came into her drawing room.

Miss Lee was always something of a surprise. She was tall and skinny and pale-faced and plain, and Nell had never really liked her. She was a good deal too sure of herself, as though she thought herself cleverer than other women, and Nell thought that a good many women, despite the fact that Miss Lee ran the sweet shop, probably felt the same way.

She said how sorry she was at Mrs Almond's loss, and how awful it must be for her to lose both her husband and her only child so quickly, but she didn't understand why her intended bridegroom had been dismissed.

'He did nothing wrong,' she said.

Nell was offended and did not offer her a seat. She felt queenly in this room, because it was hers. Her husband had intended it to be the best room in their new house and so it was. She and Arabella had picked out the green and pink furnishings and when she sat here she could hear Arabella's laughter and almost see her just beyond the door.

Every time she thought of her only child it made her want to weep. She had lost both her husband and her daughter in a matter of months, and she felt as if she could no longer hold herself up, no longer endure what God had thought fitting to burden her with. There was a saying that God only gave people that which they could bear. Nell thought it was the biggest lie that she had ever heard.

Arabella's ghost was always ahead of her, so that no matter which room Nell was in, Arabella had just left, or so it seemed to her. Sometimes she thought she was going mad. She felt for her husband in the night, but his side of the bed was cold and empty and the bed was huge without him. After he had died, she had kept a lot of lights burning, because she had the feeling that he was trying to get back to her, but she couldn't see him either.

'You should not have come here in such a way,' Nell said now to her unwelcome visitor. 'I'm sure you think that I owe you for what you did for us when Daniel Wearmouth behaved so badly, but you cannot have what you want. You could have spared your legs and not climbed the hill so very far to reach me.'

'I thought I would try.'

'It's not a question of what Zebediah Bailey has done. My husband's last wish was that the two managers should leave the quarry. This is not of my doing and there is nothing I can do about it in all conscience. I have to obey his wishes, I am his widow.' She hated the very word. 'A new manager will be arriving any day now and Mr Bailey must get on as best he can.'

She thought it was a dignified speech, though if she had heard it from anyone else she would have known it to be pompous.

Miss Lee tried again and Nell resented it. This woman was beneath her in every way and had no right to remain when any decent woman would have heard Nell's last remark and known it for the end of the interview.

'No one will take him after you have dismissed him in such a way. Does that not seem unjust to you?'

'That is not my problem, Miss Lee, and since you are not yet married I hardly think you should come here like this. My husband took on Zebediah Bailey when nobody else would, when he came back here from prison, and you, most ill-advisedly, took him into your household. He was lucky then. Don't ask for anything more. People left you your respectability in spite of your actions.'

'If he has no job we will never be married. Surely you wouldn't rob me of that.'

'You will have to excuse me,' Nell said, beginning to tremble beneath the onslaught of Miss Lee's words. 'I'm sure you know that I have a great deal to do. Norah will see you out.'

She went upstairs where she could not be followed, hating Alice Lee for having had the sheer nerve to say such things. She stayed there, trying not to think about the future. Mr Lennox was married. Perhaps his wife and children could be persuaded to come here and live in Ash House, and she would move right away, to somewhere civilized like Hexham.

She could rent a pretty house and would be able to live well on what Harold had left her. She would go to the abbey on Sundays and pick up such acquaintances as she had had when she used to take Arabella there to dances, when they would stay over at a good hotel and wear lovely dresses and they would dance and her husband would tell her that she was and always would be his only love. The anger she felt now because of Miss Lee coming there when she should not have done made her feel better, aided her such as sorrow had not.

'Where did you go when you went out?' Zeb asked Alice when she got back to the sweet shop. She'd hoped he would not been there when she returned, had wished he would go for a walk as he so often did, having nothing better to do. He was too astute not to know what she had done.

She was angry, not with him but with herself. She should never have gone to Mrs Almond. She ought to have known that the woman would not help her.

'Alice?'

She looked straight at him. It was not always easy. She thought he had the world's coldest black eyes, and though she knew she had helped him so much, she found it difficult to face him like this, especially when she had done something that he would think was not right. She had rescued this man from dying, given him everything she could, and yet she never felt sure of him. There was a part of him that remained untouched, aloof – not just from her, but from everyone and everything. She wanted so much to make him hers; she wanted them to marry and have a family. She wanted to bring him back to life as only she could.

'I went to see Mrs Almond,' she said levelly. 'I wanted her to give you your job back.'

He glared at her. Alice went on meeting his gaze and was brave enough to carry on. 'We cannot get married until you have a job, that's what you said.'

'And you thought you could do it?' His tone, she thought, was scathing, but she would not back off.

'I thought it was worth a try.'

'You shouldn't have.' He was right, she thought, men expected their wives not to do such things. And then her anger corrected itself.

'What am I supposed to do, wait until I'm fifty?'

'It won't take that long.'

'I hope not, because I want to have children and I'm nearly forty. I cannot afford to wait much longer.'

'How could I marry you when I'm useless?'

'You are not useless.' She could hear her voice and she was shouting, from frustration and also from him telling her what she should and shouldn't do. She wanted to tell him that he had no right, but that was not true either. He had asked to marry her and she had agreed, but that had been before he lost his position at the quarry.

'Alice, today I have brought in the logs and coal. I have kept the fires going in the house but after that you and Susan have done everything. What use am I? Do you want to marry me like that? What if I never get a job?'

'That is the point,' Alice said. 'I want us to be married.'

'Well, you aren't going to do it by going up there to see Mrs Almond. The way things are, I could be sleeping with my father and you could be sleeping with Susan for the next thirty years.'

'That's nonsense,' Alice said, but Zeb didn't wait. She called his name but all she got in return was the slamming of the back door.

If he comes back drunk I will kill him, she thought, and then she felt sorry for both of them. He was too proud to marry her when he had no work and was therefore making no money, but although she understood that and even admired it, she was running out of time if they were to be a real family with children. She had spent many hours thinking of their sons and daughters. The dream was too real for her to give up on it now.

She had planned the wedding, been ready to go to the rector and talk about it, imagined herself in a pretty dress, but most of all she had thought of herself in bed with the man she loved, the man she wanted so much it made her cheeks burn with blushes and her body ache with need.

She was desperate for a child. She could see herself behind the counter of the sweet shop for the rest of her life, and while that had once been enough, it was no longer. She wanted him in her bed and at her table and out all day at work, so that he would come back to her, and she wanted his children. She wanted the normality she had never had. She had always thought her greatest passion was for her work, but nothing had ever mattered to her as much as her future with him.

She listened for a long time, but he didn't come back. Susan slept. Alice had left a lamp downstairs for Zeb's father, who was usually late back from the Vernons, where he helped Mr Vernon with the local newspaper, but she heard his father come back and, no doubt thinking that nobody else would still be out, brought it upstairs with him.

When he reached his bedroom he would know that his son was not there, but it was too late by then, Alice thought, trying not to care. She waited and listened for him coming back, and when he did it was so late that she tried to pretend she was asleep but couldn't. She heard him close the door very softly.

She trod downstairs with a candle and saw him in what light there was on such a dark night, nothing but shadows. He said in a hard voice, as though he had thought long on it and decided he was wrong, 'I'm sorry, Alice, will you forgive me? I want us to be married. I want us to be together but I have to make some money first.'

All Alice could say was, 'Did you go to the pub?'

'Nothing that sensible,' he said, with a small lilt in his voice, which told her that everything was going to be all right. 'After so much that you've done for me, I couldn't even be kind.'

Alice tried to speak but couldn't. All she knew was that she loved him more than anybody had ever loved anybody else in the entire history of the world. She tried to tell him something sensible and couldn't think of anything. She couldn't help herself any longer. Putting down the candle, she ran at him as though he was about to disappear forever and when she reached him he gathered her into his arms so surely that her feet left the floor.

He smelled of cold air and icy river but his mouth was warm. His lips were sweet and she couldn't let go. He pulled off his coat while keeping her close and by then she was clinging. Forty years was an awfully long time not to have a lover, she thought, and after that there was no help for what had been her innocence.

All she wanted was his mouth and then all she wanted was the feel of his hands on her body and for her fingers to slick themselves over him, and then she wanted more and more and by the time he had divested himself of coat, hat, gloves, scarf and boots, they were down on the rug by the fire and she wanted to feel all of him against her and even then she was not happy.

She was happier when he was free of his clothes and she could feel his smooth skin, the heat of his body so close, as near as he could be. The rest was rather a shock in a way, but somehow it was good like chocolate, like the best chocolate in the whole of the world. She knew that exactly, and how to make it and how to make it so important to people that they craved it and had to have it, and how they came back again and again because it was so sweet and so necessary.

This was not just necessary, it was vital, and she was alive like never before. Though the fire had almost died it was warm down there with him, in his arms. She thought she had loved him so much before, but she had not been in love with him as she was now. She felt as if she would never deny him anything again, no matter what the cost.

If he died she would die with him, and while he lived she would be there. She saw their children, how his sons and daughters would be so much like him and so much like her and how they would laugh together over this.

She saw it all and held him there so tightly in her arms that she knew he would never go to another woman. She was all-powerful; she was queen of the moment and he was everything to her now. She would go through fire and water for him. She adored him; he was the best of all men in this time and in the time to come and forever.

Two

Nell knew that she must stick to her husband's wishes. He had known the quarry best and would know now what to do. She would employ the man her husband had wanted and as long as he did not interfere in her personal affairs she would abide by her husband's decision. She felt bad for the men, but she couldn't stand to have Daniel Wearmouth running her quarry, trying to take it for his as he had taken everything else, so she was satisfied in getting rid of him.

He had married her daughter after jilting Susan, and Arabella had died less than a year into the marriage, having his child. Worst of all, he had gone back to Susan and married her soon after Arabella died. It led Nell to think that all he had wanted from her beautiful daughter was the quarry her father owned. Daniel Wearmouth had caused so many problems. He hadn't wanted the child, and she had been obliged to send the boy away to stop Dan from doing more damage, but now she had got rid of Daniel Wearmouth. The word in the dale was that he had left the area and she felt easier for that. She hoped he never came back; she wanted never to hear anything of him again and she hoped that his new wife suffered alone for what they had done, for their greed and their disregard for anyone else or anyone else's feelings.

Now that her husband was dead, Nell heard the silence and it was harder to bear than any sound had even been. She wanted to run and run until she couldn't run any more. Even when she opened the bedroom windows at night, despite the cold wind, to hear the birdsong, it wasn't long before the birds too went to bed and once more she could hear nothing.

Dr McKenna was kind enough to visit, and when she explained this he said it was all part of the grieving process and that it would take a great deal of time to become used to her widowed state. He knew what it was like, she thought, because his wife, Iris, had died a little time ago. There had been talk in the village that he would marry again, but he looked old and tired and resigned to what life had chosen for him.

Nell didn't get better and she didn't know what to do or to whom to turn. The doctor was not her friend; indeed, she seemed to have no friends of her own. She could not go back to the friends she and Harold had had before they prospered, and neither did she fit in with the people above her, none of them had risen from nothing; all were well established in the dale. Those who had cultivated her friendship had done so for her husband's sake and nothing else. They had gone to his funeral out of respect for who he had become. Nobody came to visit.

She would go up Crawleyside Bank beyond her house

to see her grandchild, Frederick. This was her one joy. The little boy, having lost his mother to death and his father to grief, lived with one of her quarrymen, Pat McFadden, and his wife, Shirley. Nell went as often as she thought Shirley could bear it, which was not more than once a fortnight. Although she longed to see the child, she understood how Shirley might feel it to be an intrusion.

Nell wanted the child to live with her, but she could not suggest it while Shirley was still feeding the little boy. Though Nell did not think Shirley was feeding him any longer, Shirley would make it as difficult as she could, because she didn't want to have to give up the boy. As the weeks went by, Nell was more and more inclined to suggest a date that Frederick might return to Ash House. He was, after all, the heir to the quarry and would have everything that was hers.

Shirley was not openly hostile, but it was obvious she did not like having Nell there. Nell wanted to say that this child was all she had left, but Shirley had the opposite problem. There in that tiny terraced house, she lived with her husband, his parents and two small girls.

There was so little space that Nell was tempted to give McFadden a bigger house, but she felt she couldn't. Pat, although he was in charge of the quarry at the moment, knew that his position was temporary, and it was difficult enough without her doing him favours that might be short-lived.

Nell tried to give Shirley money, but Shirley was too proud to take it. Nor could Nell put up Pat's wages, though she knew she should recompense him for what he was doing. It was a very difficult situation. The new quarry manager was due any day and Pat would go back to his usual job among the rest of the men.

Nell was never asked if she wanted to hold the baby, and the few times she did he cried so much that she had to give him back to Shirley almost immediately. Nell thought it pleased Shirley that the boy's instincts were to go to the only mother he had known. Nell therefore hated going. She could not even take a cake, since Shirley, like all the dales women, made wonderful cakes.

Her house smelled of stale urine and sweet baking. It always took Nell the rest of the day to get the smell out of her nostrils. She would go back to Ash House, a single room of which could hold Pat's entire home, and hate how huge it had become to her.

She felt as though the space and silence mocked her, and yet she shuddered when she thought of how thin and pale and tired and badly dressed Shirley was. It seemed as though the giving was all on one side.

The child changed every time Nell saw him, and she resented not seeing him each day and being part of his life. To her dismay, he looked so much like Daniel. She tried to comfort herself that children altered, looking in vain for a glimpse of her daughter, her husband and even, grudgingly, the brother who had been her favourite, Tommy.

She hadn't seen her brothers in thirty years. None of them had bothered with her after she had left her home. They had not turned up at her wedding, though they had been asked. Brian, the eldest, had declared she was marrying a fool and he wouldn't stand in the same room as Harry Almond. When she thought of Tommy she remembered how he had always worshipped and followed what Brian said and did. That hurt her most of all.

Over the years she had stopped looking for sight of them whenever she was in the area around Cowshill and Killhope, the places where she and Tommy had spent their childhood by the streams and in the hills. She had a much better life now, though it lacked the affection she had known from Tommy. But her brothers had grown up to be greedy, inward-looking and insensitive.

She was a sister and therefore did not matter and could be discarded like old clothes, cast off, no longer fit for wearing. She hoped that they envied her rise to prosperity, but even in her loneliness she never once thought about Tommy with anything other than ragged bitterness.

Nell kept remembering Arabella's first words and how she had pulled herself up by the kitchen table leg and how excited Nell had been, rushing to tell her husband when he came in from work. He had been the complete opposite of her brothers. He was kind and loving, constant and clever. She missed him more every day.

And he had never talked of wanting a son. He had adored Arabella, lifting her high in the air, watching her laugh. She wished that he had died before Arabella. She would have given much for him not to see his only child die in pain, but she was glad also that he knew of the little boy. The quarry would have an heir. She reminded herself of it each time she saw the child.

It was difficult to hear her grandson referred to as 'Freddie' and to see him in handed-down clothes in a house without books, music or anything fine, but Nell remained more than civil to Shirley. The debt was huge and she never would be able to repay it, so she could ask for nothing.

The one time she had taken sweets for the children, Shirley refused them, saying she would not have such muck near her children. Her words were accurate, Nell had to admit, but savage, and another indication that Nell was not welcome in her house. Her children were clean-limbed and bonny, despite their washed-out clothes. As far as Nell could see they lived mostly on vegetables, bread, cheese and fish, which being near the river was plentiful and cheap.

Meat was rabbit. She knew how it smelled and how once it was skinned it looked almost like a small dead child.

In the back garden, besides the vegetables and the rhubarb, Shirley kept hens, so she had both eggs for every day and chicken for special occasions, and Nell sometimes saw her halfway down the bank gathering blackberries or in the nearby fields in the early morning looking for mushrooms. The image of Shirley carrying the little boy in her arms, the small girls at her sides, stayed in Nell's head. Shirley, though poor, had so much. She was rich and had so little.

She had once asked Shirley to her house, had told her she could come often, but Shirley merely shook her head and said she had too much to do, and it was true. Shirley was burdened in one way and Nell in another.

Three

Susan Wearmouth had run after her new husband, Dan, through the ice and snow. She ran fast, not fearing that she might fall, she was so keen to make sure she caught him before he got on the train to take him away from her. They had treated one another badly but she knew now that she loved him, that despite having wanted to marry Charles Westbrooke, Daniel was her first love and she had punished him enough by refusing to let him sleep with her on their wedding night. At the time she had felt justified: she was getting back at him for jilting her and marrying the quarry owner's daughter. He had cared more for money and comfort than he had for her. She could not forgive him, but she knew that she had gone too far, and he had left. She would never stop loving him, she knew that now, and as she ran she cried, and what with the crying and the running and the breathing she kept stumbling and having to stop.

She had not thought that he would go. She had thought that he would wait until she had forgiven him and they could learn to be better to one another.

Charles was just a distant memory now. She had been

desperate for another love after Dan married Arabella, and, as a Methodist preacher, Charles was kind and wise, but he too had turned out to be false and had left her. What was it about her that men always ran from her? What had she done that was so awful?

Charles had returned to the Lake District and married his dead brother's widow, as far as she knew. The only way forward for her now was to get Dan back and to try for a little of the happiness that had so far eluded her.

She had to catch him; she didn't know where he was going. Perhaps he wouldn't stay in the area – he might go north into Scotland and she would never see him again. She ran and ran until she was out of breath but it was almost three miles to the station and she was crying and breathing very hard before she got halfway there.

The train had gone. There was nobody about. The stationmaster's office was closed. There would be no more trains that day, the notice told her. The snow was blowing sideways and soon there would be no visible line, no evidence of anything real and therefore no traffic. It might be days before there was another train, she knew from past experience.

Susan began to make her way home, but she had still about a mile and a half of the six-mile journey when she saw someone coming towards her. It was Zeb Bailey. She had rarely been so glad to see anyone. He took her heavy bag from her and she said what he could see.

'I missed the train.'

'There'll be another one,' he tried to comfort her. 'He'll be in touch.'

'What if he isn't?'

'He said he will.'

'Why couldn't he tell me? Why did he just go like that? I know I was so awful to him, but I didn't think this would happen.'

Zeb said nothing to that. They walked back towards the village, the snow collecting until their boots made marks in it as they covered ground.

When they got to the village he made as if to take her to the house by the river, where she and Dan had gone two days since, after their wedding, but she panicked at the idea of being there alone after what had happened. The sickness rose in her throat and the tears stung her eyes at how awful she felt, how guilty, how mistreated. She needed comfort; she needed someone to tell her that she was not to blame, that she had been justified in her behaviour towards Dan. She had never forgiven him for how she had felt, sitting in the garden at the back of the sweet shop, on the day of his wedding to Arabella Almond, how cheap and worthless he had made her feel. The villagers talked of nothing else for months afterwards and everywhere she went she thought they looked curiously at her. It had made her face burn and she had hated waiting on in the shop, for she felt they came there only to increase her discomfort.

'I want to go back to Miss Lee.'

He hesitated, but she went off down the passage from the front street and in at the back door of the sweet shop and then she threw herself at Alice.

'He's gone. I may never see him again.'

'Of course you will.'

'Can I stay here with you? I hate that house.' And Susan detached herself from Alice's embrace and ran up the stairs.

Nobody looked at anybody. All Zeb's father, John, said was, 'Miss Vernon is expecting me for a poetry reading.' And he went off, collecting his hat, his coat and putting on his boots before stepping out into what was by now thick snow.

The Misses Vernon lived just a few doors along. Their brother ran the local newspaper and they were the people cultivating the arts in Stanhope. They had a huge house and there local artists and poets and a great number of readers gathered almost every day. They had their own library, which contained a great many of John Wesley's books, but also science, nature, art and great works of literature.

Alice always sent cake with him, and he beamed at her as she put into his arms a newly iced chocolate cake, humming a Charles Wesley hymn under his breath.

Four

Leaving Shap in Westmorland was the best thing that Mary Blaimire had ever done, even with her mistress so very poorly. Mary wasn't sure whether it was the damned bairn she was with, or shock and tiredness, but Lady Catherine slumped in the hard seat and barely recognized the shudder of the train when it pulled away from the station.

Lady Catherine. It made Mary want to laugh at the sound of it. This young woman had disgraced herself so badly that her parents had been disgusted. She had managed to get herself pregnant by a man who preferred other men to women. How in the name of hell she did it, nobody knew but Mary. She had loved him, she had thought that he was hers, and they had been betrothed and she had been happy. Like many a woman in love before her, she had given herself to him – and then he had done whatever thing it was that men did to one another and he did it at a local public house where everybody knew what was done.

How stupid of him, Mary thought. He could not get anything right. Neither could his brother, Charles, who had run away from his home and his title. Henry had so obviously known his own nature and yet had ruined this girl's happiness. So much for aristocrats, Mary thought.

Mary was relieved that her father and Ned bloody King hadn't found them before they got this far. Every minute since they had left she thought they would be discovered, and she could feel her heart beating so hard that she feared it would crash beyond her flesh and somehow clunk to the floor of the train. She sat rigid for the first few miles and even then she could not relax. The train seemed slow to her.

From Penrith they took the train that was going to Barnard Castle over the moors. She didn't know that at the time – she just wanted to get Catherine onto the first train that would take them away, and though she hadn't heard of this place, according to the people standing next to her on the platform it was right across the middle of the country and into Teesdale. That would do for them – the further the better.

The day got as bright as it was going to, considering it was winter, and though Catherine was pale she slept. Mary wondered what it would be like if Catherine miscarried on a train, but Catherine didn't say that she was hurting, and she wouldn't have held back – folk like her never did.

Mary remembered her mother losing two bairns at once, and her father had been damned glad of it, so he said, because it would have been two more mouths to feed and they would be girls, all of them were. Her mother had been glad, too, but not of the pain and the blood and how she could not go to her bed because there was always too much to do and if Mary's father had found her in bed or even resting he would have pulled her out.

You were not allowed to ail of anything; you were never allowed to be tired. You had to find occupation, even if he was sitting on his bony arse, smoking by the fire. He was a bugger, Mary thought, and the train seemed to take on the rhythm of the word – *bugger, bugger, bugger* – as it took them away from Westmorland, the place she vowed she would never go back to.

The journey went on all day, and the odd time that she fell asleep she could see in her dreams Ned and her father finding them, and how she would be treated.

Catherine would be made to go back and marry the brother of the man she had loved and lost, and God knew what they would do to her, since she had tried to escape marriage. Her father had a temper. And for her waited Ned, nothing but a stable lad, though her father said he would do better. She would never go back, she vowed it now. She would rather die.

And in any case, if she did go back her father would kill her because she had disgraced the family and his so-called wonderful name. He would be ashamed of her, and you were not allowed to make him ashamed. You were not allowed to cross him even in speech. Mary had been knocked off her feet often as a small child, and had learned to stay out of reach and away from his hard words. She had hated his very presence.

Ned had horrible big red lips and brown teeth which seemed to get past them like some sort of small rodent, an appearance accentuated by his sharp nose and tiny black eyes. He was little and skinny and when he looked at her breasts he always slobbered and his eyes grew little and piggy and the sweat stood out on his forehead and he fingered his trousers when his cock turned up at seeing her.

It was enough to make you throw up all over the place. He smelled of the stables. Mary had never liked horses because of it, which wasn't fair to the horses who didn't smell like him.

The train reached Barnard Castle, and the next train after that was apparently going to Durham. It was another place she had not heard of, but it was further away so she dragged Catherine onto it. Catherine was so tired by then that she barely heard Mary, and it was not just the journey. Catherine too was running away, and she had had to put up with a good deal. Today she was meant to be marrying the brother of the man she had loved. Henry Westbrooke was dead, hope was lost and they must leave if they were to survive, they both knew it.

It was a long way from Barnard Castle to Durham, but by then it was obvious to Mary that Catherine could go no further. She had gone grey in the face, her eyes were dulled and she was no longer sleeping.

'We should get off here,' Mary recommended.

'I don't think I can go anywhere,' Catherine said.

Mary urged her to her feet as the train began to screech to a halt. She didn't want to get off; she could see from the window that it had begun to snow, but they had plenty of money to secure good lodgings.

People jostled them, and as they were getting off some boys pushed at either side, and one of them knocked so hard into Catherine, Mary afterwards thought deliberately, that she staggered with the impact and the bag which she had held close against her shot into the air. The train stopped, jolted and the bag was lost to Catherine, coming down so far beyond them both that they could not reach it.

Mary had begged to carry it but Catherine wouldn't let her, and that had been fair, as Mary was carrying both the other bags and they were heavy. But Catherine was fit to carry nothing and that was when the problem occurred.

The bag split open; guineas rained golden. A string of pearls, a bracelet which glittered blue, various rings, which no doubt Catherine had hoped to pawn or sell. Within seconds, people were scrambling after this wealth, and though Mary pulled and pushed and shrieked and tried to grab anything at all, she ended up lying on the platform as other folk ran away with their booty. Catherine stood in the doorway so that a man helped her down, shaking his head and saying how awful the railways were these days, they had never been so bad.

Mary picked herself up, looking around in case anything should have been left or discarded, but though her eyes swept the entire length and breadth of the platform she could see nothing.

'Is everything gone?' she enquired, hoping Catherine had money stored in other places or on her person, though she doubted it. They were new at this and Catherine had no doubt taken what she could.

'Everything,' Catherine said, and she swayed.

Even the bag itself was no more, and Mary wanted to be bitter, saying that it had looked obvious, but it hadn't.

It wasn't special-looking, just the sort of thing you carried ordinary stuff in. Nobody was to blame.

One of Mary's bags held their clothing, the other nothing valuable. They could have done with getting rid of those, she thought, but instead they had lost their money and everything that could be turned into money. They set off down the hill from the station, on the road that presumably led into the town.

It wasn't much of a place, even as the snow covered it, she thought. It was steep and she had baggage and a girl who didn't look likely to carry her baby the night. Catherine kept stumbling and apologizing, but her words were slow and she was not making much sense and the snow came down thicker so that Mary couldn't see.

She began to call upon the Lord and then remembered that she had no right to. She hadn't been to church that she could ever remember. Her mother had been going through a religious phase, apparently, when she had her, and called her after Jesus' mother. There had been no religion since; her father would have nothing to do with it and hadn't seen the inside of a church since he was married, he was fond of boasting.

It was a long time before they got onto flat ground, and there seemed to be nowhere open. The lights were out in the houses they went past. On her right she could hear the sound of a tumbling river. One of the houses had no lights, but when they got nearer the outside door was ajar.

She had to get Catherine out of the night so she pushed the door open further and hastened the lady inside. For the first time now she was afraid, and almost wished herself at home, and then she remembered Ned King and how he was always urging her to get her tits out and she felt better about being here.

The snow obligingly stopped and she could see the moon through the roof of the property, which was the nearest in a long street where all the buildings looked derelict, so it was not exactly snug. She shouted as she went in, but nobody replied, and she wasn't surprised – the house was in a bad way.

'You aren't in pain?' Mary asked Catherine.

'No, no, just tired. Thank you, Mary.'

She could see some kind of chair, so lowered Catherine into it. She went instantly to sleep.

Mary listened to her breathing, was reassured, and put down the bags. She listened but there was no one about. Besides, how could they be robbed any further? She had but two pounds, and felt guilty because she had held back this money when she should have given it to her mother for the younger children. But she had known that her mother could not save her from her father or from marrying Ned King, and she had had to get out. God forgive me, she thought, my mother and sisters stuck there among such awful men.

They weren't all awful. Charles Westbrooke, who had wanted to marry Catherine, was lovely, she thought, and she would have married him in a second. He was kind, generous and rich. All right, so unlike his brother, he was not particularly tall or handsome, but his brother had liked other men.

Charles had wanted to marry Catherine, and had cared

about the bloody child she was carrying with his name – men and their bloody names, Mary thought once again – yet Catherine had run. If she had stayed, would I have left by myself, Mary wondered, and then, just as she fell asleep, she thought, yes, I would have taken my two pounds and got out.

She thought a bit more about Charles Westbrooke and how much he could give the right woman. She would have settled for marrying a baronet-to-be, and she would have been a good help. He didn't even know that she was alive, but she remembered how kind he had been, not just to Catherine but to her. He was respectful and called her 'Miss Blaimire'. Nobody had ever done such a thing before. He was a real gentleman, the first she had ever met.

She awoke what felt to be every few minutes during the night. It was so damned cold and the winter gale howled through the room. In time, she promised herself, they would move into somewhere with a fire and a decent roof and even windows, but for now this would have to do.

Somehow they must make money. Catherine had been well off, never earned a penny in her life, and was having a damned baby. Mary went on worrying about all these things – more, it seemed, each time she awoke – but Catherine did not awaken and so she kept going back to sleep, comforted by the thought that she had got free of Ned and her father.

Despite their limited money, she and Catherine would somehow manage. She could not help thinking of all the golden guineas, of the necklaces and the bracelets and the rings, but it was no good.

She could have carried no more, and at least Catherine

had not lost her baby. She must be grateful for that, though between the two she would rather they had lost the baby and kept the money. It seemed mean, but Catherine did not want the child – it had cost her everything and the money would have kept them for so long. But then, she argued with herself, if it had not been for the baby they would never have got away like this, and she doubted whether she would have had the courage to leave alone, so there you were, you could never tell.

She watched the dawn as it came in late and grey, both through the partial roof and the windows, and she saw why nobody lived here.

The roof was almost gone, and there were no windows, just gaps where the glass had been, and although there were chairs, even a settee where her mistress was sleeping, the whole place had been trashed by folk hoping to gain something. There was glass all over the floor. She could never see the sense to such things. Why make it worse? Some of the furniture had been broken too; chair legs that would at least have made firewood were strewn across the floor. She resolved to pick them up in the morning and hang on to them.

Beyond the house, the river played its own song, and in time she went to see it. Snow lay on the banks as though it couldn't think of anything better to do, and across from it she could see a great big church with square towers and then lots of houses.

She was hungry. She left the house but was shocked at what she saw. She had not seen anything this poor. Most of the houses in the street, like the one they were in, were falling down at the front towards the river and at the back down a narrow and filthy lane which she could smell long before she saw it. It stank of shit, of sweat.

Some of the houses had no roofs, their walls crumbling, and nobody was about. The people were no doubt shivering in whatever hovel they contrived to call home because it was bitter here outside in the air. She could hear children crying and the loud voices of men and women quarrelling because they had too many bairns and no money, she thought, which was what her parents always fought about. If folk hadn't so many bairns and had some decent money there would be nowt to fight about, she thought. Empty bellies made for short tempers.

The river flowed beyond the street on one side, the rest of the city on the other. There were few people about and nobody spoke or even looked at her.

At the end of the road, however, she could smell baking such as she had never smelled before. It wasn't sweet, like a cake smell, more like bread, only better, and that was when she remembered how hungry she was. So she trod up a long flight of stone steps, which led to the bridge over the river.

Up there were more houses, and it was easy to smell the baking, so she made her way in among the shops on the right and there, just one along, was an open door, and the nearer she got to it the more the smell appealed, so she dodged in against a wall and took a few coins from the hoard which lay around her neck in a small bag.

Inside, the tiny house had white walls and scrubbed

worktops. A small, dark man smiled at her. The place had shelves on which she could see various kinds of bread, and the combined smell was driving saliva into her mouth.

'*Bonjour, mon enfant*,' he said.

Mary stared at him, not understanding, and he laughed.

'Good morning,' he said. He was obviously foreign, and Mary had been told not to trust foreigners, but the smell drove her on. And besides, he had a lovely warm smile and eyes as black as coal.

'You would like bread?'

'Yes, please, sir. We – we would like bread very much. It smells wonderful.'

'You are very kind. I am Monsieur Philippe.'

'Mary Blaimire, sir. There are two of us. My mistress – my friend – needs food.'

'It is what we do best. You will take café too? Coffee?'

'Oh, yes, please. We have no fire yet.'

'Ah, then you will need milk and also butter and jam for the croissants.'

Mary could do nothing but nod. She was beginning to think that it would cost her a great deal of money, but the sum he named was so small that she smiled and took from him a big plate with a knife, four sorts of small buns which were shaped like sliver moons, a big pat of butter, a mound of glistening red jam and two big cups of coffee laced with hot milk, which steamed so exquisitely that she was happy to go back to her mistress, though the tray was a burden as she retreated down the steep, narrow steps that led to the towpath and the river. She found it hard to believe that in such a godforsaken place as this, he was willing to trust her.

'And I will not forget to bring back the plates and cups, Monsewer Flip,' she called as she went out the door.

Catherine was only just awake, and Mary was able to greet her with the most delicious coffee and the delightful whatever they were – buns, light and still warm – laden with jam and butter. When both women had eaten, with many words of gratitude from Catherine, the lady seemed inclined to go back to sleep, so Mary thought she had better leave her to it. If the child was to stay where it was, she needed to rest.

Catherine's parents had treated her badly when they found out that she was pregnant. She had been through too much. Her father had beaten her so brutally that Mary was surprised she had not lost the baby. Perhaps that had been his target. She had not wept or complained, and her mother was no help, Mary thought, and she should have been. Catherine had cried in her own room, where Mary tried to comfort her.

Mary ventured further into the house and here it was better, big and quite sound. The roof was open to the sky in places but in other bits it was all right, she thought. There was another room behind the one they were sitting in and beyond that, through the hall, was a large kitchen. There had been no fire in there for a long time but the room was habitable. Nothing much was left in it, but when she ventured out into the back yard, having turned the large key in the lock and unbolted top and bottom, she discovered a coalhouse and a nettie, which thankfully was empty and clean, both locked.

There was also a well. Mary knew how to prime it, and within minutes water streamed from the outside tap. The situation wasn't that bad, she thought. Beyond it all was the back lane, shut out by a locked gate.

The coalhouse was a find. It had in it not just a big heap of coal, but logs, so enough fuel to light fires for many a day. She decided to light the kitchen fire, as she had done hundreds of times before. Luckily she found matches, though they were rather damp, so she had to use half the box, sticks and paper. She very soon heard the familiar, reassuring crackle as the kindling caught. The chimney must be good because the smoke went straight up and soon the flames were giving out heat.

Mary, having been taught by her mother to cook, bake and look after half a dozen people, could not think what to do next. She was inclined to have a look round at the place and see what it had about it.

In the first room, she found Catherine was stirring. 'I'm fine now,' she insisted.

'See to the kitchen fire then. Have you done that before, Lady Catherine?'

Catherine looked crossly at her. 'You have to call me Cate, and no, I haven't, but I dare say I will work it out.' And then her face fell as though she might cry. 'What will we do?'

'I don't know, but we aren't ever going back, so sit over there and maybe later we can venture out.'

She set off once again, but not before telling Cate not to poke up the fire too much or the coal would fall apart and burn too quickly. It needed air from the bottom of the fire, but not too much, so she should lift it a little from time to time with the poker.

Outside there was no snow, no ice and the sun was beginning to shine. The bridge was grey and sturdy and the river trundled along as though it didn't particularly have to get anywhere. She liked it, but then she thought she would have liked anywhere her father and Ned King – and her mother and her sisters and all her life in Shap – were not. This could be her place.

She hurried back up the steps and dropped off the crockery and cutlery which Monsewer Flip had given her. She had rinsed them under the tap and dried them on her dress and hoped they weren't too bad.

The man was not there, and a small dark woman looked askance at her but said nothing as she gave them back. Mary thanked her hugely and loudly, though she wasn't sure the woman understood. Perhaps she was just not given to smiling at people, though you would have thought she might, considering she presumably ate such food herself for breakfast.

A short but steep hill led into a marketplace. Around it there were shops, houses and a big church. The market square was cobbled, and since it was Saturday there was a market and also, to her delight, an indoor market. Being January, there wasn't much to buy, and she thought longingly of Cate's mother, who was a generous woman, at least to her servants.

They ate three times a day and the food was good and plentiful. At Christmas she gave her women servants lovely clothes. Mary had not neglected to bring with her the blue dress which her mistress had bestowed on her. She had also taken as many other clothes as she could put on, which had been too big to fit anybody else in the family and that she could doubtless sell to raise money.

Cate's mother also gave them apples and pears and potatoes and various vegetables with which to feed their families, and Cate's father made sure that every household had game for Christmas, as the men were allowed days to shoot across his land in autumn and winter and they fished his river during the warmer months.

They could always snare rabbits and shoot pigeons among the fields of cabbages and Brussels sprouts, and there were orchards at the house so big that they provided fruit all winter. Parsnips and potatoes were stored. Nobody went hungry, which was why Mary could not understand how awful he was to Catherine, but then she was supposed to be above everybody – and she would have been had Henry Westbrooke been a man who liked women. It was not so much her fault. She had loved him and given in to him. Many a lass had done the same with her lover. Odd to think that, even with money and position, Cate had less freedom than other young women.

In the market Mary found flour, dried peas, yellow split peas, barley, carrots, potatoes, oats, butter and cheese. She bought a little packet of tea and one of coffee, some milk, sugar and salt, and then trudged back with her booty.

Catherine was busy sweeping up the glass on the floor with an old broom, which she said she had found beyond the back door. There was colour in her cheeks.

Mary looked around the place carefully now that the day

was light. It certainly was a strange building. The bit nearest the street was the most recently built, and by far the worst – from the outside the whole place looked derelict. But as you moved further back into the house, it felt like another time entirely.

It was darker in the back, because the windows were tiny and high up, but once the stove was lit, the kitchen was lovely and warm. Mary dragged armchairs in from the street side and once they had dried out they were more comfortable than anything else.

These they slept in for the next few nights, and Mary made broth and oatcakes and flatbread, and they ate cheese and lived fairly well. Catherine began to look much better and they both felt rested.

Mary was conscious that if people were aware they were living in the back of the house, and that it was reasonably comfortable, they might try to move in or move them out, or at least take what food and firewood there was, so they carefully did nothing that could be seen. Since it was a big house, and they weren't using the rooms at the front of the property, she didn't think anybody would know what was going on. And there was so much smoke from so many chimneys that hopefully the one fire they kept lit would not be seen.

Luckily there was a huge door that kept the back of the house well away from the front. Mary thought that in times past this had been the servants' quarters. You could get upstairs from there, but only into the back rooms, which were small and freezing. The rest of the house, even upstairs, was falling down, and the front staircase could not be climbed, so she felt fairly safe.

One evening, they were talking about what they would do next when there was a huge noise outside. Not being able to keep people out of the front part of the house, they had bolted the servants' door and felt reasonably safe. They didn't want to get involved, but it sounded as if somebody was hurt, and when they finally made their way outside, a young man was rolling around on the ground, obviously in pain.

Whoever else had been there had left him, and by the light from the moon they could see that he was in a bad way. Mary got down and the ground was sticky with blood.

'Can you walk?' she said.

He got obediently to his feet, though somewhat shakily, so that she was obliged to help him. He was lying on a large bag. She took him into the back and they bolted the door against the outside. She hoped she was doing the right thing as she led him to the fire, where he sank down.

She took warm water from the pan, which had been on the stove, and bathed his face and hands and sat him up in a chair. Catherine made tea and he put the cup to his lips and thanked them both.

'Are you hurt in places I can't see?' Mary asked, and he laughed just a little, through the pain, and said, 'Is that an offer?'

Mary laughed too and shook her head.

'Can I stay here for now?' he said.

The two women looked at one another. Catherine looked

worried, but Mary knew more about these things than her mistress – her friend – and she made the decision.

'I suppose you'd better, but it's just for tonight so don't get any clever ideas, big lad. Cate here has already lost her chastity but I'm not giving up mine without a fight. You can rest and you might even get breakfast, but that's all you're going to get, all right? I keep a kitchen knife close to me and I do know how to use such things. What are you called?'

'Daniel Wearmouth,' he said.

'Are you sure he's safe?' Catherine whispered to her when he had fallen asleep. 'I don't think we should keep anybody here, especially not a man we know nothing about.'

'Why, shall I put him out when he's bled all over the place and can hardly walk?'

'I don't know. I just don't trust any man.'

'I cannot think why either of us would, but it's bloody freezing out there, lass, so if you want to tell him to go, then it's up to you, but I'm not going to. If he dies outside on the street I would not like to be responsible for it, and let's face it, he isn't in any fit state to cause us problems. That knife goes under my pillow and I'll hear him if he stirs.'

Five

Dan hated Durham. He hated everything about it, from the stupid cathedral to the way that the river seemed to be everywhere. He hadn't thought about it, but as soon as he got off the train he knew that he would loathe it as he had loathed nowhere else.

His father's body lay buried in the prison yard without marker. He would never be allowed to show respect to his father's resting place, or acknowledge in any public way that he had cared and that his father had come to a hard and ignominious death through trying to do the right thing.

He left the station and went into the nearest hotel he found, at the bottom of the steep hill that led into the town. It was appropriately called The Station Hotel and had pretty glass windows and a bar with a fire which smoked only slightly. There he sat, nursing a glass of beer and wondering what in the hell he would do now.

His first wife had died giving him a child, his second wife didn't want him, he had lost his job and he had left the place he loved so much, his only home, to come here.

For what? He didn't know. He didn't want to be here, but

it was the only place where he had any family connection, though his father was dead. He recalled the few times he had gone to the prison to see him, only to be turned away. His father had written him but one letter from prison, when he was dying, so Dan's love for the man was hard, like a huge stone in his body that never shifted. His father had been imprisoned here for twelve years. He had smothered his wife, who had been in horrible pain for weeks and weeks, and for that he had been treated like a murderer.

Dan wasn't sure whether it made him feel better or worse to be within walking distance of the awful place where his father had been cruelly incarcerated all that time.

He wished that he could have stayed in Stanhope, where he had been manager of the big limestone quarry. After his wife Arabella had died, he had married his first love, Susan Wilson, but when he lost his job she no longer wanted him, if she had ever really wanted him at all, so here he was, watching the snow fall and wondering how things had ever got this bad. He'd had so much, and now he'd lost everything.

The morning after he had been beaten and robbed, he awoke aching everywhere, and when he tried to get up everything hurt more. He remembered that the two women, one of them obviously pregnant, had taken him in. What had happened to their menfolk he had no idea, because while the bigger, dark girl spoke with a rough accent, the other girl seemed refined, and although her clothes were worn they had once been good. He remembered from Arabella what a lady looked like and she was definitely a lady.

He smelled food, and when he could drag himself up he

went through into the very back of the house, which was down a dark passage, and there he saw the two women. The bigger, dark one was stirring what smelled to him like porridge and the other was sitting down, looking pale and exhausted.

'Did you sleep?' she asked.

'Yes.'

'It's more than Cate did. That baby is getting big and she's uncomfortable.'

Dan wasn't used to women talking about such things and didn't know what to say. Since Arabella had died he was terrified of childbirth, and wished he had somewhere else to go.

'Mary . . .' said the other, as though embarrassed.

Mary stopped stirring and divided the porridge into three bowls. There was sugar and milk and so they sat down. Dan was grateful, for he hadn't eaten since the morning before.

'I need to find a job and somewhere to live.'

'Well, you cannot stop here,' the dark girl said flatly. 'We're two women on our own. We know nothing about you and I'm not sure we want to, so you'll have to find someplace else to go.'

'If I find a job today will you take me back in tonight?'

'How likely is that?' she said, lips pursed together in doubt.

'What do you do?' Cate asked.

'I'm a quarryman.' He had been going to say 'quarry manager', but then there might be enquiries as to how he wasn't one now and he wasn't up to questions.

'Not many quarries in town,' Mary said, looking at him suspiciously. 'Can you read, write and add up?'

He nearly said that of course he could, but stopped himself and merely admitted that he could.

'Cate's mam taught us.' Mary nodded at the other girl. 'Thank God she did. You might get an office job.'

'I got thrown out of the last job,' he said.

'Lie,' Mary suggested. Dan stared at her.

'Say you worked in your father's office in somewhere they don't know about, a shop or summat, and that the business went under and you were left with nowt.'

Dan couldn't help smiling. 'I will,' he said. 'Can I come back if I find something then?'

They hesitated.

'You shot that bolt through behind the door last night, so I was left on my own with a howling gale,' he protested. 'I couldn't have done much harm.'

'I don't know about that,' she said.

He duly went off and wandered the streets in search of work. There were several notices in windows saying 'Help wanted', but either he didn't look right or he didn't speak as he should, because they wouldn't take him on. He saw himself in a shop window and then he understood. He was dressed as though he had money. He wore a decent suit and his hands were clean and soft.

Had he been able to tell lies he would have done, but either they were too shrewd or they just didn't trust him – and why would they? He didn't like to go back to the two women. Why should they do any more for him unless he had money to offer or at least a job of some sort? He could lie to them, of course, but they had been kind and rescued him from the street.

He stood in Silver Street, a cobbled way that wound up to the marketplace, and in the oncoming darkness something glinted beside his shoe. Half a crown. Picking it up made him want to laugh.

He had married into one of the richest families in Weardale, he had lived in a huge house and had clean sheets on his bed. There had been warm fires and big gardens and beef and claret for dinner. Then he remembered Arabella, her laughter and her smile, the way that she spoke. He went into a pub and bought himself a drink.

The place was called the Victoria, and he liked it as soon as he went inside. There was a big fire, and little tables. Men were clustered at the bar and near the fire, and from what he could see there were at least two other back rooms. The noise coming from them was good, and so he sat down where he wasn't intruding into anyone's conversation, feeling grateful for the heat of the flames and the pint of beer. He worried that he had found no job and that the two women would not let him back in again. Even the front ruin of that house was better than the street, with its safety of a locked door.

He had not known until now that several of the prison warders were in the Victoria. Had he, he would have stayed clear, but he had most of a pint of golden beer left and not the money to disdain it, so he stayed and then he listened and thought about his father.

They were not boasting, exactly, they were just telling tales of what it was like in the prison, how bad were the prisoners, how hard the life they led. Dan had to make himself keep his seat but he discerned through it all that one of them was Mr Perkins, who was the head warder at the gaol, and Mr Perkins lingered when his friends had gone. Perhaps he wanted to have one more pint. Perhaps he didn't care to go home. Whatever the reason for his solitary presence, Dan could not help himself going to the man and saying to him, 'You are Mr Perkins from the gaol?'

'Aye, I'm Perkins. Who wants to know?' This was spoken firmly, from a man who was in authority.

'I'm Daniel Wearmouth. My father died in your gaol.'

He waited for Mr Perkins to dismiss him, but the man looked down at the wooden floor and then he said softly, 'It's not my prison, lad. I needed a job badly and they gave it to me.'

'How can you justify that?'

Mr Perkins looked straight at him.

'I had a wife and three small bairns and we had nowt to eat. How do you justify what you do?'

'He was there without reason and you didn't help him.'

'He killed your mother.'

'She had been in agony for months and he put a pillow over her face. Wouldn't you have done that for your wife?'

'I haven't had to do it. I don't make the laws and neither does anybody else that I know. The folk who make them are rich and don't need to alter things.'

Dan said nothing.

'I'm sorry, lad. Come and have a drink with me.'

Dan shook his head.

'Howay,' Mr Perkins said, ' there's nothing the likes of you or me can do about such things.' And so they had another pint of beer together.

Dan didn't know whether it helped, but once they realized that they both knew Zeb Bailey, Mr Perkins told him stories about Zeb's daring and made it sound interesting. Although Dan felt he should not have been there when they were both drunk and singing in the streets – in his case all the way back to Rachel Lane where the two women lived – he felt better.

He found his way in among the ruins of the house, and because it was dark and late and there were no sounds from inside, he sat down on the chair he had slept on last night and tried to sleep.

In the morning he turned over and thought about how he had got drunk with a prison officer, and he was unhappy, but only for a while. Mr Perkins had told him what good things he could say about his father: that he caused no trouble, that he was kind to others as much as he could be, and even in the end, when Zeb had helped him, he had died without making a fuss.

Stupidly now, amidst such things, Dan felt better. He had the feeling that his father had died with his mother, and the rest was just painful detail forever and forever, but not meaning anything at all.

Even the mention of his father's name was balm to his heart. He had not talked about either of his parents in so long and he ached for their presence and their names and anything about them that he might remember. Here in Durham they seemed so very far away. All that was here was his father's body, but it had nothing to do with his parents' good marriage. He wished he could have had the same for so long.

It made him think back to what his life had been when he was a small boy and his parents loved him and looked after him. He had always thought they were one without him, but he saw now that it was not so. No couple could have a child and not prioritize it, because it was the future and wasn't that what life was all about?

They had done everything they could for him. His memories were coloured by how ill his mother had been and how despairing his father, and what had followed had reached into his life and soured it.

Why was it that some people had such awfulness and others did not? And yet he knew that everybody felt the same; no matter what their experience, they all suffered.

'Why did he die?' Dan had asked Mr Perkins when they were well through their second pint of beer. 'He wasn't an old man.'

'Prison destroys men; it makes them old before their time. It's a cruel system and your father had been there for a very long time.'

'Zeb told me about him.'

'Aye, Bailey did everything he could to help your dad at the end, and that's a dangerous thing to do. He even talked me into sending the letter that your dad had written. You were lucky to have that.'

Dan had never thought of himself as lucky before.

And then he thought of Mr Perkins, having to work in a prison to get by, knowing that it was unjust but doing it because he had a wife and children he could not feed otherwise. Wasn't that what men were supposed to do – marry and have children and strive to do everything they could for them? He had wanted to do the same and had not been allowed, and his father and mother had been parted long before they were old, and yet some folk lasted until they were ninety. There was no explanation for it.

That morning he did not even try to get into the back of the house; he went off and looked again for work. His insides rumbled and then he knew how stupid he had been the evening before when he had spent money on drink. He would have given a lot now to have afforded some breakfast.

Six

Nell had never liked Ash House; it had been her husband's idea. She had liked the little house they had moved into when they were married. That was the happiest time of her life, getting away from her parents. They didn't like her husband, and hadn't wanted her to marry him, because he was not one of them. He was the lowest of the low, a quarryman. Her own father was the local grocer and was a long way up the social ladder.

Her new husband made sure that they moved away from her parents' house in Cowshill, even though they had to live in a backstreet. He was determined to get her away from her parents and she was keen enough to go.

Her mother complained that 'that man' was taking her away from them. Nell had never been more pleased than when on her wedding day she was able to travel to the little house in Stanhope that was to be her own.

That house, halfway up Crawleyside Bank, not far from where Frederick lived with Pat, Shirley and their family now, was a heaven to her. Her husband's parents, who lived in Stanhope, were kind, and she liked them more than she had ever liked her own. She had thought at first that she would be required to live with them, which was what so many young couples did, but Harold's mother said, 'Nell, the last thing you need is your ma-in-law telling you what to do. Our Harold says he has found a nice little house up the bank, and we've helped him so that you can afford to rent it, just until you get on your feet a bit, but don't you be taking it if you don't like it. It has to be somewhere that appeals to you. Harold says it's nice but God knows what it's really like because he has no idea what a woman wants. So look at it and then you decide.'

It was a shame, Nell thought later, that his parents were not there when he insisted on building Ash House, as his mother would have questioned the sense of it. His parents were both long dead by then and she missed them. She felt guilty that she didn't miss her own parents, but her father had barely noticed her, and after she had left to go and live in Stanhope her mother did not visit.

Each visit to Cowshill was more difficult and she had to persuade herself to go. It was awkward to get to and took such a long time by horse and cart, which she endured. Even when she wrote, her mother pretended she had not received the letters and had prepared nothing to eat. Nell would go all day then without food.

She didn't like to tell her husband how bad it was, and her mother told her over and over how much she would regret her marriage and how she could not look after Nell's brothers and father by herself. Nell had been wrong to leave; and for her to marry a man like that, it would come to no good.

In the beginning it was true. They had so little that she

took in washing. Her mother-in-law, instead of telling her how shameful this was, came and helped, and even when Nell went to clean people's houses, her mother-in-law would be at Nell's house, cleaning it and making cakes and dinner, and all she would say was, 'Eh, Nell, I hope you don't mind me interfering,' and Nell would take the woman into her arms and cry for how kind she was.

Harold's father went to the quarry and helped from the day that it opened. He did not say that it would not work; he was enthusiastic and toiled to help his son succeed, and on Sundays they would take a picnic down by the river and stay there the whole afternoon.

Harold would chase her into the water and scoop her up into his arms and they would laugh, and his mother would have made ham sandwiches and egg sandwiches and lots of cake. It was the happiest time that Nell had known and ever would know, she thought now, looking back.

Nell loved that little house. It was no more than one room up and one down, but it was mid-terrace and cosy and she could see the top of the bank from her back door and from the front the road wound down into Stanhope.

It was all hers, even though she had nothing more than a table and two chairs, a settee which Harold had proudly bought from a man who made such things in Frosterley, a new bed and a mattress which his parents had bought for them, linen which she had sewn herself from stuff off the market and pots and pans which Harold's mam had bought in Stanhope at the hardware shop, which his mother said was her favourite place.

Part of the problem with her own parents was that they were Methodists, and her mother deplored the fact that she was not marrying one. Harold's family didn't seem to care for such things; they thought that he was the best thing ever, and because she was marrying him, Nell was also the best thing ever. They thought the sun shone from her and she blossomed under their praise.

There was no drink at the wedding but Harold's family had a few pints that day and Nell and his mother had a glass of sherry afterwards to toast the bride and groom. Nell's mother cried throughout the ceremony. None of Nell's brothers turned up for the wedding, as though – and it was true – she didn't matter to them.

Nell even had to say to her new ma-in-law that she had no decent dress to be married in, and so Mrs Almond had a new dress made for her. Nell had no idea how she had come by the material for such a thing, but it was the most beautiful creation that she had ever seen, and the local dressmaker made it so that it was fashioned just for her.

Her own mother told her afterwards that the dress was indecent. Since it was high-necked and long-sleeved, Nell could only think that her mother wished Harold's parents had not been able to waste money on such a dress to give her daughter, but in the looking glass Nell saw that the dress followed her figure and made her look beautiful, so perhaps in that it was indecent.

Her parents seemed to regret losing their daughter to a man whom they regarded as a heathen, but Nell knew she had been a skivvy in their house. There were four sons and

Nell had slaved to look after them. They worked, but that was all they did.

They didn't pick up after themselves; they didn't aid her. From morning till night it was 'Nell, did you clean my boots?' and 'Nell, did you pack my bait?' It was a miracle that she had met Harold Almond. She thought it had been by chance, though he often told her that he had known she was the bonniest girl in the dale and had gone to Cowshill to find her.

She had always suspected that he was lying about it, but there was a small, fairy-tale part of her that loved the idea of him leaving Stanhope to find her and lift her out of the mire that was her life. He had done that. He had made her happy.

He was a reckless young man, that was how people thought of him, and she was cautioned by many that she should not marry him. He had started up a quarry at Stanhope with no money but what had leased it. He would never get anywhere, the people of the dale said. Harold didn't say anything; he just got on with it.

She went out working and his mother and father helped and at night when he came home they sat around the fire together and talked and read, and it was the kind of bliss that Nell had not known existed.

Now all she had left were her memories and regrets. She held to her the guilt of not being able to give him a son. It would have been so different now, had she had some support. She had written to Bernard Lennox and told him that her husband had died and that it was time for him to come and take over the quarry.

She knew that her husband had been in touch with him

several times and so she expected not just an answer but for Mr Lennox to turn up in person. He lived in Carlisle and had been a quarryman and miner all his young life. He would be there as he had promised.

Seven

Charles Westbrooke had seen Dan and Susan married, and since his hopes of marrying her were now blighted he had returned to his father's estate at Shap near Penrith in Westmorland and tried to get on with his life. His brother was dead, his father was old and ill and Catherine Boldon had fled from him when he offered to marry her because she was carrying his dead brother's child.

What a mess, and he felt as though he had caused it. He should never have run away from his inheritance. He had been too young to realize that it was inevitable he would end up back there, wanting only to get free of his father and the estate and the huge horrible feeling of responsibility. He'd thought he would cast it off. It made him laugh just to think of his efforts.

He had fled to Weardale to become a Methodist minister, and he had been happy there. He had not thought that his future could be taken away from him as it so cruelly had. If he had stayed in Shap, his young brother would not have felt obliged to marry a woman. He would have been the one making the necessary marriage so as to prop up the estate and the old ways which would not die.

He had loved Henry, and he had caused Henry's death by running away. His brother loved unnaturally, that was what they said, but he had been seduced by the woman who loved him and had given way. Henry could not bear the life he then had to lead and had killed himself.

Charles had told himself over and over that he was not entirely to blame, but it felt like it now. Catherine had run from him. He thought he could marry Susan, and now she too was gone from him and all he could do was go home and face the future as it had been mapped out for him. His struggles were over. He felt like a tired swimmer, letting the waters close over his head.

He still couldn't rest. He remembered Susan Wilson daily, nightly, the woman he had loved and still did love. He did start making enquiries as to whether anyone he knew had seen Catherine or heard from her. He wrote to friends and far-flung relatives, but he heard nothing and in the end Stewart, who was his father's agent and ran the estate, sat down in the study where they worked and said, 'Charles, you have to stop doing this.'

'Doing what?'

'Going about like a lovesick puppy. You never did love Catherine, so why do you care where she is?'

'She has the heir in her.'

'That's blunt, at least,' Stewart said, sitting down across the desk from him.

'She needs to come back here until she has the child.'

Stewart said nothing to that for several moments, and then he said, 'May I ask you something?'

'Haven't you been blunt enough already?'

'Is there some woman you want to marry?'

Charles got up. That was too close.

'Why? Are you worried I'm like my brother?'

'It doesn't matter. It's just that you ought to marry, then you could stop worrying about Catherine Boldon. She wasn't married to your brother. The moment you marry and have an heir, she becomes unimportant, but you don't seem to want to get married.'

Charles hesitated.

'I did want to. I met her in Weardale and then I came back here when Henry was killed and by the time I got round to it she was married to somebody else. The only woman I've ever cared for. I didn't think I was capable of it, but I was, and she was so lovely.'

There was a long silence.

'Did Catherine know about her?'

This had not occurred to Charles, and now he hesitated. Had Catherine run away because she had somehow found out about Susan and did not want to hold him back or take a freedom that she was not entitled to? It was a horrible thought.

'I'm sorry, Charles.'

'I didn't think I could fall in love. How stupid.' He felt lighter after being able to tell someone.

'Maybe, in time, you'll learn to love again,' Stewart said.

'Maybe.'

Work was a refuge and in some senses Charles could see that his time training to be a Methodist minister was helping him now. Running an estate was much the same: he was still dealing with people and doing his best to keep everything right for them within the bounds of the estate he was going to inherit. He had to stop imagining what it would have been like had Henry lived. In the evenings, if the stairs creaked or the wind pushed open the outside door, he tried not to imagine that his brother was coming home.

He tried not to think that, if he had been married to Susan, he could have been taking on his own ministry, and like Mr Martin, the minister, and his wife, he could have had some kind of a future. They had three little girls and the ministry in Stanhope, a small Weardale town. It was everything that Charles had wanted. He tried to keep himself busy to avoid thinking about it, but in the evenings it came back. It upset him so much.

The people around him treated him as though he had always been there, and he liked Jack, the solicitor who advised him. Jack was married and had two children. His wife, Cora, was a lovely woman, and Charles would have liked to spend more time with them. They had a pretty house just outside Penrith, and Jack always asked him to go over for supper and stay the night if he pleased, but Charles could not leave his father.

Stewart MacDonald ran the estate, and had done so all the time Charles's father had been ill. Stewart and his wife, Laura, were good friends to him now, though rarely saw them.

They encouraged him to meet the local gentry. Everybody wanted to know Charles, and he was invited everywhere. Thinking of Stewart's advice, he began to go out in the evenings, to dinners and to dances and to any place where he could meet young women. They flocked to his side. He tried not to hate it, but it was hard. He didn't for a second think that he preferred any woman to Susan. They were so agreeable, so positive, so pretty, and so unlike the lovely girl he had fallen in love with at the chapel in Stanhope. She was so natural, so normal, but then she didn't know who he was. These women did, and it mattered to them. His wealth and status could give them an importance they would never know otherwise. They did not see him as Susan had. She had loved him as a poor man who was in the ministry and loved books and was doing his best for the people. He was doing the same now, and his heart ached that she was not there to help him and be his wife and provide the heir he so badly needed. He told himself that Susan would have hated how different it was here.

Once Charles was late getting back to the house after pursuing business. Mrs Diamond, the housekeeper, met him to take off his outer things, and when he enquired of his father she said, 'He's taken to his bed.'

While that should have been a relief, Charles couldn't bring himself to think so.

'He won't have a light,' she said. 'He's refused dinner. He hasn't even asked for a glass of wine.'

Charles went upstairs to wash and change, and took a lamp into where his father lay amid a faint smell of warm cats and damp springer spaniel.

Charles had tried in vain to have animals banned from the bedrooms, but the maids spent half their time putting the cats outside. If he hadn't known better he might have thought that his father left the doors open on purpose.

As he put down the lamp, the black and white dog on the bed opened one eye. They were wary of him. Charles didn't actively dislike cats and dogs, though he did dislike horses, regarding them as stupid though necessary, but these animals were aware of how he didn't favour them. They never went to him to be fussed over, and the springer spaniel didn't go out except for necessity. It stayed always where his father was, as though some kind of guard. Protecting his father, Charles thought now, against himself, the interloper.

'Thought you'd gone out,' his father said. His father hated him going out in the evenings almost as much as Charles hated going. He felt he could get nothing right.

'I just hadn't come back in. Aren't you getting up for dinner? It's beef.'

'That woman tells me what to do.'

'Come down and I'll find some decent wine.'

'I'm too cold.'

The room was warm – all the rooms were warm – but his father needed something to complain about. Or was it just that he was old, Charles wondered.

'I've had the fire built up in the little dining room. Here, put this on.'

Charles passed him a quilted smoking jacket. His father, grumbling, got out of bed and Charles put him into the jacket and his slippers, and then his father managed to get downstairs without help and into the little dining room.

They sat by a huge fire, which was where they always had

dinner when they were alone – which was most of the time. Charles wanted no one there and his father was beyond caring for company.

The big dining room was huge and chilly, despite having a fire at either end. Charles could remember dinners long ago, and how the women would shiver in their thin dresses and how the guests could never hear anything that was being said further than five feet away and how the servants moved up and down to please the diners.

This lovely little dining room, which he thought had once been a sewing room, was one of the few rooms in the house that had no windows. While that sounded bad, the lack of outside walls meant that it was warm, and all you had to do was close the doors which led to other rooms and it was self-contained. Furthermore, it was close to the kitchen and the food came hot to the table.

The food was superb and he had made sure that it was always so, thinking that if he had to live here he would make sure he enjoyed it. There was fillet of beef with potatoes, mustard and vegetables with butter, followed by a crumble, which his father always enjoyed, thick with custard.

Charles didn't like the crumble, but they had cheese and port and after that his father drank just a little brandy. He had always drunk a great deal but now he couldn't manage it. Charles hated that he wished his father was well, which had always involved swearing and drinking so much that he could be easily despised, even hated. Hatred was not something that stayed around to comfort you when the person you thought of so badly was coming to the end of his life.

They went into the tiny sitting room next, and there he had made sure that his father's favourite chair was always close by the fire. Charles wanted to shut out the animals but the springer spaniel was already beside the blaze and as his father sat down a large black and white long-haired cat purred as it leaped upon his knee. Charles gave his father a little more brandy.

Having wished the man dead for so long, Charles, devoid of any decent company, was almost glad that his father was still there. It was strange that there was nobody left to fight with, nothing left to fight for or about. He had lost everything but his birthright, and now his father would have his way. He had the responsibilities of this place and could not leave it.

Having said that, he was of the belief that the people there should own their own farms and smallholdings. His estate manager, Stewart MacDonald, had smiled over this idea, and said that it could not be done and that he had to go on as his father had. He'd looked at Charles as though he thought him an idiot but was too kind or polite to say so.

Charles wished he could have given it to Stewart, who loved this place as Henry had done, but the whole thing was tied up legally and there was nothing he could do.

'They wouldn't know how to manage it,' Stewart had said.

'They could be taught.'

'How would they ever work out the comings and goings, the financial aspects? They would have no capital behind them. You know what it's like here. We can have two or three bad summers in a row. The estate can stand it, but how would they? They might have thought the good times would last and so they spent what they had—'

'You make them sound stupid.'

'Not stupid, just inexperienced. They know nothing about such things. You do.'

'I don't.'

'Yes, you do, Charles. You just don't know that you do. The estate has to stand the losses year after year, and because the money has been wisely invested for so long it stands it, regardless of whether the crops are good or not. However many animals are lost when times are bad, there is always a sufficient amount to feed everybody. Isn't that the whole point of such guardianships? Your family has been on this land—'

'Yes, yes, I know, for hundreds of years. I always hated it.'

'You wouldn't have had your father been a different parent.'

Charles had looked at him.

'He has been a good master,' Stewart had acknowledged. 'You won't find a broken fence, a neglected animal or a hungry child on the estate, and your father built schools here so that everybody had access to education, even if some of them didn't take advantage of it.'

'Why couldn't he think of me like that?'

'You were supposed to be better.'

'Henry was. He adored Henry.'

'And Henry loved him. If we had to justify how much love we were willing to mete out, how would that work? We can't help the love that we feel, and in a way we shouldn't.'

Charles understood that. He loved Susan so deeply that

sometimes he wished he might die for lack of her, but you didn't die of such things. It might feel like a tragedy but it was nothing more than pitiable, and he had to get on with this now, and alone, perhaps forever.

'Your father, be it good or bad, has made you into the man you are so that you will inherit the estate – even though you may not want to.'

Charles thought of Catherine, and hoped that she was all right, and he thought about her child, the second in line to inherit the estate. It seemed unlikely that he would marry now. He didn't think he would love again. He felt as though his love for Susan had used up a part of him that could not be renewed.

He began to wish, and despised himself for doing so, that his father might never die. That he might always be there complaining and making his obviously painful way downstairs each night for dinner.

Having eaten what little dinner he could manage, his father was now sitting by the fire and turning down any efforts to persuade him upstairs. Charles forbore to tell his father that he should not drink; the man was dying.

'Once up those bloody stairs I may never come down them again, and though I know you can't wait to be rid of me, I won't aid you in it.'

Charles said nothing. His father was getting weaker all the time.

'You will look after the people won't you, Charles? They will need your help.'

'Of course,' Charles said.

'I never thought I would have to ask you that.'

'I never thought I would have to say it.'

His father smiled at him across the fire. That was the hardest thing of all: that his father smiled as though he could go now that the estate would be looked after.

And for the first time, Charles understood that this had always been his fate. And when his father slept he cried.

Eight

Mary Blaimire was in the market, trying to find something to eat that cost virtually nothing. She was seriously worried about money. There was nothing left. Dan was still around; sometimes if she got up very early she would see him in the other part of the house – the cold, open part. He had no work, she could tell. He looked more and more thin and ragged, and he didn't ask for food, so she was sure he was going hungry. But she had to make sure that Catherine ate, and she was beginning to panic now, wishing she could find some work herself. Nobody would take her on because of her strange accent, and presumably because they did not know her. She had gone to shops, she had banged on the doors of every house she could find but nobody wanted her help. Now she was considering whether to steal one or two vegetables. Would anybody notice?

Catherine was useless. She sounded what she was and she was getting fat, so there was no chance she could do anything to bring in money. It took her all her time to keep the fire going, but as the weather began to warm this ceased to be a problem as they only lit it when they had something to eat in the evenings. Mary showed her how to clean, and she did as much as was possible in a place like that, but it was a waste of time since it was almost a ruin. If she could find work, Mary thought they could move into a house that at least had a roof, four walls and a door.

On the very day that Mary was considering whether to steal in the market, she bumped into a young woman who had a child in her arms and another at her side, and since both were crying Mary stopped and spoke softly to them. The woman, about her own age, was respectably dressed. The little girl had fallen over and was crying, so Mary picked her up, put her on her feet and looked at her grazed hands. She and the girl began to talk until they were walking up towards the cathedral.

Mary didn't think much of churches and this one scared her more than most. It took up such a lot of space and was so tall. The woman thanked her as they went past the road that twisted up to the cathedral, and they took the street next to it, which was the Bailey. Here she stopped outside a pretty blue door and asked Mary if she would like to come in and have a cup of tea.

Mary said no hastily, she didn't think she should put people out, but the woman was most insistent so Mary followed her inside. It was a lovely house, she thought, quite prosperous though not rich. Mary followed the woman into the back and the door was opened and the little girls ran outside into a garden.

Mary knew nothing of gardens and was entranced. It fell away gradually to the river, though a stout fence meant there was no danger for the children. The view of the river and of Elvet Bridge was so pretty that Mary stared.

She also had the horrible feeling that the woman's husband was probably a churchman or a vicar, but the woman made tea and introduced herself as Lavinia Peters and said that her husband worked at the university; he was a botanist. Mary didn't know about such things, and her hostess, no doubt seeing her blank face, explained that it was flowers and such.

As they sat down for tea a tall, white-haired man came in. He was old and Mary thought he must be Mrs Peters' father, but it turned out that he was her husband. He was going bald and his hair was long and wispy down to his shoulders, but he was open and friendly and Mary couldn't remember liking a man in such a way before.

'You aren't from here?' he said, and Mary admitted that she was from the Lake District and he enthused about how beautiful it was. People were in the habit of saying such things. Her view of it was coloured by her life there, so she couldn't raise any enthusiasm, but he told her that his family came from there. Although she reminded herself that it was a whole area and no doubt he came from Kendal or further away, she was worried that there might be some connection. She began to make her excuses, telling them that she must be going as she had gone out to look for some work. Mr Peters looked at his wife and when she nodded he said they could do with help in the house and with the little girls, and would she be interested in that. Mary couldn't believe her luck.

Mr Peters went off into his study at the back of the house.

He was writing a book, presumably about flowers. Mary set to there and then, and since it was such a lovely house and the day was fine it made the work easy. Mrs Peters gave her dinner in the middle of the day and it was teatime when Mary thought she must be getting back. Mr Peters pressed some money into her hand.

Mary stared at it, protesting that she had only just started, but he nodded and said it was the day's wages, it would help, and they would see her in the morning. Could she come at about eight to help Lavinia with the girls as they had their breakfast? Mary said she could.

She hastened back. It was only a few minutes away, and since the shops had not yet closed she bought food and went back to the house. Rain had begun to fall, so she was quite happy to find that Cate had managed to keep the fire going and had tidied up as much as she could. As they put the kettle on for tea, there was a hammering on the outside door and she opened it to see Dan, very skinny and clothes hanging off him, but smiling. He had been taken on at the pit office up old Elvet.

'How did you manage that?' Mary said, letting him inside.

'I did like you said – I lied. Said I'd been working for my grandfather in his office in a quarry in Teesdale and then he had died and the new man didn't want me there. It's so like what I did before, and they have offered to pay me reasonably well. Since I'll have money by the end of the week, I wondered whether you would take me back in'.

Mary and Cate looked at one another, and then Mary made the decision. 'All right then,' she said, 'but if you have no money by Friday, you'll have to go. And you can't stay in here at night, I don't know you well enough to trust you.'

'It's not so cold now,' he said, almost cheerfully.

'Mr Peters gave me some money,' Mary said, 'and we are having fish and chips. Dan, will you go to the pub over the bridge and get some beer? Take this.' She handed him a huge jug, which she had found in the back.

When he returned, they sat by the fire and ate and made plans and talked about what they might be able to afford if they were both able to keep their jobs. This place was awful, and would be worse in the winter, and by then there would be a child. Cate didn't want to move into a better part of town, even if they could manage it, and the other two agreed that they should be careful. Even a better house here would do, provided there was nothing nasty in the walls or on the floors.

When Mary set off for work the next morning, she looked at the rest of the houses on Rachel Lane and none of them was decent. She didn't like the river either; she had seen too many rats about in the evenings. There were always dogs barking and people yelling at one another and children screaming, and she didn't like that either. She thought they would have to move. Having come from the Lake District, she missed the hills.

Listening to the chiming of the cathedral bells, she worried that she might have been mistaken, that people like the Peters didn't exist, but when she got there, Mr Peters answered the door with a smile. He quickly said goodbye, as he was going out. Mrs Peters smiled at Mary and said she had never been as glad to see anybody, the children were coughing and she had been up half the night with them.

Mary told her to go back to bed and when Mrs Peters protested Mary said that unless the children were very difficult, she could manage. She took them back to the kitchen, Mrs Peters' voice ringing in her ears. She'd told her that if she fancied some breakfast to help herself.

The two little girls were pale-faced but hungry and she knew that was a good sign. Ill children didn't eat and these two dug into the bread and honey, drinking a glass of milk each. Mary made tea for herself, and since she hadn't tasted honey in a long time she too had bread and honey, with lovely thick butter. It was wonderful.

Then she washed and dressed them and then she cleaned the dishes. There was a lot to be done but she sat down and read them a story. There were lots of books in the house, and she wasn't used to such things, but she loved reading them fairy tales. Even though these seemed very scary, the girls were quiet, listening, and after half an hour they went to sleep side by side on the settee.

Mary tiptoed out and began cleaning the house. It wasn't really dirty, it just needed a thorough once over. The kitchen cupboards were sticky with sugar and the skirting boards were dusty, so she set about, and because it was a really lovely house she thoroughly enjoyed it. She scrubbed the kitchen floor and the big wooden table.

She had a look through the cupboards and found yeast and flour, so she made a loaf of bread. There were vegetables in the larder so she made broth with pearl barley, and when Mrs

Peters came downstairs, looking guilty but with colour in her face, the girls woke up and Mary fed them all.

'Broth's always better on the second day,' Mary said, but Mrs Peters said it couldn't be any better.

After that, Mrs Peters entertained the children and Mary got on with the rest of the downstairs. A little later, Mrs Peters said they should all go for a walk by the river. Mary offered to stay behind and start on the upstairs, but Mrs Peters said they all needed fresh air. They set off down the Bailey to the footpath, across Prebends Bridge and down the other side of the river until they came to the town. Since Mrs Peters had nothing in for tea, and Mr Peters would need something substantial, they did some shopping.

When Mr Peters came back at teatime, the little girls greeted him at the door, and Mrs Peters looked as fresh as a daisy, he said. Mary gave him broth and bread and then she left so that the family could have their meal in peace. They said she could stay, but she needed to get back.

Mr Peters gave her some more money, as though he understood, and this time she just thanked him softly. When she got home, Dan was also just arriving, and she was grateful to find that Cate had been out and had bought a meal from Monsewer Flip that you could just reheat. Mary had never heard of such a thing, but they unwrapped it and set it on the stove, carefully so that it should not burn. By the time it was hot it was giving off smells that made Mary want to grab the pan.

They duly served it out, a mixture of meat, cheese and some kind of long stringy stuff, which proved to be good and filling. There was so much of it that they had second helpings. After that, they drank tea and dozed by the fire and Mary thanked her luck that she had come so far.

Mary said to Cate that, since she had no cooking skills, maybe this was a good idea, and it was so cheap that they might do it quite often, at least for the next few days until both she and Dan got used to the work.

Cate said that she was ashamed she couldn't help. The trouble was that she was already as big as a house, and what with that and how she spoke and how she looked, Mary knew that nobody would take her on.

'You and Dan are working.'

'We aren't having a bairn,' Mary said.

'Lots of women work and have children.'

'We don't want you to lose this one, do we?'

Cate looked down. 'I thought I did.'

'You don't really want to. Whatever else Henry Westbrooke was, he was doing his best, just like all of us, and you cared about him. If there was any justice anywhere, which we know there isn't, you would have been married and living in that lovely place and glad because this is your first child.'

Cate shook her head and turned away. Dan said nothing, but Mary always thought it best to be frank so she said, 'They were going to get married and she really cared about him—'

'Mary—' Cate interrupted.

'You did. He was the only man you ever cared about, and that was how you ended up like this, but Henry—'

'He didn't love me,' Cate put in, her voice hard. 'He

preferred men, and when people found out he tried to take an impossible ditch out hunting and broke his neck.'

She got up and went through to the back, slamming the doors.

'She thinks it was her fault,' Mary said.

'Why would she think that?'

'Women always do.' Mary sighed, getting up and beginning to clear the dishes. 'Her folks were awful to her. His brother offered to marry her, though he did it because he thought he should. What woman thinks that's a good idea? Though I wouldn't care, he was such a nice man, the nicest I ever knew. Charles Westbrooke.'

Dan stared at her. 'Westbrooke?'

'You know him?'

'Yes, he – he was a minister where I come from. I didn't know he was a lord.'

'I don't think he ever wanted it. The things life does to us . . .'

After she had washed up, she went out to the back lane where Cate was sitting on a large stone.

'It's going to be all right,' Mary said, getting down beside her.

'Things are never all right. You know that. He didn't want me. No man has ever wanted me.'

'Well, having no man want you is a far sight better than having Ned King want you, with his nasty gob and his little cock,' Mary said, and they laughed.

'You are going to have this baby, and you and I are going to make sure that it doesn't want for anything. Aren't we?'

Cate nodded.

'All right then. All you have to do is stay here every day and try not to let the fire go out.'

Mary could see how white and exhausted she was, and she worried about the baby and about Cate. What if she died? What if the baby didn't live? What if Cate died and the baby lived?

Mary was keen to get on at her job now that she had one, and it was such a good feeling, not running about after some lass her own age, though she had always liked Cate. But this was something she was good at and was being paid for, so the next day she hurried out and was glad to reach the house in the Bailey and to be greeted like an old friend. She determined to sort out the bedrooms. The children had slept so Mrs Peters had slept, and they worked together and talked over the kitchen table. The little girls were such a treat that Mary wished she could have married a decent man and had a child. It was the first time she had felt like this, because all she had ever known were her father and Ned.

She thought about Charles Westbrooke and wished she could have been a lady like Cate who had been given a chance to marry such a lovely man. But then what use had it been to Cate? She was already having his brother's child and she was too fine to take on a man when they didn't love one another.

Cate's parents had treated her appallingly because she was having a child outside of marriage. Mary was glad, triumphant, to have helped Cate out of there. Neither of them would ever go back to such treatment. Somehow they would always manage, she swore.

That evening Dan came home with the news that there was a house not far from his work that had nobody in it.

'It's about ten minutes from my work and the same from yours, Mary, the city being so small.'

'I worry about moving anywhere,' Cate said.

'We have to have somewhere better than this, and for respectability's sake we have to let Dan have a place he can disappear into. And so do I, especially after the baby's born,' Mary said. 'I don't want to have to spend all my time with a screaming child.' She softened the words with a smile, but Cate pulled a face and Mary knew she was worried about the birth. She too was worried, thinking about her mother losing twins. But that was different, she thought, her mother was worn out by then, whereas Cate was young and fit and hopefully only having one.

'We could at least have a look at it. It can't be any worse than this,' Mary said.

The first time they could have a look at the new house proved to be Saturday afternoon. Mary by now thought the Peters family could not manage without her, but Mr Peters assured her they would get through Saturday evening and Sunday and he had given her the money she was owed.

So the three of them went up the hill, Cate panting just a little and putting a hand to her lower back for relief. They went in the direction of the pit, but long before they got there they came to the property, a nice-looking terraced house.

They stopped there and it occurred to Mary that they would have to explain their relationship.

'Otherwise it's going to look really bad,' she said.

'We'll have to be married,' Cate said, looking at Dan with doubt, 'and you could be my sister.'

'His sister, considering your colouring,' Mary said.

'And you both have to change your accents,' Dan said. 'Neither of you sounds like you come from here – and you, Cate, sound like you belong in a castle.'

'I'll talk then,' Mary said.

A very respectable-looking man answered the door and Mary was glad they had sorted things out or she felt sure he would never have given them the house. He told them they could go and look inside and he would wait.

'There's no furniture,' he said, 'you'll have to sort it out yourselves, and I'll need a week's rent in advance.'

There was nothing at the front other than pavement where they stood, but when he unlocked the door it was surprisingly light. Unlike most houses, which opened into long dark hallways, this house went straight into a room. The staircase led up from there, but downstairs were two small rooms and a kitchen and then a backyard.

It was all in very good condition. Upstairs were two small bedrooms. Mary said to the others that she thought they should take it, and they agreed.

*

The new house was so much better than Rachel Lane that it was exciting.

'We could get stuff from the market for the kitchen,' Mary said, 'but the furniture will have to wait if we have to pay the rent up front.'

'I met this bloke at work whose brother sells furniture,' Dan said, 'and I can get coal free.'

There was a man in the covered market who dealt in beds and mattresses, clean and new, and plenty of people who sold pillows and bed linen. Mary bought towels and they also bought a settee and a chair, all for so much a week from the bloke at work's brother. She put in a quick prayer that they would go on working so that they could afford these things.

Table and chairs would have to wait, but nobody cared. They would have a place of their own, clean and private. There was a stove in the kitchen. Very womanlike, she knew, and perhaps stupidly, she felt affection for it. It sat there looking so reliable, with a boiler to one side for hot water and arms that came over the fire for pots and another arm that sat over the coals and even a place where the plates could be warmed.

Mary had never considered herself so particularly a woman, but she loved that stove as much as she had loved anything in her short life. They would have a house and nobody would shout and nobody would hit anybody and nobody would feel guilty and she wished it would last forever.

By the time they moved they had everything they could ever have wanted – Cate aside, Mary thought, though she would never have objected to anything. Her two housemates were supporting her and she was very aware of it. She had changed such a lot. She pronounced the house lovely and she and Mary made up the beds and they spent a lot of time in the kitchen, proclaiming over the beauty of the stove. Mary was so glad they had got away from the river and the rats and the poverty. She felt sorry for other people, but at the moment she could do nothing beyond look after her own.

She and Cate scrubbed the place and made up the beds, and when Cate slept on their new settee, exhausted, Mary made dinner and gloried in her kitchen and was glad of Dan, bringing his money to her and giving it into her hands.

'That's wonderful,' she said.

'It's no more than you did. You are remarkable.'

Every time he said things like that, Mary wondered if he had come from educated people. He didn't say anything about his background, but she thought he was almost a gentleman. His hands were white and neat and had known no physical work in a long time, she thought, and the suit he had arrived in was a good one. The other two he had, which was more than anyone she knew, were also of very good cloth, and she washed his clothes and starched his collars. He must have a good job, because every week he gave her a large amount of money and it helped lift them out of poverty.

Every time she told him that he was a decent man, which she did often, not being used to a man who helped, he just shook his head.

As for Cate, she could hardly move, she was so big. Mary did worry, but she didn't want to call a doctor because Cate hadn't complained and Mary thought she would have done had she been in real discomfort or pain. Cate slept fitfully, and Mary knew that she turned over a good deal, probably because the baby was big now and she could not be comfortable.

Mary knew that doctors were expensive, and besides, she would rather nobody knew what they were doing. There was always somebody who knew somebody else, and they were taking sufficient risks here without adding to it.

Cate left her bedroom door open – how safe she must have felt here – and Mary was glad of that since her parents had treated her so badly. She tried to be quiet about going to bed and getting up, and Dan, though nobody said anything to him, did the same. They set up a routine at the lovely little house so that it was always clean and welcoming and smelling of good food.

The days grew longer and warmer and Mary hung out the washing on Saturday afternoons. You couldn't do so on Sundays – people would have been horrified and remarked upon it. They had so many fine afternoons, so many bright and blowy Saturdays, that she began to think it would go on forever and that for once they were lucky. She tried not to dwell on that because she knew that nothing lasted.

From where she lay she could hear the bells of St Nicholas', the church in the marketplace. They lay late in bed on Sunday mornings and thanked God or whoever was in charge that they didn't have to work, that nobody cared they didn't go to church.

They ate a big dinner on Sundays at around two o'clock. They sat about in the morning and admired the day, and then they peeled vegetables and put a joint of meat in the oven. They drank beer purchased from the pub just further up the hill and they would eat as much as they could and then fall asleep. At some time in the afternoon they would walk around the river and then fall back into the house and have tea and sandwiches and cake. It was the best time that Mary could ever remember.

Nine

Nell Almond had written a brief letter to Mr Lennox after her husband had died, telling him what had happened and saying that she would be glad to see him there when he was ready.

She knew that the business side of it had been sorted out, so she did not have to go into matters that did not concern women, but she wrote that she would be glad to see Mrs Lennox and the family at her house.

She would be glad of the company and they were welcome to stay there for as long as it should take for them to find a house which might suit them. Although she knew that Mr Lennox had many other concerns, she would be happy to see him in the dale and relieved that he would take off her hands the huge burden that the quarry was without her beloved husband by her side.

For the first week she didn't give it much thought; Mr Lennox had other business concerns and no doubt he would get in touch. He had known how ill her husband was. By the end of the second week, she thought that he would just turn up with his family, having been too busy to reply, but every day after that she was worried, aware that there was no one to manage the quarry. She had put Pat McFadden in charge, but he was not a manager.

Her husband's instructions had been that she should dismiss the two young men as soon as he was dead, as Mr Lennox had agreed to come and manage the quarry immediately. He had known how ill Harold was and had said he would bring his family there to settle as soon as he received her letter.

After three weeks Nell was so worried that when she received a letter with unknown handwriting she was too relieved to do anything beyond open it in haste.

My dear Mrs Almond,

You will no doubt by now be thinking badly of us, having heard nothing. I know that my husband was to take over the quarry; they had talked of it often and made arrangements. All I can say is that I am sorry, but my husband Bernard died around the same time as you lost Mr Almond. I meant to write to you before but it has been such a shock and I have had so many things to arrange and sort that I have not been able to get in touch without weeping so much into the writing paper that the blotting made it impossible to decipher.

I am left with four children and many debts. I did not know how Bernard had gone on. I think he thought that the managing of your husband's quarry would be the making of him. He has gambled much over the years and left us penniless. He got into a fight in a pub in Hexham and was no more. I will not burden you further.

I have family whom I hope will help to keep us. I trust you will fare better.

Yours sincerely,

Eliza J. Lennox

Nell Almond was stunned. It had not occurred to her that things would be different than her husband had wished. She did not know what to do. She could not have the previous managers back. Apparently Daniel had left the area, which she was glad of, and she did not want Zeb Bailey there. She had never liked him, a convicted murderer and an ill-mannered lout.

She fell asleep by a big log fire and when she awoke it was because one of the maids, Norah, was ushering a man into the room. Norah had no idea how to answer the door and was given to bringing people in without asking, so Nell was vexed that it was Sawrey March, local gentry.

Nell barely knew him. She was told he had been at the funeral and thought it good of him. His family had once been important, but talk said that his father had left him and his sister penniless. They lived in the most beautiful house in the dale, so it was said, but old and ruined, like an old bastle house, a fortress high up on the moors beyond Stanhope. The house was tall and dark and nobody went near it.

Sawrey March was between thirty and forty and apparently the most beautiful man in the world. The local women would have avoided him had he ever asked any of them even to walk out with him, because his beauty and social status would tempt them. But of course he never did ask.

He lived in his house in poverty with his strange sister who went nowhere. Sometimes he rode into Stanhope on the one horse he owned, which was well looked after, but nobody knew anything about him.

Nell had glimpsed him from time to time, and she knew that he was a fine-looking man. He wore old clothes and had nothing to say, but everybody knew that his lineage was superb and that his family had been here since time began and so in a way they owned it. He certainly looked as though he thought so.

Nell was therefore disconcerted when this young man turned up in her sitting room and found her asleep. He was so beautiful that it was hard not to stare. She noticed his worn out, though obviously once expensive, elegant clothes. She saw that he had impeccable manners, and when he spoke it was musical and his smile was entrancing and his eyes were so blue.

His hair was bright yellow like daffodils in springtime, Nell told herself, giddy, but there was about him a touch of the Viking – tall and with something of a carelessness about him, as though he owned everything he encountered. He touched her hand with long, slender fingers and excused himself and said all he wanted was for her to understand that he had liked the little he had known of her husband and that he could imagine how hard it was to be alone.

He and Augusta had been left by themselves. Their parents had died early and left them penniless. He didn't say that, of course, but he didn't need to. The whole dale knew it. The air of strange mystery hung about him so that Nell wanted to laugh at her own reaction. No woman could know this man and remain impervious to him.

It was not a whim that made Sawrey March visit Mrs Almond that day. He had thought a great deal about it after being at Mr Almond's funeral. In fact, he had thought about it as soon as he heard that Mr Almond was ill and likely would die, though he did not think about his future in connection with the widow.

She looked awful at the funeral, but then widows always did. He was assessing her situation, and his own, and wondering about how much money this woman actually possessed. She had a grandchild, it was true, but he was an infant and she had shown what she thought of Daniel Wearmouth by getting rid of him.

Sawrey knew nothing about industry of any kind; he had been brought up as a gentleman. It made him want to laugh. Some gentleman he made – not educated and badly treated. His father and grandfather had gamed away everything except the house that he and his sister lived in, if you could call it living.

The farms had all been sold off by his father and the money wasted. All he had was a crumbling though beautiful house, empty cupboards, empty barns and byres, and a sister who would not go outside. He had to do something soon or they would starve.

The young women of the dale who had money would not have considered him as a husband. Indeed, their fathers would never have let them anywhere near him. Not that he had tried. But when he looked in the mirror, he understood why they gazed at him across the church pews, why they gazed at him with longing from the other side of the street. He was so beautiful that it was an insult when he had nothing else.

Gussie, his sister, was not beautiful. Her beauty had left her before she was eight years old. She had been treated like an animal and had withered from it. She was terrified of life, but he had to try to further her existence. He had to secure a marriage of some kind, any kind, and all he had to recommend him, like a woman, was what he looked like.

That and the fact that he was at least ten years younger than Mrs Almond, possibly a great deal more. He was hoping it would get him what he wanted.

He could not afford to marry a young woman who had nothing, and how could he take her to the house where the roof leaked in a dozen places, the rooms were damp and even the rats had deserted, since there was nothing left. The stables were empty but for his one faithful horse. He kept no dogs and no cats; they had long since left for somewhere they could be sure to eat. His land was desolate, mostly moorland and not cared for any more than he and Gussie had been. There had been other houses in easier places, London and Leicestershire and even in the Lakes, but these were long gone.

He wandered his few acres, watching the rabbits running through tall ferns that brushed against his legs, leaving his clothes soaked. He liked in some ways that it had run wild, but it did him no good financially. The lapwings swooped and cried out and he wished he could do the same.

When the land was purple with heather he loved it best of all, except for when the snow fell. Or in the spring when he could go to sleep hearing the lambs crying in the fields where men had fared better and had stock. In summer he loved the river. He loved all of it so much that he had to do something so that he and Gussie could stay here, at least for a while.

Mr March had been at the funeral, Nell remembered, and had been kind, saying that anything he could do he would, which was nothing more than a dozen other people had said. It was expected and she had been flattered that he had bothered to come to the funeral. He apologized for being alone; his sister had the headache, he said. Nell knew very well that Augusta March was said to be mad and never left her home.

The day at the house, she ended up telling him the whole story about the quarry and her lack of a manager. Just having someone to confide in helped. She knew that she ought to send Pat McFadden a message telling him about what had happened, but she was somehow too tired.

'I'm afraid I know nothing of such things,' Sawrey March said, 'but if you need a report on how the quarry is faring I could go and have a look for you.'

The truth was that Pat McFadden, who looked after her grandchild, was seeing to the quarry as best he could, but she didn't want to acknowledge to him that she needed his help. She thought it would make him think he had some hold over her.

'My husband's clerk, Mr Paterson, a very reliable though elderly man, is in charge of the office and at the moment Mr McFadden is doing the best that he can, though his job was never management so he must be finding it hard. You could go and make sure all is well in the office and ask Mr McFadden to come and see me. I should have gone before now, but I couldn't get used to the idea that Mr Lennox would not be coming to take over, and I could get no further with it somehow.'

When Sawrey March returned home, he wished he could have stayed at Mrs Almond's house, which was so warm. It had been a long time since he could afford repairs to the chimneys and so the heat left the house without warming the rooms. There was no light, there was no warmth, there was no welcome. He should have been used to it, he supposed. He had nothing left. The buildings were falling down, the animals had been sold. Finding food was becoming such an effort. He shot rabbits and pigeons and foraged the garden for whatever was left. He was too downhearted to do more, and Gussie was always there, always needing him, always afraid.

He bounded upstairs with a lamp and went into his room, and there his sister Augusta lay. He knew that she was not asleep.

'You were such a long time,' she said.

'I'm sorry. I had to go and see Mrs Almond.'

'Why?'

He couldn't tell her that he was hoping his youth and his looks would enable him to marry the widow. It was the only hope he had left.

He put down the lamp on the dresser beside the window and when he lay down with her she went to sleep. It had always been so. She could not sleep when he was not there. He tried not to think about it. She insisted on having the curtains closed tightly against the moonlight, and since the curtains were worn, he could see the fields and the moon and what light came from the stars. He tried not to despair.

He must marry, but no woman on his social level would have him. They all knew that he was penniless; they all knew that his sister was strange. They all knew that he was desperate, and desperation stank.

Sawrey March rode his fine grey horse into Stanhope and asked where the quarry was. He was sorry that he had bothered to become involved. He kept telling himself that Mrs Almond needed his help and that Mr Almond would have been pleased, but when he got past the Methodist chapel and began to take the narrow track up to the quarry he started to question his motives.

It was cobbled, and his horse stumbled so often that he began to worry he might be thrown. In the end he got off the horse, but the climb became steeper. Soon he was sweating. It was not a pleasant road. He soon reached where the buildings of the quarry were and saw how wide and deep the whole operation was and how the men toiled like over-large ants on the faces of it at various depths which jutted out as ledges. It was a busy scene, with men shovelling big pieces of stone into wagons.

There was nothing to tether his horse to, as though nobody had ever come here on horseback, so he merely found a big stone to hold the reins in place and then he went into the office. A tiny fire played in a black grate and he could see his breath. An old man laboured at a high desk filled with papers. The old man looked up.

'Good day, sir,' he said civilly.

'Good day to you. Who is in charge here?'

The old man looked carefully around as though he thought somebody might materialize out of the desks or chairs. 'I suppose I am, at least in the office until the new manager comes. Are you he?'

'No, I'm Sawrey March from further up the dale, a friend of the family. Mrs Almond asked me to tell you and Mr McFadden that the man who was to be engaged has had some kind of accident and died.'

'I'm sorry to hear that, sir. It's common enough in these sorts of things,' he said, shaking his head.

'Perhaps you could enlighten me as to what is going on?'

'Well, I can tell you what's going on in here – it's orders and invoices and payments and wages – but I know virtually nothing about the quarry itself.'

'Mrs Almond said that Mr McFadden was looking after the outside operation.'

'I shall go and find him.' And the old man got off his stool and left the office.

He was a considerable time and Sawrey grew bored and began looking at the spidery handwriting, which was difficult to interpret. None of it made sense to him. He stood in front of the fire, rubbing his hands and stamping his feet. Eventually the clerk turned up with a tall man of about forty with keen blue eyes.

'Good morning, sir,' the man said respectfully. 'Can I be of help?'

'Mrs Almond sent me here, as I'm sure your good clerk has told you.'

'We understood there was to be a new manager.'

'Unfortunately he has had an accident and died.'

'I'm sorry to hear that,' the big man said. 'You'd better come and take a look round.'

They got just outside the door when there was the most enormous bang. It caused Sawrey to start so severely that he fell over. His horse reared, the reins dislodged from the stone and the horse ran off down the way he had just come. Sawrey watched it in dismay.

'That's just the blowing of the hillside, sir,' the man said, as though nothing had happened. 'We usually do it once a day. There were problems this morning so we're only doing it now. We're a bit short-handed. At this time of the year a lot of the lads go up to the lead mines, it's better work.'

Sawrey wondered why it was better work, but didn't want to display his ignorance. He found the whole thing utterly dreadful; it was like watching small creatures grub. The man with him was nimble, but he found keeping his feet even more difficult as they explored different levels. His leather boots grew a coat of thick dust and he coughed so much that he couldn't speak. He had thought to stay in the office, which he had expected to be a civilized place.

Worse still, he fell over a second time, tripping against a stone. The big man by his side was obliged to help him up. The men didn't stop what they were doing or even look at him, and he began to wish he had never said that he would do this. It was a dreadful place. He had never been so cold. After a day's hunting in the old days, before the money ran out, he would come back warm and elated with stories to tell and in companionship with his friends. This was awful.

Down to the quarry face they went, Sawrey watching his feet carefully so that he did not fall badly and pitch into the bottom. The men didn't stop. They occasionally shouted at one another and he was only glad that he didn't understand the patois. He longed to be back in his own dining room, even that which surely would be warmer than this.

The man with him kept being consulted about various topics, which again he couldn't understand for the quick way that they spoke, and though he was giving orders he did it in such language that Sawrey had no idea what was going on.

The men stopped and sat down and began to eat, and he imagined again his home.

'So, you are in charge here?' he questioned the tall man.

'No, sir, just trying to help. It isn't really my job.'

'I see.' He couldn't think of anything more sensible to say. His feet were so frozen that he couldn't feel them, which made him stumble all the more. He began to think about his horse and to wonder how he would get back to his home.

'Do you think one of these fellows might go and look for my horse?' he enquired.

The tall man looked blankly at him.

'Do you think he'll have wandered far?' was all he said.

'I don't know. He has never heard a noise like that.'

'Oh, right,' the tall man said, but he didn't offer to send anyone. 'If you are thinking you might need a cup of tea before you go, I daresay Mr Paterson will oblige you. I had better get on.' And he ambled away.

It took Sawrey a long time to scramble up the sides and finally reach the building that housed the tiny fire. He had been longing for it, but when he got there the old clerk was nowhere to be seen and there was only a young man, apparently doing nothing.

'Is the clerk here?' Sawrey asked.

The young man ignored him, asking instead, 'Is Pat about?'

'I don't know.'

'Well, I thought I should tell him that some damned fool let a nag wander from here down into the village, just in case it ends up back here and falls into the bloody quarry. It was all over the place.' And he left the office and closed the door.

The fire had gone out and the clerk was nowhere to be seen. Sawrey made his way down to the village and there his horse was patiently waiting. He wished he had not offered to go to the quarry.

Ten

When the work finished at the end of the day, Pat called in at Ash House. It was on his way home; his cottage was one of a long terrace sideways to the road that led onto the tops, neat against the valley to keep the wind away as much as possible.

It was the house he had known for several years, since leaving Tow Law where his father had gone to the iron works. They had left Ireland in 1841. He did not look back on it with any pleasure. They had left because they were starving, and places like Tow Law and Stanhope had looked like paradise to them.

Pat had never thought he would long for the sight of Daniel Wearmouth, but it had to be said that Wearmouth had been a good manager. If Mrs Almond had kept off getting somebody new to manage the place, perhaps Daniel would be there now, though he had never been to see his child and was so often drunk at the quarry after his wife died that he made the place unsafe.

Pat knew Mrs Almond well, not just as the quarry owner, though he still thought of her as the quarry owner's wife, but because he was bringing up her grandchild as his own.

It wasn't something he had wanted to do, and neither did he want this woman with access to his house, but there was nothing he could do about it.

He made his way through the imposing gates of Ash House, reaching the door in a not too good mood, only to be told by the girl who answered the door that he was to go round the back, as he was a workman.

'I'm not going any place, Norah Hobson, so just tell your mistress I'm here. She is expecting me. And try to keep a civil tongue in your head.'

She scowled at him and disappeared into the hall, closing the front door so firmly behind her that Pat wanted to kick it in. After a long pause she came back and opened the door without saying anything, so Pat tramped into the hall.

He was covered in quarry dust and dirt since it had rained hard earlier, so he could quite understand why she didn't want him at the front, but he took no notice and followed her into a great big room which could have housed four families without lack of space.

There Mrs Almond sat like a scraggy queen and did not offer him a seat. Likely she cared for her velvet cushions, he thought. She was clad in black, and it was not a colour that became any woman over the age of thirty-five, Pat thought. Her face had dropped; her eyes were dim. She had lost her husband and her daughter and now her plans for her quarry were coming unstuck.

'Mr March came to the quarry and said that Mr Lennox had died, and since there's nobody looking after the place I thought I had better call in and see what you have planned.'

Mrs Almond said nothing and then sighed.

'I suppose you had to know.'

'I suppose I had. Here am I trying to run the quarry and nobody is going to come and sort it. It's not my job and you aren't paying me for it, so I need to know what's going to happen and so do the two hundred men you have working for you.'

'It's been no time at all since you took on the job and you knew it was temporary. I now have no quarry manager. I thought that you might be prepared to do it until I find somebody else.'

'I have been,' Pat said shortly, 'and so far I've had nowt for it.' This she ignored. He wasn't having that. 'I don't know enough to carry on the quarry by myself,' he said. 'Zeb Bailey is sitting in the sweet shop doing nowt. Why don't you ask him?'

Mrs Almond scowled at him. 'I don't want that man in my quarry.'

'Well, you have to do something shortly or there'll be problems. Two hundred men cause a lot of trouble between them, the weather doesn't help and they take no heed of anything I do tell them because they know it's just me. And Mr Paterson's eyesight doesn't help either. We could do with a new clerk but for the fact that the poor old bugger has nowhere to go and nowt to go to.'

Mrs Almond frowned – not at him, particularly, but at the idea of problems that could not be solved, and rain and wind that nobody could do anything about.

'And they're getting fed up. I told that feller who came, the men don't like it when they know nobody's in charge, and when the weather turns they go to the mines because at least they're inside – and it pays better.'

That was the final insult, Nell thought, and glared at him again.

'So we're short-handed,' Pat said. 'Wearmouth's gone off and left his wife when he lost his job. I've no idea where he might be, so unless you can think of summat better, you might find talking to Bailey is a good thing.'

'I don't like him.'

'He's the only man in the dale who can do the job, so maybe you should learn to grit your teeth and talk to him.'

Nell wasn't used to workmen speaking like this to her, but Pat wasn't bothered about who she was, she had known that the first time she saw him. And she was obliged to be grateful to him because he had taken in her grandchild.

Pat felt like she should have given him the money he was due for the role he was playing, which he felt stupid about every day. It would have eased the wound, but this woman wasn't into easing other folks' wounds, even though she had come up from nowt.

She must think she was a long way from nowt now. But it wasn't so: she could be putty in the hands of some no-good bloke. Zeb would treat her honestly. The men didn't like him but they respected him; some of them feared him because he had killed another man. He was the right person for the job and she must know it.

'Will you speak to him for me?' she said.

That was clever, Pat thought. She didn't want Zeb in her

house or her quarry, but this way he would take on the task for her.

'He'll need more money than before,' Pat said now.

'Why?'

'There were two of them running it. It's a big job for one man, a hell of a lot of responsibility, and if there's an accident or things go wrong he gets the blame. And he should be asked to get Wearmouth back.'

Mrs Almond said nothing to that.

'Well?' Pat prompted her. He was uncomfortably aware that he was bullying a recently widowed woman, but they needed to be practical.

'And I want decent wages for all these weeks when I knew nothing and I kept on going.'

'You shall have them.' She didn't look at him.

'All right then, I'll go and see Bailey and I'll tell him to contact Wearmouth – if he has any idea where he is – and we'll see if we can get this place back to where it makes some money for all those mouths it's supposed to feed.'

Pat went to see Zeb Bailey at the sweet shop. Alice was there, as usual. They knew one another well and he greeted her casually and said, 'Is Zeb about? I'd like a word.'

Alice raised her eyes to the ceiling. 'I wish to goodness he would find something to do. He is driving me mad. If he comes in here once more and tries to tell me how to run my shop I will kill him,' Alice said, only half in jest, and she nodded at the door that led into the back room. There Zeb sat, reading by the fire. He did not look up at first, but when he realized it was Pat he got to his feet.

'No work then?' Pat said.

Zeb shook his head. 'Mrs Almond has blackened my name all over the area. I couldn't get a job holding a horse.'

Pat grinned at this, in remembrance of Sawrey March, but when Zeb enquired as to what was funny he just shook his head and said he would tell him over a pint. Zeb hesitated.

'Oh, howay, man,' Pat said. 'Miss Lee can't wait to get rid of you.'

They went through the back. 'I won't be long,' Zeb said to Alice.

'Go, please. Give us all a rest.' But she smiled as she said it, and he smiled back at her before he closed the outside door of the shop and followed Pat along the street.

They wandered down to the Grey Bull, which was a farmers' pub on the edge of the village, but it didn't matter. Everybody was friendly but nobody got in the way – lots of nodding and no conversation. They sat down well away from the fire, but still amongst the smoke, which was blue with cigarettes and smelled of beer. There was the noise of the darts players and the clatter of dominoes and outside it was once again raining.

'So what's up?' Zeb said, when he came back from the bar with beer that was velvet brown and frothing beautifully. It made Pat happy, even just for a few moments, to have the beer and the fire and the bar and decent company.

'Lennox died,' he said, taking a first full sup.

After a day at the quarry there was nothing better than the

first slurp from the first pint, but he didn't often have the opportunity. It wasn't fair to Shirley to leave her up there with his father and mother and three bairns when she had had them all day. She was the kindest woman ever, he thought. She urged him to go out and yet he didn't.

His father was almost bedridden and his mother was always going on at Shirley – anything she could find fault with, she did. He had spoken to her about it over and over, but she took no notice or didn't understand or didn't see that she was doing such a thing.

Shirley knew that he would not have left her just for the sake of a couple of pints, but by hell, it felt fine. He had called in at the house and told her what he was going to do, and she had kissed him and told him that it was a good idea and then he had plunged back down the bank towards the town, the sweet shop and finally, and to his joy, the pub.

Zeb stared. 'He wasn't that old.'

'According to Sawrey March, he died in an accident.'

Lennox was well known in the area for being an expert, and although Pat knew Zeb had hated being let go, Lennox was the man to run the quarry if somebody had to do it on his own. The trouble was that Lennox had a reputation for drinking and fighting, so they didn't know whether that had had something to do with it. Anyroad, it didn't matter.

'Shit,' Zeb said, making inroads into his first pint. 'What was March doing there?'

'Mrs Almond sent him to see how things were going. God knows why. He says that he is a friend of the Almonds.'

'Oh Jesus,' Zeb said, 'he's one of those buggers whose

families rode to hounds, slaughtered birds and decimated the bloody river. How come he's friends with them? He and his sister are gentry and have that scabby old house, and Mr and Mrs Almond came up from nowt.'

Pat recounted the story of the horse, and Zeb laughed.

'Jesus,' Zeb said again, and that was when Pat got up and bought two more pints, even though the first round had lasted no time at all.

'Nobody's been there to look after the place or do the blasting,' he said. 'I'm doing three bloody men's jobs and barely being paid for one. I'd go off to the mines if I could.'

'You can't leave your Shirley.'

'God knows how she copes. That house is the same size as a hen cree. Me mam's a bloody pain in the arse and me dad is dying all the time.'

'That's not fair,' Zeb protested mildly.

'I just needed to say it. The bairns are hard work.'

'I think bairns always are. How's the boy?'

Pat hesitated. 'He's a lovely little lad but he's not mine,' he said. 'I never wanted him. Shirley dotes on him, but I cannot forget how Wearmouth ran away and left me to sort this out.' He took another sip. 'Mrs Almond wants you back at the quarry.'

Zeb looked sharply at him. 'Me?' he said, like somebody who'd never seen a quarry. 'I can't do it without Daniel, and I don't know where he is.'

'I'm doing it,' Pat pointed out, 'and I know a bloody sight less than you. Haven't you heard anything?'

'He went off to Durham. He said he would get in touch,

but he could be anywhere by now. And flaming Susan is still with us and that house over the road down the bank is empty.'

Pat sighed 'Women, they don't get it. What are we with nothing to do?'

'I'm going mad, and besides, if we could have a bigger house we could get married. At the moment the only person I'm sleeping near is my dad.'

Pat laughed. 'Shirley and me, we hold our breath and try not to make any sound because my damned mother is listening at the other side of the wall in case we might enjoy ourselves. Not that we ever do, who has the energy?'

Zeb laughed then. 'Alice went to Mrs Almond.'

'Oh hell,' Pat said.

'She didn't get it, that if we waited she might have come to us.'

'Why wouldn't Alice try? That's what she does,' Pat said, remembering how she had got him to take the boy against his better judgement.

'She doesn't know how to wait.'

'She has waited a very long time,' Pat said.

'So have I,' Zeb said, and he got up and went back to the bar for another pint. Although they both knew they shouldn't have a third, just for once they couldn't help it.

Eleven

'You need to go up there and talk to her,' Alice said.

Zeb didn't want to speak to the woman who had treated him so badly, but he didn't have any choice. When he went to bed, he thought that there must be a way of getting in touch with Daniel other than spending days, maybe weeks, searching the city for him.

'Dad, you're snoring,' Zeb said affectionately, and his father snuffled and turned over and said that he wasn't.

Zeb imagined Dan in Durham, alone, thinking of how his father had died. Worse, because Susan was here and Dan was in Durham, he had to sleep in the room with his father and Susan with Alice. Susan didn't seem to notice, but then Susan never noticed anything, and he didn't think she had any idea about how he and Alice felt. His father had no place to go, and after years of thinking he hated his dad, he couldn't imagine what it might be like without him.

Getting in touch with Dan would not necessarily solve the problem and he had the horrible feeling that it would get worse before anything could be done.

Zeb duly went to see Mrs Almond, and he made sure that

he looked his best when he did. He knew that she didn't like him, and he didn't like her, but if she was going to give him a job and pay him properly for doing it, they would manage. He was seen into the living room by a sour-faced girl who obviously saw him as a murderer. He should have been used to it by now, but he never was. He ignored her and stood in the middle of the room, gazing down at a woman who had lost a lot of weight, which was not surprising, he thought.

'I was short-sighted,' she said, 'I didn't understand what could happen.'

'There's no way you could have known. Your husband had sorted it out as best he could. He didn't imagine what might happen to Mr Lennox.'

She threw him a grateful glance. He was surprised. 'I don't like you,' she said.

Zeb couldn't help smiling at the frankness.

'I understand that you might employ me, but although I would take it on, I can't be responsible for all of it. It's too big. We need to get Daniel Wearmouth back here.'

'I don't want him in my quarry.'

'Do you have any choice?'

She didn't answer that, and for the first time he could see that her lips were trembling. He felt sorry for her. She hadn't asked for any of this.

'I will try to find him,' he said. 'I don't know where he is, though I know he went to Durham. If I find him will you take him on again?'

She turned her face away. 'If I have to. You see, I don't want him anywhere near the boy.'

'He doesn't seem to have any interest in the child,' Zeb said, though he felt like saying that the boy was Daniel's son and he would always have more right than anyone else to see him.

'But what if he does? What if he tries to take Frederick away?'

This astonished Zeb. He hadn't known that she felt so deeply about it all, but then why wouldn't she? The child was the only person she had left.

'To what?' he said, gently, unable to imagine Dan running off with the child he blamed for his wife's death.

'I don't know.' Her voice shook.

He felt sorry for her now, as he had not done before. She was in a bad way, so he spoke softly to her.

'I don't think he would do such a thing, Mrs Almond, and you have my word that I would never let him.'

The tears fell as she turned up her face to him.

'That's unduly kind,' she allowed. 'You will see if you can find him and make it right?'

'I will do my best.'

'And you will go to the quarry tomorrow? Please say you will. It haunts my dreams that, now Harold is gone, things will overwhelm me.' She broke down and cried.

He reassured her. He didn't think they liked one another any more when he left, but he had gained for himself a much better wage, which he thought he deserved, and he was resolved to find Daniel, whatever it took.

Twelve

Alice felt strange. She examined the feeling but didn't recognize it. Her body didn't feel like hers. She felt other worldly, and had to keep bringing her concentration back to the sweet making. She was frustrated. She wanted to have Zeb to herself, but couldn't.

That week, Mrs Potter, whose husband was the local blacksmith, came into the shop to buy sweets for her children and told Alice that the greengrocer's daughter was getting married in a hurry. Mrs Potter leaned over the counter towards Alice, though the shop was empty but for the two of them, and said that the greengrocer's daughter hadn't been feeling well and we all know what that means.

Alice replied vaguely, distracted at the time with weighing out chocolate almonds. Mrs Potter was addicted to them, and because she spent so much money at the shop Alice was grateful, but when she had finished and Mrs Potter had left, Alice found herself staring into the street and recalling what Mrs Potter had said.

Her bleeding had not arrived, her breasts ached and she was unduly tired, and that was when it dawned on her that her monthly bleeding was well overdue. She was not sure whether it might be the chocolate that was making her feel ill, because suddenly she had to run into the back, and she only just made it to the lavatory before being very sick. When it was over she felt dizzy, and saw that Susan had come into the yard and was hovering at a distance.

'Are you all right, Miss Lee?'

Alice had long since told her to call her by her first name, but Susan had never got the hang of it and it made Alice feel so very old. She was horrified at the realization, and could not stop trembling. She did not want Susan to come any nearer and realize something was going on, so she replied faintly that she thought it was just a tummy bug and she would be okay. Susan went back inside but Alice remained in the back garden and the trembling grew worse.

She tried to reassure herself. She could hardly be expecting from one encounter. Some people tried for years to have a baby and with others it took months and sometimes not at all. How long had she laid alone in her bed and imagined her life without a husband and child, and now she had the nerve to regret what she had done.

She wished she could ask the greengrocer's daughter about her experience, but then she brushed the thought aside, went back in and rinsed her mouth with cold water.

Susan offered to make tea but Alice shook her head.

'Why don't you go and lie down for a little while?' Susan advised and Alice, who could not stand the idea of the sweet smells in the shop, nodded and went upstairs. She lay there shaking and could not put from her mind the idea that she might be having a child.

She lay for about an hour and even dozed. Feeling better, she told herself that she had panicked, the whole thing was ridiculous and the following morning she felt well again and tried to put it from her mind.

She was fine for three days and then she began being sick again, and by the end of the week she could no longer pretend that everything was all right.

'If it is your tummy,' Susan said, helpfully, 'it could go on for days. Mr Irons told me he was sick for a full fortnight. It's something going around.'

Alice see-sawed between the two ideas and then she admitted to herself that she was having a baby. Since they were to be married, it would make everything right, and if the baby arrived a little bit early hopefully people would be kind to her. What she wanted now was a wedding and to urge Zeb to go and see the vicar with her.

Alice wished Susan would go and live in her own house but she didn't know how to say it. People talked about the way that her new husband had gone and left her, about how she was sleeping at the sweet shop. Late one Saturday afternoon when Susan had gone to the chapel and Mr Bailey had gone to see the Vernons, she stopped making sweets and went through into the back where Zeb was sitting at the table, doing nothing as far as she could see, possibly dozing when he was meant to be busy with papers from the quarry.

Zeb was very busy at work now and she knew he must be

finding it difficult. He had Pat there to help, she knew, but he needed Daniel. He was very tired and very quiet and she didn't like to say anything to him.

She came to the table and hovered, but he was so deeply into what he was doing that he didn't notice, and she had to call him by his name twice before he looked up.

'I don't know how to get in touch with somebody who hasn't written and doesn't have an address.'

'Zeb, I've got something I need to say to you.'

He smiled at her. 'Is it about the wedding? Yes, we will go and see the vicar very soon.'

'We need to do it quickly.'

He looked blankly at her.

'I think I'm having a child.'

He stared. He looked down at the paper and his pen and then stared at her again.

'Heavens, we are good,' he said, and that made her laugh and then she thumped him and he pulled her down onto his knee, but he looked seriously at her. 'Do you feel all right? Do you want to see Dr McKenna?'

'He's the last person I want to see. He asked me to marry him and now I'm about to produce a child out of wedlock.'

'No, you won't. We'll sort it out this week.'

'We will?'

'Of course we will.'

She looked down at the table and the paper, which he had not yet written on. 'Why don't you address it to the local post office and tell them you will pay to have a notice put in their window?'

'Alice, you are a genius. Oh Alice,' he said, taking her into his arms and kissing her, 'we shall have a wedding.'

She thumped him. 'You are very rude. I wanted a proper wedding.'

'You wanted a proper husband too, no doubt. You can't have any of that, I'm afraid. Oh Alice, think what it will be like. We're having a baby. It'll be wonderful.'

Alice stopped crying and looked up at him. 'You promise?'

'I promise,' he said.

Thirteen

Daniel was fast asleep. He was sleeping better now that he had a job and was making a wage. He hadn't slept properly since Arabella died, but now he went off into a deep sleep. It was the first time he had slept properly in months. The dreams of Arabella haunted him, and so did those of how he had jilted Susan for the beautiful rich girl. He had lost his mind when Arabella died, but he was full of guilt now and could not forget how he had betrayed Susan and then had the nerve to imagine she would have him back. She had justly taken her revenge on him. He could not blame her for that. And as for the boy . . . He could not even bear to think of how badly he had behaved. Only the immature blamed grief for such matters. He should have looked after the boy and the quarry and tried to help Mrs Almond, but instead he had behaved like a child who had had his sweets taken from him. He could not stand the person that he had become, so here all he did was work, give up every penny to these kind women who had taken him in, and try to sleep.

He was hauled out of peace when he heard a scream and then another, and when he awoke properly he realized that it was not a nightmare, it was the sound of Cate giving birth. She was shouting and talking and breathing heavily and Mary's voice was low and warm and encouraging.

He was terrified. He remembered that he had not been there when Arabella was dying and he didn't want to be here when Cate died. He wanted to run away, throw on his clothes and disappear, but something stopped him. It was dark, the middle of the night, but he would not let himself run away, even though the sweat ran down his back until his shirt stuck against him as he pulled on his clothes.

He lit the candle that stood on a wooden crate beside his bed. And then the air was rent again. He flinched, but took the candle and went next door.

He had been right. The lamp was lit and he saw Cate in bed, upright, red in the face and yet somehow so white. She was yelling and screaming, and he felt horrified.

'We have to get her a doctor,' he said.

'Nowt of the sort,' Mary said, 'she's doing grand. I've watched me mam give birth half a dozen times, and the other women too.'

Dan stared. 'She's in pain.'

'Aye, well, that's what happens when you're bearing some bugger's offspring,' Mary said. 'Maybe you'll take note of it next time you fancy it.'

'Should it be like this?'

'Will you stop talking about me as though I'm not here!' Cate said through gritted teeth.

'Oh, for the Lord's sake,' Mary said to him, 'why don't you go and stoke up the fire?'

'Do you need hot water?'

'No, I need you to concentrate on summat other than the lass's pain,' Mary said, and then Cate screamed again and he was off and downstairs and intent on the fire as the night went on.

'Bloody Henry Westbrooke,' Cate said.

'Breathe now, breathe carefully.'

'Shut up, Mary! My God, I will never let a man near me again.' And Cate held hard to the back of the chair, because she was on her feet by now.

She walked up and down, up and down, as the pains came and went. Dan kept away, downstairs, sitting by the fire, listening to her. He wished he could go out and find a doctor. Arabella, even with a doctor, had died. He was so afraid now. The night began to pale, and the colour of the sky was the only thing that changed. He stayed below, listening in case he should be needed, but why would he be? Even if she died, he did not know what to do.

It was only a couple of hours before he would usually get up for work, and then things changed. Cate's screams became longer and he could hear Mary's low, sweet voice encouraging her, and just when he thought he couldn't stand to listen any more, the voices changed and he could hear the high note in Mary's voice, giving instructions.

'Easy, easy, pant, pant. It's coming now, all right, steady, give it time.' And he could hear Cate's cultured voice swearing and trembling and then she was crying, but not in a bad way, in a resigned but almost pleased and breathy sense, and in the end both women began to cry and speak at the same time and then they were like a little island. They began to laugh together.

Dan stood in the kitchen and cried. He let his body sob and shudder. He heard Mary's heavy steps on the stairs. She bustled into the room and said, 'It's a boy. Well done, you, plenty of hot water.'

'Is she all right?' Dan said, not turning to her.

'She's fine. Will you go to Mrs Peters and tell her that I won't be in today? I need to stay here with Cate.'

He said he would and Mary took a basin of hot water up the stairs and she began to sing.

Daniel set off early so that he could deliver the message to Mrs Peters. Once again he played the concerned brother. He told her that Mary had a matter she needed today to resolve, and would be sure to be there the following morning, and that she hoped she wasn't putting them out unduly but it had been an emergency. Mrs Peters was gracious and said that Mary must take all the time she needed.

Dan was wretched at work but glad of it. His mind played over and over the day he'd had to leave the quarry to go back to find Arabella dying. But this time he didn't have to do that, so he got on with his work and tried to apply all of his mind to it.

This was not because of him, this was nothing to do with him, and he could stay at work and the skies would not fall. This was not his child. When it came time to go back he wanted to hesitate, to spend time in the pubs. He didn't want to face the little house where he imagined Cate had died, but he knew he owed more to them.

He crept home, and when he opened the outside door the first thing he heard was laughter. They were both downstairs in the kitchen. Cate had the child in her arms and there was the smell of dinner cooking and they greeted him eagerly, turning towards him as they heard his footsteps.

'Come and see the baby,' said Mary and Cate, more embarrassed, said nothing, but gazed down at the child in her arms. He turned from them and couldn't look. He went out into the night beyond the front door and after a little while the door opened and then clicked.

'Daniel?' It was Mary. 'Are you all right?'

'I'm fine,' was all he managed.

'No, you aren't,' she said, and she came and turned him into her arms like a child. 'What is it?'

He didn't know how often she asked him this before he could say, very short of breath, 'My wife died having our baby.'

'I'm so very sorry.' And she held him fast there while he sobbed and shuddered against her shoulder. 'Come and see the baby,' she said, and they went back into the house, where Cate sat by the fire, the baby tiny and pink in her arms.

'You're all right?' was the only thing he could think to say.

'Would you like to hold him?'

Dan shook his head and remembered that he had never held or acknowledged his own child. But he could see that she was not going to die, and she held out the baby for him. He stood there and then he knew that he wanted to hold the baby in his arms, and so he went forward as he had not managed to do after Arabella died and he took the child to him and instantly fell in love.

It was so small and so perfect and he knew then that everything was going to be all right. Cate looked better than he had ever seen her; there were tired shadows under her eyes but her whole face was triumphant and he was able to hold the tiny being for a few seconds before handing it back to her. He was so afraid of himself and of life. When she took the child he saw how she looked down at it and he saw the love.

For the first time ever it was not just Arabella he wanted back. He knew that neither of them was to blame for what had happened, but that most especially the child was not to blame, and then the guilt covered him in darkness. What had he done to a child that was his, giving it up without a thought when it had no mother?

And he was glad, too, that Miss Lee had persuaded Pat McFadden and his wife to take it. What would have happened to it? Other people had decided his child's fate and had cared so much more than he did. He wanted to thank them, he wanted to go back, but most of all he wanted to be a part of the child's future.

Fourteen

Mr Bailey was spending a lot of time with the Vernon family. He would not have crowded them for the world, but the more he was there the more they asked him to be there, and it could not all be Miss Lee's cakes. When he was there one morning in early summer, drinking coffee and being polite to everyone, Mr Vernon came to him and asked for his help. Mr Bailey wasn't asked for his help any more, so he was delighted, but not quite sure he could do anything.

Mr Vernon took him to the print room and showed him what to do and confided that he was getting too old, he could not manage alone, and asked if Mr Bailey would help him.

'I do appreciate it,' Mr Vernon said as they ran off the latest edition of the newspaper. 'You work so hard for us and for nothing. I will take you on and pay you.'

Mr Bailey shook his head and refused, as he had refused several times during the past few months.

'It's getting to the stage where I can't manage without you,' Mr Vernon said. 'I can't keep on asking you if you won't take anything for it.'

'You and your sisters have made my life so much better. How could I take from you? Besides, half the time I eat here.'

Mr Vernon assured him that he was important to them and to their work and John Bailey heard it with joy. He liked being away from the sweet shop. He did not like the atmosphere. Susan was difficult and cried a lot, and while he could understand, it was not easy. Here among the Vernon family he felt better. They were his age, they understood and he was happy there. The two ladies were kind to him.

Miss Emily was rather shy and read a great deal. Miss Florence presided over the household. She was the practical one. She also helped organize the poetry group and the readings for the children on Saturdays, when people arrived until the rooms were full.

Miss Lee provided cakes, but when she couldn't offer more, other women began baking and there were pies and scones and extra teapots and tea and sugar and milk, so that on Saturdays the place became so lively that Mr Bailey was never home before the rest of the household had settled down for the night.

A lesser woman than Miss Lee would have complained, but she had soon seen that he liked being with the Vernons and so she sent him off each day with lots of goodies, as she called them.

He also went to help Mr Vernon, and he had begun talking to people who might have some news. He would go and collect the records of births, deaths and marriages from the vicar to put into the newspaper. It was hard not to like the vicar; he was such a genial man and so eager to help, even though their spiritual ideas were very far apart.

Mr Bailey would make weekly lists which he thought might matter for inclusion in the newspaper, and he would take note of when there were table-top sales, Bible classes, scholars' walks and outings, and these would all be published. He had realized that if people's names appeared, they were more eager to buy the newspaper. So he would take as many names as he could and the newspaper sold better and better, so Mr Vernon said.

Mr Bailey also went to see Mr Martin, who had taken over from him at the Methodist chapel. At first he had been given to resenting Mr Martin, but now he had a place here, a role to play, and he would jot down various doings at the chapel so that these could be put into the newspaper. Mr Martin, always genial, seemed flattered by the attention. It would encourage more people to come to the Methodist services, he said, and Mr Bailey agreed.

Mr Bailey went to various activities in the village, and he also encouraged women who belonged to different groups to write their reports. The Green Fingers Club had a competition each month for best flower, shrub or houseplant, depending on the time of year; the Married Women's League specialized in knitting, crochet and sewing and also had monthly competitions; and the United Women's Group were devoted to charitable causes.

Mr Bailey went and talked to the farmers about their prize stock, and he went to Miss Lee for various recipes which people might like a copy of, and not just cakes but hints on various herbs to be used in teas, such as mint and camomile and rosemary, and easy biscuits which they could make even when they were busy. He ended up writing a weekly column, which she helped him with, under her name.

The sheep show results were very important in May, and the local show in September. He was pleased at the very idea of all the things he could put into the paper, and every kind of competition found its way into the *Gazette*.

Mr Vernon published poetry and short stories, and there was information about nature walks and local history, geology input about the make-up of the stones and the lead and silver and limestone that made up the dale. Mr Peters, who was a botanist from Durham University, came there to live in the summer and would write all manner of articles. His knowledge was great while remaining friendly, Mr Bailey thought. He and Mr Vernon became more and more enthusiastic as the paper grew bigger and bigger and sold to everybody in the area.

Mr Bailey was even given to distributing the newspaper and would push it through the letterboxes. It paid him to do so because people flooded to the office to include something that he had not thought of and this had to be paid for as well. They liked to put in births, marriages and deaths at so much per inch, and Mr Bailey had the idea of charging people to advertise their various services, especially when something unusual was happening. They had taken to featuring a different aspect of business, shop or livelihood each week.

He thought about moving out of the sweet shop if he could find a room to lodge in somebody's house. A lot of families took in someone to supplement their income.

He wondered whether Zeb would be happy if he moved out, but now that Zeb had a good job and Miss Lee had the sweet shop they were making plenty of money, and he wanted not just a little space for himself but a little more privacy somehow. Zeb and Alice looked at one another like people who should be getting married.

He wasn't sure how he would manage it, or where he could go, but now that he had a small wage of his own he could think about changing his life. It made him pleased to think that he had this small power.

Susan was never happy, and he had the feeling that she would leave soon too. He thought he would move now, when he wanted to, rather than have her make the decision. Zeb and Alice would be much better married and having the place to themselves, and he would be better away from a newly married couple.

He asked Mr Vernon if he would mind if he put a sentence or two in the newspaper to see if anybody had a room for him, and Mr Vernon agreed. But that night Mr Vernon went home and told his sisters that Mr Bailey was looking for somewhere to live.

They were sitting around the tea table. They always ate at half past five and in the evenings had poetry readings and book groups. Both ladies went to spinning classes in the church hall, so they ate together and then went off to their various jobs. They had something on almost every night and they loved the activities.

They looked at one another, and then Miss Emily ventured softly, 'We have such a big house here – three bedrooms we don't need. Mr Bailey is a very nice man and he works so hard. I think he might be an asset if he came to live here.'

Florence pursed her lips and then she said, 'It wouldn't have occurred to me, but Emily's right. We have so much in common with him and I always think people are better living with those their own age, unless it's a complete family, and I don't think there's much room at the back of the sweet shop. I think it's a good idea. He fits in here so well and I do like him more than anyone I've met in a long time.'

'He has been a lot of help in so many ways,' Mr Vernon said. 'Why don't I suggest it to him and see what he thinks? He might not want to live and work in the same place.'

'I don't see why not,' Florence said. 'After all, we are very good company.' They smiled around the tea table. 'As long as we can still have Miss Lee's cakes.'

The following morning was the first opportunity Mr Vernon had to speak to Mr Bailey alone. They were in the printing works.

'I don't like to be personal, Mr Bailey, but if you would like to come here and lodge, you'd be very welcome. We feel as if you are part of our family. I know you are lodging with your son, but we thought you might prefer to be with us. You are doing so much for us, you've made a huge difference to our lives.'

Mr Bailey said that he couldn't intrude, and Mr Vernon wasn't sure whether this was just politeness, but he said again that they would be happy to have him, and so he must think about it.

Mr Bailey thought about it for a few days, then he told them that he would like to move in as long as he was not imposing.

Fifteen

Mr Bailey invited his son to the pub.

'I want to talk to you,' he said, 'and there are so few places to go. No wonder men drink too much.' They went off to the Grey Bull, to Zeb's dismay, since he was tired after his day's work. He hadn't been there very long yet, and he wished Dan were there to ease the weight of responsibility. It seemed to him that things went wrong every day, sometimes twice or three times. He left his father and went for beer. His father looked worried, he thought.

'Is there something wrong?' Zeb enquired as he sat down.

'No, no,' his father said, pushing the glass away from him as Zeb picked up his drink. 'I wondered whether you would mind if I moved out. I know that, to begin with, you would have liked to get rid of me, but we've . . . we've become close, and I don't want you to feel that I don't appreciate everything that you and Miss Lee have done for me. I don't know what I would have done without you both but—'

'But?' Zeb said, mystified.

'Mr Vernon has offered me a room in his house. I like the Vernons. They are people my own age and I am working with him and it's all very exciting. I feel as though there is so much to be gained, and I like his sisters very much, especially Miss Emily.'

Zeb thought that he detected a slight colouring of his father's cheeks at this point, but they were close by the fire so he couldn't be sure. Was his father in love? He wanted to laugh at the idea – aghast, in a way, that his father might inspire love. Or was this just his father's imagination and neither of the two Miss Vernons was interested in him?

Also – and Zeb was surprised at this – having not wanted his father there initially, now he did not want him to leave. It made him laugh. He had always thought he would be the one to move on. His father had finally come home, and in a lot of ways he was himself now, as Zeb had never seen him before – happier, and excited about the prospect of new ventures.

'You don't want me to go?' his father said, as though amazed that such a thing might occur.

'I don't want to lose you again.'

'Oh Zeb, I never thought to hear you say such a thing.' His father's face shone across the table from him. 'You won't miss me snoring.'

'In a daft sort of way I will.'

'But?'

'Well, I didn't quite know how to tell you, but Miss Lee has agreed to marry me.'

'Oh,' his father said, 'I'm not surprised. I'm so very glad for you. The extra room would be useful for you.'

'You're pleased?'

'Yes, of course I am. Miss Lee is a fine woman and she has

done more for us than anyone in the world. I will be happy to come to your wedding.'

The only thing Zeb wasn't happy about was that he would miss his father, but they needed a room to themselves and the arrangement as it was just wouldn't work. They couldn't move, as the sweet shop mattered a good deal to Alice.

Susan obviously had no notion of what was going on, and not the slightest suspicion that Alice was expecting a baby. They told her together about the wedding one night after he had come home from work and the shop was closed. The way that she stared made him certain she had not known.

'Oh,' she said. 'You'll want me to move out then.'

'No, my father is moving in to stay with the Vernons,' Zeb said hastily. 'There's no need for you to go anywhere.'

'I couldn't manage the shop without you,' Alice said. 'And besides, we've always been together. I couldn't get on without you, you're my family.'

Zeb rather wished she hadn't said this, but Alice was so kind.

'I see,' Susan said, but after that things changed, as Zeb had known they would.

Alice was disappointed. 'I don't want her to feel awful about it. She's had such a bad time, what with losing Dan and then Charles and then Dan again. It's like a nightmare.'

'We deserve some happiness,' he said, but he said it in a low voice.

The following day, however, after Zeb went to work, Susan announced that she would be leaving.

'Leaving?' said Alice.

'I think I should. I think you and Zeb will need the room.'

'No, we won't.'

Susan looked straight at her. 'You think I can stay here while the two of you are together and me lying there alone? How do you think that will make me feel?'

'I'm sorry,' Alice said, and she felt stupid saying it. She had had nothing in her life for so long and now she could make it right, she could have a husband and a child.

'I have a house down the bank. I'll go there.'

'Oh Susan, you don't have to go. I don't want you to feel pushed out.'

'I must.' Susan went upstairs and came back with a huge bag of her things. 'I'll come back for the rest.'

'At least wait until Zeb comes in from work. You were first to move in, I don't want you to leave.'

'He does.'

'No, he doesn't.' Alice felt awful about this, because it was true that Zeb no longer wanted Susan there. He would dearly have liked to sleep with her at night, and though the thought made her blush she wanted to sleep with him too.

She longed for him in so many ways and it was difficult to behave so as to make Susan think that she didn't feel like that. Once they had the house to themselves, everything would alter. They would be happy.

'He's made it clear,' Susan said.

'But you will come back and help me with the shop?'

'I don't think so,' Susan said. 'I'm sure I can find something else to do.' Alice felt even sicker than she had of late. Getting what you wanted, she decided, was as bad as not getting what you wanted. To look after the sweet shop and the house and do everything herself was a lot of work, and considering how she felt, it would be a burden. However, she didn't want somebody she didn't know well in the house. The idea of having a maid was very lowering to her.

Susan did not even come in to say goodbye. Alice heard the slam of the back door and watched her cross the street and disappear down the steep road that led towards the river and the house that she and Dan had never lived in together. Alice cried. She was given to crying a good deal these days. And then she thought that she would go a few doors down to where Mrs Garnet lived.

She knew Mrs Garnet was looking for something more to do, because she had said so to Alice in the sweet shop only the week before. She was a farmer's widow. When her husband had died, her daughter-in-law had made it clear she didn't want Mrs Garnet at the farm, but it was a good thing in a lot of ways, Mrs Garnet said. Life had always been hard at the farm, so she didn't mind leaving it. Now her son was keeping her in her little house, and he was generous, but she was often by herself. Alice had suggested she go to various meetings, as other women did, but Mrs Garnet said she couldn't get the hang of such things, having lived out of the village all those years.

Alice mentioned it to Zeb when he got home from work that evening and he said he thought it was a good idea. If

Mrs Garnet could look after the house then it would be easier for Alice to make sweets and mind the shop.

'I think her cooking will be good too,' Alice said. 'Farmers' wives always are good at it, but it will be odd having somebody about.'

'She won't be here in the evenings though,' he said darkly, and smiled at her.

Sixteen

Susan had not meant to leave so abruptly, but something drove her away. She didn't want to be there alone while they were in the other bedroom together. It seemed as if her whole life had been spent watching others' happiness and trying to find her own.

She resolved to give up the house by the river. She had hated it from the moment she saw it. It was damp and dark and all it reminded her of was her marriage to Dan, how she had hated him and how he had gone away. She remembered following him and finding the train gone. That was how her life felt now – as though she had missed everything. She wondered whether Dan would ever come back, and decided that he would not, despite what Zeb kept saying.

First of all, she must find something to do, but she didn't know what, and in a small town like Stanhope finding work wasn't easy. Most of the shopkeepers had their families to help. There were several single women who ran shops, but in the front rooms of their houses with just a big table beside the window and jars and tins on shelves so that they could manage some kind of a living. Few of them were as professional as Miss Lee, and the bigger shops were run by men, and they wouldn't employ a pretty young woman for fear of talk.

She didn't know what to do. She couldn't go back to the sweet shop, and anyway, she was tired of making and selling sweets. It was a job that lasted every day but Sunday. She would like more time to herself and a house of her own that did not remind her of Dan or of Charles Westbrooke. They had both treated her badly. She wanted nothing more to do with men. She would put them both from her mind and go her own way.

She went for a long walk down to the edge of the village, and then came back up to the house. On the edge of the narrow street where the solicitor's premises were there was a little card in the window, which said, with a kind of desperate politeness, 'Help needed to sort out paperwork.'

Susan stared at it, convinced that it hadn't been there when she set out, but it was quite a small card, as though it didn't like to advertise itself, so she might have missed it. She wasn't sure whether solicitors were meant to advertise at all. She went inside, into a dark hall and then through into the waiting room, which was surprisingly light.

Somebody had heard her and a man dressed in a suit came through. It was Mr Calland, the new solicitor. The rumour was that Mr Preston wasn't well. Jos Calland was an incomer, from Consett, and he was not much above thirty. He smiled at her and Susan managed something similar and then enquired for the job.

He frowned. 'Have you done office work before?'

Susan was rather cross he didn't know her, but then he hadn't been into the sweet shop. How hard could this be compared with making and selling sweets?

'I would like to try.' She was for a few seconds assailed with the idea that Mr Calland didn't want to take her on because not only was she a woman, but she was a deserted wife. They didn't know that she had been so awful to Dan before it happened, nor that she had felt justified in it and that she had since regretted it.

'I want something new. I was very good at school and I lived with a lady called Miss Frost who taught me a great deal.'

He stood there, considering, and she said, 'Why don't you take me on for a week and then if you think I can't do it I'll leave?'

She could see that that sounded fair to him and he agreed. Susan felt elated. She had not been as happy in a very long time. She had finally done something for herself without anybody's help. All she needed now was to be good enough that he would not dismiss her, and then find a tiny place to live. She would not regret leaving the house; she couldn't wait to go.

She started straight away. He had not been joking when he said things needed sorting out. He told her that Mr Preston was unwell and that he had not been in Stanhope very long. She already knew that; nobody arrived in Stanhope without the whole place knowing of it within hours.

She enjoyed beginning to sort things out, and Mr Calland gave her the waiting room to herself, with a desk, so that she could greet people and see them in and out. She also began writing his letters for him. Miss Frost had always said that Susan wrote with a lovely hand, so she was rather pleased about this. At the end of the first week he told her that she could stay, and she asked him if he knew of anybody in the place who had a room she could live in. It didn't need to be very big but she hadn't heard of anything. She was then frank and told him that she was estranged from her husband and trying to start a new life. He said to her that she could stay in the building if she chose.

It was an end terraced house, so slightly bigger than most, but it suited her well. Susan was so excited she couldn't think. There was a room on the first floor that overlooked the dale, and downstairs in the back there was a kitchen of sorts. It had water, anyway, and a range and a big dresser. Susan couldn't think when she had been so excited about a house, and then she remembered how she and Dan had chosen their first cottage together and then he had jilted her. She determined not to think about it any more. She was finally going forward.

She took the furniture from her old house, which would make the place look like hers, and moved her things. It wasn't far, just a few doors up from the river, and she even gloried in that. She got the man who lived next door to her to help her with the furniture, and when it was in place and she was unpacking in the kitchen, she couldn't remember when she had felt as happy.

Seventeen

With Mr Bailey moved out and Susan gone, the whole place felt different – light and private. Alice came to be glad of the respite and of how she could behave as never before, as a young girl might, first in love. They agreed to be married as soon as they could and they asked nobody to the wedding but Mr Bailey and Mr Vernon and his two sisters. They all said that they would be very pleased to come.

Alice was going to cook and bake, and after the wedding they would go back to the shop and have a small celebration. She didn't ask Susan; there didn't seem to be any point.

Alice wore her best dress and Zeb wore a new suit, which Alice had insisted on because none of the others fitted him properly. The older people were so joyful, and she was glad they were coming to her wedding. That morning she had gone into her garden and picked a few pink roses, and then they walked down to the church in the early afternoon and were married.

It was a lovely day, so after the wedding they sat outside in Alice's tiny garden. They had ginger beer and cake, and when the older people had gone Alice and Zeb sat there together in the peaceful quiet of the little town and she thought she had never been so content. They were going to be a family. They were together now and would have a child, and tonight they would lie in one another's arms and her joy would be complete.

They trod up the stairs, and it was then that Alice felt a sharp pain across her stomach.

'Alice?'

'Oh, it's nothing,' she said, and went on into the bedroom. There in the lamplight he took her into his arms and kissed her, and another pain caught at her insides. She drew back, catching and then letting go of her breath very carefully.

'Are you all right?' he said.

She drew back further. There was another twinge. She waited for it to go, and it did, but just when she thought it had gone for good, it came back worse than ever. Doubled up, with both hands across her front, Alice began to sob.

'Shall I go for Dr McKenna?'

'No.' She clutched at his wrist. 'Don't leave me.' He tried to hold her close but she couldn't bear it. He lit the oil lamp so that they could see better, and the pain went on, until finally she said in awful choked tones, 'It's our baby. I'm losing it.' She could feel it come loose. The sensation was awful; it dragged at her insides, it knifed her in half a dozen ways.

She could feel when the bleeding began, sudden and unstoppable, and the awful feeling of the lump that was her baby. She bled all over the bed and he held her while it happened. The pain seemed never-ending, and when it was over, the sweat streamed down her back and between her breasts and over her thighs, mixing with blood. He took what had been their baby and wrapped it up and then he went downstairs and got hot water and he cleaned her up. It must have been, she thought later, the strangest time a man and his wife had spent on their first night of marriage.

'It wasn't the first night,' he pointed out later, when sanity had pitched itself back at them.

But that night, their wedding night, she lay there in a clean nightie and fresh bed linen while he went downstairs and soaked the sheets in hot water and soap to get the bloodstains from them, because he knew that she cared about such stupid things, and besides, it was something to do while she cried.

Then he went back and held her in his arms.

'We may never have a baby,' she said.

'Yes, we will.'

'What if we don't?'

'Don't worry about it. We're here together.'

'I'm so sorry.'

'Don't say things like that.'

'But I wanted to give you a child.'

'Alice, you are still here and I am still here and we can mourn the child we didn't have.'

She haunted herself with the idea that he was too young for her, that he could have married a woman who would have given him half a dozen children. She felt so very old, used up and tired. Exhausted, she fell asleep in his arms.

*

In the early morning she awoke after not much sleep and remembered that the child was gone.

'What did you do with the baby?' she said.

'I wrapped it up in clean linen in case you wanted to see it.'

'I do.'

She went downstairs and he opened the linen to show her, and then together they buried it beneath what she called the big diamond rock in her garden, a piece of quartz taken from a mine some age before this.

'What if I can't give you a child?' she asked him later.

'Alice, you have given me back my life. How could I hope for more? I love you as I had never thought I would love anyone.'

Eighteen

Sawrey had taken to visiting Nell Almond almost every day, and she had begun to look forward to this. She felt as if things were improving. Zeb Bailey was back at the quarry and she thought that he would manage until Daniel could be found.

She wasn't at all comfortable about the idea of Daniel coming back. She was haunted by the notion that he would somehow snatch his child. She had cried in bed several times over the idea, and one rainy afternoon she had sobbed by a big fire, but she knew that it was part of her grief, loneliness and fear of the future, and that she had painted Daniel a lot blacker than he really was.

She could see now that his grief over her daughter's death had been such that he could see nothing past it. It had to be admitted that Daniel had loved Arabella as much as any man had loved any woman, and his refusal of the child was raw grief and pain.

She tried to accustom herself to the idea that he would come back and things would be better. She didn't think he was the kind of man to snatch a child, and when she thought about this she could hear Zeb Bailey's reassuring voice, and she had to admit to herself that everything he had said was sensible. In the meanwhile, she had a lovely young man who was so concerned about her that he visited her often.

'And you and Miss March must come and stay some time soon. I haven't seen her in so very long,' Nell offered.

'She hasn't been well the last few years,' Sawrey said, 'but it's kind of you to ask. She never goes anywhere.'

Nell offered him dinner and he accepted, having said to Gussie that he would be late because he was going to see Mrs Almond and cultivating her acquaintance, so he felt happy enough doing this. He never saw decent food or wine unless he raided the cellar at home, which he tried not to do because it was almost empty.

Mrs Almond kept a good table, and although he tried not to drink too much of her excellent claret, he found himself singing as he covered the two miles home with less speed and more enjoyment than he usually did.

When he married her he would have good food every day. He had worried for so long about Gussie. He would be able to help her as never before. He might even be able to get a special doctor from London. They would have nothing to worry about.

He would be able to leave Gussie with Nell from time to time, and perhaps gain some kind of a life for himself, though he couldn't think what, as he had never had such a thing. When he reached Holywell Hall, he looked at the bad state it was in and thought that he would be able to make repairs, and the house itself would have something of a future.

When he saw Gussie, he wished he hadn't left her, even just for a few hours. She had known he was going, but somehow, like a dog, she assumed he would not come back, and he knew she had been sitting by the same window, watching for him all that time.

When he had settled the horse in the stable he went into the house. Since being with Nell Almond, he could see how shabby and cold and unwelcoming his own house was, and now he felt guilty because Gussie had no heat and the only light she had allowed herself was one candle. She was sitting where she always sat when he left her, unless she had given up and gone to bed. But she hated going to bed without him and sometimes would sleep downstairs. She complained to him that there were footsteps on the landing and shadows in the hall and she was afraid. He had wondered if this was her mind playing with her, but sometimes he thought the same, and since it was a very old spot and people had lived here for hundreds of years, it was hardly surprising that some of them had left an impression.

He made his way carefully through the house, hating it as he had not hated it before. The house was not to blame, and had not caused his problems, but it had become the problem.

He was hopeful. Mrs Almond seemed to like him, but she would have been interested in anyone who cared enough to call, and it seemed that nobody did. What a lonely, desolate life she was now leading, and any unscrupulous man could take advantage of her. Just as he was doing, he thought with a guilty pang. Then, as he reached Gussie, he forgot, and he saw her as if for the first time.

Gussie stared at him. She hadn't moved. She had been beautiful as a small child, but now she was like a ghost, all white and grey. There was nothing left of the hopeful little girl who had been flung out of the house and slept in the stables like a cat. She was so thin and coughed so much that he had given away most of the furniture to Dr McKenna. Though Dr McKenna said he didn't want it, he was the one man Sawrey thought he could not afford to offend, and so now the doctor had almost all of the valuable furniture that they had kept in their house. McKenna was very kind, and he had helped as much as he could, but he was the only doctor in the area and Sawrey could not have asked for more help for her, much as he would have liked to. To have the house put back into a decent state so that Gussie was warm in winter might make a huge difference, as would good food.

'I was a long time?' he asked her.

'Were you? ' They no longer had a clock in the house, but then Gussie had always gone by light and dark, by hunger and fear, so she saw time differently than other people. She didn't even ask him where he had been. Time stopped for her when he was gone. She just waited. If he had been gone a week, she might still have been sitting there.

'Would you like something to eat?' As he spoke he picked up the candle. It was almost going out. Gussie followed him through into the freezing kitchen, where he listened to rain batter the roof, feeling glad that at least he had got home before it began.

He was inside, his lovely horse had been rubbed down and fed, and now Gussie sat at the table obediently while he gave her bread, cheese and water. He thought guiltily of the food he had eaten and wished he could somehow have suggested to Mrs Almond that he should take some for his sister. Yet how could he have done it?

As Gussie ate, he told her all about Mrs Almond and the house, though not about the food.

'Why do you want us to be friends with her?' Gussie asked for perhaps the tenth time. He had been waiting for the question.

'Because I intend to marry her.'

Gussie stared at him. 'But you sleep with me.'

'She won't expect me to sleep with her.'

'Won't she?'

'Of course not. She's old and lonely and we have no money. She gets to live with us and we get her money.'

'Will she want to come here?'

'Why wouldn't she? Her house is awful, but worth a lot of money, and she can afford to put this place back to where it should be. Wouldn't that be wonderful?'

'We could have something nice to eat,' Gussie said, and he agreed. He waited until she fell asleep by the meagre fire and then he carried her upstairs and into her bed. When he was sure that she would not awaken, he went back downstairs and found a glass and a bottle of wine. The cellar was almost empty and that was as good a reason as any other for him to marry.

Nineteen

Dan started to feel different about himself. He liked where he was, he liked what he was doing and from the day that he held Cate's baby in his arms he began to feel better. He was glad to have work, he was grateful to have a home to go back to and Mary and Cate were easy people to live with. Mary was happy with the Peters family and Cate was entranced with the baby.

They had sufficient money coming in so that they could keep the house warm and they could eat well, and he was beginning to think that that would satisfy him for a long time when one day he happened to be going down Claypath on his way to the marketplace and spied a large notice in the post office window.

He nearly didn't stop. He would be coming this way tomorrow and probably most days and he didn't think it mattered, but something made him pause and then retrace his steps and he knew instantly what had caught his eye. It was his name, in large black letters.

He stood, going numb, as he read it.

'DANIEL WEARMOUTH. Please come back to Stanhope. Important news awaits you. ZB.'

That was all, and then he felt guilty that he had not written to Zeb, but he had tried and he wasn't ashamed of it until right this second. He knew he had been hiding and trying not to think about his past life. Maybe he had needed to do that, but now he could not hide any more. The only thing that worried him was that perhaps something awful had happened. He thought Zeb had more sense than to make him go back unless it was for the child. He was tormented by the notice.

He didn't want to have to go back to Stanhope ever again. He had been able of late to put the place from his mind, and he was thankful to do so. He had nothing but bad memories of himself, but he thought he had remade himself here. He felt like somebody completely new. He felt as if Cate and Mary were his family now. And now to have to face the person he had been . . . He couldn't do it. Every time he thought back to who he had been there, he flinched.

And in a strange way he felt closer to his father here, having seen Mr Perkins and done away with the idea that all prison warders were fiends. Discovering that the man was just another man doing his wretched best for his family made him like Durham all the better.

He was just getting established, and he liked coming back to Cate and the baby. No, he liked coming back to the baby. It made him think that perhaps none of what had happened to him really could have. He was building up a life here which had nothing to do with the huge and horrible mistakes he had made.

What could be that important? Arabella was dead; he

wanted nothing to do with the little boy. He felt such a lot for Cate's baby and had taken to coming home in the evening and sitting by the fire with the child in his arms while the two women made something to eat. He was such a lovely baby: he rarely cried, he slept often during the night, and even if he didn't, Daniel had taken to waking up when the baby did and lying awake, imagining Cate holding the baby in her arms while the streets were quiet and dark.

He wanted things to go on and on like this, so that he did not have to go back and face Susan. He didn't want to know what had happened to her, whether she was still living in the ghastly house where water crept under the door like a low thief. He did not forget how she had turned her back on him, how she had ruined his wedding night. In honesty, he had understood that, after what he had done to her, she had done it in revenge, but he couldn't go back to a loveless marriage, the humiliation of no job, no status and the knowledge that people were talking about him.

If he got in touch and gave Zeb his address, he would panic and want to run away. He might even do that. He might be obliged to give up everything he had created for himself – and to go back to what? He couldn't do it and he was angry with Zeb for making him feel so awful, so guilty.

He tried to sleep and couldn't, and the following day at work he kept thinking about the notice. He knew Zeb so well, but whatever had happened, why would he have got in touch? Would he do that if the little boy was ill? What would be the point of that? He had never seen the child after Arabella died.

That brought back all the hell he had been trying to get beyond, and he relived over and over everything that had happened, how much he missed her, how he had tried to move on with Susan and couldn't – she wouldn't let him and he wasn't sure he blamed her. He had treated her so badly, and when he tried to make it up it didn't work. Maybe it wasn't meant to work.

Maybe he was meant to be here. He tried to get back to where he had been before he saw the message, and for a few days it worked. He ate, he slept, he stopped thinking.

Twenty

After his father died, Charles Westbrooke went nowhere, but the days plodded forward and the house seemed to get bigger, and it was so silent that Charles despaired. Having banished cats and dogs from the house, and been glad of it, he began to regret the impulse. Even a dog or a cat would have been something with life in it. The servants didn't live in and never had – another one of his father's ideas. They had their own perfectly good homes beside the house and around the property, within five minutes' walk at most. His father used to joke and say that if he smoked in bed the house would go up and nobody would be wiser. He disliked having people there, it made him nervous. Charles had always thought it was because he could behave more badly with nobody there, but his father wouldn't have cared. He wanted them safe in their own homes.

So when Stewart and his wife, Laura, invited Charles to dinner, assuring him there would be nobody else there, he went. He didn't think he was a difficult guest – in fact, he was rather enjoying himself. The children were long since in bed, and he and Laura and Stewart were still at the table.

They talked about what it had been like when they were small children.

There, at least, he could talk about Henry and how favoured he had been by their father, but he saw the glance that Laura gave her husband and he stopped.

'What?' he said.

'That was never true,' Laura said.

'What do you mean?'

'Your father always preferred you. Henry was the obedient child and you were a ghastly little ruffian. He said to my father that you reminded him of himself at that age.'

Charles stared at her.

'You were,' Stewart said. 'The only time your father ever bettered you was when Henry died and you came home. You must know that, Charles, and by then your father was conquered and you know that too.'

'Henry was tall and handsome and rode a horse well.'

'Oh, for heaven's sake,' Laura said. 'You were the heir. Every girl in the entirety of the Lake District was trying to get your attention. Henry was a bore.'

'Laura . . .' her husband said.

'I'm sorry, but it's true. We all loved him dearly because he was one of us, but he never talked about anything beyond hunting. He had no friends, and every time I danced with him he crushed my feet. You were a beautiful dancer, so elegant, and you could talk about interesting things. You made every person you met feel so important, so clever – a rare gift – and you were funny and kind.'

Laura had married down when she took Stewart, who had

nothing but brains and his connections with the Westbrooke family to recommend him. Her father owned a small estate but naturally that had gone to her brother and it was well known that her father had left her penniless. Her brother wanted nothing more to do with her, though he had thought she might do a lot better than Stewart MacDonald. While not giving her a home or an income, he was not above telling everyone in the area that Laura had married badly.

'I would have given you half a chance, but you never once looked at me,' Laura said now to Charles. 'I was little and plain and dumpy and had no manners.'

'You haven't changed,' her husband offered devotedly.

'Oh, shut up,' she said. 'It's a pity I didn't wait for you to come back, Charles. I'm sure I could have managed you better now, and I wouldn't have been obliged to wed this ruffian.'

And then Charles laughed. Laura got up and went around the table and hugged him and kissed him heartily on the cheek.

'Oh, you fool,' she said. 'We have missed you so much all this time and you didn't care.'

Charles didn't know whether this encouraged him to go about socially. He wasn't given to such things, but since his father had died he had become more and more lonely. He just hadn't admitted it to himself. At first he had thought that he did not want to go out in the evenings, but the trouble was that he missed having somebody else there. His father, despite the fact that he had been a terrible old man, had been another person in the house.

Even Mrs Diamond went home once everything was finished. She would call in at the study, which was now where Charles holed up after dinner, trying to do something constructive, and make sure that he wanted nothing more and then she would go back to her husband, who was waiting for her just around the corner, more or less. She had an estate house, one of his father's better ideas. Thirty houses had been built since his father had inherited the place, and it made such a difference for people. They were well built of local stone and gathered in squares. Each house had water and its own privy. His father had made certain that the tenants and the servants lived well. It was one thing that Charles was determined to carry on, and even make better, if he could.

In the meanwhile, if he had to spend another evening by himself by the fire with a book, he would go mad. There were invitations, so, very carefully, he began to go out. He had dinner with Jack and his wife, but they were friends and not on his social level, so when the landed gentry began to ask him to their gatherings, he went.

They had asked him when he had first come home, but he hadn't gone then. He had been too consumed by his longing for Susan Wilson and Stanhope and the minister he had hoped to be. But now, as he took over the running of the estate with Stewart, he knew that he had to accept who he was and there was no point in fighting against it. He had to face the responsibilities that he had never wanted. And he needed a wife.

This was a huge admission. He held to him the idea that

Cate would think better of things and come home. He had also come to accept that he could never have Susan now that she was married. He would have to marry somebody he might, at best, like. She would also have to be somebody from the same background, and although she did not have to be rich there was never anything wrong with money.

If she were pretty, well bred and prepared to take him on, he would have to have somebody likely to breed boys. It made him sick, thinking of how his father had treated his mother. Was that what frustration and dislike of one's partner did? He tried to remember what Laura said, that he stood a chance of marrying well. He knew that he was neither tall nor handsome; there was nothing attractive about him other than what he owned, but he also knew that this was very important.

Twenty thousand a year and a prosperous estate were as important for women as for men – more so, in many ways. The inheritance of Catherine's family's estate was not tied to the male line, and so she was unique in that the estate would be hers – if she ever came back for it, he thought. Other women had nothing if they did not marry. He thought of Cate and how he had offered for her. He liked her spirit. She made him angry, but he thought that if they had married at least it would have been interesting. She was, in fact, the only woman he had liked in that way – after Susan – and that surprised him, because they had been nothing alike.

In a way he missed them both. But he regularly got himself into suitable evening dress, which felt very odd because he rarely wore anything like that, drove to the best houses in the area, and there he ate and drank and talked and even danced.

Hopeful mothers sent hopeful glances at him. Plain young women ignored him, because they knew that they had no chance. Anyone whose waist he could not close his hands around was not acceptable. It was disgusting, he thought, like a cattle market. He swore at that point that he would try to make sure that every girl on his estate had a decent education, and he would persuade other men the same, if he could, even though to a lot of them not only girls but boys should be kept in their place. Otherwise they might try to challenge the upper classes and that would never do. Who would hold the horses and clean the bedrooms and scrub potatoes in the kitchen? One of the things that had attracted him to the Methodist church was the belief in education. People needed choices, and education gave them that.

At these parties, he was often obliged to talk about hunting, which he loathed – not just because of the fox but because that was how Henry had died. He was not convinced that Henry had not done it on purpose, but that acknowledgement hurt so much that he couldn't bear it.

One evening, the gentleman bending his ear had been a friend of Henry's, so he was not totally oblivious to what he was saying, and he talked about Henry with kindness, so Charles was glad he had gone to this particular gathering.

Henry's reputation of indulging in disgusting practices prevented all but Charles's dearest friends from mentioning his beloved brother. He was so pleased at what this man said that he danced with both the man's daughters, no doubt raising hopes in both damsels. They were both lovely girls and very agreeable, and they made him wish that Cate was there, swearing at him and calling him names, or that he was back in Stanhope, sharing the Sunday school with Susan and walking through the streets, talking of chapel business and feeling happy.

He danced every dance and hated every second of his evening. He had spent the evening trying to work out which girl had the most brothers, so that he might decide which woman to marry. He couldn't wait to get back to his fireside, and when he finally did, he sat with the spaniel and the cats. They were treating him like his father now. He didn't care, and actually kissed the dog on top of the forehead. The spaniel looked at him in a most peculiar way and Charles was not surprised. And the black and white cat settled on his knee and he sank the brandy in his glass and wished his father had not died and that Henry was there and things were not so bloody impossible. To come back and be lonely like this was turning him into his father so surely that he was horrified.

Would he beat his wife when she didn't carry enough sons to suit him? Would he push her down the stairs so that she would be dead when she got to the bottom of them? Would he grow so impatient with her that he bedded women on the backstreets of Penrith? He began to understand why Henry had broken his own neck. It seemed to Charles that this was the easiest way out of something impossible, but he did not have the luxury of doing such a thing. There had to be an heir. Somehow, he had to produce one.

Twenty-One

A couple of times a year, Stewart and Laura went to Durham and stayed with their friends John and Lavinia Peters. The children liked one another's company, and when John had time off in the winter or at Easter they spent a week walking the riverbanks, going to the cathedral for evensong. Stewart would get to talk to men about things other than his work and he enjoyed how they had dinners at the various colleges. He also liked the Peters' house in the Bailey.

He didn't want to live there, but it took care of a part of him that sometimes felt left out. His father had been a scholar and, while he acknowledged he could never have done such a thing, he did like to be involved from time to time.

The Peters family had a new servant called Mary Blaimire who was from near Penrith, and Stewart wondered if he might know her. He didn't, but she was so good at what she did that he could not help being pleased to be around her. She was lovely with the children and made them laugh and took them for walks and read to them.

She was also proud of her housework and she could cook

and bake better than he had ever seen. Lavinia had to stop Mary from doing everything, but Mary was young and enthusiastic, so all they could do was admire, be grateful and wish they had somebody like her in their own house. Each late afternoon she would leave and go back to her own family, whoever they were.

One such afternoon, Stewart was venturing out just after her and so he followed her into the town and there in the marketplace he stopped and stood back, astonished.

Mary was meeting up with another young woman, a fair, tall and very good-looking woman, and Stewart knew who she was immediately. Lady Catherine Boldon. She looked very thin and rather poor, but it was definitely Lady Catherine.

He was shocked. The whole area had been looking for her after she disappeared, pregnant with Henry Westbrooke's child, and here she was. What's more, she had had the child, and was now cradling it against her.

Stewart couldn't think. He didn't know what to do. He carried out his mission in town, though it had but little of his attention. He thought he should tell his wife what had occurred. Should he tell Charles? Would he be betraying Catherine? If he said nothing, would he be betraying Charles's trust in him?

He went back and was soon caught up in the doings of the children and the evening party that the Peters had given for he and his wife, but Laura was not deceived.

'So, what is bothering you?' she asked, as they got into bed that night.

'Nothing.'

She looked shrewdly at him.

'I don't want to talk about it,' he said.

'All right then.'

He got into bed and she kissed him, snuggling down against him once he had blown out the candle. She was almost asleep when he said her name.

Laura groaned. 'Oh, I did give you the chance. The children have been hell today.'

'I know. I'm sorry. Go back to sleep.'

She closed her eyes, but she could feel how tense he was against her.

'All right,' she said, turning over towards him. 'I won't tell anybody else, I swear. What is it?'

So he told her and she took in her breath more than once and when the story was finished she said, 'No wonder you didn't want to tell me.'

'What am I to do?'

'I never liked her, but that's not the point. If you don't tell Charles and he finds out, and people always do, he will be livid. He's more like his father than he knows, and will probably kill you.'

'Well, thanks,' Stewart said.

'Was it a boy?'

'How in God's name am I supposed to tell from that distance?'

'Do you think he would take it from her?' Laura said.

'No, of course not, don't be dramatic. But it would be the heir.'

'That in itself is a responsibility, unless Charles marries.'

'If he does then it doesn't matter.'

'Do you think he won't?' Laura put the question tentatively.

'I think Charles is a dark horse and has a past he doesn't want us to know about. If the woman was married and he couldn't have her, he's just the sort of man who would be obstinate enough not to take anyone else. And he has always hated the idea that he had to marry and produce an heir. Laura, you could go and talk to her.'

'I knew you were going to say that,' his wife said, in much too loud a voice for a woman whose children were sleeping in the next room.

'I think it might help.'

'Whom might it help?'

'You could ask her to come back.'

'Likely,' Laura said.

'Can we really just say and do nothing?'

'She ran away.'

'Mary is poor. If Catherine is that poor and looks it, then she might reconsider marrying Charles. She has never been poor in her life. It must be awful for her.'

'I didn't think of it like that,' Laura said.

'If I follow Mary and find out where they live, will you go to her?'

'That is despicable,' Laura said.

Two days later, shortly after Mary arrived home, she heard a knocking on the door, and it was Mrs MacDonald. She was not surprised. She had recognized the people from her area, because everybody knew the better-off folk.

Luckily, she thought, they had not recognized her, and she was happy to keep it that way. Cate wanted nobody from there near her, and especially not somebody like Laura bloody MacDonald, who was an interfering bitch if ever one was born.

Mary swore silently, but it was at herself. She should have left the Peters as soon as these people arrived, but work was hard to find. How in the name of God had Laura found her?

'I'm sorry about this,' Laura said, 'but I would like to have a word with Lady Catherine. I know her family.'

'I'm not sure that's possible,' Mary said, half closing the door.

'Just ask her, please. I will wait here.'

Mary closed the door and went slowly into the house. Thankfully Cate was in the back room and must not have heard the door, or she would have seen Laura straight off.

Cate could see, Mary knew, that something was wrong.

'I've been recognized by the people staying with the Peters family. I should have left, I should have told you.'

'Who are they?'

Mary told her and Cate swore profusely, but also said, because she was always fair, 'It wasn't your fault. Hell, she'll go back and tell Charles where I am.'

'Shall I tell her to go?'

'No, you'd better show her in. What's the point in trying to hide now?'

Mary went back and opened the door. Cate came through into the kitchen with Harry in her arms.

'Laura,' she said, 'what in the hell do you want?'

Laura had always hated how beautiful Catherine was, but now she was skinny and gaunt. Her cheeks were almost grey, her hair lifeless, colourless and down past her shoulders as though it could do no better. She wore a dress that looked like a sack on her. It was washed out and shapeless. Laura could not help but stare. Was this really Lady Catherine Boldon?

As Laura stood there she heard the outside door and a young man came into the room. He was tall, handsome and wearing a good suit. Whatever had Cate got herself into now, Laura wondered.

'Stewart and I wondered whether you might consider coming home with us when we go back at the end of the week. Your parents are frantic, to say nothing of Charles. He doesn't know where you are or what happened to you. Don't you owe him better than this?'

'I don't owe that bastard anything,' Cate said, glaring into Laura's face in a way that made Laura want to step back. She had never heard any woman, especially a supposed gentlewoman, express herself in such vile tones.

'He offered to marry you in very difficult circumstances, and you behaved so badly in every way possible.'

'Oh, did I? And what would you have me do?'

'I think you owe Charles the marriage and to let him see

Henry's child. He has to have an heir for his estate. It seems to me that you might be carrying that heir in your arms.'

'Only if it's a boy though. How did we get to such stupid ideas? You can tell Charles that I will see him in hell before I go back there. The Westbrookes have no right to my child. Now get out.'

'I don't think that's quite true.'

'Henry is dead and it ends there. Charles was relieved when I left.'

'You don't know that.'

'Oh Laura, don't be naive. He only offered me marriage because he felt obliged to.'

'What about your estate?'

'It isn't mine.'

'Of course it's yours. You are the only child and it's not entailed on the male line. You know this. What are your parents supposed to do?'

'You think I care?'

'I think you ought to care. You were brought up to a high position. Are you going to run away from that? What about your responsibility to your parents? What if they think you are dead?'

'If you tell anybody that you have found me, I will see you in hell. Now get out!'

Laura, shocked and offended, didn't move.

'Show her out, please,' Catherine said, and the handsome young man moved slightly towards the door, so that Laura felt she had no option but to go. She hadn't wanted to be there. She blamed Stewart, she blamed herself, she blamed Charles and

Henry. She felt as though she had betrayed another woman, and most of all she was angry with herself for doing it.

'What did she say?' Stewart asked when they were alone that evening.

'She told me to get out, and said that if I told Charles where she is she would see me in hell.'

'Oh lovely,' Stewart said. 'Did you see whether the baby was a boy?'

'Like you, I didn't see anything.'

'You could have asked.'

'Stewart, why don't you go and see her if you care so much?'

'I will tell Charles where she is living and then he will come and see her himself.'

'If you think that best.'

'What else could I think?'

'You could think how badly she has been treated both by Henry's family and hers and leave her alone.'

'You're afraid of her?'

'Of course I'm not, but it doesn't seem decent to betray her like that.'

'You don't like her.'

'That's not the point. She should do what she chooses. I put across all the points you would have wanted me to, and there is no way she will ever come back. God knows what she would do if Charles tried to take the child from her, even if it was through marriage.'

Twenty-Two

Zeb was going back to work on the Monday. He said he wouldn't, but Alice told him that he was fussing. They had had two days, and now they had the rest of their lives to enjoy together. Besides, he was lucky to have work to go to.

'I still think you should have the doctor.'

'I don't need a doctor, Zeb, I'm fine. I told you a dozen times yesterday. I have no pain and no blood. It's just as though the baby had never been.' There was a little quiver in her voice as she said this, but when he came towards her she squared her shoulders a bit and said, 'I have to get used to it.'

'We have to.'

'Yes, we have to. I have the shop to attend to and you have work to go to and I think it's best we just carry on. If we are meant to have another child, we will. In the meanwhile, just think how lucky we have been.'

So on Monday morning, she got up early with him and gave him breakfast and made up food for him to eat later and then he went.

She was glad when he had gone, because she had the place to herself until Mrs Garnet arrived. Mrs Garnet knew only that Alice hadn't been feeling well, but thought it was nothing serious. Mrs Garnet was not a curious woman, so she asked nothing and got on with the housework. Now that Alice could go back to what was normal for her, things should get easier.

She talked to the customers as usual, but when it got to midday she felt very tired and knew that it was the loss of the baby, so she put up the closed sign, locked the door and went to bed, leaving Mrs Garnet to cope.

She did not know how long she had been asleep when she heard the outside door and started up.

'Zeb?'

'Aye.'

He pounded up the stairs and sat down on the bed. Alice was horrified to discover that she had been in bed for six hours.

'I was so very tired.'

'I'm not surprised. Do you feel any better?'

'Much better. I have to make fish pie for dinner.'

'Mrs Garnet has already done it. It smells wonderful.'

'Oh, bless her,' Alice said, feeling good for the first time.

'We have our own fireside,' he said, 'and it's such a pretty evening. We can sit in the garden.'

She thought this a very good idea, and they enjoyed a few quiet hours together. As she fell into bed later, she slept instantly and told herself she would be better the next day.

The following day, however, she was more tired and she heard him leave the house without even getting out of bed. She went back to sleep. She was repairing the damage with rest, she thought. Mrs Garnet came up a couple of times and brought her tea and asked if she would like anything to eat, but Alice said it was just the end of the not feeling well, so Mrs Garnet merely mentioned Dr McKenna and Alice said she would send for him if things didn't get better.

'The shop,' she said, coming out of sleep with a start when Zeb came back at about six.

'It doesn't matter. You'll get to it eventually. In the meanwhile, you just have to concentrate on resting and sleeping and you will be better. We'll put a notice in the window saying that you aren't very well. People will understand.'

'Will you come for a pint?' Pat McFadden asked.

Zeb hesitated. He had been married for three weeks.

'We haven't been to the pub in ages and I really need beer. Just an hour?' Pat said.

'Alice isn't very well,' Zeb said.

'What do you mean?'

'I don't know. She's acting really funny.'

'Since when?'

'Since we got married.' That sounded all wrong, he knew, and invited daft remarks, but Pat was far from stupid. Zeb frowned. 'I need to get home.'

'Do you want me to come with you?'

Zeb was astonished at Pat's instincts. How did he always know when to say the right thing?

He wanted to tell Pat that everything was all right, and that he just needed to get there, but somehow he couldn't. For the first time in his life he didn't want Alice to himself. He was afraid to go home. She had become so distant, so abstracted. The shop had been closed all this time. He knew that Mrs Garnet soldiered on regardless, and he was grateful to her, but a couple of times now she had mentioned the doctor. If Alice had not forbidden him to call in Dr McKenna, he would have done so, but he knew it was important for Alice to feel that she still had some control over things. To go to the doctor above her head would not be easily forgiven, and he respected that, but he was worried.

Alice usually sat watching the fire in the back room if it was cool. She had lost weight she didn't have to lose, and sometimes he found her outside and he was not certain she knew where she was. He was growing afraid of what he might find, so he let Pat follow him into the village and down the passage and in by the back door.

He was sure Pat did not miss that the shop was closed. He would not have known. Shirley never came to the shop; they had no money for such luxuries. Inside, he saw the room with Pat's eyes. Rain drummed on the windows, making the evening appear darker than it would have been. He called out her name and had no answer.

'She must be in the bedroom,' he offered, but when he went upstairs the bed was unmade. The other bedroom was empty. He came back downstairs.

'She's gone,' he said.

Pat didn't say fatuous things like 'she could be shopping' or 'she could be visiting somebody'. The rain had stotted down all day.

Quarrying was at its most miserable in the rain. Everything was twice as bad. The stone was heavy. Soaked, the men toiled, and today there had been a wind behind it, which made the work so much colder. When the day was dark, the depths of the quarry were dark too.

Zeb ran into the street in full panic. She had never disappeared; she was always just outside at the front or in the back garden. He feared that he might have waited too long. He told himself that he should have gone for the doctor, despite what she said to him.

What if she had wandered somewhere and could not find her way back home? What if she had truly lost her mind? He had lain awake three nights now, trembling that she was lost to him in one way and still could be in another.

He feared the river. He and Pat took different directions and searched the main street, calling her name, and he ran down the bank, although it was difficult to see the river because the rain and the river blended in shades of grey.

He went to Mrs Garnet's little house just further along in the terrace, but the poor woman went white with horror and said that Mrs Bailey had been asleep when she left and that had only been an hour ago, so she could not be far. Mrs Garnet offered to go out and help but Zeb dissuaded her. The weather was awful and getting worse, and Mrs Garnet must be fifty if she was a day. He told her he would report back, so she stoutly said she would go to the house and keep the fires burning and that she would make sure there was hot food for when they got back. That at least was of some comfort.

Up and down the various roads which led down to the river he and Pat ran, and up to the tops beyond the chapel and through the houses where they petered out into country. Nobody was about. Everybody had gone home, huddling by their fires. The shops were shuttered and closed.

By the time darkness fell, Zeb was frantic, sobbing. He wished for a horse to cover more ground. Feet had never seemed so slow. He wanted to tell Pat to go home, he had more than enough to do there, but he couldn't. He didn't want to be alone now. He couldn't go back to Mrs Garnet and tell her he couldn't find his wife.

The rain only grew worse. When they were up on the top road, halfway to Rookhope, Pat shouted, and when Zeb ran to him there was a bundle of rags laid in the road.

At first they thought she was dead, she was so cold, but he picked her up and carried her the two miles over the moor and down the bank and past Greenfoot and into Stanhope.

Mrs Garnet had the lamps lit and the fire was blazing. Zeb got a rug and then he took off Alice's shoes and rubbed her feet. Finally she opened her eyes. She didn't focus.

'It's all right, Alice, you're at home now. You're here and you're going to be all right.'

Alice gazed around her uncomprehendingly and then she said in a hoarse tone, 'He was up there, I could see him. I could see my baby. Where is he?' Her eyes were everywhere and she said again urgently, 'He is here. I can see him. Give him to me. I need him near me.' Her cheeks were bright scarlet and her gaze wavered so that he was more scared than he had ever been in his life.

'I'll go for Dr McKenna,' Pat offered, and away he went, returning in about half an hour, during which time Zeb and Mrs Garnet had managed to undress Alice and put on her a big nightdress. She kept on and on about the baby, looking past him so that Zeb wanted to panic.

They managed to get Alice into a warm bed and Mrs Garnet put on more coal. Aware that this woman now knew what had happened, Zeb had the feeling that she might desert him, being a country woman of traditional ways, but she said nothing other than that she would go and heat up the soup and see if Mrs Bailey could take a little of that before the doctor came. It would do her good.

It seemed like a hundred years before Dr McKenna made his good-natured way down the passageway and into the house. Zeb was so relieved he didn't know what to say. The doctor said reassuring things and then he went upstairs. Zeb could hear him talking softly to Alice.

Pat went off home, and when he had gone and the patient was asleep, Dr McKenna came downstairs and gave Zeb a very straight look. They had left Mrs Garnet trying to spoon soup into Alice's mouth, like a bird with its chick.

'When did Alice lose the baby?'

Zeb couldn't look at the doctor. His throat had turned to stone, but he answered as best he could. 'Three weeks ago. She wouldn't let me go for you, even after she got worse. She kept saying it would be all right.'

'Did she bleed for long?'

'No, not afterwards. Is she going to die?'

The doctor shook his head.

'Has she gone mad in some way?' Zeb asked, his voice wobbling like half-set jelly. 'We found her on the top road, in the rain, and she was unconscious.'

'It wasn't your fault.'

'It was though. And now she's going to die.' He choked and couldn't look at the doctor.

'No, she's not, ' Dr McKenna said soothingly.

'I did it. I wanted her and it was sinful and—'

'No, no,' Dr McKenna said soothingly. 'Sit down. Sit down.' And the doctor waited until Zeb took up a place by the fire, and then he got down like he would have with a child and he said, 'Women often lose babies in the early stages of pregnancy, and for some of them it's a kind of heartbreak in that they miss what they might have had.'

'Alice's heart is broken?' That didn't sound quite so bad, somehow, when you were in the depths of despair – though it was a ghastly thing to hear.

'It will repair.'

'I would have been dead but for her, and I've done this to her. I will never go near her again, that she might have to suffer so much.'

'Listen to me,' Dr McKenna said. 'God doesn't go around striking people down willy-nilly. Do you think he has nothing better to do? You and Alice love one another. It was slight over-enthusiasm, that's all. You had both waited such a very long time for one another, had been through so much in your lives. You didn't deserve this.'

Zeb wanted to laugh, and he choked and the tears chased themselves down his face.

'She could have died,' he said, trying to breathe properly and not managing it.

'This temporary madness when the child is lost, or sometimes after it is born, is quite common – and no wonder. Can you think what it must be like, giving birth to another human being and then having nothing to hold? Here, take this.'

This was a bottle of grey-green liquid.

'It's a natural remedy,' the doctor said, 'and it will help her sleep and heal. She needs to stay in bed. Is Mrs Garnet here every day?''

Zeb nodded.

'I will come back tomorrow and every day after morning surgery. You must go to work and get on with things. She will get much better, I promise, but it will take a while.'

'You are so kind.'

'I have had a great many chocolates free of charge over the years,' Dr McKenna said.

Zeb panicked after he had gone. When Mrs Garnet left, he went to bed, where Alice was sleeping. He lay down beside her and relived the horrible, horrible evening when he had thought that she was dead. God was punishing him for having wanted her, for having taken her, for having behaved in such a dreadful way. Lying beside his wife, he cried himself silently to sleep.

Twenty-Three

Nell dreamed of Sawrey March. She dreamed of how his mouth would feel on hers and woke up sweating with guilt. He was a young man by comparison, and she was nothing more than a stupid old woman.

The trouble was that her dream the next night was even less decorous and she woke up blushing. She was missing her husband, she told herself, it was nothing to do with Sawrey March.

Then he called in at the house the following day. She didn't know where to look. He was so handsome, so engaging. His voice had a magical quality, and he was well bred.

Nell badly wanted him to come and stay, and she had to ask his sister, though she was aware that he would refuse because his sister went nowhere. Although he had said Augusta saw no one, Nell thought it might do the young woman good to go out somewhere with people who made her feel safe. She could hardly ask to go to Holywell Hall, though she was curious. She had always wanted to see it.

'I can't ask you to come and stay,' he said, looking so straight at her that she faltered. 'My sister is more ill than I have let anybody know and the house is falling apart, it really is. We have nothing and you would hate it.'

'I came from Cowshill,' Nell said, and they both laughed.

'It's a lovely place,' he said. 'Such views across the valley.'

'Really, Mr March, I would very much like to meet your sister. I have no company, and if she is ill then perhaps I might entertain her – unless she would rather have nobody there.'

'I don't know how she would receive a guest,' he said, 'but if you were willing to come, I would like you to. You won't be offended if she acts strangely. She was not always like this, but our father was not a kind man. We had a difficult childhood.'

'My childhood wasn't that good either. Perhaps nobody recalls such times with honesty, or perhaps it is just that as children we are powerless. Please let me come, just for an hour or two, and I will bring tea with me. I will bring cake.'

'I will see whether we still have any cups and saucers,' he said, so the following Saturday, when it was agreed she would go for tea, she took the pony and trap plus cake, tea, milk, sugar and a good many other things, packed in a hamper that she imagined herself unloading in the kitchen.

It was not far, but she was excited. She had always wanted to see the hall for herself. She had heard many tales about it, of hauntings and sightings and how the top of it had a walk around it, and various folk of the family in older times had thrown themselves from it when they could stand no more of the wretched March family. She thought, more probably, that it had been used to see the enemy more easily, but local tales were always colourful.

Nell was half pleased and half sorry that it was not a blizzard or pouring with rain or deep in mist. It was bright and sunny.

The trouble was that Nell could not help loving the hall from the moment she saw it. She had liked the tiny terraced house where she and Harold had lived when they were first married, but this was a different thing altogether. She was not sure she would ever be able to leave, in some ways. She craved it as she craved Sawrey March's mouth.

She was ashamed of both things and tried to push them from her, but it was no good. Sawrey looked right here, as right as any man had ever looked. It was stark and forbidding, built of grey stone, high and wild, like something that women in fairy stories might have let down their hair from. It stood amid heather and ferns in a place where even sheep had to be careful, it was so steep and open. In winter Nell thought the wind would howl. It was an old bastle house, tall and spare.

There were a few rooms which made up the habitable and most recent part, she surmised, but even that was hundreds of years old, and nobody had imagined anyone would need any better. The stone floors and windows kept out so little draught they might as well not have been there, and there were even narrow slits from which people had fired arrows. Nell was amazed.

The land around it was uncared for. The grass was long, and what had been a road was obscured. Everywhere, wild-flowers bloomed and moved in the wind – yellow, orange and blue.

Sawrey took her into the house and here the decay was

worse. It smelled cold and empty, as though there had not been a fire for so long that the idea was lost. There was very little furniture.

'I had to sell what there was,' he explained. 'Augusta needed the doctor, she has been so ill, and I could pay him in clocks and tables and tiny chairs and exquisite ornaments. He wouldn't take most of it, so I sold it and gave him money, and he kept returning when she was ill, any time of the day or night, and I don't think it was the clocks that did it.'

They were in the hall and as they stood there she heard soft footsteps and saw a figure begin to descend the stairs. She saw now why he had said that his sister was ill.

She had long grey and white hair, like a piebald pony. It fell to her waist, and it had about it a wave that reminded Nell of a winter sea, though it was thin and wispy. Her features had long since retired into her face and her cheeks were sunken like sails without wind.

Her eyes were blank and colourless, and she wore what Nell was sure was an old nightdress, grey and full length. Her hands were bony and gnarled like branches, blue veins showing through, and her neck was scrawny and pale. She regarded Nell with suspicion, as though she had forced her way in.

Nell went forward but not far.

'I'm pleased to meet you, Miss March. I'm Nell Almond. Your brother was kind enough to invite me here.'

The thin, gaunt figure came down the stairs and then ran back up again. Nell felt rather than noticed Sawrey's whole body bend in pain.

'I can take all these things to the kitchen, if you will direct me,' she said.

The kitchen was neglected. You couldn't call it dirty, because there had been no food made or eaten in a very long time. The fire, which at one time must have kept the whole kitchen warm and busy, was so grey it was almost black. Nell wanted to light it; she wanted to bring it alive. She was aghast. She had never seen anything like it.

She wished she had servants here to help, but she must do her best. She took off her coat, but finding nowhere clean to put it, she laid it carefully on the stoutest chair and then she lit the fire. When she had it going, she felt admiration for herself that she had handled the situation so well.

'We will need more wood,' she told him.

'What?'

'For the fire.'

He was gone a long time, which implied that he had not known where it was, but by then Nell had the kettle on. It was a dirty kettle, but she rinsed it under the tap so at least the water went into it clean. She had to go outside for water to the well, so she could see why the place had been built here. Water was more precious than anything else.

When the water boiled, she made tea. On the tray that she had brought, she put a milk jug and a sugar bowl, the cups, saucers and the cake, which was chocolate. Could anybody in the entire world not want chocolate cake when they had not had any for months? Also Norah had made egg sandwiches and there were scones, just gone cold, with strawberry jam and cream.

Augusta must have been able to smell the food, because as Sawrey and Nell sat at the kitchen table she ventured slowly down the stairs. Nell ignored her until she sat down, and then she smiled and gave her a cup and saucer and offered her a sandwich.

Thank God for Miss Lee, she thought, and then felt guilty, since she had not always done what she should for Miss Lee and her family. But the cake was so good and the response from these people was so fine that she was pleased at what she had done. They ate and ate and it made Nell so glad to see them. She determined to do it again.

The trouble was that she ached to sort out this place, to better it, to have warm fires and stables with horses and cats and dogs around the place, and sheep and cattle in the fields and for the orchard to give up its fruit.

The hall itself wound up and up and had ridiculous staircases, narrow and made of stone, but as Sawrey showed her around she wanted more and more to help, to improve, to be there with him and to own it. She wanted to do everything to make it better and to make it easier for Sawrey and for his sister.

She did not want the afternoon to end, and she was disappointed when she felt she had to leave. She saw now that Sawrey and his sister had had nothing to do. They had been born into the kind of prosperity that allowed servants to do everything. They did not understand how to live with their poverty.

Nell saw how much she would miss the place. She ached to ask him when she could come back, but it would have been unseemly, and so she went home and the evening was the longest that she could ever remember. She got a pen and paper and began to write down all the things she would do to the hall if it were hers.

The time flew past and when she went to bed, very late, she could not sleep, and then she knew that it would never happen. It was just another dream and nothing to do with her. She lay there in her perfect bed in her perfect house and wished things were different, trying to devise ways of going back to Holywell Hall.

After that it rained for two days and Nell ached to be out doing something useful. She fussed in the house over things that did not need her attention; she couldn't settle to a book; she had a fire lit which made her too hot. When the rain finally ceased on the third morning she went out to admire her beautiful lawns and her rose beds and horrified one of the gardeners by telling him that she wanted a whole flowerbed pulled up and replanted. She did remember an hour later and told him not to do it. The look of relief on his face made her feel utterly foolish.

She wished she had friends or even decent relatives to keep her busy, but there was no one. The following day, she could stand it no longer and took the pony and trap and packed it with a good many things she felt she should not, but wanted to, and then she made her way to the hall.

It was even worse than she had remembered, and she was so keen to begin on the garden that she got out of the trap and began to pull up weeds. As she approached the house, a voice just beyond her said, 'We can't afford to pay you, you know.'

Laughing, she got to her feet, aided by his slender hands. She thought he had the most beautiful eyes she had ever seen.

'I'm sorry to invite myself.'

'Oh, please. I would have asked you, but I don't like to impose. We have nothing, as you know.'

'The hall is so beautiful.'

'It was, unless my memories of it are coloured by how much I love it.'

Nell thought it was like a castle from a fairy story, cobwebby and neglected. The hall was like a sleeping woman who needed a kiss, and she was not the only one, Nell thought, turning away hastily. To her surprise, Augusta came to the door and smiled at her. Nell took her hand.

'I do hope you don't mind me coming back here,' Nell said, and Augusta shook her head and said that she was very pleased to have her company. Sawrey seemed delighted at this, and they went on into the house.

She had been bold and packed a hamper. As she unpacked it on the kitchen table, Augusta sat wide-eyed like a hungry child. Nell put out plates and knives and forks, and then unpacked a huge roast chicken and a white loaf, Cotherstone cheese, a half-pound of rich butter and two bottles of wine. Augusta began to smile.

Nell gave her huge pieces of chicken and some sliced bread. Sawrey did not seem to want to eat, and she looked at him, half ashamed that she had come here. He didn't meet her eyes.

'I hope you don't think I'm overbearing,' she said.

'Not at all.'

'Will you have some wine then?' she asked.

'It's champagne,' he said wistfully.

'Won't you try a little?'

She gave him the bottle to open, and even though it had been shaken by her journey it opened with a quiet pop and he poured it out. He closed his eyes over the first sip, and then she sliced more chicken and put it on a plate and gave him bread and cheese to go with it. After that they were quiet for a little while as they ate.

Augusta fell asleep on the old sofa under the drawing room window, and Nell asked if she might see the orchard. Sawrey unlocked the door. It was a big walled place, which it needed to be to provide shelter up here. Inside, the trees were bowed down with half-ripe fruit. The grass was up to her knees, but Nell went forward full of enthusiasm. Apples and pears from years before had rotted on the trees and made great heaps on the ground and were now part of the floor. There was even a little summerhouse at the far end, almost impossible to get to, but Nell managed to battle through the long grass and over fallen boughs. When she opened the door, the sunshine was falling on to the old chairs. She seated herself in one with delight and Sawrey sat in the other.

'The trouble is that by the time I was a small child there was nothing left,' he said. 'The paintings were all sold, the animals too. The books in the library fell to pieces in my hands – and I had longed to read them. The library was always locked.'

'Did you never think to marry?'

'I couldn't. I have no money and there are no heiresses to take on a fellow like me who has no uses, no gifts, no education.

No sensible woman would ever marry me. And besides, there's Gussie. You can see what a troubled soul she is.'

'I think with some company and good food she would probably be a lot better.'

'She was starved as a child, not just of food, but of company and education. She wouldn't have learned to read and write if it hadn't been for me, and I had no tutor after the age of eight. My father didn't believe in education beyond learning to read, write and add up, and women were just like dogs. In the end there was nobody but the two of us. I sold everything that was left and here we are. I don't think I can take her from here. She only just survives now. Away from here she would be nobody, not even herself.'

Nell couldn't think of a single useful thing to say. Had he been a different kind of person, he could have done a good many things with this place, but born well and with no help, money or education, and the hall like a huge empty shell on his back, he couldn't see the way forward.

'Show me the vegetable garden,' she suggested, getting up, and when he did it was again a revelation. It was huge, and there were broken-down greenhouses and even an orangery, with most of the stone still in place but no roof.

Red, black and white currant bushes flourished. There were rhubarb plants, raspberry bushes and lots of strawberries, which had been half-eaten by the birds and trodden to mush in the grass. In the greenhouses, sunflowers had somehow taken root and were plentiful, and there were lilies of all kinds, so many that they were like weeds, orange, white and pink.

Further down, what had been a leek trench was covered in grass, but vegetables still grew there. She saw the fronds of what must be carrots and the tall leaves of potatoes and beans, which should have been on sticks, folding over like old sheets. The crops were lost and Nell was dismayed at the waste.

She felt like a child in a newly discovered cupboard. She found sticks and some twine in one of the greenhouses, and showed him how to tie up the beans. He couldn't even do that, and she had to get him to hold the sticks while she did it. She thought it was a good job, but the whole thing made her sad. Harold had grown vegetables in the little back garden of the house where they had lived when they were first married. Away from the quarry, he was content in their tiny back yard in the evenings, and beyond it they had a patch of ground where they would labour, drinking tea and sitting on the wall in the sun and planning their future.

It was all gone.

'Nell?' He said her name softly for the first time, and she shook her head.

Nell could see how bad things were by the way that the fences were falling down. She wished she could stay, but she had seen the bedrooms and there was no chance she could sleep in such a wretched place. Her hands and feet were so cold that she soon retired back to her warm house. That evening, she sat by the fire and thought of the two of them, perhaps huddled by the kitchen fire, and wished she could do more to help.

Being alone was even worse after that. She felt like she was losing yet another battle.

Twenty-Four

Earlier that summer, Mr Peters had called Mary into his study just before she was due to leave.

'You know that term end is very near?' he said.

Mary had come to realize that in Durham an awful lot of things revolved around the university. She had not thought it would influence her life, but of course she was working for the Peters family, and he worked there as some kind of professor. She liked the idea and would have boasted about it had she anybody to boast to about anything.

'We usually go to Weardale for the summer months. I have a house there which belonged to my family.'

Oh hell, Mary thought, just when things were improving, she was going to lose her job.

'We wondered whether you would come with us. The children are very fond of you and, well, we are all fond of you. You have been such a help. I don't think my wife could manage without you.'

Mary stared. She was horrified. Uproot again? Leave Cate and the house? She couldn't.

'That's very nice of you, Mr Peters, but I have people here who rely on me. I couldn't do it.'

'There is a cottage on the end of the house. Could your family not come with you? There are big gardens.'

'I've just rented a house and, well, Cate has a baby.' Mary thought it best to be frank. 'I can't go into it all, Mr Peters, because a lot of it is her business. The man she cared about, he died and . . . well . . .'

'Could you not talk to her, to Cate?'

Mary was astonished, but then she had given him to think that Cate was widowed, though she had not actually said so. Needs must when the devil drives, her mother would have said.

He smiled at her. 'Mrs Peters would be very disappointed if you didn't come with us. Why don't you talk it over and let me know?'

Downhearted, Mary walked back up Claypath to the house. Daniel got there at the same time. They found Cate white-faced, for the baby had screamed all day, she said. She had, however, cleaned the house, kept the fire going and made a stew. She was doing everything one-handed because the child yelled every time she put him down.

As they sat down to eat, the baby finally sleeping, though Cate grumbled that he would be awake half the night because of it, Mary told them what Mr Peters had said.

'I didn't mention you, Daniel, I didn't like to. You two could stay here for the summer and I could go to Stanhope, though he did seem happy to have Cate with me. I couldn't include you, Daniel, I didn't know how to. I didn't think fast enough, and anyway, you have a job. I don't suppose you could get a job in a little place like that.'

'Stanhope?' Now Daniel was pale too.

'It's a little town in Weardale. Mr Peters says it's very pretty. I won't get another job like this one if I don't go with them.'

'I suppose we could stay here,' Cate said, 'but I'd rather go to Weardale with you.'

'I don't think it really matters, does it?' Mary said. 'Are you all right, Dan?'

He had stopped eating.

'You don't have to worry, Daniel,' Cate said. 'I'm not going to make you marry me.'

It was a joke, of course, Mary thought.

'That wouldn't be possible,' he said, grimly. 'I'm already married. I've got a wife in Stanhope.'

Nobody was eating by then. Cate's painstakingly made stew went cold as Dan told them about Arabella and her parents and the quarry, and how he had first jilted Susan and in the end had married her, and because she had then not wanted him he had left. And then he told them about the message in the post office window.

'I didn't know whether I should go back, because I'm not sure what I'm going back to. I have a job here and I was starting to feel happy again, and now this.'

'It could be that there is something wrong with the child,' Cate said.

'I haven't seen him since the day he was born. Why would anybody contact me? What use would I be?'

'You're very good with Harry,' Cate said.

'Harry isn't mine,' Dan said hoarsely.

'You can't not go,' Cate said.

'Then we must all go,' Mary said.

Every feeling in Dan was that he could not leave Durham City. He had hated the place for so long, and now it had become a sanctuary. He felt stupidly close to his father here, and in some ways meeting Mr Perkins had eased the pain that he had felt about it. For the first time, he could think back cheerfully to his childhood and have it not be overshadowed by his mother's death and his father's imprisonment. He had the notion that the moment he went back to Weardale, his newfound joy would disappear like sunshine when the clouds turned dark before rain.

'I should have told you all this before,' he said.

'I can't judge anyone,' Cate said.

'Nor me,' Mary said.

When they went to bed, Cate said to Mary, 'Charles may not find me there.'

'You think Stewart will betray you?'

'Oh, sure to,' Cate said, more cheerfully than she felt. 'Charles is his god. And that stupid, fat wife of his feels just the same. I've been waiting for him to arrive ever since they left.'

'I didn't know them.'

'I wish I hadn't.'

They lay in silence in the darkness for a short while, before Cate said, 'At least Harry is sleeping. Goodness knows for how long.'

'She was very fat,' Mary said.

'And plain.'

'Plain ugly,' Mary said, and they had a giggle, which helped.

Twenty-Five

Zeb wanted to tell Mrs Garnet about their life, and how they had made mistakes, but the minute he tried to she put up both hands and looked him straight in the eyes and said, 'I don't tell folk this, but Mr Garnet and me, we had to get married. It happens, so don't think I'm judging you here, Mr Bailey. I know you can't say these things, but I wish you'd told me. I wanted to help so much.'

'Thank you, Mrs Garnet. You did help. You are more than kind. I don't know what we would have done without you.'

'You get yourself away to work and never mind. I'll be here to see to the lassie, and the doctor is coming and she will get well. You go and make some money. I've packed you something to eat. I won't leave her until you come back. Off you go now.'

Zeb was so unhappy at work that he wanted to run back to the sweet shop and see how Alice was, but he knew that Mrs Garnet was there and the doctor would call and there was no point in his presence, so he tried to work.

People soon got to know that Alice wasn't well, without the details.

'And you just married,' was the general consensus, and over the next few days he had a lot of help. They made stews and they came and cleaned in the house and they offered to help with the shop, getting it back to normal when Alice was well. They didn't ask to see her; they had more sense. They said that when she was well enough to have visitors, when she was spending time downstairs, they would come to help and they would look after her when he had to work. He mustn't think that they didn't care. It was such a lovely response that he began to take heart.

It was a strange but comfortable way to live. He liked that the weather was bad, even though it was summer. He liked keeping the bedroom fire on all the time. He read to Alice and talked to her. He held her in his arms while she slept.

When Pat could get away, which wasn't often, they sat in the kitchen and talked while she slept.

The only thing that upset Zeb was that Susan had not come to the house. He wanted to ask her why not, after everything that Alice had done for her, but he didn't. Alice would not have thanked him for it, and he could not have brought himself to be civil for any length of time, so perhaps things were better as they were.

Alice did not get better. He began to think she would never come back downstairs again. Dr McKenna called at least three times a week, and he was always hopeful, but it seemed to Zeb that she would not be his wife any longer, she would be an invalid upstairs for the rest of their lives, however long that might be. It made him despair. After all they had been through, were they not entitled to a little happiness? Perhaps not. Perhaps they were entitled to nothing.

Twenty-Six

On the Thursday of that week, the weather had turned itself around again and was warm. Nell had been outside, fussing over the garden. She knew that the gardeners wished to be left alone, and she wished she could have left them alone, but she had to do something.

She had read until her eyes ached, and taken an early morning walk up to the top of Crawleyside and back over the moors above Stanhope. She had walked for several miles and her feet were aching, but by mid-afternoon she was desperate for company.

Norah, the maid, came into the garden with the information that there was a man to see her and he had said that he was her brother. Nell did not know what to do. She could hardly avoid him. She got Norah to ask him into the drawing room.

She was inclined to hide in the garden and say that she was not at home, or to ask him here, where the gardeners, Mr Thompson and his son, Jeff, made her feel safe, but that was a ridiculous feeling, she knew. She returned to the house and found a short, stout man standing in the middle of the room.

He looked uncomfortable, and she only just recognized that it was her brother Tommy, the one she had been close to when they were children.

He heard her and turned. He was red-faced and his hair was thin on top of his head and he had not shaved in several days. His clothes were wrinkled and worn and his boots were shabby. She searched his figure in vain for anything that she had once loved about him.

She brought to mind all those times after Arabella had been born, when she had made her way to the house in Cowshill which she had once thought so pretty. Not one of her brothers had ever been there to greet her, and her mother did not acknowledge the child but to say that it should have been a boy and that it had a look of Harold about it, which in her eyes could not be a good thing.

When Nell enquired for her brothers, her mother said they had more pressing things to do than wait about for her, and they were at work. Her father was never there either, though he was no great loss.

He had barely spoken to her when he was there. Her mother informed her that her father had been so upset when she had married that man that he would no longer speak to her, even if he were around. But of course he was at work because they had no money, and he had to go though his feet gave him a great deal of trouble.

Her mother spent a long time complaining about her own feet and her own headaches and her terrible backaches and how a decent daughter would never have left her for heathens like the Almonds.

Worst of all, Nell remembered how that house, which looked clear across the valley, stank of men in a way in that she could not remember noticing before. It was socks and boots and cabbage breath, grimy fingers and unwashed nether regions. She felt sick, remembering.

'Tommy,' was all she could manage to say now. She tried not to be surprised or taken aback, but she was already trembling, she was so upset. All the memories of childhood and how close the two of them had been came back to her in pretty pictures, such as the kitten he had rescued because she liked it, fishing it from the water barrel where his mother had drowned half a dozen others. She had helped Tommy with his letters. The other boys cared nothing for school and were scornful of her efforts at reading and would throw her books across the yard. Not that she had much opportunity for such goings-on, as her mother called them. She washed clothes and brushed boots and peeled hundreds of potatoes. She was last to sit down to a meal and was on her feet all the time to get whatever they asked for.

Since there were but two bedrooms, she slept downstairs alone in the darkness, and the smell of soot and frying was always in her nostrils.

She and Tommy had walked miles in the heather when they were small children, confiding their grievances to one another. Now she gazed at him and thought how out of place he looked in her drawing room, where the curtains were moving slightly in the breeze from the gardens.

One of the first things Harold had done was have the place terraced so that the lawns ran down one after another like a green waterfall. At the bottom was a pond where herons would gather and talk to smaller birds in the afternoons. At first she had been worried that the herons would eat the little birds, but they didn't. They were hoping she had fish in her pond. She would watch the gatherings of starlings and doves and sparrows, all bathing together and the herons gossiping with them.

She had no idea what to say to her brother.

'Now, Nellie,' he greeted her, not really meeting her eyes. He turned his hat around and around in his hands, so that she longed to grab it from him. 'How ist tha doin'?'

She felt sure he didn't need to talk like this. Perhaps he was so nervous that he could do no better.

'I'm quite well, thank you, Thomas, and how are you?'

He didn't even say how sorry he was that her husband and child were dead. He had no manners. Had he ever had them? Maybe not. He laughed uneasily now.

'You talk funny. You never did.'

'Thirty years is a long time,' Nell said.

He looked as if he didn't understand that.

'What do you want?' she said.

'Nowt, just to see thee.' He looked around him, suddenly emboldened. 'It's a grand place thoo's got here, and ne master for it. I'd like as fine a place as this for me and mine.'

He had married. She didn't even remember the name of the woman or whether he had children.

Then he looked at her for the first time. 'Our Bri is reet poorly and canna work. Joe got hurt at the mine and Wal went off and left his wife with six bairns to bring up. I came to thinking like that you will help us. You have space for us all.'

She wanted to tell him that she wouldn't pick him up if he had fallen into the quarry and broken both his legs, but somehow she couldn't. She couldn't do to him what he and his brothers had done to her. She tried not to be the sister he had so much liked, but her memory dredged up all the nights when they had lain watching the stars and talking, when they had been very small. She remembered the day she had rescued him from bigger boys who had set on him, and her throat dried. She said nothing.

'You were never there, even when Mam and Dad died,' he said, looking at her as though these things had been all her fault, and Nell thought yes, she was the only daughter, the only girl, it must have been her fault. She was not good enough to carry them all on her back.

'It was cruel of you and we had nowt,' he said. 'Mam was in pain for days and Dad's feet gave out and then his legs. They were talking about cutting off both his legs, but he died, so they didn't have to.

'You never even came to the funerals. Never to visit, not thinking of us for a minute. You owe us, Nellie, for walking out like that and not seeing us after. I wouldn't have come to you but we need money bad, and you have such a lot of it. How could you not care about your family? Anyroads, we need somewhere to go, and it's time for you to take care of your own. I'll be back with our Bri.'

When he left, Nell was so upset she wanted to cry, run upstairs, anything but have to deal with more this day. She felt guilty, as though she should never have left, that she should have been there for her brothers and their families and her parents. Even though she knew it was stupid, she could not rid herself of the guilt that she felt. These people were her blood and she ought to have done better, as a sister and a daughter.

She was about to go upstairs when she saw a man from the big windows, shabbily dressed but nevertheless elegant. He was unmistakable. It was Sawrey March. She could see that he was talking to Mr Thompson, the gardener, and that Mr Thompson had brought him in through the garden gates and up the path towards the house. They were chatting and she liked watching them.

Mr Thompson knew everybody, and was now smiling. She could hear the sweet drift of Sawrey's beautiful voice. She had the feeling that Mr Thompson was saying he could probably go in by the double doors which led into the drawing room and that Norah was about somewhere, picking parsley for dinner, and she would guide him since he was certain Mrs Almond was there.

Norah duly appeared, and since the doors were open, Nell went out onto the terrace and was able to greet Sawrey in a tone that she hoped was not one of utter relief.

He gave her good day and told her how well the gardens were looking and how Mr Thompson was such an expert and knew everything there was to know about hydrangeas. Nell knew it for a joke and wanted badly to laugh. It was the kind of thing she had come to expect from Sawrey.

'It's the soil apparently,' Sawrey said, with a huge disregard for niceties, and with a very droll countenance. 'It alters the colour. If it's acidic, they are blue, and if it isn't they aren't. And then they are pink, and sometimes they are both, and the odd time they are purple, and sometimes they are all three, I have it on good authority.' He pulled such a face at his pretend knowledge, and so like her head gardener, that Nell couldn't help a quick choke of laughter as she saw him into the house.

'May I give you coffee?'

'Indeed you may.'

'How is Augusta?'

'The weather doesn't suit her. She feels the cold when the winds blow up there, and is stifled in summer. Your house is so sheltered you wouldn't notice. Are you well? You look a little pale, if you will allow me to say so.'

Nell didn't want to discuss her brothers, so she merely smiled and talked about the gardens.

Her guest demolished two large pieces of walnut and chocolate cake and two cups of coffee and made cosy conversation as though he had nothing better to do, and she could feel herself relax. He was such a comfort after her brother.

Then there was silence, and he put down his plate and cup and saucer as though remembering that he had come here for a purpose. Haltingly, he began to speak.

'I have never done this before, and shouldn't be doing it now, but I need help. I have no money and Gussie and I are in a bad way. I have nothing left to sell. I don't love you, but I like you very well, and I wondered if there was any chance that you might marry me.'

Nell stared.

'I know.' He got up to leave, as though embarrassed and feeling stupid, though he didn't turn away. 'Who on earth would, but you have been very kind and I think you could do with some company, and although I am absolutely frightful to be about, I just thought that with your money and our company perhaps we might smile at one another and make the best of things. If I've been presumptuous, please forgive me and I will leave. You won't have to throw me out.'

Nell hesitated, and then she said, 'No, don't go anywhere. Let us have some sherry.'

He protested feebly, but when Norah brought the sherry he accepted it. It was dry and kept cold in the larder and was Nell's one failing. She could refuse anything but the sherry. She was not sure she could refuse him.

'You aren't serious?' she said.

'Aren't I? If you don't want me to be then I shan't be.'

'I could be your mother.'

'I don't think so.' He pulled another face and she wanted to laugh again. 'My mother was an awful woman, nearly as bad as my father. Nothing like you. You're kind, and compared to her you are a lady. She cursed the servants and ignored us and ran off to France with some man, and the next thing we heard she'd died. Gussie and I were ever grateful. One of the best days of our lives was when she walked out, though it didn't do our father any good. He was twice as bad after that.'

'I'm fifty,' Nell said, trying to be sensible. 'Actually, I'm more, but I don't tell anybody. How old are you?'

'I admit to thirty.'

'Oh my God.'

'I'm nearer forty, so you see there's not such a huge difference.'

'But you're so very good-looking.'

'Is that a problem? I do try not to look into the glass more than a dozen times a day.'

Nell couldn't help laughing, and then they had more sherry.

'You don't think you're beautiful?' she said.

'I would rather Gussie had looked like me, then she might have married. I had dreams once that she would marry someone very rich and he might like me and let me live with them, but of course I couldn't leave the hall. I couldn't ever leave it. You wouldn't just think about marrying me? It would make things so much simpler for me.'

'It wouldn't work.'

'I suppose not. I thought it was worth a try. I hope you don't think I'm a dreadful person for trying, though I suppose I am. I had better go now, I am so embarrassed.'

'Let me think about it.'

'You would?'

Nell thought of Augusta and the beauty of the hall and how it could be made so much better with money. She also thought of the implied threat from Tommy. She had the feeling that if she were left here without a man, her brothers and their families would invade. Mr Thompson and Jeff could not stop it, but she did not think her brothers would challenge a gentleman such as Sawrey March. It was just one more reason to take his offer seriously.

Nell lay awake at night and wondered what to do, and

in the end she asked her lawyer, Jos Calland, Mr Preston's partner. He was shrewd by all accounts.

'If you marry, you will lose much,' he told her. 'Women have very little financial power when they marry, and although I would try hard to help you, it wouldn't be easy.'

'What am I to do if I don't marry?'

He frowned at her. 'You will keep everything.'

'In the evenings, when you have nobody to talk to, time hangs hard. I'm not sure I can endure it for the next twenty years, should I be spared that long.'

He said nothing. How could he? He was prosperous and young, and he probably thought that she was old and would not live for very long. That was what young people thought.

Twenty-Seven

Stewart and Laura had talked about whether they should tell Charles that Cate was living in Durham, but the moment that Stewart went to the house to see Charles, he knew that he had to tell him.

Stewart was unhappy about telling Charles of Cate, but he felt that he had no choice. They sat in the big study, which had once been the library, never used by Charles's father. Charles had made that his headquarters. It was orderly such as it had never been. Stewart had made it his weekly job to go and sort out the papers and find out what there was to do. When Charles's father had been alive, they would sit by a roaring fire, drinking whisky and talking about the estate hour after hour.

Charles was much more efficient: nothing was out of place, but he did not have the love of the place that the old man had. He was doing his duty – and duty without love, Stewart thought, was a sorry thing. Now that the old man was dead, it appeared that Charles had reverted at least partly to the minister he had intended to become.

Stewart could have coffee if he was there, but he was not

asked to lunch or to dine, and he missed that too. The old man had kept a good table and was generous with it, but he understood. To Charles, this place reeked of his unhappy childhood. He was making the best of it but it was not where he wanted to be. Stewart didn't want to tell people that he needed to marry, because although Charles was polite, he made no move towards any of the women they knew.

The other problem was that since his brother had liked men, the rumour got about that Charles, since he had no wife and took no interest in women, was the same way. Stewart thought that Charles took no particular interest in anybody, but he could say nothing about such things directly to Charles.

So Stewart waited for a few weeks, and after the estate business was concluded on the Saturday morning, he told Charles that he had seen Catherine in Durham.

'And Mary Blaimire?'

'The servant, yes. I didn't know her. And there was a man, I don't know who he was.'

'She could be married?'

This possibility had not occurred to Stewart. What kind of man married a woman who had a child out of wedlock? Perhaps Cate had told him she was a widow? She was unscrupulous, and would have done that if it got her what she wanted.

'I don't know whether he was attached to either of them, but he was certainly living with them. Laura saw him at the house.'

'And the child?'

'Yes.'

'The address?'

Stewart hesitated, and then gave it, knowing that he could not hold back such a vital piece of information. 'But she could have moved on,' he added.

Charles looked hard at him.

'She thought I would go after her?'

'I don't know. I thought she wouldn't let me in, so I sent Laura. I didn't see her.'

'That was brave,' Charles said, with a hint of humour.

'You know what she's like. Laura said she's skinny and poor and sharp-tongued.'

'I'd like to leave her alone. After all, there's no rush.'

Stewart was surprised at this. He had envisaged that Charles would go dashing off to Durham.

'What if you lose contact altogether?'

'I don't know.' Again, he was vague, and Stewart thought that wasn't like him.

'You should marry.' Stewart was worried about saying this, but somebody had to, though he thought he was being more direct than he should have been.

'I know. That would seem to be the solution, but . . .'

He stopped there.

Stewart didn't dare to ask any more. He had done what he thought he should; now he just had to work on, hoping that Charles did not go to Durham, and hoping that he found a woman he liked, or at least felt he could marry, after which things would be a lot better all round – and maybe he might be offered a decent dinner again beneath Charles's roof.

Twenty-Eight

It was the end of May when the Peters family left for Stanhope, and Mary and Cate went with them. Dan had said he would make his own way there and find out what the problem was, which he had tried to put to the back of his mind, but which plagued him like an illness. The uncertainty was, for him, the hardest part.

Cate was only glad to get away. She felt so nervous. Sometimes she thought that Charles would turn up, find that the child was a boy and become as unscrupulous as she had always suspected. Then he would either make her marry him, because of the baby, or take Harry from her, which she had the feeling he was legally entitled to do – and even if not, his lawyer would make it so.

But the next minute she remembered how kind he had been, and thought that he would not do anything awful to her. She reminded herself that men changed when they had power, and if he didn't marry and produce an heir himself, he would not be lenient.

So she was glad to get away, even though she worried that he might follow her to Stanhope. Stewart would know that the Peters family went there for the summer, and he would tell Charles whatever Charles wanted to know.

She wished she could run to somewhere she could not be brought back from, but with a tiny baby and no money, she could do nothing. She was the lowest of the low, penniless and with a bastard child.

Mary regretted leaving the first house she had ever liked. She thought of it as hers, and she had some say in how it was run. But she was also pleased that Mr and Mrs Peters had been so generous.

On top of everything else, she was worried about Dan. She felt that she and Cate had already lost him to the person he needed to be. She had liked him before she discovered what he had done. Now she couldn't work out how she felt.

Twenty-Nine

Nell thought about marrying Sawrey for so many hours that her head ached and then her back ached and she was so out of sorts that she took to her bed, assuring Norah that it was nothing. All Nell could do was to go to bed and stay there for a number of hours.

The sun poured in. She lay there with the windows open, hearing the sounds of the birds and the odd remark between Mr Thompson and Jeff, and it was so comforting. She realized she didn't have to do anything, and then she slept.

When she awoke, the shadows were long and it was evening. She felt so much better that she got up and read for a while outside, and then she had dinner alone, as she always did, but then she remembered Sawrey and his sister and longed for their company.

Nell found that she was ashamed. She didn't want to tell people that she was foolish enough to decide to marry a man at least fifteen years younger than herself. They would think she was stupid. It was a risk, but it was no bigger a risk than staying here, growing older and more and more alone. She couldn't live like that any longer. She felt stupidly playful, like a kitten, and wished to be twenty-five. Though if she had been twenty-five, she had the feeling she would have married Harold again and not Sawrey March.

She went to the castle to tell Sawrey that she would marry him, and she took champagne, good red wine and a huge beef pie.

When Nell saw the hall again, she rejoiced that it would soon be hers, and she would be able to do what she liked with it. She was more thrilled than she had been about anything she could remember in years, though she was rather worried about Augusta. When she got there, she told him that she would marry him, but only if Augusta agreed.

'You won't mind, will you?' she asked Augusta. 'Because if you don't want me here, I won't come. I'm too old to be your sister, but I hoped we might be friends.'

Gussie looked confused, but then she said, 'I won't have to go and sleep in the barn?'

'Of course not,' Sawrey said, leaving his chair and going around the dining table to put his arm around her. 'It'll be even better. We can have big fires. It'll be just like it was when there was just the two of us, but warm and with lots of nice food, and Nell will help you with things. She might even buy you a decent dress – you've never had one.'

Gussie wasn't always this bad, Nell thought, but she was worried and it obviously made her less coherent.

Gussie managed a smile, and Sawrey came back and sat down with Nell.

'We can put things to rights, build the greenhouses and even have ponies, if you want,' Nell said.

'Horses,' Sawrey said.

'Yes, well, horses then,' Nell said. She had never been interested in horses – they struck her as beautiful but incredibly stupid.

Later, when Gussie fell asleep, which she often did at strange times because she didn't sleep very well at night, he said, 'It will be wonderful to have you here, sweet Nell. The place is haunted, you know, so I hope you don't mind ghosts. Sometimes I think it shows Gussie and me as children, and the people we might have been.'

Nell tried not to remember his words, but when Sawrey took a newly awakened Gussie into the overgrown gardens, she looked over the place on her own. It was the first time she doubted that she could be happy here and make it hers. She went into the library, and remembered what Sawrey had said about it: how the books were moulded and many had gone to dust. She thought she might replace them in time, if Sawrey wanted. The bookcases were oak, and although cold and damp had damaged them, they were still good enough for fires to dry them out.

She wished she were young and could have had children to bring up here. The place had suffered from the lack of young voices. It had about it an air of vacancy. No, it was worse than that: it was lack of love. There was so much to do here that she thought a less enthusiastic woman would have been daunted, but she was so tired of Ash House, where there was nothing to do, that she couldn't wait to get started.

She thought the whole place reeked of failure and neglect. In different parts of the house, all of which were in bad repair, ceilings had fallen down, plaster had come off walls, paper was peeling, the paint gone, the wooden windows bare. Doors had fallen off hinges and been left on the floor. Discarded furniture lay everywhere. She wondered when was the last time that somebody walked here who cared and had enough money to do something about it. A very long time ago, she thought. Or maybe never, she worried. Maybe this place had been like the children who had known it – unloved, unwanted, uncared for.

Most of all, she remembered something that Sawrey had told her about Augusta: that she had had chilblains as a small child, and when she put on her too-tight shoes, which were all she had, her toes bled and the blood ran into the leather.

There was something so cruel about it. She knew that men and women had done much worse to their children, but the image of Gussie's feet bleeding stayed with her for so very long. She heard the sound of hushed laughter all around her, and determined to try to help the house and its people back to some kind of happiness.

When she spoke to Sawrey about an heir, he was vague. As she asked more, he told her that if he produced no son there was a relative, a distant cousin who had gone off to Canada – he was that sort of chap, Sawrey said, as though nobody in their right mind would do such a thing.

'Do you know where he is?'

'No, and I don't need to find out, do I? When I'm not here the lawyers can sort it out, but I'm not very old yet so I don't think it's a pressing problem. At least I hope not.'

'But you have no child, or have you?'

He looked innocently at her.

'I have had to look after Gussie. I couldn't ever leave her, even for a night. The women I might have had, I would have to pay or marry, and things would have been worse either way, so I discounted everybody. I have to sleep with Gussie. I'm sorry if that sounds awful – I don't treat her like a wife, I don't touch or hurt her. You must understand that I wouldn't be sleeping with you either. I just don't do it; it's too complicated and I don't understand it. I'm telling you all this because I don't want you to have ideas about us together, because it won't happen. I don't want you to marry me and then wish you hadn't.'

He stopped there. Nell was not sure whether she was aghast or grateful that he had told her. She certainly couldn't think of anything to say. In the end, she could see him take a deep breath, hoping that she might accept these strange conditions. Though obviously it was not strange to him.

'You know, Nell, if you are worried that I've done horrible things, don't marry me. I am going to hell anyway.'

'Why should you be going to hell?'

'All our family goes to hell. Where else would I find companions?'

Thirty

Stanhope was a very small town, Mary thought. Not as big as Durham and nowhere near as impressive, but then it was a lot bigger than Shap, and the house that the Peters family owned was special. The main part of it was big, but the cottage on the end was a good size too, and best of all it looked down the bank towards the river. The garden went right across the back of both houses and was filled with flowers which all seemed to be in bloom.

She gloried in the colours and how tall some of them were. There was a huge lawn, which Mrs Peters had impressed upon them was theirs to use at any time. Since the children played there and came over to inspect the baby each morning, Mary and Cate spent a good deal of time there during the first few days.

Mary was almost happy. She thought Cate was, too. Mary was still concerned about Daniel, but she knew he would manage. For her, this was a good time. She was living next door to the Peters family so that they were almost joined completely, and the little girls happily ran in and out of the house and the cottage. After Mrs Peters had apologized several times for her children intruding on what was meant to be Mary's time off, Mary insisted that they were welcome. They were at home, and the buildings were all one to them. They could even spend the night should Mrs Peters and her husband want to go anywhere or have some quiet time together.

Mary had become infected with Cate's anxiety. She knew that Charles would find Cate, and then her father and Ned would find her, and they would kill her without thought for having disgraced them as men, for having made the family ashamed of her.

She tried to focus on the children, and it was a lovely summer in that way. The two little girls adored the baby and wanted to cradle him in their arms. The river trundled on its way down to the sea and they sat in the garden, which was full of flowers: peonies in great bunches, roses in pink, red, yellow, orange and white, all waving freely in the breeze and with the sun beating down. It was almost like a fairy tale. Nobody disturbed them.

There were lots of books in the cottage and Mary had taken to reading. She had always done well at school, before her father dragged her away to work. While Cate and the baby slept, she would sit in the slight gloom inside with the windows open, the bees buzzing amid the chives, purple in bloom, and she would let the afternoons go from her as she read.

Thirty-One

From the first, Mr Bailey loved being in the Vernon house, but now Alice was ill and he was so worried about her. The illness went on and on, and she was always in bed. He hated going past the sweet shop now that it was always closed. He didn't like to visit very often, because Mrs Garnet was there in charge all day and he didn't know her well, and in the evening Zeb came home so he thought he should leave them together.

He had become increasingly upset with Susan, for she seemed continually in a bad mood, and he was glad she had left. But he was doubly glad he had left. What would it have been like for him now, with Alice in such a state when he could do so little to aid her? He did enquire of Zeb occasionally whether the doctor attended, but Zeb said so little that Mr Bailey couldn't make sense of it all.

He was concerned for his son. Alice had taken in Zeb when he came out of prison after nine years. Mr Bailey was sure that, but for Alice, Zeb would have ended up in the river. And on top of that, Alice had taken in Mr Bailey himself, and but for her again, where would he have been? He loved her more than he had ever loved any woman except his wife. John and Zeb had not had a good relationship since Zeb had run away from home, but now they had found a love for one another and she had done that too, bringing them together. If Alice didn't get better, Zeb might go back to the devil. Mr Bailey couldn't sleep for thinking about it.

The saving grace was that he was living with kind people whom he liked, and that he had plenty of work to do to keep him busy. Miss Vernon's cooking was nowhere near as good as Alice's, but he learned to expect less. There was nothing wrong with it, only that it was dull, as Alice's meals had never been.

Miss Vernon cooked because they had to eat, whereas Alice loved cooking. Miss Emily did not cook. They had two girls who came in to do the washing, the ironing and the housework, so the two women were free to do as they liked, more or less, and so they helped with the newspaper, writing columns on various subjects like sewing, crochet and how to make garments last longer, and also recipes for various cakes, all of which were Alice's. They talked softly of her and asked Mr Bailey, when he went to visit, how dear Alice was. When he shook his head they grew silent.

Mr Bailey also knew Mrs Garnet of old. She was a faithful Methodist and she always had a word for him, but when he enquired about Alice she merely shook her head and said the poor lady was very ill.

The problem that Mr Bailey had was twofold. First of all, he had fallen in love. He was very cross with himself for having done so, because he knew that he was too old for such a thing, that age had put such things beyond him. It was one more aspect of his life that must be laid to rest. He didn't miss his wife so much any more, and he was happy with his life with the Vernon family. He was very fond of Mr Vernon and Miss Vernon. The trouble was that he had come to care a great deal about Miss Emily.

What a silly old man I am, he said to himself. This was not what he had intended. He had also thought that when people were older, love was a dry and insipid thing. The trouble was that he soon began to adore Miss Emily. He wanted to save her from light rain, he wanted to be brilliant where she was, he watched for her entrance to the room and sighed like a lovesick idiot when she left. Every word she spoke was sweet; every idea she had was magic. She alone encouraged him in his work. To the other two, he was just one of the family, involved in everything they did.

He told himself that he could live like this with her, but he wanted to kiss her, to hold her, to wake up in the mornings with her. As hard as he fought, he could not quash these stupid feelings. He began to absent himself from places where she might be, until she asked politely whether she had offended him.

'You? Oh no. Never. You – you are very important to me. I thought that perhaps I was being tiresome.'

She assured him that he was nothing of the kind, and then she said that she had found a new piece of music for him to play. They had had the piano tuned after he came to live with them, and though he said that he hadn't played a piano in years, they insisted on him doing so. He rushed through his scales for half an hour a day, then began on easy pieces and now had ventured into the likes of Beethoven's sonatas.

He enjoyed playing very much, and he liked that the family would sit about in the evenings and listen, and now he and Miss Emily had devised a short concert for him. He had been hoping that Alice would be well enough to attend, but now he did not like to mention it.

This was his opportunity to ask Miss Emily to marry him, but somehow he couldn't find the words. He lacked experience in this matter. He had only had one prior go at this, when he asked his wife, and he did not see how he could manage again. He began to lie awake in bed, trying to construct the correct sentences to see him through the ordeal, but they would not come.

He was also very afraid that Miss Emily, being a maiden lady, would be most affronted. They were friends, such good friends, and he was risking it all. When she refused him, he did not see how they could ever be in a room together without awkwardness and embarrassment.

He would have to leave. Where on earth would he go? He did not want to go back to the sweet shop, and he felt sure that Zeb would not want him there. His son had more than enough to cope with. If Alice died, he would have to move back then. He would have to give up his sweet life and his lovely Emily and go back to be of comfort to his son.

He groaned and turned over. God had not provided night for such terrible and irrational thoughts. He must stop thinking such things. Alice would get better and he would ask Miss Emily to marry him and everything would be well.

*

Zeb didn't know how to deal with Mrs Garnet. He tried to ignore that she now knew exactly what was happening, but somehow he couldn't. Neither did he know what to say to her. In a sense, she was the hired help, and there was no reason why he should say anything. He suspected that many a man would have ignored the fact that she knew, but Mrs Garnet was so kind and reliable that it made him feel worse.

He was not worried that she would talk about them. As a farmer's wife, she had a lot of experience of life, and he was sure she knew when to say something and when not to. He wished he could do the same. He lasted for a week and then he deliberately came home early on Saturday, which he very often did, and found her busy in the kitchen, scraping carrots and singing 'Love divine, all loves excelling' in a very soft tone, aware always of Zeb's wife sleeping above.

He was so wretched that he didn't know how to begin, but she smiled at him and told him the kettle was about to boil.

Somehow, for Mrs Garnet, the kettle was always just about to boil. He had no idea how she timed it so exactly, but he was grateful for the comfort.

And then she said the innocuous words: 'I made a coffee cake. It won't be a patch on the sort of thing that Mrs Bailey can make, but . . .' And then she stopped, because Zeb lost all his breath.

He had never cried in front of a woman. In fact, he had rarely ever cried, and was not yet good at it, though he seemed to be getting a lot of practice. When he came out of prison it was as though his tear ducts had dried up, along with his heart and several other seemingly essential organs.

Unfortunately it seemed he had finally got the hang of spilling his emotions, and he choked over his lack of breath, and something caught in the back of his throat. From there it was no time at all until the whole thing reached the back of his eyes and after that it was all over for his sense of respectability. The tears ran as though they were determined to be held back no more. It was a horrible experience. His face burned and his nose blocked. His breathing got worse and worse and he gave in and sobbed.

Mrs Garnet dropped all pretence of formality and touched his shoulder as he was half turned from her.

'Eh, lad,' she said, 'try not to fret.'

Zeb wished he was by himself. He wanted to run out. He wanted to die. Alice was the only person he had ever truly loved and he was terrified. At first he couldn't say anything, but Mrs Garnet's sympathy was too much for him. His breath got worse, the tears increased and to his horror the snot suddenly unblocked and he searched desperately for the handkerchief that he had in his trouser pocket.

Since it hadn't been used in ages it was still folded in the special way that Alice folded such things. He had seen her ironing. First she took the handkerchief in both hands and shook it, and then she ironed the whole thing. Then she folded it once and ironed it again, then she folded it twice and did it again, and then it became a neat square parcel and she pressed the iron to it one final time. Perfection, just like everything she did.

'She isn't getting better,' he managed, and blew his nose just before the snot emerged on his upper lip.

Mrs Garnet didn't say anything, and then let out a heavy breath, as though she had made up her mind to speak. 'I lost three bairns like that. People think you're all right, but you're not.'

She smiled at him and tightened her fingers on his shoulder.

'But I was wrong,' he said.

'In some communities, so I understand, lads and lasses don't marry until they know the lass can have a bairn. I only had one in the end, God love him, and he's a good lad, but they got married before they should have had to, and now I have grandbairns. Don't you take on. Sit down and have your tea,' she ordered, and Zeb felt so much better that he was able to eat a huge piece of cake.

Thirty-Two

Dan did not want to go back to Stanhope. He was having dreams about holding on to things that were whirling away from him. The foundry where he had found work, up Elvet, was sorry to lose him. The manager shook his head and said he would pay him more if he would stay there, because he was the best they had had in the office in a long time. Dan really wanted to be there, but he couldn't.

He comforted himself that if it was nothing important, he could come back. The manager said that he would keep Dan's position open until the following week, and then if he heard nothing he would find somebody else. Dan told him how grateful he was and set off for the train station feeling sicker than he had felt since arriving in Durham.

He didn't have a plan. He thought he would go to the sweet shop and find out from Zeb what was happening, and if it was nothing to concern him, he would stay overnight in the pub and take the train the next morning back to Durham. He would not see Susan, nor anybody else, and this time when he left he would not come back.

But when he got to Frosterley, where the train ended, his

confidence swept past him like a long-distance runner and was out of sight before he could think.

Zeb would not have called him back here without a good reason. He just hoped that Susan hadn't damned well died on him while he was not there. He felt she might have done so just to spite him, and having lost Arabella like that he didn't want to make a habit out of such a thing. This frivolous and awful thought carried him the three miles to Stanhope. He could hear the thud of his heart when he saw the sweet shop, and he wanted to turn around and run away.

To his dismay, the shop was closed. It was never closed, except for Sunday, or sometimes a half day on a Wednesday. It was shut up and dark when all the other shops were open. Daniel's heart then did horrible things and he imagined everybody dead.

He went to the house where he and Susan had spent the first night of their married life, and he could not help recalling how much he had expected and how Susan had taken her revenge on him and then how he had left. He thought of the wedding night of his first marriage, how wonderful it had been with Arabella, when Susan would not let him touch her, and the two stood there in his mind until he wanted to run away.

Susan had obviously moved. When he looked in through the windows the rooms were empty. The garden was neglected and overgrown, and even though the days were now long and warm, it smelled like marshland. It was as though the whole place was unhappy but he knew that it was only how he felt.

He went back over the road and found that the sweet shop

was not just closed for the day, but looked empty as well. Had everybody moved? It was like an alternate world.

He made his way down the passage into the back yard and knocked on the door. When he had no answer, he climbed the steep hill to the quarry. He opened the office door and there he found Zeb and Pat, looking at some papers on the desk. He was so grateful he could have wept.

For several seconds as he had approached the building, he felt as though he would find Mr Almond there, and that he would be back in the days when he was happy, Arabella at home with Mrs Almond and he and Mr Almond running the quarry together.

It was so similar. Mr Paterson was still there, but in the boss's chair sat Zeb Bailey. The next thing that hit him was that Zeb looked awful – skinny, grey-faced and dull-eyed. He wondered how hard things had become at the quarry, but the look on Zeb's face was all gratitude.

'Now,' Dan said.

'Now, you bastard,' Pat said with a grin.

Zeb said nothing. Mr Paterson barely looked up.

It was the end of the day and the men stopped work. Pat went off and Mr Paterson packed up and he too went.

'We need you back here,' Zeb said. 'Things have all gone wrong. The bloke who was supposed to run the place died and Mrs Almond realized she needs us.'

Dan sighed and sat down in the rickety chair across the desk from him. 'Susan moved?'

'She's working for the solicitor. She lives in rooms there.' Zeb glanced at him. 'She ran after you.'

'What?'

'When you left. She ran all the way to the station to stop you from going. She was halfway home by the time I got there. I told her you would come back but she lost heart.'

'She hated that house from the minute she saw it. I don't know why I insisted we go there after the wedding. Both of us taking revenge. Is that why the sweet shop is closed?'

Zeb paused. 'Alice isn't very well,' he said. 'She hasn't been well since we were married not long after you left. Have you got some place to stay?'

Dan shook his head.

'You can come back and stay at the sweet shop with us, but don't expect much. Mrs Garnet, who lives a few doors along, comes in to clean, and she leaves something for me to eat when I get back, but Alice doesn't come downstairs.'

'If Alice is poorly I wouldn't put on you like that. I'll stay at the pub—'

'Come back with me. I would rather you did. It'll be good to have company.'

They walked slowly back down the hill and into the town, and Dan had the curious feeling that he had been gone for years. So much had changed.

At the back of the sweet shop, Zeb took him inside. The fire was low but still burning, and when he lit the lamps it didn't look so bad, but it had lost the personal touch, as though Alice had moved out. Zeb put the kettle on to boil and then he went upstairs.

Dan was unhappy. He had somehow thought life here was standing still, perhaps waiting for him to come back and pick up where he had left off. Now he was beginning to see that nothing was the same. He could hear Zeb's soft footsteps up above, but he could hear only one voice. He wondered how ill Alice was, and for how long the shop had been closed.

He didn't know whether to ask or not. When Zeb came downstairs Dan didn't like to say anything, but neither did he want Zeb to think that he didn't care.

Zeb built up the fire, put the stew into the oven and got out a big loaf of bread. The woman who looked after him was obviously a good cook, Dan thought, but he wished that Alice would come down and tell him that everything was all right.

When they had eaten, Zeb got out the whisky bottle. Dan was surprised at that, but he worked out that Zeb needed the whisky and wouldn't leave his wife in the evenings to go to the pub. They sat by the fire and drank slowly and watched the flames.

'The bed is made up in the other room,' Zeb said, without looking at him, 'and the sheets on the bed are clean. Mrs Garnet is very good.'

'Is Alice getting better?' Dan couldn't wait any longer.

Zeb looked down into his whisky glass and gave a twisted sort of smile. Dan's heart ached for him.

'No.'

Dan thought it was just plain awful. He had hoped they would marry, had hoped they would be happy and something had gone wrong.

'Is she going to get better?'

'I don't know.'

'I'm so sorry.'

'You can stay here as long as you like. It isn't wonderful, but it's better than the pub. And it's nice to have you here, even though I'm not much company myself.' Zeb summoned up a decent smile. 'I'll leave Mrs Garnet a note and she'll make more dinner for tomorrow night.'

That night, Dan found that his bed was clean and the fire burned brightly, and it only made him think that perhaps sometimes when Alice was very ill his friend slept here. He was pleased to be there, even just to help with the quarry, and he sensed that Zeb was glad too.

Dan thought about Susan and envisaged her running after him. It had not been as he had thought. And all the time he had been in Durham, he had thought that she didn't care.

He went to the quarry the following day with Zeb and was immediately glad. How had he thought that he belonged in Durham? Yet he didn't regret the time spent there. He felt closer to his father now and he remembered vividly how he had felt for Susan when he had asked her to marry him for the second time.

Meeting Mary and Cate had made such a difference, and especially the little boy. Knowing the small baby made him wonder how his child was, and whether he had a look of Arabella.

Being in Zeb's house and having Alice never come downstairs was not the easiest place in the world to be. Zeb was so unhappy that he wasn't as good at his work as he might have been, and Dan understood how much Pat had therefore taken on, but he didn't say anything. He just wrote Mrs

Almond a letter saying that he was back and was taking charge as she had wanted, and that he thought Pat McFadden needed a pay rise because he had been working successfully as undermanager for quite a long time, and now he was the man in between the men and the management, as Zeb had been when Mr Almond was alive. He hoped she would agree to this.

He absented himself from the office when Zeb told Pat about the wage rise. He knew Pat didn't like his attitude or the way he had let Pat take his child and had never thanked him. He saw Pat's face when he came out of the office and it was inscrutable.

When he got time off, he began thinking about where he would live and how Susan was, so on the Saturday afternoon he waited until the solicitor was closed and then banged on the door down the side street. It made him think of the awful house they had been in together so briefly, and when she came to the door she looked as if she was half expecting him.

She wasn't beautiful any more. It was a shock, and then he quickly became accustomed to how thin and pale she was, and he felt guilty because he had caused it.

'Daniel,' she said, without a smile. 'I heard you were back.'

'May I come in?'

'I suppose, if you want to.'

The building, which he had not been to before, was strong and square. When she took him through to the sitting room, he found that it looked down not only towards the river, but towards the house where they had been so unhappy.

'Zeb told me that when I left you followed me,' he said.

'It was a mistake,' she said.

'It might not have been if you had caught me and we had gone to Durham together.'

'It was just an impulse,' she said. 'I thought I had treated you badly. I know I had, in fact, but I remembered how you had treated me and after that I knew I couldn't love you, however much I might want to. You look just as good as ever, and now of course you have returned in triumph to take back the managing of the quarry.'

'And you have a new job?' he said, as she ushered him to the sofa they had bought together before he jilted her.

He wasn't sure whether it was uncomfortable or it was just how he felt.

'I like the work,' she said.

'Did you leave because Alice is ill?'

'I know nothing about her. I think you will understand that I decided to leave when they got married.'

'She's been in bed all this time. I'm staying there, but I will have to find somewhere to live.'

'I'm very pleased for you, Daniel, and glad for the rest of this place that you've come back. You were always very good at your work, even though you turned out not to be very good at anything else.'

Dan said nothing to that.

'I thought I might try to see Frederick,' he said finally.

That surprised her, he could see. It surprised him too. He had thought about it a great a deal, but had not been this positive. His conflicting ideas about how he had behaved towards the child made him hesitate. He wasn't sure he deserved to see the boy after all this time, and yet now it was what he wanted most of all. But he feared rejection. If the little boy took against him, what would he do? After all, they did not know one another. Also, and this too was a sudden surprise, he wanted to see Cate's little boy even more. He had learned to love Harry, and because of that he thought he might learn to love his own child and perhaps even be a decent part of his life. And he must see Cate and Mary. He had missed them so much from the moment that they had left Durham. They were his family now. He had not realized he had so much in Stanhope. It was as though a whole clan was waiting for him. Susan, on the other hand, was not. He had had vague hopes, but he could see that she would not take him. He was not sure whether it was pride, because she had loved him well at one time, but the look on her face was hard and unrelenting.

'Really?' she said, and he thought that the look in her face softened just a little, but she obviously didn't want him there and wasn't interested in the boy, and he was surprised that he had thought she might be. The boy was nothing to do with her, and so far had been nothing to do with him. Alice had saved him, with the help of Shirley, and now Alice was seriously ill and he was terribly worried that she would die. Zeb wasn't talking about it and he didn't dare to ask.

Thirty-Three

Charles ventured to Durham. He pretended to himself that he had thought carefully about this, and was not in pursuit of Cate because she could have the male heir to the family. He was not going to persecute or hurt her, he just wanted to know, in case he had need of an heir in time.

He had tried to persuade himself that he should marry. He knew that he ought to, but he saw nobody he liked as well as he had liked Susan, and he had fallen in love only once. He didn't understand that: some men seemed to be able to love half a dozen women at different times in their lives, sometimes two at once, but it was not so with him. Susan was in his dreams and in his heart, and she prevented him from loving anyone else.

Durham felt a long way away. He thought that if he did find Cate, and she agreed to go back with him, he would spend the next few years of his life trying to persuade her to marry him. It was lowering to know that she did not want to, and that they were both bound by stupid rules made by stupid men and there was no reasonable way out of them.

He could, of course, have stayed at home and pretended

that everything was all right, but that would not have helped, and so he made what felt like very slow progress to Durham. When he got there, he followed Stewart's instructions and had his servant bang on the door of the house where she had been living. He was hardly surprised to find that there was no reply, and when the servant went on banging, the door next to it opened and a fat man with a bald head and an unshaven chin said, 'They've gone. And will thoo stop making that row. I'm working shifts and it doesn't help when buggers like thoo bang bloody hell out of the house next door when I'm trying to sleep.'

'Do you know where they are?' Charles said, getting out of the carriage.

The man looked him up and down.

'I don't,' he said, and went inside and banged the door.

In spite of his disappointment, Charles couldn't help but smile. He thought that in some cases he could have offered the man money for more information and been told elaborate lies. Here in Durham, nobody cared. It had been one of the things he loved best about this area. He missed it.

He missed being ordinary, he missed Susan and the dale, and in a stupid way he missed his father and most of all he missed his brother. He could have wept long and hard now, as he had done so many times over his brother.

Oh God, Henry, he thought. I do miss you. I can't believe I will never see you again. No wonder people need heaven.

Sometimes he thought he would never stop crying over his brother. It seemed to him now that he had given up every opportunity he'd had, that he had caused Henry's death because he had not stayed in Westmorland and taken on his responsibilities. Everything was his fault. He had no recourse but to go back to Westmorland, and when he got there and sat by the fire, full of dinner and drinking brandy, he saw how he had turned into his father. Nothing could equal the bitterness he felt now.

Thirty-Four

Nell had no idea what to wear when she got married for the second time. She didn't know who to invite, and so invited nobody. She took the pony and trap and trotted down the hill. She would have walked, but everybody would have looked at her and she did not want to see or speak to anyone.

She had dreamed about Harold. It was annoying and badly timed. And it wasn't as though he had been saying to her that he was pleased she was marrying; he was just displeased at how she was running the quarry, and he wanted his money back. From what, she did not know, but it didn't help her day.

She drank two glasses of dry sherry before she set off, wearing a pretty cream dress with a hat to match and a light coat. She told no one where she was going but Norah and she felt horribly sick, thinking that perhaps Sawrey had thought better of it and would not be there. He had to be there, her better sense told her; he could not afford to stay away.

She had wanted to employ Norah at Holywell Hall, but Sawrey was reluctant to have anybody there and each time she broached the subject he changed it.

'We can sort all that out later,' was his response, and while

Nell wasn't very happy about it, she thought she had come too far to back out now. She reminded herself of the loneliness she had endured since Harold had died. In a way, she blamed him and Arabella for having left her so abruptly, but at least now she could see some way ahead.

She had insisted on having the roof seen to before she moved in, so that the bedrooms were dry. She bought new beds and threw out the others, which were so awful she couldn't look at them. She made a bonfire of everything she could. She bought new linen and mattresses and pillows, and swore to herself that when the weather was cooler the chimneys in the bedrooms would be fit for big fires and she would employ people to make things right. Even if Sawrey wasn't altogether happy about it, she didn't think that he would object to such things. He had seemed happy when the roofers arrived and when the furniture came, and even Augusta liked her new bed. She had told Nell so.

Eventually Nell hoped to keep cows and hens and various other animals, and to grow as many vegetables as she could. She had also decided on glasshouses so that she could grow tomatoes, cucumbers and possibly even grapes, and she had plans to fit stoves into the glasshouses so that perhaps in time she might grow exotic plants within the walled garden, where it was sheltered. The walls had been tumbling down, but she had hired experienced men to build them back up and she had so much enjoyed doing it. She loved this place as she had loved nowhere before, and couldn't wait to get her hands on the rest of it.

She had also talked to Mr Peters, the botanist, and got him

to come to the hall and advise her about what the soil could produce and what she needed to put into it so that everything would prosper. In her mind's eye, she saw sheep in the fields and pigs in the sties and ducks on the pond, and she could not wait to get on with it. She wanted the place to look as good as she could make it. She would have a new hen house built and repairs done to all the outside buildings.

When she got to the church, tying up the pony on the rail nearby, she found that she was last to arrive. Sawrey was there, though not Augusta. He did not mention her and Nell was not surprised. Sawrey's suit was creased and had obviously spent a good deal of time in the wardrobe, where moths had had a feast. The sleeves were thin in some places and holey in others, but it didn't matter. He could not help but look elegant. It was something to do with the way that he moved, though she couldn't for the life of her tell how.

They went into the church and one or two people, who presumably had nothing better to do, drifted in and sat at the back. She made herself not turn round, in case they might be people she knew. Nell trembled all the way through the short service. It was as unlike her first wedding as possible, and she wished with all her might to be magicked back to when she had been young and marrying the love of her life.

She looked at Sawrey and felt sorry for him. She was much too old for him and he was marrying her for her money. She wanted to run back down the aisle and outside and drive up to Ash House and forget it all, but she remembered how lonely it was, how nothing went forward there. She could retreat, but there would be no way out before death and she couldn't do it. It was better to take her chances and try to go forward, no matter what it might cost.

The wedding, so brief, was over quickly. To her thanks, Sawrey followed her on his horse back to Holywell Hall, where he went off to stable the horses. Supplies had arrived from the local grocer, and there were two cases of wine standing in the kitchen.

Nell could see already that she'd had only a vague idea of what this would be like, and it was not going to work out. When would she ever learn? The day had turned wet. The dark corners of the hall smelled dank and there were no fires. She set to in the kitchen and lit the fire. While Sawrey opened the first bottle of wine, she put into the oven the chicken that had come with the rest, slathered in butter and salt and pepper.

She hadn't done work like this in years. It was not unpleasant, it was just that she was unused to kitchens. How far up in the world she had come, and yet here she was?

Augusta did not come downstairs, and Nell was not surprised.

'How long will the chicken take?' the bridegroom enquired, peering into the oven as though he had never seen it before, which possibly he hadn't.

'The oven hasn't even warmed up yet, so I'm not sure. Less than two hours.'

'Isn't there anything else to eat?' He began rummaging through the supplies and came out with a loaf of bread and began tearing chunks off it and devouring them at speed.

Then he took the bottle and a glass and went off. Nell

found carrots in the groceries and French beans and began to feel clever, doing the things she had thought she would never have to do again, and which, until she became the real mistress, she would have to.

She was beginning to enjoy herself. She built up the fire and when there was sufficient hot water she took soap and a scrubbing brush and scrubbed the big wooden table, and after that she cleaned out the cupboards and washed the surfaces and the floor. She even made an attempt at the window. It looked out over what had been the kitchen garden, which she had such plans for.

She went out of the back door and found herself in an overgrown square which had had tumbled walls around it. She had seen it before, but it looked so different and even more interesting now that it was hers. This was her place and she felt right in it as she had not felt at Ash House. That made her feel guilty and disloyal, but she also felt pleased at the prospect of trying again, starting afresh.

Many of the plants she recognized, and as she moved she saw the big leaves on the potato plant, and when she heaved at it, it came out of the ground and small potatoes rained all around her. It made her laugh. She picked up those she could find and went back into the kitchen.

The smell of cooking chicken was glorious as never before. When it was done, she and Sawrey sat at the kitchen table and ate. Augusta did not come downstairs and Sawrey said to leave her, she would come when she was hungry. He then lay down on the old sofa in the drawing room and slept. It had been a difficult day for all of them, but right now Nell was too exhilarated to rest. She thought it must be the strangest wedding day any woman ever had.

They had not yet exchanged a kiss, and wouldn't. She knew that, but had to keep reminding herself. They stayed up late, or at least she and Sawrey did. Augusta slept, having come downstairs to eat hastily and without looking at either of them. Sawrey said that she was worn out by the day, as she was unused to such things. In the end, he carried her up to her room and then came back downstairs and he and Nell toasted one another with the dry sherry they both liked.

They had cheese and biscuits, and she outlined to him all the things she wanted to do, and he told her that as far as he was concerned anything she did would be fine, as long as the building retained its atmosphere. She knew what he meant. He didn't want the place spoiled, and he didn't want it like Ash House, but that had been Harold's venture. This was hers, and much as she had loved her first husband, this was different.

When it was late, he said he was going upstairs, and wished her goodnight. After he had gone, Nell sat for a few minutes and then went up herself. She found it very difficult. She kept telling herself that he had not promised her a real marriage, that he had not deceived her. So why was she finding this so very hard? She was too old to behave stupidly. She had known what she was going into when she agreed to this. Whatever else might happen, she would never be lonely again.

She went down to breakfast at half past eight and found Sawrey coming inside.

'How are you feeling on this fine morning, Nell?' he said.

She couldn't think of anything to say. She had had a real marriage with Harold. This was nothing like that.

'I feel strange, very odd, very dissatisfied.'

He said nothing.

'I know you told me that it wouldn't be a real marriage, and I know you think I'm far too old to want a man, but you cannot imagine being around you when you are so beautiful and not being able to touch.'

He sighed and sat down with her. She was surprised. She was being unfair. He had not tried to deceive her, and she thought he might just turn and walk out of the room. Harold had often done so when they were arguing, or were upset with one another but they had had no problems in the bedroom other than that she had so desperately wanted to give him half a dozen children and couldn't. She had tried to accept that too, but she had been obliged to accept so many things and she was tired of it.

Vainly, she told herself how lonely she had been. She had wanted this. Now she wanted more. She could not believe how greedy she was, and was ashamed. He sat down without looking at her, but he didn't say, 'I did tell you' or 'you couldn't expect anything more'. He just sat there and then he raised his eyes to her face and he said, 'I care about you very much. I don't think of you as old, I just am not used to anybody but Gussie. I've never been allowed to touch anybody and I don't know how to do it. If I'd been rich or even vaguely respectable, I suppose I would have married and had an heir and maybe some semblance of a normal life. I don't remember normal. I don't think we ever had it.'

Nell very gently put her hand up to his head and smiled into his eyes and then she kissed him, just a brush of her lips, and then she drew back. Maybe in time, she thought, something would happen, and suddenly she felt happier than she had felt since Arabella had died. And he put his arms around her and held her close and she shut her eyes and thanked God for her good fortune.

She liked being in charge of restoring the house. She put the workmen to the task of mending the roof properly, which meant recovering the inner layer and putting on stone slates to secure the whole thing. After that, she made sure that the walls were stout and the fires in the various rooms worked. She put on doors that had fallen down. She tried not to encroach on the house; her aim was to make it look as it must have looked when it was sound. When all the fires worked, and the people in the place were well fed and had good clean beds to sleep in, she felt easier.

Sawrey wanted the stables rebuilt and so she saw to that as well, but he didn't buy any horses. She didn't like to ask why; she knew he had married her so that she could keep the hall going and enable him to buy hunters, but he didn't. Perhaps he had just needed to know that he could.

One evening that summer, they were sitting outside drinking champagne. He liked champagne best, except for sherry, and it was one of the things she could do for him. Augusta was in bed, as usual, and she said to him, 'There is plenty of money for more horses.'

He fidgeted for a few seconds and then he said, softly, 'You have been so very generous.'

That was when it occurred to Nell that, as he became well fed and well looked after, he was more beautiful than ever. His hair shone and his eyes were clear and he had new clothes, and the worry and the horrors of his previous life were all gone. He looked happy and she thought, with pleasure, that she had done that. That was her best gift to him.

'I was lonely.'

'I like that you love this place,' he said, looking down over the dale.

'I never loved Ash House. I should sell it.'

'Do we need the money?'

'It's your money too now, you know.'

He laughed and said that he had never had any money and would probably not get used to the idea, and that she should sell the house and put the money away for the future.

He looked down into his fluted glass. 'I don't want to buy horses. Isn't that strange? I imagined that if I had a house like this, and money, I'd want to hunt and shoot and have people here to stay, and wear fine clothes and go away and see other places, but I don't. I just want us to live here, like this, in peace. You've done so much for us, Nell, I don't think you realize. Gussie and me, we've never had anything. It's wonderful.'

She said nothing.

He glanced at her. 'Do you see the people at night?'

She did. She hadn't liked to say so, because she didn't believe in ghosts, it seemed such a silly idea, and yet she had seen figures and she had seen their pain as the faces flitted through her room. She wasn't afraid, because she had not been born here or died – at least as far as she knew. She liked the idea that in one of her lives – because the idea of having several was more and more appealing as you grew older – she had lived here or had known it, visited it, maybe even been married here and had children. Was that why she had such affinity with it? Or was it just that perhaps everybody felt the same about such places, wanting to remove the hurt and the pain and the cries and replace it all with flowers and animals and maybe even a future.

There was no future for any of them here in a lot of ways. It was all about the past, or seemed to be, and as far as she could tell there would be no child in the house.

She was going to ask Sawrey whether she might bring Frederick here to live. She had said nothing to him, but it was one of the dreams she had about this place, that Frederick might grow up here and belong and that the house could go forward. It hadn't done such a thing in a very long time, and being childless, none them would make it so.

She knew that somewhere Sawrey had a relative who would in time inherit this place. It could never be Frederick's, but if the quarry could make sufficient money, and she sold and invested the money from Ash House, there would be enough to educate him well, send him to a decent university and then enable him either to do what he wanted with the quarry or to put the money into some kind of business.

'I don't want you to be lonely here, you know,' Sawrey said, carefully not looking at her. 'You needn't be afraid, because I will come and look in on you through the night.' And from that minute she began to love him.

'Time is different for Gussie,' he said, 'and I can't always be on the same time as she is. I think a lot of her is still back in the past when she was very young and we had both our parents and we were happy – at least I think we were. I can remember a big tree at Christmas, and the carols, and how we sang them. And I remember the dogs sitting by the fire. But then I remember how the dogs were allowed to sit by the fire, and we were banished to the outside buildings. We would stand outside and see the fire and the dogs and the light in the drawing room and then we would know that the doors were bolted so that we could not get inside, and we would go and try to find somewhere which was not as cold and huddle there all night.'

'It's all right now,' Nell soothed him, 'and we will make the place good again. You are happy about the repairs?'

He stared at her. 'Oh Nell, I never hoped the place would look this good and that Gussie would be comfortable. She isn't yet, but she will be, and I never imagined myself drinking champagne and having such good food and being offered wealth like yours. I hope you won't regret it.'

'I'm enjoying myself,' she said, and he kissed her on the mouth and took her into his arms and hugged her to him.

That night he left Augusta sleeping and went to Nell's bed, and although all they did was talk softly for a long while, she found herself turning over in bed and remembering how she and Harold had slept together and how she was grateful that Sawrey was with her. He left her in the dawn in case

Augusta should awaken, but from that night onward they almost always slept together, and in the night she could reach for him and be taken into his arms and kissed and held.

Her hope was that she could bring Frederick to live with them, but she chose her time carefully. It was late evening several weeks later, and as usual Augusta had gone to bed and she and Sawrey were sitting by the fire.

She said to him that she wanted her grandchild there.

He looked worried. 'Isn't he better where he is?' Sawrey said. 'Isn't he very small?'

'He's quite big enough to leave Shirley.'

Sawrey squirmed in his chair. 'I know nothing of children, except that I used to be one.'

'You wouldn't object then to my bringing him home.'

'This isn't his home.'

'Of course not. But I need him close to me. He is my heir and the heir to the quarry.'

'I suppose not then, but you won't let him take up all your time.'

He and Augusta were still children in many ways, and they did not want a real child there who had to have all her attention.

Nell went up to talk to Shirley, and braced herself. She knew that Shirley considered the child her own, and she was prepared for a row but also she knew her rights. This boy was her blood, her only descendant, and he would inherit the quarry. He was all she had left and she was not going to give him up, no matter what Shirley said.

'He doesn't need to be here any more,' Nell said.

'How do you know that?' Shirley said.

Nell hated the small house, and Pat's awful parents. His father stank and his mother hovered, with her thin nasty mouth and small lightless eyes. Shirley held the boy to her as though she could not let him go, and the little girls came to her, one of them with a thumb in her mouth and the other with sunken cheeks, as though she had never had enough to eat, which Nell knew was not so. Perhaps they had some childish ailment.

'You aren't feeding him any more and he's on his feet and he's talking. I want him now. He is my heir and I have married and can do a lot for him. You need to give him to me.'

Shirley turned her back and Nell could somehow imagine that she was crying, but she wanted the child too much to care about that. Shirley had two children, a good husband and a house, no matter what she had to bear. She must give up the child.

'If you don't give him to me now, Shirley, I will come back when your husband is here and he will.'

Shirley sobbed and Nell could see she was pressing the boy into her breast.

'He is my grandson. Give him to me.'

'I can't.'

'You have to. He's mine.'

'You are cruel.'

'He's all I have. You already have two children.'

'But I wanted a boy.'

'Give him to me, Shirley. He isn't yours.'

'I'm his mother, the only one he has ever known. You gave him to me. He would have died without me.'

'That's not true. I would have found somebody else.'

'Where?' Shirley had turned and was glaring at her now, eyes full of defiance. She looked to Nell like an animal being asked to hand over its cub.

'If I give him up now he will never remember me. Think what it must be like for a tiny child to be torn from his mother's arms and taken away. It will damage him. You will be damaging him for the rest of his life. He's my child now and you can't have him.'

'That was never the arrangement.'

'Arrangement? This is a child we are talking about. You make it sound as though it was a business deal. What on earth can you give him that I can't? He eats well, and he sleeps soundly here between his two sisters. He's well looked after. Pat reads him bedtime stories. My parents adore him. All you have to give him is more food and a bigger house. He isn't yours any more.'

Nell Almond – or whatever the hell her new name was – left, and Shirley tried to breathe easily. The boy had begun to cry because she was clutching him to her so tightly, and he sensed discord, she thought. She watched Mrs March go back down the road and the sense of relief left her. She would come back. She would try to force Shirley to give him up. Briefly, Shirley contemplated running away, and then dismissed it as nonsense. But she wanted to run until she couldn't run any further.

By the time Pat came back from work, Shirley was crying, all the children were crying, his father was mumbling in his sleep and his mother came to the door and told him how stupid and useless his wife was.

Shirley listened to the beginning of it and then went outside. She looked out over the little town and had to stop herself from taking Freddie and battling down the hill in some fruitless attempt at running away. She knew that she could do nothing of the kind.

As though in sympathy, the valley was wreathed with flowers in the early evening and the shadows were long. Her husband came outside, and even though she turned her back to him, he said impatiently, 'I lost a morning's work. I had to walk two bloody miles up to the hall and do battle with Mrs March. What in God's name are you thinking about?'

Shirley didn't answer.

'You have to give him up to her.'

'What is he, a package?'

'That's not the point, Shirley, and you know it. I understand—'

That was when she turned on him. 'Understand? You were the person who didn't want him. You are the man who can't wait to get rid of him—'

'That's not true.'

'Isn't it? You are impatient with him. You have no idea

what I have to put up with day after day, with your blessed parents and the children and never having enough money and—'

'Don't do that to me, Shirley. I'm doing the best that I can.'

'We all are, and I will not give up this child when he is far better with the only mother he knows.'

'So what will you do when she takes my job off me?'

Pat went into the office the following day. He didn't spend much time there now that Daniel was back, and he was glad of it. He was competent there, but nothing like the other two men. He was content just to do his job and go home to his family, though he missed going to the pub with Zeb. He liked the summer nights, being able to sit outside and read to the little ones. He was glad to get out of the house, where he thought his father smelled worse every day, even though Shirley diligently changed the bed, so that most days, especially in the winter and early spring, the house was full of wet washing, and somehow the smell of his father's open bladder and bowels never quite went away.

Pat sometimes wished that his parents would just die, and then he felt guilty and mean and remembered them looking after him all those years before they became ill. His father had worked hard. His mother had adored him. True, she had never liked Shirley, and this was one of the problems. His mother would have been jealous of any woman he cared for, because he was not just her only son but her only child. Nothing Shirley ever did would make up for the fact that she had taken his mother's boy and made him hers. And his mother could not forgive Shirley either for not having had a son herself. So on fine evenings, Pat liked to go outside. Sometimes he wished he could get away, but it wouldn't be fair when Shirley had been on her own all day, coping with everything.

He got more tired at work than he had even five years ago. Now he would not have welcomed a walk up the hills – he was too tired and had too much to think about. So he resented being called into the office, where Dan told him that there had been a message from the hall that he was to go up there and talk to Mrs March.

'Me?'

'So she says. Got the note here.'

'Now?'

'As soon as you can.'

'I'm in the middle of doing stuff here, and it's two miles uphill.'

'I know,' Dan said flatly, so Pat gave in and went. There was no point in arguing. The woman owned the place.

His anger got him there quickly. He had never been to the hall before, and had imagined it as a tumbledown place, but it was not any more. There were a lot of workmen about, and in among them he could see her. She didn't acknowledge him, even when he knew that she had seen him.

'So,' he said, when she finally looked up. 'What is it?' He knew he didn't sound respectful. He didn't feel respectful.

'Come inside.'

Inside, the place looked good – repaired but not spoiled.

She led the way into a big room: a library with oak shelves, and some of them smelled of new books. Pat was not sure it was a smell he might ever like again, considering how she was watching him.

'What am I doing here? I'm losing time.'

'At least you still have a job,' she said.

'Have I done something?'

'I want my boy.'

Pat stared. He thought she looked dreadful, much worse than before. She looked old. Her face was caving in, and she had been out in the sun too much and there were deep threads of white as her pouched brown face wrinkled and dropped.

'I want my grandchild. If I don't get him, you won't have a house or a job. I am grateful for what you did for Frederick, but I want him now. You have two days to bring him to me.'

Pat tried to breathe. He always tried to breathe instead of losing his temper. It would do him no good here, and though he thought her unfair, he could see how upset she was. He said nothing, but simply turned around and walked out, feeling glad to get away from the terrible feeling of the house. No amount of oak bookshelves would change the ingrained sadness of the place.

Now Shirley turned around and looked at him. 'Your job?'

'And the house. What will we do then, Shirley, with two old people and two children, when I have no job and we have nowhere to live? I won't get another job here, because she will tell everybody that I am not to be taken on. What then?'

'You're afraid of what a woman says?'

Pat couldn't believe this, but he saw how badly upset Shirley was. He was caught in the middle of a fight and he knew very well that neither of them would give in. They both wanted the child. He wished he had been Solomon and could have offered to cut the baby in two so that one of them would yield, but then neither of them was the little boy's mother. Arabella Almond lay cold in her grave and her mother had nothing left but this boy.

'You have two children,' he said. 'She has nothing.'

'He knows no home but this one. How will it affect him when he has to leave me?'

'You cannot do it to her, Shirley.'

'Watch me.'

'It's Thursday. If she doesn't get the child by Saturday, I will have no job and Daniel Wearmouth will be obliged to put us out, so think carefully about it.' And then he went off down the hill to the Grey Bull, and there he found Zeb and Dan. They never seemed to go out any more so he was surprised and not very pleased. He didn't want to talk to anybody. He merely nodded to them, got a pint and went outside, where he sat on his own. A little later, they both came over and sat down beside him.

'I'm trying to have a quiet pint here,' he objected.

'Grand evening,' Dan said.

'There's no point in you talking to me.'

'It could be my last chance.'

'Oh, shut up,' Pat said.

'I'll go and get some more beer,' Zeb said.

'I've just got mine.'

'Well, if you drink the bugger off you won't,' Zeb said, and he got up and went inside.

On the Saturday, inevitably, Pat had a fight with his wife. It was their first and he hoped there wouldn't be any more. He came reluctantly back to his house at the end of the afternoon, and Shirley ran out with the boy in her arms. There was no point in waiting for her to offer the child to him, and besides, he had exhausted his patience.

He grabbed her as she went past him, even though she had a tight hold on the child. She shrieked and shouted and hit him and put her nails into his face, but he managed to get her arms free. She clung both to him and to the boy all the way up the bank. She grew exhausted from the effort, but even then she hung on, grabbing at his hair and his neck until Pat was bleeding. In the end, he pushed her hard into the grass verge, knowing that she hadn't the energy to get up until he had got the boy a long way from her.

After that, all he had to do was keep walking. The child howled all the way, and so Pat was eager to give him up when they reached the hall. A young woman answered the door. All Pat did was to give the screaming child into her arms. As he made his way home, he wished he didn't have to face his wife.

He forgot all the days when the child had been hard work. He remembered Shirley feeding Fred, sitting by the fire and looking lovingly at him, as she had looked at all her children. He knew how much she had wanted a boy.

When he got home, she was not there. Later, she came back, and she made the tea, and everything went on as it should. Nobody said anything until they were in bed that evening, and then all she said was, 'I will never speak to you and I will never lie with you again,' and she turned away from him, towards the wall.

Thirty-Five

Cate knew that she should not have been surprised to see Charles that day in the garden, when he walked in looking rich and decadent and in charge. Stewart had betrayed her for a second time, as she had known that he would.

She wanted to shout for Mary or Mrs Peters, but they had taken the girls to the river to throw stones and plodge in the shallow water at the stepping stones. Mr Peters was up at Holywell Hall, where he was having a wonderful time, helping the new Mrs March with her gardens, so he said. Gardens were his passion. He had already written several books, but he was writing another and he was giving lectures in the dale and talks to different groups. Each week he wrote a column for the local newspaper about walks in the area and flowers to see on the way.

Harry had cried all night and she was too tired to do more than be grateful he had fallen asleep in her arms. She was about to put him upstairs and try to snatch some sleep for herself when Charles appeared. Instead of coming to the front door like a gentleman, he had sneaked around to the side and opened the gate.

'Well,' she said, 'what a surprise. Stewart couldn't keep his mouth shut during a sandstorm in a desert. What the hell do you want here?'

'Just to see you.'

'Well, of course,' she said. 'Not trying to work out whether my child is a boy so you can take him back to Westmorland and give him a similar kind of childhood to yours and Henry's – as though that worked out so well.'

'Catherine, I wasn't.'

'Go to hell, Charles. You want to subject my child to the horrors you and I faced. Do you really think it is the best way?'

'I just wanted you to be aware that I hadn't married and the child could be the heir to both our estates.'

'Your stupid estate comes down the male line, isn't that true? So if this little person here is a girl, you will have no further interest in her, will you? You will have to go elsewhere to sort out how your stupid estate will go on.'

'It isn't like that.'

'I can remember the days when you thought it was very like that. Could you possibly have made a mistake?'

She could see the top of his head, since he was looking down at his feet. He looked so like Henry now that although she was furious with him she couldn't help being aware of the similarities, and it was true that Charles was everything Henry had not been.

When he looked up, she caught her breath. He was well dressed and with a new air of confidence about him, like he knew who he was now and what he was doing. He stood up straighter and looked so much taller – really very good indeed.

She knew that his father had died and he was now in charge. He looked more mature and more aware. He was now the eligible man his father had wanted him to be. Clever, good-looking and rich, and she knew instinctively that he was not like Henry.

He was not afraid, as Henry had been. Henry had suffered, like a lot of men did, she thought, from being the second child. But Charles was born to the estate, and perhaps that was why he had tried so hard to get away, to deny his heritage and his responsibilities. Now he had accepted it. He had come home in all the most important ways. She just hoped he would be a better parent than his father had been, but he would not do it with her child.

'I know it sounds stupid,' he said, 'but there are so many families relying on us so that they might have a living.'

'Oh, I see. It's all for the sake of other people. My God, Charles, you are almost still a minister of the church, offering people better lives in the hereafter. Well, I don't think people believe that any more. You could help them to own their homes, you could devise things to suit them better, but you don't choose to.'

'I have tried to do this—'

'Have you really? Do let me know when it brings results. In the meanwhile, I would like you gone from this garden. I despise you almost as much as I despise your dead and disgusting brother.'

Charles ventured a little nearer. 'I'm not trying to take him – or her.'

'I do hope not. From here I can scream loud enough for the people in Eastgate to hear.'

' I just wanted to say that the offer is still open. We can be married.'

'How very generous you are,' she said, 'but I don't need you. You should marry and have a child of your own. Or are you not given that way?'

'I suppose not,' he said, smiling just a little. She hated that smile.

'Oh dear, your father so into women and neither of his sons could raise even a smile.'

'I think my brother managed more than that.'

'Only once, I assure you. He was too drunk to manage more. I was surprised he did even that when I found out what he was.'

'You hate us both.'

'You doubted it?'

Charles shook his head. 'You have so little here.' He was looking around at the pretty garden, which must have seemed very small to him. 'I could give you the money to educate your child and make a good home for you both.'

'And I suppose I would be obliged to live with you, like a whore?'

'I wouldn't bother you. Besides, you have an estate of your own.'

'With my parents in it? You really think I would go back after the way that they treated me?'

'They aren't as they might be, but they are your family.'

'My God, Charles, how can you say such a thing, coming from your background? Just because you were stupid enough to return.'

'I loved my brother.'

'I loved him too, and look at us because of him. He cost us our happiness.'

'We could try again.'

'I don't choose to.'

'You'd rather live off other people?'

That stung, because she was always conscious of it.

'These people have been kinder to me than anybody ever before. I wonder what that says about the landed gentry and their ridiculous ideas.'

'I know.'

'Then why do you want me to go back?'

'Because I think that you have the heir, to your land and to mine, and that is a great many people to be looked after.'

'I will never go back there – never, do you hear. Even if I were dying I wouldn't do it. I was treated lower than a mare or a bitch, and it is unworthy of you to come here and try to persuade me. Heaven and earth could fall first.' Her arms by now were trembling so much that Harry awoke and cried again.

'The answer to this is that you should marry and have a child. Then you wouldn't need to worry about mine,' she said.

Charles stood for a few moments, and then he sighed, and Catherine couldn't help saying, 'I'm sorry about your father.'

Charles gave a small smile. 'I miss him.' And then he said, 'I am going back to Westmorland and will not hound you any more. If you need to come back or you get really stuck for money, I will send it and arrange everything—'

He stopped there because she held up a hand. 'Please, Charles, just go away and leave me alone.'

'All right,' he said, and then he turned around towards the gate. Cate could not help saying his name, so that he turned once more to her.

'When you marry and have children, try to be kind.'

He nodded, and then he left.

Mary came into the garden and Cate could see that she had overheard the conversation and hidden from fear.

'Was that Charles Westbrooke?'

'He's gone.'

'If he knows we are here, then my father and Ned will know too, and I cannot stay. They will kill me when they find me.'

'He's not going to tell them.'

'You don't know that,' Mary said, gazing at the side gate as though Charles was about to come back inside and pounce on her. 'I need to get away from here. I have the money I've been paid.'

'You're panicking.'

'Of course I'm panicking. You know what my father is like, and Ned King is even worse. I've got to go, and as soon as I can. I'm sorry, Cate, but I have to, you know I have to. I wouldn't dare to stay. I couldn't be happy for a minute.' And Mary started to cry, very softly.

'That money is nowhere near enough. We have to think of something, and quickly, and make sure that it's a very long way away so that neither Charles nor your father can find us.'

'You would come with me?'

'What else?'

They couldn't think of anything. They had nobody they could ask for money, and they both knew that if Mary's father and Ned found out, they would undoubtedly come here and kill her. Her father would think it shame on his family that she had run off, and would not spare her. Mary and Cate were so afraid now that Mary couldn't help but choke on a few tears.

Cate had never felt as helpless. In Westmorland she had an estate worth twenty thousand pounds a year, yet here she had nothing and she was a burden to Mary.

They didn't have a chance to talk of it any more. What with three children, the housework and the cooking for both houses, they were very busy, but that night when Cate went to bed she realized what she could do, and that was when she began to cry too.

She thought that there must be some way around it, and the only way she could sleep was to think that there would be several alternatives and they would choose the one that they preferred, but after another two days, when Mr and Mrs Peters went up to Daddry Shield to look at a moorland garden and left the children with them for the afternoon, Cate outlined the only plan she had thought feasible.

For the last two nights, Mary hadn't slept, so scared was she that her father and Ned would appear and kill her right here in the garden. Now they sat for a long time watching the two little girls playing on the lawn with the baby.

Mary turned away and then she said, 'We can't do that.'

'Do you mean you won't?'

Mary shook her head vehemently.

'No, no, of course not, but there has to be an easier way.'

'If you can think of it I would be glad to hear it. I've thought about nothing else for days.'

'You could go back there and marry Charles Westbrooke – that would be the sensible thing to do. After all, Harry is the heir to both estates, and if Charles were to marry someone else and produce an heir, you and Harry would lose that place.'

'I don't want Harry to be a Westbrooke, and this way I can go home and take charge of the estate. In a few years I'll be able to bring you and Harry home, or I'll be able to come to you.'

'That's not the right way to do it, I'll leave—'

'Charles would take my child, you know he would, even if he was being nice about it. All he cares about is family and you know how stupid it all is.'

'But for me to go away with your baby—'

'I'll say you and Harry died of a fever and that's why I've come back.'

'He will still make you marry him.'

'How could he? The estate will be mine the minute my father dies, and by then Charles might have found some woman foolish enough to marry him and produced an heir himself. Then we can claim what's ours.'

'It's not mine,' Mary said.

'Mary, if it hadn't been for you I wouldn't have lived through this. I would never have got away. I would have been married to Charles and he would send my child away to a horrid school, and expect him to mix with the kind of people who think hunting is a profession. He would want him to marry for the sake of the estate. Look what happened to Charles: he did everything he could to get away, and now he's back there, being his father.'

'I can't go.'

'You have to, or you know what will happen. Your father is not the forgiving kind. You could have a whole new life in Canada. You could get across country to Liverpool and sail away.'

'With your baby? Cate, you would never bear it.'

'It's the best thing all round. I would bear it a good deal better than you going off on your own and me having to take the baby home for the whole damned world to see that I have a bastard son who is a Westbrooke. Charles would try to make me marry him, for the sake of respectability.'

'He tried to help.'

'There were other ways, but he didn't care for them. I think we should sort this out as soon as possible, and in the meanwhile I will go back to Westmorland. But before that I will see Mr Calland, and you shall have enough money to go somewhere and hide with Harry until I can get money transferred to you from Westmorland in a few weeks' time. It doesn't have to be far away, only far enough so that you can't be found.'

'Harry would hate me.'

'He's tiny. He won't know the difference after the first few days.'

'How could I go without you?'

'You have to. It would be the best thing of all. Won't you do that for me?'

'But you don't want to go back there.'

'I will do it for my child. At the end of the summer I will go back and say that my child has died of a fever of some sort, and I will tell your father that you died of it too, so that they don't come looking for you.'

'It can't be what you want.'

'This isn't about what any of us wants. It's about the future and Harry. And you. I will manage.'

'Without him?'

'I will have to.'

'It feels a long time until the end of the summer.'

'Just a few weeks. We need that time so that I sound credible, and I need that time to say goodbye to my boy.' Her voice shook, and Mary couldn't look at her, but she knew that it was the right thing.

When Cate went to bed, she could not believe what she had said. She wanted to take it back, and yet she was sufficiently afraid of Charles that she could not do so. He was unscrupulous enough to take her boy from her once he knew it was his heir. He could have done differently. He could have married. What was stopping him? Was he really like Henry, or had he seen his father treat his mother so badly that he no longer wanted a woman?

*

Susan, leaving her house, was just in time to see Charles Westbrooke coming out of the Peters' garden. She was astonished. He came to her with a polite smile on his lips. He looked so different that she barely knew what to say, and then she remembered that he had loved her and she had loved him and how wrong it had all gone. She tried to dredge up hatred or even dislike, but she couldn't manage it, even though he had cost her her happiness.

'Susan.' He said her name so sweetly that Susan was taken aback. She had no idea what to say, and then she remembered how important he was, who he was, and she was struck dumb.

He came to her and took hold of her hand. 'You look wonderful.'

Susan knew that she looked everything but. She was tired and thin and unhappy. She thought she had plumbed the depths of her unhappiness, until she saw this man and knew that he would have taken her away to a life of riches. They would have been married and perhaps even had a child by now. She wanted to weep for the injustice of it all.

She did look wonderful to him; she could see by the way that he looked at her.

'What are you doing here, of all places?' she said.

'Just business,' he said.

Susan couldn't imagine what kind of business would bring him back here. Perhaps he wanted to come back to see the people he had lived among, and the Methodist minister and his wife who had been so kind to him. It was obvious to Susan that he had not come to see her. He would have said something, written to her, let her know. He must by now know that she was married.

Charles wanted badly to ask her about her marriage and her life and to tell her how much he still loved her. He thought he had conquered the way that he felt about her, but now every feeling he had ever had for her came tumbling back to him like water over a fall.

It would not be quenched, and he had been mad to think he could marry Cate. It had been out of a sense of duty and nothing more. He would have given anything in the world to marry Susan. Without her, his life was a failure, and he began to wish he had not come here on such an ill-starred hope.

It wasn't what he wanted, even a little bit. Cate had been right all along. They couldn't be married. This little dales woman held his heart, and she looked so unhappy, so pale and wan, and she had already lost her looks so he couldn't think why he felt so much for her, but it wasn't something that could be bettered or moved. Was her marriage not good? Even if it were, there was nothing he could do about it. She had made her choice, but he had the feeling she had chosen from the wrong place and married the wrong man and was regretting it hugely.

He couldn't help holding on to her hand. Even if the skies fell, he didn't want to let go, but he was aware that he must. Respectability must take him from her. This little dales town, which he had known and loved so well, was a very small place, and if he went on holding the hand of a local married woman it would be no more than five minutes before the whole place knew.

No one had missed the carriage, the horses and the servants, and though people had stared it was clear that they did not remember him. But of course they would not remember him like this. They had known him as a minister – *almost* a minister, he reminded himself. How different he had been; how far away it all seemed now.

Susan didn't know what to call him, so merely said his name, and her heart did horrible things to her.

'Charles, how very fine you look.' She managed a smile and she felt young again and so much in love with this man. No wonder she had learned to care for him. He was everything that Dan was not: educated, elegant and well bred, and his voice was so sweet.

She had to get away from him. Whatever he was doing here could not possibly have anything to do with her, though stupidly she wanted it to. She wanted him to tell her that he could not live without her, and he had come back here asking her to marry him, but of course it was no use. She was married. She tried to think coldly and that was when she drew back her hand and with a shaking voice she said goodbye to him.

There was no laughter any more between them, and she could not bear to be so close to him. She turned and then she fled. Men were hateful and horrible and she would never forgive either of them for what they had done to her.

She was going to go to her grave unloved. How many women who had been chosen by two men had such a fate? Perhaps more than anyone knew. She could have been a nun, she thought wildly; considering her Methodism it was laughable. And besides, she knew that nuns were married to God. That didn't seem a particularly good idea either.

She thought back to Dan. He had changed so very little that she resented it. He had had two marriages and borne a child, and yet he looked just as he had when they were going to get married. How could he do that? It was so unjust, when she looked into her mirror and saw lines and sadness.

She had tried not to want Dan when she saw him again when he came back to Stanhope, but it was impossible. He had been her first love, and even his horrible betrayal was not enough, so that she did not think about him. She called herself names, she told herself that she would never speak to him again, even think about him again, but it was no use. She was just glad that she had work to go to and a place to stay.

She could do what she wanted. The trouble was that she did not want to do anything. Once again, Dan had ruined her peace and now Charles had made things worse. Why could Charles not have stayed in Westmorland? Why could Dan not have stayed in Durham? Why did fate arrange it so that he could come back here and pick up his job and his life and she was left fending for herself? And then she remembered Alice Lee and she felt guilty.

She had wanted to go back so many times. She knew that Miss Lee was ill, and worried that she might die before she could tell her how sorry she was. But somehow she couldn't go back there. She didn't understand this, just that she was far too hurt to be glad when other people were happy, and it was awful, she knew it was.

Alice had been so kind to her and Alice had had nobody to help. They had so much in common, but then Alice had found a man to love her and Susan couldn't bear it. She had tried twice and had failed. Alice had tried once and succeeded. Susan could not have stayed at the sweet shop where Zeb and Alice were so obviously in love. She could not have slept there, in the other bedroom, still by herself still without a man, still without the opportunity to have a child. And now Alice was ill.

Susan lay awake at night, worrying about Alice dying, but during the day she filled her time with her work and cleaning her rooms, and she could not make herself go to the sweet shop and be kind. She cried and cried but she couldn't do it. She kept telling herself that she had nothing to worry about, Alice would get better, but the shop did not reopen and every time Susan came past it she felt scorched and hurried away.

Thirty-Six

Nell watched Pat McFadden stride away from the hall. The tiny boy in her arms began to howl. She had never heard anything like it. Worse than that, he struggled in her arms and cried, no doubt for the only mother he had known. Nell had trouble getting him inside the hall and shutting the door. When she had to let him down because he struggled so much, he ran from her, colliding with Augusta as she reached the bottom of the stairs.

Nell did not know who was the more surprised. The child gazed up at Augusta and then ran from her, screaming as he did so, as Augusta stared after him. Nell tried to explain who he was, but Augusta understood nothing like that and merely turned and walked back up the stairs.

The dogs were in the hall and they too stood and watched as the small person whizzed past them. Nell ran after the boy, reaching him before he got to the kitchen. Her thoughts were all of fire and of him falling and of all the awful ways he could damage himself in this place. She grasped him into her arms again only to find he kicked her so ferociously that she could not hold him.

In the end, she took him into the library where the fire was not lit and there was nothing to hurt him. She let him scream and sob and run round and round as though demented, until she heard the sound of the door opening and Sawrey came into the room, gazing wide-eyed at the small child who was destroying the peace.

'Should he do that?' he asked.

'He's frightened.'

'Wouldn't he be better with the woman who was bringing him up?'

'He won't go on like this forever,' Nell said.

The trouble was that he did. He would eat nothing, and when she tried to get water to his lips he dashed it away. The only time they had any peace was when he had exhausted himself and lay down and slept where he had fallen.

She began to doubt the wisdom of what she had done. She knew she had all the right reasons for doing this, but she questioned the effect it might have on him, and also the household itself. She decided that she should find a nursemaid, but when she told Sawrey he only asked her whether that didn't defeat the purpose, and Nell had to admit that running away from the child when she had insisted on having him there would not do.

The child stopped sleeping, so that Nell got no sleep either. Augusta took to staying upstairs, and Nell began to think that she had damaged the hard-won peace for these two people. She wanted to call in Dr McKenna, but he would no doubt think her foolish for what she had done, even though he wouldn't say so.

She didn't think there was any solution to the problem; she just had to get on with it. She remembered how troublesome Arabella had been when she was small. But it had been different – she had been young and Harold had been there during the nights and at weekends, so the whole situation was different. Here she had the boy entirely to herself, and she knew that she could not ask Sawrey to do anything.

He was absenting himself from the house because of the racket from the child, and no doubt remembering what his own childhood had been like. She had the impression, though he said nothing, that he thought she had done the wrong thing. He did not want to be involved, and why would he?

The child reminded her of a bird caught behind glass. He ran from wall to wall, trying to get away, and she had to stop him. He had taken to biting and kicking her, and even spitting, and Nell knew that she had broken the whole purpose of being in this place. And then she knew that she had been planning this all along and had always planned this. He was the whole point now; he was the heir to the quarry and Arabella's child and she would just have to put up with his behaviour.

To make things easier for them, Nell had promised that she would talk to Dr McKenna about Augusta and see if he could recommend a doctor who might be able to help her. She mentioned this to Sawrey, but not to Augusta, and was glad, because it was the one thing he really wanted – the most important thing that might come out of his marriage to her. She asked him if he would go with her to see the doctor, but he said that Gussie shouldn't know at this point and he did not want to get their hopes up, so she was to go alone.

After they had decided this, he said to her, 'We should get a nursemaid for the boy. I know it sounds stupid when you got him here to be with him, but he is so very unhappy.'

Nell badly wanted to say that Shirley ought to have the child back, but she couldn't give in at this point, and in any case, Shirley might refuse to have him. Also, Nell wasn't sure that to be in different places so quickly would be good for him. She felt defeated. She had tried to do what was right for her grandchild and had apparently failed. Nell wrote to a friend in Hexham who had several children and who had a good nanny, and when the friend wrote back she had a recommendation, so Nell wrote eagerly to the girl and asked her to come as soon as possible.

She went to see Dr McKenna on her own about Augusta, and he listened carefully and then he sat back in his chair and said, 'You must know that it will cost a great deal of money, and since Augusta is thirty or more, she has been neglected for a very long time, so I doubt it would help.'

'She is better than she was, at least until I ill-advisedly took my grandchild to stay with us.'

'Small children are very difficult.'

She told him that she had hired a nanny and that the young woman was to turn up very shortly, and he said he thought that was a wise decision. In the meanwhile, he knew of a fine doctor who ran a mental hospital in Newcastle upon Tyne, and would ask if this man would come to see Miss March. But if anything could be done, it would take a long time.

Nell felt much relieved. This was what money was for – not pretty gardens and fine houses, but to help people.

She went back and told Sawrey.

'They won't come and take her away into some awful place?' he asked.

'Certainly not. She goes nowhere.'

He smiled at her with more warmth than ever before, and she basked in the glow of it.

Thirty-Seven

Cate went to see Jos Calland. His office was in a lovely old building, with high ceilings and stained glass in the top windows.

She didn't know the man very well, and she was taking a huge risk not only with her own future but with the futures of Mary and the boy. However, this was the only thing she could think of, and she had turned the idea over and over in her mind for days and now she could wait no longer.

If she delayed too long, they would be caught, and so she had to take Jos Calland into her confidence.

She hadn't been inspired by men so far, but they had power, money, land and influence, and she needed all those things. She had to get this man on her side and have him respect her, so that he would trust her in turn to pay him for what she wanted.

She didn't care whether he liked her. She looked straight across the desk at him and hoped she looked capable of paying a man like him for aid. It was, after all, what he did, though she suspected he was not used to doing such things for women. After all, women had no power and no money.

She spoke decisively and looked hard at him and hoped that he was decent.

'I need to trust you,' she said as she sat down across the desk from him. 'And I need your help.'

If he was surprised, he hid it very well, but then that was part of his trade. She had no idea what he was thinking, and that was scary. She did not allow herself to smile at him. How many thousands of women were smiling now at how many thousands of men, hoping it would get them somewhere. He must take her seriously.

'I gave my name as Catherine Boldon. I am Lady Catherine Boldon and I need your help.'

'Everything you say to me is confidential.'

'Luckily I have no husband for you to betray me to.'

'That's nothing to do with luck. It's a simple transaction. I work for you and you pay me. As long as you can pay me, there is no problem.'

'I will be able to pay you but not immediately. A certain amount of subterfuge will be involved, and I think I should tell you everything so that you know the truth of who I am and what happened, and how I intend to get away from here. I come from a powerful family but I am in bad straits here.'

He nodded and sat back and waited, so she told him all about Henry and Charles, of how she had to leave, and of Mary and how she now needed somebody they could trust to help them.

'I am going to back to Westmorland, where my father and mother have an estate which is worth a great deal of money. I am the only heir. I need to get money and I need you to borrow it for me. If you do this, then I will pay you back with interest. I need to get Mary Blaimire and my child away from here as soon as possible. I cannot do this without help. If you betray me, everything will be lost.'

'I will help you, I swear to it. I will talk to the bank manager, though not including the details, and I will give the money to Miss Blaimire.'

'We will also need a cottage where she can stay for a little while. I wondered if you could look for somewhere out of the way. It shouldn't be too difficult around here. I could do it myself, but it would look strange, and it must be far enough away so that people won't know her. Nobody knows about us at all but through the Peters family, but if it could be Westgate or Rookhope I would be most grateful and would pay you handsomely.'

He agreed, and there was only a very small part of Catherine that worried, and that was because of what other men had done to her. There was no way back from here.

She spent all night worrying, and most of the following few nights, in case Jos Calland was like every other man and would leave her stranded or worse.

Susan was surprised to see the woman from the garden come in to see Mr Calland. The previous day, she had heard a man's voice from beyond the road as she walked, and it was one she recognized. Trees and a wall surrounded the Peters' house in Stanhope and she couldn't see anything, but she knew Dan's voice so well. There were two other voices, both women.

She had heard that two women had moved in with the Peters family, and when she saw the side gate half open, she peered into the garden.

They were turned away from her, so could not see them clearly. Dan had a child in his arms, a very small child, and Susan's heart did horrible things to her. He had served her badly in so many ways, this was just another.

Now she could see the two women: one small and dark and dumpy, the other tall and blonde and slender and rather pretty. They obviously knew one another very well and were laughing and talking as people did when they were intimate, and she thought about Arabella and the child he had left and could not believe that he had another woman, even while she was thinking of how bad she had been to him when he married her.

That night she had lain in her bed and wished she had behaved differently. She longed to have him back. She loved him still and he had betrayed her yet again. He would never be any good. He had found another woman and she was tall and slender with lovely golden hair and Susan could hear her educated voice. She was like Arabella in so many ways.

He had gone to Durham and found somebody new. It was just what he did. Presumably he would always do it, and why not? He was young and fine-looking and now he had a good job again, so he was a prospective husband for any woman – except that he was still married to Susan. Her face felt wooden for having not cried and she thought of how awful she had felt, of how much she had hated herself for letting him go when she could have had some decent kind of life with him. He would never wait for any woman, never be true to anyone.

Now, from Susan's place in the office, seeing her close up for the first time, she knew that this woman had been beautiful not very long ago. Her voice was sweet and eloquent and reminded Susan so much of Arabella, and she was already inclined to dislike her, but then the woman said that she would make an appointment and gave Susan her name.

'Catherine Boldon.'

Susan was astonished. She didn't show it, of course. Mr Calland had impressed upon her that everything that happened within the walls of the solicitor's office was strictly confidential. When he took her on, he assured her that if he ever found she had spoken in the village about what went on here, she would be dismissed. Susan was inclined to be offended, but she understood. He was almost like a doctor. People had to be able to tell him what was wrong. Mr Calland had also implied that if she did well he would help her to study the law, and that meant a great deal to her.

'Me?'

'Why not?'

Susan had never felt clever in her life, but this man was looking steadily at her.'

'I need help. Few professional lawyers would come here, and you seem very bright to me.'

She stared. She didn't understand how he could tell, but she was prepared to do whatever was necessary so that she could be a part of this very interesting business. She didn't know how she had understood such a thing, only that she did.

She would be his confidante. He might go back and talk to his wife about his business affairs, but other than that she was the only person who would know whatever went on there. He had his own office, of course, but her big office was just outside and she had sharp ears. It was a question of trust such as never before. She was proud to be invited and so determined to work hard, but it was difficult when Catherine Boldon's appointment, the day after she had asked for it, came up.

Susan had made the appointment for her, asking smoothly whether there was a time she preferred, because Mr Calland had a ten o'clock appointment and later he would be out to lunch, but she could come at eleven if she chose. She said she would, and so now she arrived and Susan ushered her through. The baby was nowhere to be seen, and although she was still skinny and pale and badly dressed, Susan recognized a lady when she saw one.

As she listened in on Catherine and Mr Calland's conversation, she learned that this woman had borne the illegitimate child of Charles's brother. Susan was astounded and horrified. This woman had cost her the future that Charles Westbrooke might have given her, because she and that stupid brother of his had been so disgusting as to conceive a child before they were married. It had cost them all so very dearly.

Susan was not inclined to forgive her. And now she was going to send her child and her maid – at least, Susan thought it was her maid – out of the country with Mr Calland's help.

Susan had not considered that he might do such a thing. Perhaps he didn't usually, perhaps it was the first time he had encountered such a problem, but he sounded almost happy to deal with it and why wouldn't he? How exciting to be involved in something unlike the dreary legal problems that people put before him every day.

Susan was so intent on listening that it wasn't until Lady Catherine had gone that she realized the child was nothing to do with Dan. Was that a relief? She wasn't sure it was. Even without a child to care for, Dan had got mixed up with other women. Perhaps he always would. He would go on tearing people's lives apart.

Susan got on with her work, but that night when Mr Calland had gone back to his house and she was sitting by her fire, the thought occurred to her that she could write to Charles Westbrooke and tell him that the child was a boy and was about to be smuggled out of England in case he should try to snatch it. And then she realized that it would avail her nothing. No matter what she did now, she was married to Daniel. The child did not belong to Charles; he belonged to the woman who had given birth to him, and Susan didn't think anybody had the right to try to stop her aim. None of them owed the Westbrooke family anything.

Thirty-Eight

Having seen Harry again, Dan began to miss his own child as he had never thought to. Cate and Mary told him that they were leaving, and he was as upset about that as he had been about anything in a long time. He had thought they would come here and live and that they would find some sort of work and that he would see them.

He even felt better about Durham and his father, they had given him a sense of well being such as he had not felt since Arabella had died. He was healing and Cate and Mary had helped him so much, with their kindness and the little boy and the home that they had shared for such a short time together.

He waited until Saturday afternoon, and then he walked up to Holywell Hall. He was surprised at how the place looked. He had known it just as a tall stark building, which had been there for hundreds of years. Back then, border reivers would come down from the high hills to steal, and this was how the people held them off.

The place had a good air to it now. The grounds were not neat, that would have been silly when it was high and almost wild up here, but he could see smoke from the chimneys and the building looked strong. It had a new oak door at the front and the glass in the windows had been replaced so that the afternoon sun glinted off them.

He banged on the door, worried as to the reception that Mrs Almond would give him. He kept forgetting to think of her by her new name. Would she turn him away? She had given him his job back, but that was only because she had no alternative. He was the best in the dale and they both knew it.

He was surprised when the door opened and there she was, with a small, crying child in her arms. She looked so much older that he felt sorry straight away. Though he had felt something like that when her husband died, he had been so upset about Arabella that he had not shown the sympathy that he knew he ought.

Worst of all, even though the boy was a squirming figure with a tear-bloated face, he could see that he was his.

Mrs March was skinny and she looked exhausted, but all she said was, 'Daniel,' and pushed back the door and led him inside.

There was the smell of new wood, and because it was a summer's afternoon, shafts of sunlight poured into the hall from the doors of the rooms that were open.

'I hope you don't mind me coming,' he said, and she had to let the boy down because he was howling and kicking her. He ran from room to room and then finally threw himself onto the floor and sobbed.

Daniel could not take his eyes off the child. He had beautiful black hair and cream skin.

'He's just like her.'

Mrs March nodded but her mouth was set in a grim line. 'I think I made a mistake in taking him away from Shirley. I feel so awful about it now, but I wanted him to grow up with people who belong to him.' She threw him an apologetic glance. 'I thought I was the only one.'

Dan didn't know what to say, but she carried on in what he thought was a defeated voice. 'I have a nanny coming to look after him. She is due in a day or two. I'm too old to cope with a child who is so actively distressed. You may think I should have left him where he was—'

'Who am I to have any opinion, after what I did? ' Dan was glad to say it. He had been rehearsing the words, and then these new ones came forth, encouraged by how blunt she was and the kindness in her face, which he thought was new to her. She had lost so much and was now struggling with a new life.

'I'm sorry,' Dan said, looking into her face. 'I'm very sorry.'

'You loved Arabella. You lost your mind when she died.'

'I blamed the little boy. Wasn't that stupid?'

'You loved her so very much. I lost my child and my husband and then I sent you away and was left with nothing.'

'You thought it was the right thing to do.'

'I didn't know what loneliness was like, and then I didn't even see you after you came back here. You are staying?'

'I thought that perhaps you might let me see him from time to time.'

The little boy had cried himself to sleep. She went off and made tea and came back with everything on a tray. She proudly told him she had made the cake herself, though added that it was when the boy had slept.

As Daniel ate his cake, the little boy awoke and Dan spoke softly to him and he felt such a pull on his heart that even Harry didn't give him. The child stared and then he got up and went to Dan. Dan gave him cake and poured a lot of milk into the tea and gave him that too and the child moved very close to him. It was one of the most magical moments of Dan's life. He wanted to cry and he wished that his parents could have been here and that Arabella and her father could have seen this.

The little boy ate two pieces of cake and drank two huge cups of tea and then he scrambled up against Dan, and that was when Dan knew that he thought he was Pat. They were both quarrymen and no doubt smelled of stone and dust and whatever it was that set quarrymen apart from other men, and he felt for Shirley and Pat and knew that they must see the child too. He wouldn't suggest it yet to Mrs March. For now, he took the child into his arms and sat back in his chair and enjoyed his son's embrace.

'He is very advanced for his age,' the boy's grandmother said proudly. 'He walked before he was a year old, and now he's so mobile he cannot be contained, as you can see.'

It seemed such a long time since Arabella had died and yet the child could not be more than eighteen months old. It felt like a decade since he had been happy with her, looking forward to their wonderful future together, and then it was all gone. He didn't think he would know such happiness again.

Thirty-Nine

The specialist was called Dr William Charlton, and he was from Newcastle. To Nell, he looked like a doctor should. He wore small, round spectacles, had a long white beard and gave the appearance of having just come from the tailor. He was also very friendly and smiled a lot. He sat down at the table in the kitchen in a very informal way, but Augusta, rather like a cat, Nell thought, knew when something horrible was going to happen and would not come downstairs.

Dr Charlton sat and drank tea and asked how Miss March was and how long she had felt unwell. Sawrey answered his questions nervously. Nell longed to be reassuring, but she knew that one of the main reasons Sawrey had married her was because he might be able to get much-needed help for his sister. Nell doubted anything could be done – she had no great belief in doctors for the mind – but she was willing to give it a try.

Augusta was better in some ways than she had ever been. Sometimes she came downstairs for meals, but mostly she would take food in her hands and scurry back up. She rarely spoke. Nell had made her room as comfortable as she could. If Augusta was going to spend time there, then she should spend it well.

Nell had fixed a lovely sofa in front of the window, and from here Augusta could lie and watch the birds and animals. Nell had put a table outside and regularly scattered it with crumbs, nuts and seeds, and Augusta would occasionally call out delightedly when the resident grey squirrel stole from it.

There were books in the room. Nell had chosen these from a bookseller and had them sent from Hexham. They were easy tales. She knew that Augusta could write and read, so she also bought pencils and books that Augusta could colour in, and easy reading books with lots of pictures. She had put up illustrations of birds and animals, which Augusta had agreed to with joy. It was, but not quite, a child's room. Nell would have loved to take Augusta to Hexham or Newcastle to buy some lovely clothes and have her hair done, but Augusta couldn't bear to be touched, so Nell bought clothes from catalogues and hung them up in the big wardrobe. She also bought a silver-backed mirror, comb and brush. Augusta hated mirrors, so it was the only one in the room and could be turned on its face and left there. It was so pretty, and the sunlight glinted off its back.

Augusta came to let Nell do her hair. She even let her cut it, and it began to grow thick and became shiny. In the evenings Nell would brush it until it was sleek and then put it into plaits, and Augusta had come to like the feel of Nell's hands. Nell told her stories which she had told to Arabella, and it was only then that she felt she had got part of her own child back. Augusta was still a child in so many ways, a badly treated child who needed her care.

Nobody was allowed into the room unless Augusta said so. Sawrey still slept with her sometimes. More maids were now employed at the Hall and one of them would slip in whenever Augusta ventured downstairs and clean and see to the fire and change the bed. There was always a fire unless it was very warm, and even then, if Augusta asked, one could be built. Nell fancied she had made Augusta feel safe possibly for the first time in her life.

She still had nightmares, and Nell knew that was why Sawrey was so often there for her. She cried out in terror when the nightmares plagued her.

The doctor talked to Nell and Sawrey about Augusta for a long time, and then requested that he might speak with her, but even though Sawrey and then Nell went upstairs to beg her, she would not come. Augusta had taken to her bed and had turned her face away. Nell began to wish they had not asked the doctor to come such a long way.

In the end, Nell got the doctor to cuddle one of the kittens. Augusta adored the kittens and they ended up in her room, but also they liked to escape. Since the weather was good at the moment, they were often outside playing, and searching for mice as their mother showed them.

This particular kitten was Augusta's favourite. It was creamy and long-haired and had gleaming brown eyes. It purred happily in the doctor's arms. Luckily the door of Augusta's room was still open, a sign that she had not decided completely that she would see no one.

Nell ventured through the door and said that Mr Charlton was a kitten lover, and would be interested to hear about this one in particular because it had no name, and he thought Augusta might give the kitten a title.

At first nothing happened. They stood in the gloom of the narrow hall and waited, and then little by little the shape in the bed moved, and after another two minutes Augusta sat up and peered suspiciously at the doctor. She seemed to see nothing but the kitten.

'It already has a name, silly. It's Kitten.'

Well, that was new, Nell thought.

'Only one name?' the doctor said, moving a little closer. 'Cats very often have several names, such as Little Miss Tabbytoes, or Lucky Randolph the Black and White, or Doggie the Ginger Moggie.'

Augusta stared at him. 'Who are you?'

'I'm a doctor of kittens and such, and this one wanted to see you.'

'That's my kitten,' she said.

'May I bring it to you?'

She nodded. The kitten, playing its part, was happy to see its idol. It licked her face, and that always made her smile.

'There is no such thing as a kitten doctor,' she said.

'There are animal doctors. I look after animals when they are ill.'

The kitten isn't ill. She's very small but perfectly well.'

'I can see that she is,' he said. 'May I sit down?'

She thought about it for a few moments, looking at him with suspicion, in case he had really come to steal the kitten, and then nodded and indicated the armchair that stood by the bed. If Nell came into the room or Sawrey sat with her, here was where they sat.

'It's a very pretty room.'

'Nell did it for me,' Augusta said, moving her chin in Nell's direction. 'She's very kind.' She leaned nearer, and confided, 'Nell makes us eat properly and the house is always warm.'

'What a view.'

'I like the day.'

'You don't like the darkness?'

She shook her head. 'I get frightened. Sawrey has to stay with me. If he isn't there, I can't sleep, and when I do sleep I see horrible things.'

'What kind of things?'

And she told him. Nell, hovering just beyond the room, heard Augusta haltingly tell him about her childhood, not intending to, Nell thought, but out it came. The kitten went back and sat on his lap. Nell thought she could almost hear it purring.

Mrs March encouraged Daniel to come to the house, but it was a long walk when he had already done a week's work and she knew that he often did paperwork at the weekends because Mr Paterson's eyesight was going. She knew that Dan wanted the old man to stay on, and not just because Mr Paterson knew everything that went on and had been Mr Almond's right-hand man, but just because he was part of the place.

Nell did offer to pension him off and Daniel stared at her.

'What, pay him for not being there?'

Saturday had become Nell's favourite day because Dan always came now and saw the boy. Remarkably, she thought, he adored Dan.

'He was there when we opened. If it hadn't been for him, we would never have got the quarry up and running.'

'Yes, but he lives on his own. What would he do at home all day?'

'Then we should get somebody in to help.'

'I help him, and Zeb does and so does Pat.'

Nell couldn't look at him when he mentioned Pat McFadden; she was feeling worse and worse about it every day. Pat was still getting the same higher wage that Dan had insisted upon, and nobody questioned it.

That autumn, Dan asked if he might take the boy into the village and have him for most of the Sunday, and Nell was so relieved that she would have a free day that she agreed. She sent the groom (the only one she still kept) with the pony cart to bring Dan there and take them back to the village and then go back for the little boy at teatime.

It was only an experiment when they did it for the first time, but the release when they had left was so good that Nell could have danced. She told herself that she should take the opportunity to go to church, as she had done before the boy was there, but she didn't.

She made a huge beef dinner and after it fell asleep by the fire while listening to the cold wind howling around the hall. Sawrey was there with her all day, and Augusta too, and it made Nell feel even more guilty. She couldn't think now why she had thought she could manage all these things. How stupid she had been. She had made everyone – herself, Sawrey, Augusta, Shirley, Pat and the little boy – unhappy, but she could not make herself go to Shirley and ask her to take the child back. Besides, she thought that Shirley was a good deal too proud to do such a thing anyway.

She was beginning to wish that Daniel would say he would like to have his child full time, as of course he was entitled to, but he didn't live with his wife. Alice Lee was ill and he would not want to leave the little boy with a stranger, thinking he was better off with his grandmother.

If only she had known, Nell thought, that the boy had been better off with Shirley. Having tried to do the right thing, she now felt selfish, but after Arabella and Harold had died she'd felt she had no one. Although she was learning to love Sawrey and Augusta, it was not the same. She had adored her husband and her only child, and she could not get used to the idea that they were gone for good. She had hoped that the child would help, but he was making things worse.

She tried to distract herself by going to see the solicitor, Mr Calland, and asking him whether he would help her find a buyer for Ash House.

'It's worth a great deal of money,' he said.

'That is the point. I want to put the money away for my grandchild, Frederick. Also, we have a special doctor who comes from Newcastle to see Augusta, and it costs money, so the income that I have from my investments must be eroding.'

'You are still making money from the quarry and your husband left you very prettily situated, so you have nothing to worry about. I think a wise move would be to keep the house or at least rent it out. Property makes more money than anything else, and I will always keep an eye on things.'

'I want to make a lot more changes up at the hall.'

'Do so. You look as if you are enjoying yourself.'

Nell thanked him and let herself out and planned what more she would do. It took her mind from her worries.

Dan had been concerned about taking the child from the hall. The boy had not been long away from Shirley. How would he take to another change? There was no point in saying to him that it was just for a few hours, because he was too young to understand.

Frederick seemed excited about the horse and trap and was content to sit on Dan's lap, being told all about the cows in the field and the hens further over beside a big cree. They were big brown hens, Dan told him.

When they got down and he thanked the groom, Dan found that he knew him, as his brothers worked at the quarry.

Mrs Garnet had made them a big Sunday dinner, and within half an hour of Dan getting there with Frederick it was dished out, and then she went home.

Frederick sat with Dan and ate a surprising amount of food for such a little boy. Dan had no experience of small children, other than Cate's child, and he was younger than Frederick and hadn't been eating proper food for long. It seemed to Dan that Frederick ate everything they would put in front of him.

He still couldn't believe that this child was his, and that after all the mistakes he had made he might have a chance to be some happy part of his son's life. Every time he saw Frederick he could see Arabella, and it made him sad, but as he watched his child at the table he was reminded of the boy he had been. He wished very much that his parents had been there to see the miracle that was a child that had your blood. He felt cheered. There would always be a part of Arabella here on earth, as long as her child lived, and maybe Frederick would grow up to have a child and it might look like Arabella, and even a bit like Daniel. He thought he understood for the first time why people wanted children. This little boy now meant the whole world to him; he was the only person he would die to save, and he hoped he would live long enough to watch Frederick grow up. He hoped that they would never be parted again.

Forty

There was a poet in the village called Cuthbert Ironside. Any other man in the place with such a long name would have been known as Bert, Mr Bailey could not help thinking, but Cuthbert was always known by his full title and was a respected man. He was about fifty years old. His parents were still alive, and he had lived with them since coming back to the dale several years ago from Scotland, so it didn't look to Mr Bailey as though he had anything other to do than write poetry.

His father had been a businessman and had retired to Wolsingham, the first and prettiest town in the dale, so there was sufficient money, no doubt, that he did not need to work and could afford to indulge himself.

Cuthbert Ironside began spending a lot of time at the Vernon household over the autumn and when the weather gave way to ice and dark nights. Mr Bailey disliked the man from the beginning. He knew that he was unfair – why should he take such an active dislike to anyone? – but the trouble was that he felt his position was being usurped by this intruder. Although nobody said anything, he felt as though he was a hen who had moved down the pecking order.

Mr Bailey couldn't understand it. He was much younger than they were, and he could have had other friends, but of course the Vernons were the people who looked after things of culture in the area, so why would he not?

Mr Bailey would have liked to have somebody to complain to about Cuthbert, but he knew that Alice was ill and that Zeb was working hard, and he could not go there for any sympathy. When he did visit, he felt that he was in the way. He did not want Zeb to think he did not care, but it was difficult and he felt out of sorts and generally rather unwanted.

There were a lot of folk in Stanhope who thought of themselves as poets. Privately, in the evenings at the Vernon house when it was just Cuthbert, the Vernons and Mr Bailey, Cuthbert would say that at best these people were rhymers. They thought that because they could get two lines running to rhyme, it meant they were good at such things. He would shudder, but he knew also that the Vernons liked to encourage everyone to their poetry afternoons, so he was not too down on anyone. It would not have been fair since he was so clearly the dale's poet.

On Saturday mornings they hosted storytelling for children and in the afternoons book discussions for adults, but on Sundays people would come to the poetry afternoons. After they had been to church or chapel, had their Sunday dinner and found themselves at a loss, perhaps not wanting to go for a walk because they were weary from their week's work or the weather was inclement, they would come to the Vernon house. The cold dark nights had long since set in, and they would huddle around the fire in the sitting room.

There was always tea and coffee, and biscuits and cake that the two sisters would serve at the end of the readings. They would have talks and discussions, and a lot of people were eager to go. They had culture, cake and gossip all in one.

As time went on, people were encouraged to bring their own contributions. These varied. Cuthbert, Mr Bailey could tell, thought the whole thing tiresome, though he was polite. Miss Emily had asked him to shoulder the burden and he did so. He would sit with a slightly disengaged air as everybody was quiet, before the air was rent with yet another effort of rhyming, snowing, blowing and flowing, mostly about the river and the weather, though occasionally a wit would attempt a funny poem. Sheep and hills also figured hugely, and remote farmhouses with falling-off doors and broken windows.

Miss Emily would sigh with happiness. She was shy and didn't say much, so Mr Bailey would applaud their efforts and tell them well done at the end, no matter how uninspiring the rhyme had been.

Mr Bailey spoke to everyone. Cuthbert Ironside did not. Rather, he held forth from his chair and expected people to go to him. They were not often the kind of people who were forward, and sometimes it was all they could do to be there. Only the brave ones would get up and recite, and they needed to hear praise. Everybody did, thought Mr Bailey.

Mr Vernon talked a lot about publishing Cuthbert's first book of verse, if he would complete his poems over the winter. It would be called *Night Falls on the Elephant Trees*, the famous trees that stood on the horizon above the town. They had talked about how it would be distributed, and the two ladies were all for having a special occasion that day.

The book was to be dedicated to them and would have their names in the front. Mr Bailey found himself thinking uncharitable thoughts about Mr Ironside. He tried to be more generous, but the trouble was that Cuthbert had only one subject when he spoke, or rather two if you were feeling generous – himself and his poetry.

He was always being asked to supper, and Mr Bailey tried to think of ways to absent himself without appearing rude. He could not go to the sweet shop, and he had no other place to go, so he could not get out of these evenings, but it was by now no fun at all living with the Vernons. He could not even go to his bedroom since the fires upstairs were only lit an hour before anyone ventured there, fuel being expensive and the coals having to be carried by the young man who looked after the garden and the horse. Mr Bailey was therefore caught in the boredom. He dared not take up a book for fear he should be thought rude and unsociable. It also seemed to him that, though Miss Emily was a dozen years older than Mr Ironside, they liked one another. He found this particularly trying. He had spent a great many hours trying to make Emily like him, and she did, but he had long since realized that she would never marry him. He was just a friend. Even he could tell the difference.

Cuthbert was so warm towards her, smiling at her when he was reading yet another of his seemingly endless poems. He would make sure she sat next to him, and he was always flattering to her. Miss Emily had begun to write her own poetry.

Mr Bailey hoped that it would be good, but in vain. Vain was the word, he thought, for would-be poets. Even though he knew that Miss Emily had read Keats and Byron, she did not appear to see the difference between her work and theirs.

Perhaps this should have made her less interesting, but though he felt a little pity, he found that he liked her all the better for trying to do something that took more skill than one person out of a million could have achieved.

Cuthbert told her how good her poems were, heaping praise upon her, and perhaps her brother and sister were also impressed, or they loved her too much to disillusion her. And why should they? If she could shine, no matter how little, in such a shy person surely it was good.

As Cuthbert talked of his first publication one evening, he went even further and said that perhaps the next set of poems should combine his verse with Miss Emily's. Never had Mr Bailey seen her eyes light as they did when he made this suggestion. To think that her small verses were equal to his, she trilled.

They would have further poetry evenings on Wednesdays from now on, since they had proved so popular, and for the first publication they would invite everyone they knew who was interested. Mr Vernon (and with a little help from Mr Bailey, who had drawn a lovely sketch of the elephant trees for the cover and hoped for an acknowledgement, at least) would give the publication party in the spring, at Easter. What could be more fitting? Mr Bailey, had he been honest, would have said a church service, and he would much have preferred this, but of course he could not.

Mr Bailey shuddered and tried desperately to think of a way to get out of the event. People would be encouraged to listen to Cuthbert reciting several of his poems, and then buy a copy or two as Easter gifts, no doubt to palm off on unsuspecting relatives who were hoping for nothing more sophisticated than a few chocolate eggs from the sweet shop. Then Mr Bailey remembered that the sweet shop was shut.

Miss Vernon said that she would make a buffet – such things were becoming fashionable – where small savouries and pastries would be put over a white cloth on the dining room table and people would move around the room, with a plate in one hand and a cup of tea in the other, conversing with one another about literature. Mr Bailey began to long for the sweet shop.

Forty-One

Alice turned over. She heard Mrs Garnet's reassuring voice downstairs and knew that she didn't have to do anything. Mrs Garnet would take care of it for now, and in a little while, when she wasn't tired any more, she would go downstairs and make the evening meal. What day was it? It must be Sunday. She could smell the joint cooking. It didn't make her hungry, it only made her glad that she could go back to sleep. In a little while she would wake up and go downstairs.

She couldn't think. If she did try to, the sleep reached for her and she gave in, thankful. She began to be aware that she was always going to get up, always going to go downstairs, always going to see Zeb, but somehow she couldn't get there. It was as though getting out of bed was too much effort.

She was vaguely ashamed that Mrs Garnet had to empty the chamber pot, and the woman was forever offering her tea and food which she could not eat. She did sometimes eat the small pieces of toast that Mrs Garnet would feed to her, and Mrs Garnet would sit by the bed and urge her on. She found that difficult – almost impossible, some days.

But that Sunday was different, though she had no idea why.

She had come to hate the smell of food as it made its way up the stairs, and had long since put to one side the idea that eating and cooking and anything else that happened downstairs was to do with her. That surety made it easy for her to sleep. Only now she was disturbed. She felt frustration, even anger. Who was getting in the way of the rest she so badly needed? She ignored the noise and turned over and closed her eyes. Sleep would come to her, it always did. She waited, and then she waited some more, and then she opened her eyes. She turned over. Once she had turned over she would sleep, she knew, she always did.

She turned over and then she turned over again. She didn't want to go back to sleep. She heard Mrs Garnet say goodbye to Zeb as she left, and she still didn't want to go back to sleep. This was amazing and awful. She listened hard.

She heard another voice, a man's voice. It was Daniel, surely. She thought she had heard his voice several times lately and been glad he was there. He would be good company for Zeb. The last thing she could remember was that he had gone off to Durham and left Susan and was not coming back, as far as they knew.

She heard the door, which meant that Mrs Garnet had gone. Usually then there was silence, apart from the two men talking together in low voices. This would send her off into sleep, but today was different.

The curtains were not closed. Sometimes she liked them open and today she had preferred them like this because the sun was coming in at the window not too hot, just there and comforting. She could feel the warmth of it. And then she heard another voice. She listened hard. It didn't happen again straight away, and then it did. It was a child. How could that be? Where had the child come from?

She listened again, and when she heard no more she got out of bed and stood quite still. It was her imagination. She had wanted a child so badly that she thought she could hear one below. That was nonsense, but then she had not dreamed such a thing before and she seemed to be on her feet.

She looked at the door and it was not quite closed, so she could slip out if she wanted to. She put on a robe, went out of the room and began to make her way slowly down the steep stairs, hanging on to the rail because it had never felt so steep before. But then she couldn't remember the last time she had come down the stairs, and she had an idea that she had done it so quickly that she hadn't noticed.

At the bottom of the stairs she stopped and then looked into the room. There she saw Daniel and Zeb sitting at the table, and on Zeb's knee was a small boy. She thought he was the most beautiful child that she had ever seen. He looked straight at her, as children often did, as though they knew you. As she progressed into the room he slid off Zeb's knee and came over and held out his hand, as though trusting her to take hold of his fingers in case he should fall.

In that way they reached the table and then she sat down and he reached up to be on her knee. When she got him up there, Zeb put food onto the plate he passed to her and she fed him from a spoon.

The two men went on talking about the quarry as though she had not come in, but Zeb's voice wobbled, she could hear it, and Dan hesitated. She remembered now that Dan was staying, because before he had stayed, sometimes Zeb would leave her and sleep in the other room. She must have been disturbing him in some way, she thought, but she didn't sleep well without him. She longed to go on to the landing and into the bedroom and beg him to come back, but she couldn't.

Now she felt that everything had changed. When she tired, Dan took the boy from her and she went back upstairs and slept.

The next day, when Zeb got up to go to work, she said, 'When is the little boy coming back?'

'At the weekend. Were you glad to see him?'

'He's so lovely,' she said, and he said, yes, wasn't he. And he kissed her and went off to work.

The following weekend, the little boy was there as Zeb had said. She could hear his voice from upstairs and again she went down and again she took the child onto her knee while the two men went on talking. She was not quite as tired this time, but after an hour or so she gave him to Dan and went upstairs.

The next day, Mrs Garnet came to clean and cook, and in the afternoon Alice managed to go downstairs again. Mrs Garnet seemed very pleased to see her and insisted on making tea. She put before Alice a large chocolate cake, which was very nice but not to her own standard. She told Mrs Garnet it was a wonderful cake, and Mrs Garnet said it must have been because Alice never ate any of her cake usually. Alice managed a tiny bit. It was difficult trying to balance somehow, so it had to be either the cup and saucer or the cake. Her hands shook, and when she had drunk the tea she went back to bed.

The following day, Alice got up in the morning and demanded her clothes. It took a long time to dress, but Mrs Garnet went off and left her to it when she said that she could manage. She had to keep sitting on the bed, but she was determined. When she went downstairs and wandered around, she felt almost as though it was somebody else's house. Then she wondered why the shop was shut. She had somehow forgotten all about it, and stood there, staring. She went through and it became obvious to her that it had not been open in a very long time. The smell of sweets had faded – no chocolate, no coffee, no toffee, no fudge. She was astonished.

There were no customers. She watched people going past through the gap where the blinds did not meet, some of them quickly, and older people or those with small children more slowly, but nobody looked towards the sweet shop. The place was clean – no doubt Mrs Garnet kept it so – but Alice hated how empty it was, how unused. It was not hers. It was nobody's now. Had somebody else started up a sweet shop so that people were going elsewhere?

She slept in the early afternoon. Every time she got up she was dizzy, but she knew that the dizziness would leave her if she persisted. For the first time in a very long while, she was feeling hungry. It was when she ventured to look into the mirror that she saw the scarecrow she had become. She stared in horror at the sunken face, her bony arms with their scraggy dropped flesh. Her whole body was sagging and the tears chased one another down her caved-in cheeks.

Her hair was thin and grey and hung in wisps around her. It had always been long and she had always been proud of its dark thickness and would pleat it at the back of her head. The shine of which she had always been proud was gone. She was wearing some tatty nightwear and would have loved a wash. She was aware of Mrs Garnet getting her out of bed and washing her, and she knew that the woman changed the sheets and always spoke so softly and kindly.

The crying made her feel even weaker, and so she got back into bed, but she didn't sleep. She lay there while the room moved, and she kept closing her eyes, but after a while she just lay there with her eyes open, listening to a bird singing beyond the house and Mrs Garnet's slightly off-key voice warbling Charles Wesley hymns in the kitchen. It made Alice smile.

It was not long before Mrs Garnet appeared in the doorway with soup and a large slice of bread.

'You're awake. How are you feeling now?' She almost always said the same thing, and Alice always told her that she was feeling very well, but today she sat up and smiled and said, 'The soup looks good.'

Mrs Garnet stared down at it in surprise.

'It's just the same thing we always have – potatoes and vegetables with pearl barley and split peas. And there's a nice piece of ham if you fancy a pease pudding and ham sandwich for afters.' She put the tray down on the side, as usually she fed Alice, but today Alice sat up and gestured for the tray. Mrs Garnet gave it to her without a word and went on tidying up the room around her.

Alice found it slightly difficult because she hadn't fed herself in so long. To begin with her hands shook, but as soon as she tasted how good the soup was she forgot about it and fed herself readily.

After the soup was eaten, Alice went back to sleep, but she heard Zeb's voice when he came home and Mrs Garnet's voice too, and then he pounded up the stairs. She did not know until that moment that she would be glad of the heavy way he took the steps, as men did when they were eager to see you.

He came tentatively into the bedroom, in case she still was asleep, though how anybody could have slept through that noise Alice wasn't sure. She felt the smile stretch on her face.

'Alice,' he said and sat down on the bed.

She thought he looked so young and fresh even after a day at the quarry, and he brought a bright presence into the room. She managed to reach up both arms to bring him to her, and after he was close to her, he said, 'Alice, I have missed you so much.'

She could not believe he was hers. She could not believe he was married to this old crone.

Daniel thought about Mrs March, and every time he went to pick up the boy on Sundays he thought she looked worn out. She seemed so relieved to give the child to him, and Dan could tell that the child was different with him than with his grandmother. Eventually she said, 'I wish you could take him more often.'

'Why don't you talk to Shirley about it?'

Nell shook her head and didn't look at him. 'I couldn't, not after the way I treated her.'

'Doesn't he hate being away from her?'

He could see tears standing in the woman's eyes. She nodded. 'I don't know how to cope. Even with help, it doesn't work. I feel so entirely defeated. Shirley was right, he needs her, and I feel every day as if I am damaging him. And Sawrey and Augusta must think I've taken this place from them.'

Dan thought a lot about it, and he didn't know what to do. Pat was very quiet at work. Usually he was strong and funny, and since he was the go-between he was often in and out of the office. It wasn't as if he was being useless; Pat prided himself on his work no matter what he did, and like Zeb had been, he was good with the men. The life had gone from him, though, and Dan knew it was since Mrs March had made him give up the boy.

He asked Pat if he could have a word. This was usually something unpleasant, otherwise it would be said in the office in front of the other two men, so Pat scowled. Pat was doing a lot of scowling. In fact, it had taken over his face, Dan thought, but that was unsurprising too.

They walked just a little way from the office and stood there looking down at the working men. Dan didn't know how to put this, even though he had rehearsed it several times.

Having waited, Pat then said impatiently, 'So, what is it? Have I done something?'

'Of course not.'

'Why 'course not? If it's a job to do, I'll do it.'

'It isn't. It's something else.'

'Well, howay then,' Pat said, with just a touch of the humour the men were used to.

'It's about the boy.'

Pat looked confused. 'What, Freddie?' He spent a moment taking this in. 'That's done, surely. It bloody cost me.'

Dan wasn't with him for a second or two, and then he understood. The little boy had been theirs and then he had not.

'I'm sure it did. I just wondered if you and Shirley might like to come to the sweet shop on Sundays and see him.'

Pat stared. 'You get him on Sundays?'

'Yes.'

'Just on Sundays then?'

'I can't have him the rest of the time, can I? I've got nobody to see to him. You know how things are at the shop.'

'Alice.'

They all called her by her first name. Among the quarrymen, Alice was a much-loved woman. She had taken on Pat face to face, something anybody might admire. And they all knew that the sweet shop was long since closed and that Alice had some horrible thing wrong with her, like when men came back from tropical climates and got sleeping sickness. They were afraid she was going to die, and some of them were thinking that it could be the sort of thing that was contagious. Even if the sweet shop had not been closed, a lot of people might have stopped going.

Not that Dan thought Pat believed any of these things.

He didn't know what was wrong with Alice, but he had the feeling that Pat did. Since Zeb wasn't saying anything and Dan wouldn't have asked, he went around in ignorance, and was slightly glad of it in some ways.

'Alice is getting better,' he said.

Pat looked straight into his eyes for the first time that day – or for the first time in weeks, Dan thought.

'She is?' he said hopefully.

'The boy did it.'

Pat stared. And then he almost smiled.

'Freddie thinks I'm you. I think it's the quarry smell,' Dan said.

Pat laughed, and then he turned away a bit. 'I miss him. We all miss him. My Shirley, she's . . .' Whatever Shirley was feeling, Pat couldn't say the words.

'Alice heard Freddie's voice and she came downstairs, and ever since then she's started getting better. He goes to her. I can't believe it. It's just as if he's a sort of miracle.'

'She was really bad, you know.'

'I don't.'

'Well, she was.'

'Will you talk to Shirley?'

'I'll try. She doesn't have a great deal to say to me any more.'

That was a huge understatement, Pat thought, as he went back to the men. Shirley had kept to her word. She hadn't spoken to or touched him since he had taken the child from her. Pat had been through a lot of very difficult things in his life, but being ignored was a whole new category for him. He hated himself and Shirley hated him too, and it wasn't a good way to live, with all that hatred carried on his back, like a small snail with a big shell.

He thought about nothing else all day, and when he went home all he wanted was to get Shirley to himself, but she blocked that every way she could. They were all suffering, although as far as everybody else was concerned, nothing was wrong. She talked just the same to his parents, she fed everybody, she was good with the two little girls, but he thought they all sensed that things were not right.

His mother was even more bad-tempered than usual, and his father was mostly sleeping. Pat wished he could have climbed into bed with his dad and passed out for a few hours. It wasn't easy lying in bed, night after night, with Shirley turned away from him. In his mind, he replayed how he had pushed her over and taken the screaming child up to Mrs March, and how Shirley had wailed and cried and he had hurried away until he was out of earshot.

In bed, of course, he tried to speak to her, but Shirley ignored him. Having hurt her once he would not lay hands on her again. It was more than physical; he had hurt Shirley in so many ways that there was a chance she would never forgive him.

So there in the darkness, with a wife as stiff as a board next to him, Pat talked softly to the air and told it that he had spoken to Dan, and that Shirley could go and see the boy on Sundays and he would be glad to take her. Or if she felt worried about leaving his parents and the children alone for so long, he would stay with them. He knew that the little boy would be so pleased to see her.

Shirley said nothing. She said nothing that night, she said nothing the next night or the one after that, and eventually Pat, when asked by Dan, said that Shirley wanted no more to do with the child.

Forty-Two

Alice got better. It happened rapidly. One day she could barely stand, and within a week she was staying up all day, though not necessarily getting dressed. Everyone could see how much better she looked. The gloss on her hair was coming back and so was the shine in her eyes.

The following week she was up and dressed by midday, and sleeping less and less, and Zeb had begun coming back from work and smiling. Mrs Garnet was still doing all the work, but there was less for her to do now that Alice was no longer an invalid, and Dr McKenna had smiled and said she was well on the way to recovery.

By the third week, Mrs Garnet had to stop her from doing everything.

'You'll set yourself back,' she said, and Alice could not help reflecting that Mrs Garnet, having looked after her so intimately, was treating her like a daughter; and because she had no daughter, Alice was pleased to let her. Alice did still get tired at night, and slept eight or nine hours. Zeb would be at work when she awoke, and she missed him and wanted him with her. She felt as though she had lost so many days with her husband and it made her feel lonely.

Sometimes she turned over in the night and remembered his mouth and his body and wanted him, but she didn't like to say anything after putting him through this. Her body had put them through hell and she wasn't sure she wanted to do that again, and she was very sure that he didn't want to.

After a month, Mrs Garnet was so tired of Alice trying to take over that she said, 'Why don't we go into the shop and start to clean it properly?'

Alice stared. She had considered opening the shop, but there were no customers and she doubted they would come back.

'Let's go and have a look,' Mrs Garnet said, and when Alice would have protested, Mrs Garnet didn't take any notice.

The shop looked dismal, even though Mrs Garnet had gone in there often. Alice hadn't wanted to go in because she had known how she would feel, and somehow it was even worse. She wished she had come in by herself, because then she could have gone straight back out and thought about changing the downstairs so that they had two rooms. Life would be much more pleasant; they could do with the space.

The trouble was that it was a lovely day and the sun unhelpfully poured in at the big window, and Alice could see dust thick on the high shelves where Mrs Garnet, with what little time she allowed the shop, had not been able to reach. Mrs Garnet went off to get hot water and the stepladder and began scrubbing the shelves as Alice watched. She didn't say anything, and Mrs Garnet had all the shelving cleaned by the end of the day.

When Mrs Garnet went home, Alice found she could not leave the place, and she ended up scrubbing the floor and seeing how much better it was. Zeb came home and she was in the back room by then and said nothing to him about the shop.

She was cross with herself that she had been deluded enough to think the village couldn't manage without her. Nobody really needed sweets; they needed warm fires and good food and wages. Sweets were a luxury and not necessary. She lay awake most of the night, but had fallen asleep by the time Zeb got up for work.

Mrs Garnet came in singing as usual and began on the housework. 'Why don't you try to make something nice like butterscotch?' she said to Alice.

'I should really help you—'

'There's only two of you, and that man of yours is the tidiest person I think I've ever met.'

Alice didn't like to say that he had been in prison for nine years and didn't have any possessions, but Mrs Garnet knew that anyway so it didn't matter.

'Is it difficult to make butterscotch?' Mrs Garnet asked innocently, and Alice replied that it was the easiest thing in the world, and it was only when Alice was taking the butterscotch off the stove that she saw she had been had.

'Mrs Garnet, you are a very wicked woman,' she said.

'Is it ready yet? I haven't had sweets since you took bad, so if it doesn't cool within the hour I shall have to burn my mouth on it.'

When Zeb came back, Alice had the shop door open and

was cleaning the outside of the window. He saw her and laughed and then he came to her and almost kissed her.

He stopped himself in time and then they went inside together. Alice thought that she would make sweets over the next few days and then she would open the shop. If nobody came to buy them she would simply eat the whole lot herself.

They fell easily into a routine, Mrs Garnet looking after the house and Alice making sweets. Together, they tasted them, and Mrs Garnet said that they were all good, but she would need more mouthfuls to make sure.

Alice left the shop door open while she worked, because when she made sweets the whole place felt like an oven. She was in and out of the back and people kept coming to the door, asking when she would be open again. The children hung about in the entrance and she took to giving great trayfuls of sweets to people who went by, so that they stopped and told her how pleased they were that she was better, they had missed her and, even more so, they had missed their favourites. Alice laughed and was happier than she had been in a very long time.

The following week she was well enough to open the shop properly, and for days she had a queue quite a lot of the time. It made her want to cry, how kind people were, how glad they were to see her back there in her shop and how good she felt.

She began to wish that Zeb would come home earlier. She was very proud of how good he was at work, and of the progress the quarry was making. He didn't say a lot, unless she asked, but he was making what she considered to be a lot of money and he didn't keep it.

When she refused to take it from him, he put it into a pot on the mantelpiece and she was left to move it because otherwise Mrs Garnet might notice and think they were bragging, though she also thought that Mrs Garnet wouldn't care.

Zeb had insisted on paying Mrs Garnet more, and Alice was proud too that he was open-handed – many men weren't – and though she told him to take something for himself, he said what on earth would he want it for.

Dan also insisted on paying board, as he called it. Alice told him that she didn't need his money and he should keep it, and when he too said for what she couldn't say anything. She didn't like to say that Susan was still by herself; it was none of her business.

Nobody spent anything except for the odd occasion when they went to the pub for a couple of pints. The two men drank whisky at home in the evenings and that was the extent of their social life. She grew to like the smell of whisky, though she didn't want to try it, even when they urged her. She sometimes fell asleep listening to them talking around the fire. It was so comforting, and the night that Zeb picked her up and carried her to bed, she was in heaven.

Having Dan there made her feel good. He was not in the way at all. He was no bother, as they said. He was always agreeable, but best of all he brought the boy. She longed for Sundays, and now that Frederick had been here several times he had grown used to the custom. He would run down the passage and in by the back door and almost say her name. He called her 'Leece', because he had heard the two men speak of her that way. She would lift him into her arms and cover his face with kisses, and he would laugh at her and with her. She loved him so much that she ached for her own child.

In bed at night, in her own reticent way, she tried to entice Zeb to her, but he wouldn't touch her. Her skills, she thought with scorn, were slight, and she was skinny and old and grey-haired. Though of late her hair seemed to be in recovery, there was no getting past that she was forty and he was not. Now that he was so important, he could have had another woman. He was also tall and lean and very attractive. She considered briefly whether he had another woman and dismissed the idea. He came home to her every night.

Then came the night when she was so frustrated that she said to him, 'You don't want to be here, do you?'

'What?'

'I'm too old and too skinny and too plain, and I have lines on my face and my body would drop if there was any of it spare to go south.' She stopped there because if she hadn't she would have cried.

'That's not so.'

She tried not to think that his voice was like silk. 'You are very important here now,' she said, almost sobbing. 'You don't have to stay with a wizened old creature like me. You can have another woman. You can have any woman you want.'

She stopped here only because her sobs got in the way.

'Oh Alice,' he said, and his breath touched her neck, 'I have never in my life loved anyone but you.'

'You don't want to touch me.'

'I don't want to put you through what you went through before.'

'Or what I put you through. Is that it?'

'No. Ever since the day I met you, I have wanted you for my wife. I love you. I adore you. You were my saviour and now you are my wife, and when I saw what it was like without you I couldn't bear it. I don't want to be here without you. Another child might kill you. Then what would I do? It's entirely selfish, you see.'

Alice tried to see him in what little light there was. 'Come to me then. Hold me.'

'What if we cannot have a child? What if it happens like that and I lose you forever?'

'I want you. I want you to give me a child, and if we can't have a child I want to know at least that we tried. And more than that, I want you because I love you. I love you more than any man was ever loved by any woman, and I know that I'm older than you and no longer very attractive—'

And that was when he stopped her mouth with kisses, his hands on her body, and after that Alice no longer cared for anything but her husband.

Forty-Three

Cate had returned to Westmorland in the autumn. A heavy heart had meant nothing to her before this, being something that other people talked of. Now, she felt as though her heart was broken. She had had to leave Harry and come back without him, but she was certain that it was the right thing to do. Mary would look after him.

Mary had already got away, helped by Mr Calland. He had done everything that he had promised. He had got her in his pony and trap, taken her to the house which was well out of the way, and the money had been ready as soon as the two women needed it to be.

He had discreetly been to see Mary, and Mary wrote to tell that he had given her even more help. He would drive her to the nearest train that would take her to Liverpool, and he had written and found berths for her on the next ship, which was going to Nova Scotia. He had paid for the berths and seen to everything that Mary and Harry needed.

So Cate went back to Westmorland and endured the journey, unable to avoid thinking of how awful her leaving the place all those months ago had been, and how much she had learned to hate her father and how she had thought she would never have to go back there. She had sworn to herself that she would not go, and now she was remembering all the awful things that had happened to her after Henry Westbrooke had fallen from his horse and died.

When she was put down at the entrance to her parents' house, her stomach did horrible things, turning over and over and making her feel sick. She wanted to run away and get on a ship with Mary and the baby. She sternly told herself that there was no way she could do this, nobody she could go to for succour. Nobody would help her except the man she had trusted. She had learned a valuable lesson here: you needed money to achieve anything, and when you had enough of it you could do what you chose.

She had loved this place as a child, but now, as she arrived outside the house, she thought it ugly. It seemed dark and rigid and withdrawn, with its stone lintels and its huge front door. Perhaps it was made ugly by the way that she had been beaten and starved in the cold before she had run away, and all because she had lain with the man she loved. She had thought he loved her in return. She had envisioned their life together and how happy they would be. She was determined to come back in some form of triumph, and so she made her way to the front door and banged upon it.

The maid who opened it did not recognize her, and would have directed her differently, but she pushed past and into the hall. The black Labradors got up from the fire to greet her, as they had always done. They knew her at once, wagging their tails in harmony and with joy.

The maid went off and shortly after that both her parents came forward to greet her. She was astonished and rather pleased at how old they looked. They were very thin and grey-haired, and they clasped her to them with words and tears, but she was not impressed. She had not forgotten leaving here. She had not forgotten Mary Blaimire, and how she could not have managed anything without her. She was polite and told them that her child had died. They sat by the drawing room fire while she told her lies. She had become very good at it, she found.

She would play their game and get money for herself and enable Mary to leave with the boy and have a life somewhere better than this – if there was a place where women were allowed decent lives.

That first night, when her mother would have had her room opened up for her, she declined, and told the maid that she would have another room, one which held no memories for her, though she didn't say that.

Her parents seemed to have forgotten the past; they did not ask about how the little child had died or what had happened to Mary Blaimire. They were cocooned in their tiny world, where apparently nothing could hurt them. And yet they had treated their only child in such a way that she would not be here now except for Mary and the boy. Her heart ached for him.

Her father was not well, and he had never employed an agent, doing everything himself, so when she offered to help him with this she saw the look of relief on his face. She was privately astonished. Had he forgotten how he had treated her? Which daughter could not hate a father who had beaten her, forsaken her, locked her up and starved her until he thought she might give in? He was a man and therefore he had to be right, she concluded bitterly.

It made her laugh to think of it now, that she would make a suitable alliance, albeit with the man whose brother she was with child to, because they treated her so badly that she could not stand any more.

She hated both her parents for what they had done, but she needed to find money. She would not have been here at all without Mary, and she swore that she would make sure that Mary and the boy were safe and well looked after and that in the end she would have them back here.

She was therefore attentive, and asked her father to show her the accounts and the estate and how things worked there, so that she could do it. He seemed overjoyed, and they rode out together on horseback to view the grounds.

He was feeble, and although she noticed this she did not particularly care. She was happier when, having shown her the estate as though she were a stranger, he left her to her rides and to the work, confident that she could manage.

Her mother talked to her freely about all manner of things that were not Cate's immediate concern, about other women marrying and having children, and when her mother realized she did not want to hear such things, she talked about the church and the sewing group. Cate was older now and she was expected to enjoy having charity afternoons at the house.

She politely refused, and her mother did not understand it, as she had not understood so very much. After that, Cate went to the estate office and there she took over the whole running of the place, as was expected of her, even though she had just come back. The people there assumed she had come back because her father was ill. Soon she could use money as she chose; her father signed papers so that everything was hers.

And then Charles came to call. Did he have no delicacy, she wondered? He waited until she went back to the house in the evening and then he came by and she wanted to spit on him.

He smiled just a little and said that he had heard the child had died and he was very sorry.

'Thank you. Yes.' Here Cate managed tears, and it was hardly surprising, she knew, because she did feel in some ways as though Harry was no more. Storms happened at sea, and she envisioned Mary and the little boy dying. Even once they got there, she had no idea what would happen, so it could be that she would never see her child again. She was not any happier that she might never see Mary again, who had been closer to her than anyone before and had got her from here when she most needed to leave. Her debt to Mary was huge.

'There seemed nothing for it but to come back here,' she said to Charles. 'I had little to keep me in Stanhope.'

Though he looked carefully at her, the tears were there and he would see her grief.

'I'm glad you came home,' he said.

She wanted to kill him. Did he really not care for her loss, or was he so good at hiding his feelings? Finding an heir to his estate was something that mattered to him a great deal.

He went away very soon afterwards and left her with the estate, her parents, the accounts and the farmers. She envied Mary, and yet Mary would have a bad time too, with a child that wasn't hers. It wouldn't have been like that had the three of them been able to leave together. Cate spent several minutes envisaging how wonderful it would have been, but she could not afford to indulge herself.

As soon as she could, she sent money to Jos Calland to replace that which he had already given to Mary. He told her, while saying nothing obvious in case the letter should fall into different hands, that everything was being done and that her packages were safely away and everything would be all right.

Mr Calland had a new address, but again he did not employ specifics. This man was made for intrigue, she thought with slight humour, and was glad of him and how he had helped them. She understood that Mary would write to him and he might send the letters on if he felt it safe. Still, Cate knew she wouldn't be able to relax until she heard from Mary that they had reached Canada.

Forty-Four

Shirley didn't find not talking to her husband a problem. She was so angry and she missed Freddie and it hurt physically. She wanted to run after Nell and all the way to that bloody awful house where that dreadful woman now lived with those strange people. She wanted to claim him back from them and their influence. They were mad, people were always saying so. Mrs March had been wrong to marry that man and evil to take the child from where he was happy.

Shirley could not imagine what it would be like for him to be apart from her. Would he forget her in time? Part of her hoped not, but she could not help but feel for his misery. She wanted him to be happy, but with her, and she didn't see how being taken from her arms when she was all he knew of a mother was a good idea, regardless of who did it.

Everything was so much harder without him. She did what she had to do, but it was drudgery. She spoke rarely, and then only to the children. Pat's father had long since forgotten not only who they were, but who he was, and sometimes now at night, having been in bed all day when she had been busy, he would get up and move around the cottage, lost. Shirley often wished he would go and fall into the quarry and die – and with any luck take Pat's mother with him.

As for Pat, she ignored him, and he spoke less and less. When his father got up at night, Pat spent as much time as needed to get him back into bed. Shirley did not stir. She went through hell during the day, why shouldn't Pat do it at night? After all, they were his parents.

Many a man would have left, in spite of his parents and his children, or taken to drink or knocked her about, but Pat was difficult to hate. He went to work, uncomplaining, then came home and spent most of the time trying to settle his father. Shirley told herself she didn't care, but sometimes Pat's face was beyond pale to ashen. She was determined not to feel sorry for him. Why should she?

After Daniel Wearmouth came back, and Shirley heard that he was seeing the boy, her jealousy cost her a great many hot tears in what little privacy she could gain for herself.

Then Dan had the nerve to invite her to that awful shop where he was living. Shirley hated places like that, spending money on muck. He wanted her to go there and play pretty and pretend that she was not breaking her heart over a child who had been ripped from her arms. She felt almost as though he had been taken from her belly. After all those months and all that work, tending him every hour, being there for him every moment, now it was as though she could be picked up and put down like a toy that was no longer needed.

Daniel Wearmouth had deserted his child and now he had the gall to allow her to see the little boy, whom she loved more than anyone on earth, even more – and she felt guilty about this – than she loved her own two wonderful little girls. They were older; they did not need her as much as he did. How was it that he dared treat her in that way? He had not once thanked her. Without her, his child could be dead. She wished him in hell and she wished her husband there with him.

Forty-Five

Nell found her so dearly won household disintegrating before the eternal screams of her grandchild. She had not known that one small boy could upset things so very badly.

She was glad when Dan took him away. He now stayed at the sweet shop the whole weekend, and during that time things went on as normal, or as normal as everything ever got at Holywell Hall.

Alice apparently managed to run the shop and see to the child, but it was by now common knowledge that she had help. Also, the men only worked on Saturday mornings, so presumably Dan was there to spend most of the weekend with his boy. Nell looked forward to Friday afternoons as never before. She dreaded the boy coming back, and she hated Monday to Thursday, when both Augusta and Sawrey were scarcely to be seen, except at dinner. Sundays were the worst. The little boy would fight and kick and bite and scream when his father left.

Norah was a big help. Sawrey had never liked her but Nell had taken her on to help with the child and not just with the general work. Nell had wanted to bring in a nanny but it seemed that no woman wanted to be there. Nell had the feeling she had taken on too many impossible things at once and could not cope with them. She did not know what to do, and even when the boy slept, she could not.

Augusta had been getting better, and sometimes she ventured outside, though not for long. She kept away from the little boy. Nell went back and forth between handing him back to Shirley, which she did not want to do, and the alternative, because no matter how much attention he had, no matter how many women fussed over him and helped, the little boy was not happy.

Dan was by now feeling awful. He had caused the problem. Would Frederick get used to the comings and goings of his life, or had Dan's intrusion made things intolerable? He told himself that he was entitled to see the boy, and Mrs March was eager to let him have Frederick, but he couldn't help but wonder if he was making things worse with his selfishness.

The only person who had really benefited from the boy, other than Dan, was Alice. Frederick had found the cure for Alice's awful illness and Dan could see how much she loved him. He would have liked to leave the boy with her always, but it wasn't fair to any one of them. Frederick was not her child and she had the shop to see to and the sweets to make. Dan thought she would gladly have given up the shop to look after Frederick, but he thought Mrs March would be very upset at the idea and would never allow it. Having taken the child from the only mother he had known, it would make matters worse that the little boy should be given to yet another woman.

Forty-Six

Mary's father came to see Cate at her home. He barged into the library where she was seated at her father's desk.

'Aye, they said you were here.' He stood with his legs planted well apart, as though to intimidate her. All she felt for him was disgust.

'Mr Blaimire. How may I help you?'

'You can tell me where my daughter is.'

'Your daughter died. She helped me get away from here when I was having a child, and then both she and the child died of a fever.'

She could still summon tears. If anything, the loss was getting worse.

He gazed at her weeping. 'My Mary is dead?'

His Mary, as though he had not treated all his children and his wife so badly. Cate was astonished that he could delude himself. Was he, like her father, convinced that he was always right?

'I'm afraid so. I would have come to your house and told you but both my parents are ill and I have had time for nothing more. I am helping my father with the estate. Please, let me get on.'

He left and she swore she could see tears in his eyes, the gutless bastard.

Her father was already forgetting day-to-day things.

'It was after you left that he went like this,' her mother said, blaming her, and then Cate thought how weak her mother was. She had starved her daughter, listened to the beatings, left her in the cold and then tried to marry her to a man she didn't care for.

They could have protected her in some way, surely, but they had thrown her to the nearest wolves for respectability's sake. Well, it was over now. She was doing this for her boy, so that some day he would come back here and take her estate and perhaps the Westbrooke estate too. Then she began to worry. If the boy had any sense and was old enough, then he would never come to this and she would have done it in vain. But no, she and Mary had not had the money to leave together and the sacrifice was best this way.

She lay in bed at night and thought that Charles just might marry. He was rich and eligible and she didn't really think he was like his brother. She thought he had found somebody he cared about and lost the chance of marriage somehow, but men were fickle creatures, and he might learn to love again. At night she tried to talk herself into marrying him. But why would he have her now, when her child had apparently died?

She didn't like him or love him, but for her child's sake she might be able to take him on. But would he take her on now? She looked at herself in the glass and was not deceived. She looked awful: skinny, unkempt, uncared for, careless of dress. Her hair was like a nest of some kind and there were big bags under her eyes. My God, she was awful. Nobody would ever want to marry her, unless perhaps for her money.

She was, however, grateful that she had money to hand. Her father had no more sense than to let her do whatever she wished, and her mother had no notion of how the estate was run. Cate sent Mary a great deal of money and gave Jos Calland sufficient and more for doing it. Mary wrote to Mr Calland to say that she had received the money and that she would do what she should and that when it was possible she would contact Cate.

That was all. Neither of them was explicit, and it was wise to be careful. You never knew who read your letters, but she thought Jos Calland treated her fairly and that was enough.

She went nowhere that autumn. She was grateful that Mary had got away with the boy, but sometimes she felt full of self-pity and cried in bed. She could not show her grief elsewhere, nobody would care and she could not let them see that she felt her loss. Children died all the time – the churchyard was full of them – so why should it not have happened to her?

She made sure that she knew exactly what was happening on the estate, and so she went to see the Blaimire family. There she found the full horror as Mary had described it, and so she gave Mrs Blaimire a living for her children and she told Mary's father that he must find somewhere else to live, and she also made Ned go to the nearest place he could find to live away from her. Mary would have been pleased, but Cate didn't tell her.

She took on two of Mary's sisters to work with her and she made sure the others had more than enough to eat. She directed all the women and children who had been neglected and ill-used by their husbands and brothers. Some men were good, and she employed these and paid them well. Sometimes she had to admit that a man may be a bastard at home and a god at work, but it was hard to stomach.

Every night when she went to bed, she thought about her boy and how Mary had been so generous. If Harry were here, she would not have treated him in the way that she and Charles and Henry had been treated. Dogs and horses did better, and it would not do. She would not have it. She lay in her bed and was so angry that she couldn't sleep, so she did as the men did and took brandy to bed with her.

Her father grew steadily worse and her mother blamed her. 'You did this by running away. He was never like this before.'

'I did it? You were trying to marry me off to Henry's brother.'

'He's a good man.'

'He's nothing of the sort. He's a—' She wanted to say bastard, but she couldn't, her mother would probably have fainted. And in any case, it wasn't fair to Charles.

He had tried to help her, but only because she had the heir to his estate. That did not explain why he came over the day before Christmas with a huge hamper of game, chutneys and sweetmeats, several good bottles of claret and two bottles of fine brandy.

'Charles,' she greeted him, 'and rather than just sending your gifts, you delivered them.'

'Don't take it badly,' he said. 'I'm just being polite.'

'As you never were.'

'As I always was. I hear your father isn't well.'

'Your ears do not deceive you, but I have plenty of help here.'

'If you get stuck, let me know,' Charles said.

She did think about him when she went to bed, and she wondered whether he too could smell and taste brandy when he went to sleep. Whether he too thought of someone he had loved, as she could think of Henry when she was sweetly drunk. She didn't know, but she suspected it. Was he as disappointed in his life as she was in hers?

Someone had to take the blame, and she knew that she wasn't being fair or right. Everybody did what they could, and so she attempted to excuse her parents. She was kind to them, but her father soon knew nobody and in the night would call for his own parents. She had never known them, but the way that he wanted them encouraged her to think that they had been kind. Or was it just that he wished they had been? He had become the child and she the parent, and she hated it.

Through the solicitor, everything passed to Cate, and she was amazed that her father had done such a thing. Yet what else could he do? He had no male heir.

'He always intended it for you, his only child,' the lawyer said.

She hated her father for seeing so far ahead, and herself for not thinking so far. And then she was astonished that he had known she would come back here and have it for hers. Or had he just hoped?

She half wished she hadn't come back, even though it

would have been unfair to everybody here on the estate. What would have happened had she not? It would have gone to a distant cousin, the lawyer assured her. But her father had known she would come back, and had made certain that it would all be for her. She hated that he had known her so well.

Forty-Seven

Mary had gone. She was on a ship bound for Nova Scotia and could not be traced, could not be turned back. Cate had told Mary that she would send money on as she could, if Mary would enable her to send it.

Things were hard, and Cate knew that Mary was not happy either. She loved Cate's child, but not as her own. She was pleased that Mary had taken her boy, but she missed him as she had not thought to miss anyone. Her breasts ached, her stomach ached, her arms ached; in her mind she saw pictures of him over and over again, until she wanted to weep.

Cate's whole self was bereft. She thought of how he would change and grow, how she would not hear his first words. Even though she knew that Mary would do everything she could for him, Cate wept when she was safely in bed at night, wishing she could hold her boy close.

She hid her sobs against the pillows. She cried and her body ached and then sleep would take over and it was the only relief. She felt herself falling beyond the tears and was grateful for the quiet and the rest.

One night she heard a wailing and woke up. Being a

mother, she always awoke at the first instance of anything different, and she knew what it was. Her father was crying. She ventured out onto the landing with her candle and across to her parents' bedroom, and there her mother sat, staring at her father in bed.

Cate put down her candle and lit the other two in the room so that she could survey the scene. Her mother was pale and white and skinny, and her father was crying as though he would never stop.

Her mother was gazing at her husband as though she had just met him. He stopped crying and then shuddered, and over the next few minutes he gradually fell asleep. She had never thought of him as old, yet he was thirty years older than her mother.

Cate gazed at her mother's white face and dull eyes.

'Would you like to come and sleep with me?' she offered.

Her mother looked gratefully at her and nodded.

Cate didn't want to sleep with her mother, but she couldn't go back on the offer. She left the door wide open so that she should hear her father across the hall if he woke up, and then she took her mother into her bedchamber and they lay down together. It reminded her of her childhood, how her mother had hushed her to sleep with nursery rhymes and how she had sung sweet songs to her when she was afraid of those night demons that everybody feared.

Now she could shush her mother to sleep and tell her that all would be well, and though her mother must have known that it was nonsense, she nodded and smiled and laid herself down with a sigh. She had relinquished her responsibility for her husband and the estate and her life, and that was what kept Cate awake.

She had become her parents. How awful, how unexpected and how soon. But if she had the run of this place, if it was legally hers, then she could bring back her child. But that also meant that her father must die, and although she had learned to hate him, he had been a good father to her until she crossed him.

Perhaps it was always like that. You grew up and they didn't want you to. They kept telling you what a beautiful and obedient child you had been, and you learned to dislike them so that when they died you didn't break your heart. You had broken your heart long before, when you tried to get away and they tried to contain you. Perhaps each generation must do that.

In the morning she sent for the doctor, but her father was much better and then so was her mother. They seemed quite happy to leave her to the management of the estate.

'It was always for you,' her father said.

Why could you not be what your parents wanted you to be? You had to push forward, you had to go on and it was so tiring, so all-encompassing.

Forty-Eight

Mary found Cate's child troublesome. He knew his mother was gone, and why would he not? Women smelled different, and although he was weaned he knew that his mother's breast was nowhere near. He screamed so much that she wished she could have thrown him overboard on their way across the Atlantic.

She had just begun to think he would go on like this forever when he stopped. After that, things got better so very quickly, and although Mary missed Cate, she was excited by the idea of a whole new life. She would never go back to Shap. She stood by the rail and watched the sea, happy that each day this ship took her further and further away from all those people she had hated, from poverty and neglect.

Quite suddenly, the boy accepted her. Mary wanted to tell Cate that her child was as happy as he could be without her, and that he was falling in love with the only mother he knew now. Possibly the only mother he would remember.

She and Cate had decided that she should be a widow who was moving away to start afresh and find new things to enjoy. To that end, Mary had bought a cheap wedding ring in Liverpool, where nobody cared, and then she had booked a decent passage with Mr Calland's help so that they had to share with no one.

Cate had suggested it, and Mary felt she could not do any less, because at that time the boy cried so much that she feared he was ill. On the ship, they were warm and fed and could go up on deck as they wished, and Mary was known as Mrs Holyoake. She thought it was a good name.

The voyage was fair and they made good time, according to the captain and the crew. Although it was a long way to Nova Scotia, she was happy as long as it was flat and the boy slept.

He was easier and easier as the days went by, and she learned to love him as she imagined Cate loved him. As the ship took them further westward, Mary was pleased with Cate's decision. This could work until Cate should send for her baby – and perhaps she never would. Mary was so glad to be away from her father and Ned. She would never go back there, and perhaps this baby would not either, except in triumph to take up the inheritance that was his.

When Mary got to Nova Scotia, she was astonished. Halifax was a big town and the harbour was full of ships, so many that you couldn't see how many there were. As they got nearer, she saw around it lots of woodland, prosperous and green. The place had about it the most wonderful atmosphere that Mary had ever felt. She was free. She could do anything she liked here. She had never felt so excited about anything.

The streets up from the harbour were all steep and there

were plenty of good buildings. The streets were thick with Scottish and Irish accents, and she understood these. She could feel the enthusiasm coming off these people. Although there were also plenty of disagreements and harsh language, nobody upset her and those men who met her were most polite.

She found what she thought was a very good hotel and they did not look askance at her as they might have done in England. It was different here. She was welcomed with a smile and when she produced money the smile grew.

She was given a room that overlooked the street. The manager said that if it grew too lively in the night he would move her to a back room, but Mary liked the idea of activity beyond the hotel. She was safe there. Nobody knew where she was but Cate. Nobody would come here after her.

While the little lad slept, she gazed through the big windows and watched people on the street – beggars picking up pieces of food, those who worked late homeward bound with packs on their backs, and at 3 a.m. those who came out and stayed in the shadows like ghosts. She didn't mind seeing them; she had never felt so safe in her life. This big hotel held her within its warm grasp and nobody could hurt her.

In the mornings when she went down to breakfast, the people in the dining room greeted her and spoke to Harry and there was everything you could think of to eat. There were hard-boiled eggs and lots of rough brown bread with butter and honey; there were fried potatoes and cheese and ham. Mary had never seen the likes, and it took her days to get used to the fact she didn't have to do anything, it just emerged.

The hotel didn't do lunch, or 'dinner', as they called it, but there were a dozen places on street corners where she could have soup and good bread at a table. Harry was learning to eat real food and he liked the soup and the bread.

In the evenings, she ate at a place just beyond the hotel, up a few steps from the pavement and into a large room with a fire. There was always fish and vegetables. She grew fond of it, and the people, though they didn't say much, were kind. Mary had not known anything like it. She began to think that she would enjoy this place.

Cate sent her a great deal more money than Mary needed, and so she opened a bank account and put it in there. She wrote to Cate and told her that it wasn't needed, but she could see that Cate needed to do it, that it was a point of contact with her child and her friend. She called Mary her friend so often in her letters that it made Mary proud and made her weep all together.

She sent Cate descriptions of Halifax, and made it sound as though her child was safe but missing her. In truth, he was not, he was forgetting her, but Mary didn't want her to know it. She did not see how Cate would ever have him back as long as her father lived, and possibly as long as Charles Westbrooke lived, unless he married.

She was falling in love with the little boy. He changed every day and it was endearing in a way she had not expected. It made her want a child of her own, because although she loved him, she was always aware that he was not hers.

She wanted to go home, and yet she didn't. Home meant her father and Ned. She could not go back there unless somehow she was beyond their power. Cate said that her mother and sisters were being looked after, but Mary saw no rescue for herself. They would find her out and kill her in a horrible way. She would not go back there unless Cate asked for her child.

Cate sent her enough money so that she could buy a house, and there were wonderful houses in Halifax. They were detached and made of wood, and they had two or three storeys, each with its own garden. They were beautiful houses such as she had never seen, and to think that one of them might be hers was so exciting. Cate told her to go ahead and buy what she wanted and so Mary did. She bought a house that was the prettiest thing she had ever come across.

Cate wrote to say that her father was ill and she didn't expect him to live. He had given everything to her so that she could do as she pleased, but she still said that there was no chance they could come home. She would never be accepted as an unmarried mother, despite who she was, and things were difficult enough. She missed Mary, and she missed her little boy so much that some days she felt she could hardly breathe, but they would have to go on as they were.

Mary was the happiest now than she had ever been. She didn't have to clean anybody's boots or scrub anybody's floor. She had this little lad all to herself, and now she had a home of her own and could even employ people to look after her. She told people that her husband had been a farmer in Northumberland and had died just a few months after the baby had been born. She said that she was lucky in that she had an aunt who left her money, so she decided to go away and start afresh.

She only hoped that Cate might meet another man and marry him and have other children. Although she would never forget Harry, she might learn to be happy without him.

Mary didn't think she could be happy without him now. It was selfish, she knew, but he had come to be hers. He remembered nobody but her, and no doubt he would come to believe the lies she was obliged to tell him. Some day, perhaps, they would go back. Some day she might be able to tell him, but not now.

Now, she slept close against the little boy and dreamed of when he would take his first steps and say his first words. He would be a year old that spring and he was completely hers.

Forty-Nine

Stewart MacDonald came to see Charles.

'I heard from John Peters. It seems that the story about the child and Mary Blaimire is a total lie,' he said. 'Lady Catherine came back here to make money, and Mary and the child have vanished into thin air, much to John's disgust. He thought he had found the perfect cleaner and nursery-maid. And the child is a boy.'

Stewart looked triumphant, but Charles's first reaction was one of disgust. He didn't think he wanted to know. Since she had come home, he found that he did not want Cate to be unhappy. She had been through enough. He had tried to believe Cate, and although he was disappointed that she could not tell him the truth, he understood why.

He must accept that she would never marry him. She had no need to marry anyone, now that she had taken power over her father's estate. Charles did not doubt that she had sent Mary Blaimire far away with the boy.

It seemed to him the right thing to do. Her father was a ghastly man. Charles applauded Cate for having found work far away for Mary's father and the awful lad who had wanted to marry her. He just hoped that Mary would find some deserved happiness and that the boy might one day come home to his inheritance. In the meanwhile, he decided that he did not want his brother's child to inherit the estate, so he must look around for a bride.

If only it were that simple. He could have had almost anybody he wanted, but for all the wrong reasons. They knew who he was, and even had he been ugly and bad-tempered they would still have taken him. It was disgusting.

He longed for the days when he had been poor and almost a minister, and had fallen in love with a dales lass. She had not known who he was, yet she had fallen in love with him. He doubted she would have him now.

The honesty of that relationship almost knocked him over. She was the only woman he had ever loved. He had planned to marry her, had intended never to come back, and here he was. In spite of his determination to get away, he was here and he must do something positive. He disliked the prissy person who could not fall in love again, and maybe the time had come for him to try.

The following day he went to see Cate, who was at her desk, as always. He thought she was looking better. Her father had rallied slightly, Charles knew, and she had colour in her face and there was a huge kind of relief in her eyes that she could not hide.

'Will you go to a dance with me?' he said, when the pleasantries were finished.

She stared. And then she laughed, and he liked how she laughed, more carelessly than he had seen in years.

'Are you mad?' she said.

Charles, sitting down opposite her in the lovely drawing room where she had once passed out at his feet, sighed. He drank his coffee and ate his walnut cake and still wasn't happy.

'I really need to get married,' he said.

Cate cast up her eyes to the ceiling. 'Oh, not again.'

'Not you, somebody else. But I need camouflage. I don't want to look obvious or needy.'

'How could somebody as rich as you look needy? For God's sake, half the women in the north-west would take you in an instant.'

He merely shrugged and watched the fire. Cate was starting to enjoy herself. 'You need me to go with you?' she said. 'Charles, that's ridiculous. And besides, I can't go to things like that.'

'Why on earth not?'

Cate hesitated. 'I have a bastard child and no husband,' she said slowly, and she watched his reaction with slight concern but no fear.

Charles looked carefully at her. 'How is the bastard child?' he said, and he smiled at her and it was a very good smile.

She looked straight at him and took a chance. 'He's doing very well, thank you.' She hadn't meant to say that – at least she thought she hadn't – but once it was said she felt better than she had since Henry had broken his neck and died. She felt as though she and Charles could be friends now and he would never ask her to marry him again. He didn't want to marry her, not even in the way of getting himself an heir. He had given in, so it was time for her to give in too.

'You used to enjoy dancing,' he said.

'I haven't danced since Henry died,' she said, and she heard the little catch in her own voice and knew that she still loved him in spite of everything. His child lived, so a part of him would always be with her.

'I miss him too.'

She heard how tight Charles's own voice sounded, then their eyes met in understanding and she knew that they were going to be friends and she was glad of him.

'I haven't a thing to wear,' she said.

The ball took place in Penrith at the Assembly Rooms, and Charles made sure that he danced the first two dances with Cate, just to establish that she must be seen as important. She was now worth a great deal of money, and while she had caused the biggest scandal of the area in years, she must be seen as respectable if she had come with him.

Charles danced every dance and put up with a lot of maidens who agreed with everything he said. He didn't remember having been more bored. He didn't notice who or what they were, they could have been plain or beautiful; he just wished he could have stayed at home by the fire with the dogs and a decanter of brandy. He really was his father.

He and Cate were staying the night, along with dozens of other people, and it was all perfectly respectable, so how it was that they came to sit in a tiny back room and drink brandy he didn't know. He wasn't even tired, and although

Cate kept saying she must go to bed, she had told her maid not to wait.

'Are you horribly bored at home?' Charles said.

'Actually, no. I used to be terribly bored there, when I was expected to play the piano and listen to sermons being read by the fire in the dark evenings. Nothing could ever be that dull again.'

Charles choked and laughed.

'I like my life best now,' she said. 'I know it's awful to say it, because if things had been different I could have been married to Henry and had my little boy here and . . . I might even have been expecting my second by now.'

'You could bring him back.'

'I don't think I want to. Not before I have you safely married with an heir. Haven't you ever been in love?'

'Do you know, you and Henry being here and married and having children was what I really wanted. I wanted to be a minister of the church, I really did.'

'I think you would have been awful at it.'

'Actually I wasn't. I liked it. And I liked the place.'

'Stanhope is worse than Penrith for how boring it is. Now Durham, that's a real place.'

Charles told her the story of how he had gone there after her and about the man who verbally abused him because he was working shifts and they had woken him up. It made her laugh, and she said she loved the way he tried to imitate a Durham accent.

'Stanhope is my favourite place of all,' Charles said.

'You have no taste.'

He hesitated. 'There was a woman in Stanhope.'

Cate stared at him. 'You fell in love in Stanhope? I don't believe it. Was she the local squire's daughter?'

'She worked in a shop.'

'Oh Charles, really!' she giggled, and then she saw that he was serious and sobered. 'Why didn't you marry her?'

'Henry died and I came back to rescue you from my father and your father.'

'I hate to say this to you, Charles, but I'm very grateful. If it hadn't been for you insisting that I marry you, I would never have run away, and it was the best thing I ever did.'

Charles couldn't think of anything to say to that, but he knew that in a way she was genuine. She had needed to get out just as now she had needed to come back.

'Was she anything like me?'

He shook his head, knowing that she didn't ask because she was vain. She was just interested that he might have tried to marry her, because he felt he ought, when he loved somebody quite different.

'She was little and dark-haired, found on a doorstep. She had a thick dales accent and was a Methodist.'

'You're going to make me choke. Why didn't you marry her?'

'She married somebody else. After you ran, I went back to Stanhope and found that it was her wedding day. I had thought I could have the life I wanted.'

'Lord, how awful.'

'I think that was the worst day of my life. No, the worst day of my life was when Henry died.'

'That was my worst day too. I wish they hadn't tried to make us get married. I loved Henry, and he liked me very well, even if . . . I don't think I shall ever marry.'

'You don't know. You're a woman with a big estate.'

'Yes, and some money-digging fiend is sure to come along. So what was she called?"

'Who?'

'The woman you loved.'

'She was called Susan Wilson.'

Cate frowned. 'The woman who worked for the solicitor?'

'Did she? I saw her when I came to find you. She didn't look happy.'

'Well, she wouldn't. Like me, she caused an enormous scandal. Perhaps we do have things in common, after all. She married one of the quarry managers – you know his name.'

'Daniel Wearmouth. I never liked him. Jilted her and married another woman, and after she died he had the gall to marry Susan. She must have wanted him anyhow.'

'Yes, but Charles, everybody knew what happened. They got married, she rebuffed him and he went to Durham. That's how I met him. It was never more than a marriage in name.'

Charles frowned. 'How do you know?'

'He told me so. She got her own back on him, if you choose to call it that. She married him and then wouldn't let him near her and off he went, and I'm glad he did. He was a big help to Mary and me.'

'Not a real marriage?'

Cate smiled. 'You could marry her, Charles. It would be

a bit sticky, but you could. I can recommend a very good solicitor to you.'

Charles didn't sleep. He didn't allow himself to think that his luck could be changing. He could talk to Susan and ask her if she still cared for him and if she could get an annulment of the marriage. That was what money and influence was for, after all. But would Susan have him when he had let her down so badly in the first place? She must have known that he had to go back and offer to marry Cate – but would she understand the stupid way that the landed gentry went on?

He got up and paced the floor. He kept going to the window, as though there was anything to see other than the deserted grounds and the far hills dark beyond. He waited for the dawn, and he thought so much about Susan that he knew he had to go and ask her if she would have him. Yet how could he?

She had married Daniel Wearmouth, who had been her first love. Susan had been let down so many times that it seemed stupid to imagine she would now marry anyone. Why would she? She had a good job, somewhere decent to live and she probably cared little either for him or for Daniel Wearmouth.

He remembered seeing the man, on a lovely grey horse, gazing across the street when he had been in Susan's company. Even then he had dreaded the other man, knowing how attractive he must be to the woman he had once loved. And she had gone on loving him. You did not take such cold revenge on a man unless you cared. Would he be mad to go there and try to persuade her to marry him?

What would he do if she refused? How would he ever live with himself? But if he didn't try for the woman he loved, he would end up marrying some stupid girl because he was desperate for someone to bed. He must do something, and if it did not work he would come back here and try to choose some woman who was at least sensible and who could talk about books and didn't ever hunt.

He had never been as afraid in his life as he was now. He couldn't bear to be at the other side of Susan's decision. He couldn't stand to stay here; he couldn't bear to go. It was awful. He was in danger of shouting at people who didn't deserve it. He delayed day after day until he couldn't stand his own presence, and so a week later he set off for Weardale.

He could have been sick a dozen times on the way, and he was glad it was so far. Then he thought it was too near and wished himself home. When he finally got down from his carriage, Stanhope looked so ordinary, so normal, that he wanted to laugh.

The shops were open, including the sweet shop. With each step he took, he remembered Susan and how much he had cared for her, and thought of how afraid he was now. If she turned him down today, he would spend the rest of his life regretting it and would never marry.

He wished he hadn't come. He wished he were at home with the dogs or in his office with Stewart, making decisions that he hoped would aid everyone and keep the estate going.

There was nowhere for somebody like him to rest. There

was no decent hotel. What could he do? The horses and servants needed a place to go and so he found rooms for them at the Bonny Moorhen, where he remembered there were good stables. He gave instructions that they should have the best rooms, plenty of beer and food and whatever else they needed.

They had spent so long on the way, changing horses, in and out of hostels, and now, at journey's end, he must ask nothing more of them. Even if he didn't want to stay here, he must for a day or two, until they were rested and ready to return.

He knew where Susan would be. He knew where she lived, in the building that the solicitor had for his business. He walked there very slowly, so worried was he about what would happen. She had not yet rejected him, and he could still indulge in a little anticipation.

He stumbled into the building. He was usually fairly graceful, so he wasn't happy from the start. The door was unlocked and he made his way into the reception area, where Susan was seated behind a desk.

She got up looking surprised, as well she might, he thought.

'Charles,' she said, and then stood back.

'Susan. I have come to see you.' Oh, fool, he thought, whatever else would you be doing here?

'Oh. Well, I am at work.'

'I would like to talk to you. When do you finish?'

'About five. Is something wrong?'

Did women always think there was something wrong, or was it just that there was always something wrong?

'No, everything's fine,' he said. Assuring her that he would come back at five, he staggered out.

He was exhausted.

It was the longest ever afternoon, and he had forgotten how cold early spring was here. He did not know what to do. He couldn't walk; he couldn't eat or drink. He couldn't pace, because somebody would notice. The Bonny Moorhen was unused to people like him. He was only grateful that the people who had run it when he was here were no longer about, but then he worried about what had happened to them, as though he were still the almost minister.

He tried to read. He went for a walk, but time had taken on a new rhythm. Snails would have thought it too slow.

At half past four he could stand it no longer and was pacing up and down outside – but across the street, so that she would not see him. Would she come out? She was living there in rooms, so probably she wouldn't. He crossed the road and entered the building and there she was. She looked surprised to see him.

'You're still here.'

'I said I would be.'

'Yes, but people have a habit of vanishing and not being there when they said they would.'

She put on her coat and her hat and her gloves, and what looked to him like innumerable scarves, and then they left the building and were out in the street, and that was not what he wanted either. He was worried that somebody might see them and interpret it wrongly, or perhaps rightly. He urged her up the first street they came to, which led up to the tops.

It was steep, and even after just a few minutes it seemed a ridiculous idea to him, but they ploughed on, and the further they went, the steeper it was, with houses at either side.

How the hell had people got builders up here, he could not help but think. Then, after a long haul, he panting and she was pretending she wasn't, they came out at the top. They looked down at the village and it was so beautiful it made him want to weep for how awful things were in other places, and for what might have been.

'What are you doing here?' she asked when they got their breath back.

'I wanted to see you. I didn't understand. I came here to fetch you and it was the day that you married Daniel Wearmouth, so I turned my horses around and went home.'

'You were here?' She didn't believe him, though she wanted to.

'I thought I was too late. I saw you marry him, and I knew that you had loved him so very much and so I – I went home. It was only a few days ago that I discovered your marriage had not worked out.'

'Oh,' Susan said, and that single syllable made him look hard at her, while she looked out over the view as though she had not seen it a thousand times.

'Cate told me about it.'

'That woman,' was all Susan said, but her cheeks flushed as she said it, as though she had a violent dislike of Cate.

'You don't think she should have done?'

'I don't know.' Susan moved away from him and turned her back, and Charles wanted to run. He was too late, he was too stupid. He had put her behind everything else. She had thought she didn't matter to him, and he had demonstrated how little he had cared because he had not put her first.

'I thought you'd married her after your brother killed himself. I thought you would have to marry her.'

'She didn't think so.'

'She does what she wants.'

'Did you know about the boy and Mary Blaimire?'

'Yes. Cate contacted Mr Calland, and I write his letters and deal with his business. I knew all about it.'

'You didn't think to tell me?'

'When I knew that she had been through so much, what with you and your brother? She had as bad a time as I. Why would I betray her? I'm glad that Mary Blaimire and the boy got away.'

'So am I,' Charles said.

Susan said nothing to this.

'I'm sorry for the way that I treated you.'

'Oh, I understand,' she said, with unreal lightness of voice. 'You had your family to consider. I didn't understand then, because I'd never had a family. I had no one to put me first. And then I met Miss Lee and she put me first, at least for a while. I resent the fact that she doesn't now, and that is so unfair when she has had so much to deal with. I have wanted to come first with someone for all my life.'

'I'll put you first now, if you'll let me.'

She said nothing to that, and Charles waited. It didn't

matter how long he waited now, but the time went on and she stared down at the village as though something important to her was happening there.

Finally he couldn't stand it any more. 'Susan, I love you. I have always loved you.'

'Do you know,' she said, almost interrupting, 'I think that if you had really loved me you would never have gone back there, no matter what happened to your brother and your father and your – your estate, or whatever you call it. I'm not like these society women who need to marry somebody with a title. You have got a title, haven't you?'

Charles felt like he was being scorched.

'Men are so swift to tell women how much they love them, but all they really want is to imprison them in some stupid house and have them produce a child a year and do as they are told. To be frank, I can't think of anything worse. You see, I have finally met a man who is interested in me, and strangely enough, it isn't to do with how pretty I look. Though I don't look so good any more after the way that you and Daniel Wearmouth treated me.

'He cares about my mind. He pays me for my work. He has given me a set of rooms all to myself and he is teaching me about the law. I love that. I love it as much as I ever loved you or Daniel.

'My rooms are full of books, and I am learning. One day I hope that I will be able to study at university as men do, and that I will be able to become a solicitor. But if not, I will be here and I will be taking part, helping people to sort out their difficulties. And when it's over I won't be going back to screaming children and people with stupid minds and a dull, selfish husband like you or Daniel.'

Charles couldn't think of a single word to say to this.

'You didn't think I would turn you down?' she said.

'I didn't think you would,' he allowed.

'I have my own fireside. I can eat what I want, get up when I want at weekends. I can buy the clothes I like and I can read all on my own. During the week I help Mr Calland, and I like it as I had never thought to like such a thing. He will be opening another office in Wolsingham, and he and I will run the offices between us. He has a wife and a child, so there is no danger, and I know what I want now. Thank you for coming all this way.' And she smiled briefly at him and began to walk back down the hill into the little dales town.

Fifty

Zeb had now a well wife, a good friend to stay and the little boy to see often. Things were also going well at work and he had time to worry about his father. Mr Bailey had not often come to the house when Alice had been so ill, but Zeb knew it was not because his father did not wish them well, it was just that he was happy and did not want to intrude. Zeb invited him to Sunday dinner, and he came but had little to say.

It had not occurred to Zeb that his father might have difficulties in his own life. He had seemed so eager to go and live with the Vernons, who were good, interesting people, but he could tell that his father was unhappy. He wished he could have asked his father to come and stay, even just for a day or two, but there was no bedroom for him and he did not want Dan to move out. He could suggest they share the back room, and he didn't think either of them would mind, but Dan might then go to stay at the Grey Bull, where they had decent rooms and food. He could well afford it. He could well have afforded a house, even. But Zeb knew that Alice had come to depend so much on the child, it would be like kicking a chair away as she sat down. Dan was also aware of it, and they all got on so well. They could not even move to a bigger house because of the sweet shop.

On the second Sunday that Mr Bailey came to eat with them, Zeb offered to go for a walk with his father. It was a bright, cold day. Alice and Dan were happy with the little boy, and he was glad to get his father to himself. They didn't go far; they walked along the footpath beside the river and before they got to the edge of town there was a bench and he sat his father down there and made tentative enquiries. These bore no fruit. Mr Bailey seemed to find the brown river water suddenly fascinating.

'What is it?' Zeb asked gently, looking into his father's face so that Mr Bailey turned his blushing cheeks the other way. Zeb waited, and just when he thought he should say something else, Mr Bailey spoke.

'Miss Emily is getting married to the poet.'

Even Zeb knew of this glamorous figure, and he was astonished. Miss Emily was old. Cuthbert Ironside was not. How extraordinary, and how the village would talk – a maiden lady, long past marriageable years, marrying a man so much younger. And a lady like Miss Emily, whom he had always regarded as a mouse, small and grey-haired and hardly daring to speak aloud.

'I don't understand how I didn't see it coming,' Mr Bailey said, warming slightly to his subject and throwing up his hands in the air. Zeb sensed his father had long wanted to talk about this, but couldn't, or perhaps had felt he shouldn't burden anyone. 'He's never away from the place and they are writing poetry together.'

Zeb was terribly inclined to smile over this, and had to guard his lips carefully. The images in his mind were very funny. He didn't understand poetry – at least not the kind that everyday people might make up.

'His first book comes out on Easter Sunday. There is to be a big party and they are to be married in the summer, while working on new poetry together.'

Mr Bailey was obviously very hurt. Zeb was surprised that his father liked Miss Emily so much. Was she anything like his mother had been? He didn't think so. It was a shame his father had not tried to approach her, but then perhaps he could not bear the indignity of being refused. Zeb was sorry for him, especially in the light of his own now happy life and so far reasonably successful marriage to a woman a lot older than he was. He could not now imagine his life without Alice.

'Isn't he a lot younger than she is?' Zeb enquired, just for something to say.

His father sighed.

'Yes. She is entranced by him.'

He hadn't thought they would get married, not at first. It had seemed to him a most unlikely scenario. Cuthbert Ironside, fifty, well off and intellectual, could have had any woman he wanted, at any age, but Mr Bailey could see why he liked Miss Emily. She was gentle but interesting; she was kind but also somewhat discerning. She read history and science and even played the piano. Mr Bailey thought bitterly that he had been the one to encourage her. He played and she had wanted to join in. They had even at one time played duets together, and she had enjoyed that, but this had fallen away once Cuthbert Ironside began to spend so much time with her. Mr Bailey would politely suggest to her they play something, and she would put him off with a smile and say they would do that later. He could no longer talk to her by himself. She was always busy; she always had an excuse. He felt so out of place and sad.

'He is moving into the house,' he told Zeb. 'There are plenty of bedrooms, of course. I wanted to ask her to marry me.'

Zeb was really concerned now. He had not seen his father like this before. 'Why didn't you?'

'She doesn't think of me like that. And look at me, I'm old—'

'You aren't old.'

'I'm a lot older than he is and I have nothing. I'm not – not glamorous.'

Zeb had to agree: his father was hardly glamorous. He couldn't imagine why any man would want to be such a thing, but obviously Miss Emily had fallen for it. He barely remembered her. He had the dim recollection that she was not very pretty and not particularly engaging, but everybody's taste was different. After all, Alice loved him.

'Why don't you come back and stay with us? Dan won't mind sharing the room.'

Mr Bailey shook his head. 'They would be most offended,

and besides, it would look obvious, like I was a small child in a playground having his toy confiscated.'

Zeb really did have to bite his lip at that, but his father meant him to smile so they smiled together.

Fifty-One

Alice didn't bleed. She now kept a careful account of such things, as never before. She noted the days and the weeks, and her monthly bleeding did not arrive. She tried not to think about it. She tried to concentrate on her shop and her husband and the little boy who came to see them every weekend. He was not an easy child and she found herself getting impatient with him. The men seemed to think she would instinctively know how to deal with him, but she had had no experience of small children and had not known how thoroughly they invaded your life. Sometimes she felt glad when he went back to Holywell Hall and left her in peace.

She could not put from her mind, however, that she might now have a child of her very own. It would be quite different. Even if it did take over her life, it would be different than housing someone else's child. She waited and waited for the pain and for the bleeding to start, but it didn't. She didn't say anything to anybody. She was too scared that it would prove to be nothing and she would have become excited in vain.

She was more tired than usual, and maybe that was why she found Frederick particularly troublesome. The last time she had been pregnant she had been tired, and it was hardly surprising. This time she found herself hugging to her a shawl or a cushion when she sat by the fire.

She tried not to make plans; she tried not to think whether it would be a girl or a boy. She tried not to hope that it would work, and she was terrified that the dreadful illness would come back to her if she did not carry the child full term. Dr McKenna had said that sometimes after birth women felt the same way. She was so worried with thought after thought that she began falling asleep in the evenings, sitting by the fire. The evenings used to be when she made her sweets and looked after the house and her husband. Now all that seemed gone, and she felt a gnawing apprehension.

It was exactly three months to the day when Alice felt the all-consuming pain that she had known before, and she wished that she had told Zeb about it as she crumpled to the floor. The whole situation took on a nightmarish quality. It was late afternoon and Zeb was not at home and Mrs Garnet had gone. She felt the blood slip down her legs when she was halfway up the stairs – how ridiculous and how unseemly – and she sank down and the blood flowed and she lost her second child when nobody was there.

She did not know when she passed out. She only knew that she awoke to find Zeb's face close to hers and how glad she was to see him. He picked her up in his arms and trod up the stairs with her, and when he put her down on the bed, which was so usual to her when she was ill, she broke down and cried.

'I should have told you.'

'Don't worry.'

'It might have been different if I had, but I didn't want you to be disappointed. I wanted to have a child for you and for me.'

'I know,' he said, and then he insisted on her lying down and he lay there with her.

He held her there and told her to go to sleep, and she did, because she knew that her body and mind had stood enough and could manage no more. Her last thought was that if women had to do these things, to handle horrifying things, they had to have a man there. If not, then what would they do?

Fifty-Two

'We could move somewhere better.'

Pat felt gratified when his wife looked at him for the first time in many days, in many weeks. He was trying not to know exactly how long it was. She didn't say anything, but she didn't turn away.

'I'm making more money. We could have a bigger house. We're so cramped here. We could find a house in the village with three or four bedrooms. We could go and look at somewhere to rent, somewhere pretty perhaps and – and we might have a maid. It would make all the difference.'

Shirley turned away. She didn't say anything, she just turned as though he had not spoken, but his mother had heard him and she said, 'Oh, it would be wonderful to have a bigger house, it really would. I don't remember the last time I slept, what with your father on his feet all the time.'

Pat said nothing. He had spent hours listening to his mother snoring while he waited for his father to come back from yet another perambulation around the house. He was terrified that his father would leave, even though he made sure to lock the doors so that his father could not get out of the house. Pat saw images in his head of his father falling down the quarry. He slept with the front- and backdoor keys under his pillow. Or, rather, he didn't sleep. But his mother snored hour after hour. He was surprised she didn't wake up everybody else.

The two little girls slept well, but then they had no worries. Shirley didn't sleep and she looked worse and worse. He thought this might sort it out, but he realized now how foolish he had been.

'For God's sake, Shirley, what am I supposed to do?'

'It's nothing to me what you do or say. I'm going nowhere. You can't turn me sweet like that and you should know it.'

'Giving the boy to Mrs March was the right thing to do.'

She glared at him with such venom that Pat moved back slightly. 'You took that child from my arms and gave him to that dreadful woman.'

'She is not a dreadful woman. She is his grandmother and she has a right to him in blood.'

'He is mine. You had no right to do such a thing. And who is she to take a child from my arms? Do you think he is happy?'

Pat knew very well that Frederick was unhappy except when he was at the sweet shop. 'You could see him, Daniel said so.'

'Oh, did he, and wasn't that nice of him?'

'Freddie spends his weekends in the village at the sweet shop.'

'Oh, so Alice Lee can have my boy but I can't.'

Pat didn't know what to say any more. He wished he

could ask Dan to give the child back, but he couldn't. It wouldn't be right, Dan being his father and Mrs March his grandmother.

Pat was desperate to win back Shirley and he had the feeling that if they moved to a bigger, better house it would make things different. His rise in wages went on and he knew it would always be as much so that he could afford to give his family more space. So he went to Dan and suggested it, and Dan, possibly out of guilt, accepted the idea. 'For you and Shirley, of course,' Dan said, and he was talking fast, as though he knew he should have thought of this himself and was ashamed. 'There's one in the village and it's got a garden for the little girls and it's quite big. Shirley would love it, wouldn't she?'

Pat could see the shame written in Dan's eyes, and so, it being the end of the day and with the men gone, he let Dan walk him down into the village and to the street that stood beyond and down from the quarry. There, not far beyond the chapel, was a street of well-built, three-storey houses in grey stone, tall with big windows. It was high in the village, up the steep street that led from the parish church, and likely to make people pant before they reached the top.

Dan had possibly even thought of this before he mentioned it, Pat thought, with a strange pleasure, as they went up the outside steps and into the house itself. The rooms were big, and although it was a dark, late spring day, there was still enough light to see. He couldn't have organized this so quickly if it had not occurred to him that it was the right thing to do.

There was a big back garden, which the children would love, shaded all around by mature trees. The two men went outside and saw that from a big tree somebody had hung a rope swing.

The garden was laid out to vegetables, which Shirley would enjoy. She grew what she could halfway up Crawleyside, but this was sheltered and far enough down that she would be able to grow so much more. She would love it. He couldn't wait to show it to her.

There were fruit trees, and even a lawn that Shirley could sit on when she had leisure to, because he would get help for her, it would make everything so much easier. She could sit outside in the early evening and the girls could play.

Dan and Pat went back in and up the stairs. There were two bedrooms on each floor, and they were big and wide. His mother and father could have one on the first floor, or even downstairs, because their health wasn't good and here they would manage better, he told himself almost with glee, and the rooms were so big. He and Shirley could have the bedroom that looked out across the valley, and the girls could choose a bedroom each. It was, Pat thought, heaven.

'We'll need new beds,' Pat said, and he thought he might even be able to buy his wife a pretty dress. She had never had such a thing. Even his mother might be pleased.

The house was near enough perfect, and in the kitchen was a new stove that would keep them all warm. He could see them sitting around the table, with more than enough to eat. He could see his family taken care of as he had always wanted them to be, and his heart ached just a little bit less for Shirley and how she was given to grieving about the boy.

He saw himself going and telling her about this house, and how much she would love it and how easy it would be by comparison when they had live-in help on the top floor and she could have a woman come in to do the washing and ironing and maybe even find some kind of nurse to look after his father. His mother wouldn't like any of it, she never did, but he would disregard her. Shirley would have all this.

'When can we move?' became Pat's mother's litany, and while Pat was away she went on and on at Shirley about them moving. It would be wonderful, why weren't they going, was Shirley refusing on purpose to upset her mother-in-law, had she not done enough by taking Pat from his mother?

'I didn't take him from you,' Shirley said at last, 'you're bloody well still here with us.' And she slammed outside to try to get away.

His mother followed her outside. 'This is spite,' she said. 'You know we'd be better off with a bigger house and some help. You never could manage. You don't want me there, or Pat's dad. You never wanted us.'

The two little girls came to Shirley in tears, and clung on at either hip.

'You don't deserve our Pat,' his mother said, and she went back inside.

It was Friday. Shirley had come to hate Fridays. She knew

that the little boy went on Friday night to spend his weekends in the sweet shop. She didn't think she could bear it any more.

She took the girls inside and gave them their tea and then she shouted through to her ma-in-law to watch them as she was going to the shops, she had forgotten something for Pat's dinner. She put on her shawl and left the house.

She could see Freddie in her mind, being taken there by Dan. Did he put the child on a horse? Did he walk? Did Mrs March lend him the pony and trap, or did a servant take him there, now that he was so important? She thought that was probably so. She had come to hate Daniel Wearmouth. She wished to God he had never come back. She wished he had stayed in Durham, or anywhere else – anywhere but here, where he could say what should and should not happen to her little boy.

Shirley increased her pace. She might see the trap go by, if she timed this well. Pat would be home soon, so Daniel might have gone up to Holywell Hall before now and be on the way back. She would see Freddie, even just at a distance. She was almost running when she got to the main road, which led down Crawleyside from the tops where the hall lay. She might just see them as they went by.

Dan had not thought that his mother-in-law would invite him into the house. Everything was peaceful.

'Frederick has rather taken to the nanny I've found – what a relief – and we have more help, which makes things easier, but I want to talk to you about it,' she said, encouraging him into the deserted drawing room.

She didn't give him chance to speak. As soon as he closed the door, she said earnestly, 'I feel very bad about this but I couldn't say anything. Frederick is your son, but I think Shirley should have him back. I think it's bad for him to be away from her. He is better than he was, but there is a look in his eyes which is not happy. I meant well but I think it was misjudged, misguided. Would you have anything against Shirley having him back?'

Dan was astonished and just a little upset. The arrangement as it was suited him. He could not think that Shirley would give up the child every weekend like this. Why should she? And even though Frederick was his, Shirley had nursed him and cared for him. She had been the parent when Arabella had died and he had run away like the coward he was.

Alice would no doubt be disappointed, but then in time, perhaps, the boy would come for the odd day or they would all get together. He had a vision of them all together on Sundays: Pat and Shirley and the two little girls; Alice and Zeb and perhaps a new baby; and himself with Frederick. It was an image that came to him every day now, and he treasured it. It was the last thing he thought of before going to sleep each night.

'Do you think I am stupid?' she enquired.

'No, no, I think you are probably right, but you were right also to try to give him the life you thought was better for him. Pat is talking about moving, and he and I looked at a house in Stanhope that would be suitable. Mrs Garnet has even found them a maid and that would make all the difference to Shirley. She would be so pleased to have the little boy back.'

'You would miss him?'

'I would still see him, and so would you, but it is right, I have realized that. I think it's very big-minded of you, Mrs March.'

'You do? Thank you, Daniel. I have been so worried about the boy, but I cannot undo what I did. Shirley was right.'

'You couldn't know that.'

'Well, in any case I didn't know it. Would you talk to Shirley and her husband? Would you ask them if this is all right with them? I couldn't go directly to her, not after what I did.'

Dan assured her that he would, and then he got into the pony cart with the little boy and the driver went forward and it was just like every weekend. He talked to Frederick and Frederick was happy. He loved the sweet shop, he loved Alice and Zeb and Dan. Perhaps they were all the same person to him.

Off they trotted across the hill, and then they turned into the road that led down Crawleyside Bank into Stanhope. Crawleyside was winding and steep, twisting in three tight bends, so the groom slowed the horse and talked to him. Frederick loved the horse and trap, and sat on Dan's knee and watched.

Shirley saw the pony cart and thought of the little boy she loved so much. She must catch him now; he must not go to the sweet shop. She ran past the end of the terrace and suddenly could see the pony cart. She ran into the road, screaming his name, and straight in front of the horse. Somebody shouted, the horse was drawn up short, rearing, and after that Shirley had the boy in her arms. She had him all to herself, as she had dreamed of all those awful nights since he had gone. She had him close in her arms and they would never be parted again.

Dan stared as the woman ran in front of the horse. The horse startled and let out a high-pitched whinny as it reared back, its legs flailing in the air, and somehow the whole thing became entangled and all Dan could remember afterwards was that the little boy screamed too and everything changed pace.

The groom tried desperately to bring the horse to a halt, but everything collided. The groom called out and Dan was horribly aware of Shirley under the cart, of the slap as the cart met her body. He held on tightly to the child, who was writhing to get away from what was happening, and the whole conveyance began to turn and slide down the hill, as it must on that bend.

Somehow the horse tore free and ran away into a field, but the cart slid and slid, turning over as it did so, Dan hanging on to his son as they were turned and bumped and ground.

The groom was flung away, and the trap went on and on, faster and faster, gathering speed as it reached the road which went one way into Stanhope and the other up to Eastgate, Westgate and St John's Chapel. They flew across and careered into the wall and there finally came to a stop. The cart was tipped so far onto its side that it was almost upside down, and he and the boy, sobbing now against him, were trapped.

Dan knew that he was bruised and bleeding; he had tried to hold the child close and away from it all, and his hands were bloody from the road. His legs hurt too, and his head, but he did not think he was seriously hurt and he hoped the child was nothing but distressed.

He could hear voices of men as they made their way out of the Grey Bull, no doubt, the first public building at the bottom of the road, perhaps with the first pint of the evening in their fists. He lay there upside down with the child in his arms and could not move anything. The men shouted at him: was he hurt, they would try to get him out. Workmen went away to get tools so that they could free him, and he was not to worry, he was just to sit tight.

As though he could do anything else, Dan thought grimly. The child was still holding on tightly to his jacket and pressing hard against his chest. Dan started to talk to Frederick in a low, reassuring voice. He talked about how the horse had got free and run across the fields, and how they would be away from here and to the sweet shop very soon now, and there was nothing for Frederick to cry about, now, was there?

It seemed a long time before they set to work, trying to turn the conveyance over to get the passengers out, but the wreckage stopped them. Dan knew that if he became more upset it would affect the little boy, who had begun to scream again.

Dan wanted to scream also. Over and over, he saw Shirley run out into the road, the horse rearing up and breaking free, the groom being flung from the cart. He closed his eyes and tried to calm the child. As far as he knew, Frederick was nothing beyond shocked, and he didn't think the child was hurt. But what about the groom and, most importantly, what about Shirley?

When Pat got home he found his two little girls crying and his mother saying that Shirley had gone to the shops to buy something for his dinner.

'Without so much as a word, she ran out of here as though she couldn't stop herself,' his mother said. 'Where on earth she thought she was going, I don't know. She's so unreliable. I've never understood her. When I think of all those girls you could have married, and you chose her.'

The shops were well closed by now and he knew it, and Shirley would have known it too, so where was she?

'I'll go and take a look,' he said. With his mother's protests following him out of the door – she should not have to mind the children and look after his father like this, she was not up to it – he left.

Shirley could not have been gone long. She was upset, he knew she was, and nothing he could do would alter it. He made his way along the terrace and onto the path, but he could see nothing, so he slowed down, wondering which way she had taken. One way went into Stanhope, down steep hills, and the other was a walk through fields. She would not have gone there. Her aim would be the village, presumably, though why it should be he had no idea.

He took the main road, thinking that even if she was far ahead of him he would come across her, and if not he would go into Stanhope and then up the hill in the middle of the town and he might come across her there. He could not put from him the thought that she had done something he had not thought of. But what? And why?

Then he rounded the bend and saw two figures: one in the grass beside the road and the other in the road. He couldn't see beyond them, or what had happened, but he recognized Shirley. He knew that grey, washed-out dress that she had worn seemingly forever.

He knew that she was dead when he reached her. There was not even a second of hope. People lay like that when the life had been knocked from them, in an ugly, twisted, ungainly way. Pat wanted to go back even a few seconds, so that he did not know what was happening, but that was no good either. He slid down onto the road. He didn't even say her name; he knew that there was no point, she could not hear him. And now she would never speak to him again.

He touched her face and gazed into her sightless eyes. She was bleeding all over the road, so that the red ran down and into Stanhope in some kind of accusing way, as though to wash from him the guilt which he could feel spreading all the way through him.

It was mostly her head that had taken the impact, he could see.

'Oh God, Shirley, what were you doing?' he muttered, and he thought of her running out to see the boy, which he knew could be her only reason for being here at this time of the day, and then he thought that she would go there, regardless of anything but how the boy looked to her, how he had been taken from her, how she loved him even better than her own children. How could that be? Yet it had been. A tiny boy she had been given to nurture, a child with no parent, taken in and loved in a different way than her own safe daughters who had sufficient love. And he had taken the child from her. He had made her miserable.

'Oh God, Shirley, I'm sorry.'

Then he heard groans from the grass at the side of the road and he remembered the other person, so obviously hurt, and he went over there and recognized the groom from Mrs March's. His family lived in the village and were so proud that he had got such a job. Pat went and got down beside him and asked him if he was all right. He knew it was the stupidest thing in the world to say, but he knew that he could bring no relief to Shirley, while just a few words, if the lad could hear, might aid this boy.

The lad spoke to him, so at least he was not dead. Although his voice quavered there was not nearly as much blood, though his leg lay under him and might be broken, Pat thought, and that might hurt like hell. He just wished that Shirley could be in similar pain, something that might be rescued. He couldn't think or feel or move.

As he kneeled there he heard shouting, and when he looked up he saw several men running up the road towards him. They stopped when they saw Shirley, and one came forward and saw him with the groom.

'Somebody's gone for the doctor,' he said.

Pat didn't know his name. It didn't matter. He couldn't remember the groom's name either, even though he tried hard.

Men clustered around Shirley. He wanted to shout at them not to move her, not to touch her – though what difference it would make now he could not tell. He talked to the lad, telling him that everything was going to be all right and Dr McKenna would soon be there, but the boy cried for his mother. Pat was aghast, thinking he had injuries nobody but a doctor could see and that he might die before Dr McKenna got there. Time crawled onwards like a wounded creature on bloody paws and nothing happened.

The evening set in cold. Even in his misery, Pat could feel the wet mist settle on the shoulders of his work jacket, thickening the quarry dust. Somebody put a jacket over Shirley's face and somehow that made things worse. It was so final. There was no going back now. Pat took off his own jacket and put it around the lad's body to keep him warm.

The boy's face was bloody where he had hit the ground, and his hands were skinned, though his thick gloves had ensured the damage there was minimal. They were now torn and bloody and his hat was half off. He was lying on his side as though it was more comfortable that way, though Pat wasn't sure whether he could move, and he didn't dare to touch him for fear of making him worse.

Pat thought that even a brave lad would have wept and

moaned further if his body was properly hurt, so he was hoping it would not be much. The boy shuddered and Pat hoped that was just shock, and he wished the doctor would hurry up.

In his mind, Pat saw the horse and cart coming this way, taking the little lad to the sweet shop for the weekend, and after that he tried to shut out what had happened. He couldn't bear to go over and over it, not yet. Later, he promised himself, if there was to be any later.

Maybe he was dead and not Shirley. If not, the woman he had loved so dearly was lost.

The men stood around, nobody saying anything. One or two kept coming to him and then going back down to Shirley, and it began to rain in earnest now, hard pellets that soaked through Pat's shirt and hit his skin like bullets, like God's bloody tears.

Somebody jimmied hell out of the bit of the cart that was caught, and after what seemed like a small eternity to Dan, he suddenly saw the evening sky. As soon as there was enough space, he gave the child through the gap into eager hands, and after a few minutes they managed to pull him too. He was hurt, but not badly so, and when the doctor arrived Dan said that he was worried, as there were two people badly hurt halfway up Crawleyside Bank.

Dr McKenna looked him and the boy over briefly. He said he would be at the sweet shop later but he didn't think there was any great harm done. Then, after being helped onto his horse because they were on an angle and the horse was big, he trotted around the corner and disappeared.

Pat heard the horse and had an idea that it was something to do with the accident. It was the doctor's horse, well known because it had a shiny black coat. Everybody knew the doctor's horse, Black Boy.

Dr McKenna went first to Shirley and was such a long time that Pat got off his knees – they ached so much, and he hadn't known it until now. He sat back on the soaked grass and watched the doctor. It seemed to him that Dr McKenna, having seen accidents and illnesses all his professional life, would get used to such, but it was obvious to Pat, watching him walk up to the boy, that he never would.

The doctor put a hand on Pat's shoulder and waited until Pat looked up at him. 'I'm sorry, Pat, Shirley's dead.'

'Aye, I know.' Pat couldn't look at the doctor and was afraid that his throat would close. He had to distract himself.

'Is the little lad going to be all right?'

Dr McKenna nodded.

'And Daniel?'

'He's bruised and battered, but he'll recover.'

'This one's hurt.'

'It was good of you to sit with him,' the doctor said, always conversational, and then he put his bag down on the grass beside Pat and he talked to the lad. Jim. The doctor remembered everybody's name and now Pat remembered too. Jim Pennyworth. Pat had always thought what a lovely name it was, as though the lad was always worth something and that at some time the family had been named because they had money.

A horse and cart came up the bank, and after the lad was bandaged as best the doctor could, and after gentle hands had lifted Shirley's body onto the cart, they set off. Pat followed them down the hill and into the main street and along past the sweet shop.

Beyond that was the doctor's house, and the cart turned in at the drive. Pat insisted on carrying Shirley's body, and Jim was aided by more hands than he needed. When they got inside, Dan and the boy were there. The child was sobbing, but quietly, as though he was about to fall asleep in his father's arms. Dan was bleeding, but his eyes told Pat that he was not badly hurt.

'Shirley?' he asked.

'She's dead.'

Dan's eyes widened. 'No,' he said, shaking his head like a horse with flies around it. 'No, she can't be.'

'Did she run into the road in front of the horse?' Pat questioned him.

Dan hesitated. 'Yes, and Jim didn't see her, I didn't see her, but we should have done. We should have known she wanted the lad and – and—' There he stopped. 'Mrs March wanted Shirley to have him back.'

Neither of them spoke for a very long time and Pat thought Daniel was in shock or he would never have said such a thing because it could do no good now.

'She's been . . .' Pat couldn't tell Dan what Shirley had

been, and it didn't matter anyway. They all knew his wife's grief over the little boy.

And thinking back now, Pat could barely manage to acknowledge that things had been on the verge of getting better, and Dan had been instrumental in it. How could it all go so badly wrong just before things got better, as though they didn't deserve good things? It was like the story of the farmer who had had a barn raising. It was the most beautiful barn in the whole world, and when it was finished, the farmers and the neighbours who had helped stood back to admire their work, and a storm broke out. There was thunder and lightning and that night the barn burned down.

It made Pat want to weep to think how nearly he and his Shirley had come to great happiness, and it made the loss all the more bitter.

Fifty-Three

Zeb hadn't wanted any interruptions. His wife had lost their child the evening before and they had done little today. Mrs Garnet had been there earlier, and was so in their confidence that he told her. She had offered to run for the doctor, but he told her that there was no need.

'Isn't that what you thought the first time?' Mrs Garnet said, in a voice that wobbled like jelly. He knew that she was upset for them. All he said was, 'Go up to her.'

So Mrs Garnet went upstairs, but he didn't go to work. He couldn't go and leave Alice that day. Dan had tactfully gone off to stay at the Grey Bull. It was better all round, just for this one night, and Zeb was glad to close the door after him.

Neither of them had slept, and so in the early evening when Mrs Garnet went home, having cleaned the house and the shop and made a meal that nobody might eat, they lay on the bed and tried not to think about what they might have had. It was so hard for both of them.

'I think I'm just too old,' Alice said, and while he disclaimed this, he thought she was probably right.

He didn't mind if she didn't, but the trouble was that she did mind. He thought of what it had been like the first time, and tried to comfort himself that there was no bloody scrap of a baby, nothing but what had been discharged before it looked like a child. He was glad of that. It was surprising how grateful you became for every tiny thing.

Not having cared about children before, he now found that he cared very much. He had wanted to give Alice everything she desired, and he knew that she wanted children.

They might have to grow used to the idea that they would never have a child, that they had met too late. And then he thought back to what their lives had been. She had been unloved and lonely and he had been – God, what had he been? Nothing, less than nothing, slime on less than nothing and she had rescued him. He would not have been alive now but for her, and that made it worse somehow, that he owed her hugely for what she had done and they could not even make a child together, no matter how badly she wanted it.

He wished there was something he could do.

And then when it was very late some bastard started banging like hell on the bloody back door. Nobody did that. It was rude and unseemly and unnecessary, and it was bound to be a friend because nobody but a friend came to the back door. Then he remembered that it was Friday and Dan was bringing the little boy for the weekend. But not late like this. He should have been there hours before this.

Zeb crept downstairs and wondered whether he should guard the door, and then he thought how stupid that was and so he shot back the bolts and turned the key and even in the dim light he could tell it was Dan. He would want to be there that weekend with his child, because he knew that it mattered so much to Alice. He was most welcome. The boy would distract Alice; he always helped her.

Dan looked dreadful, Zeb thought, as he stepped into the light. Zeb had seen Dan look bad before, but not like this. His face was all cut and his arm was bandaged, but he held the little boy close to him, clutching him tightly.

'Daniel?'

'Oh God,' Dan said, the child waking and beginning to sob in his arms. Zeb took the boy and let his friend into the by now decidedly chilly kitchen.

The little boy cried and cried, and it was as though a tap had been turned and would not go off. Zeb did not like to question Dan, who walked around the kitchen as though he couldn't remember where he was going. And then the words came out all in a rush as Zeb rocked the boy back and forward, his cries eventually lessening.

'There's been an accident. Shirley's dead. She ran out into the road in front of the pony cart and now . . . and now . . .'

'Easy. Easy now,' Zeb said softly, barely able to hear what Dan was saying, his voice was so constricted. He looked as though he was going to pass out.

The boy clung tighter.

'She ran into the road to see the boy and went under the horse and cart. She's dead.'

Alice came to the foot of the stairs; she had come down so softly that Zeb had not heard her.

'There's been an accident?' she said, and then the boy

heard her voice and held out both arms. She took him and he wept into her shoulder.

The child was sobbing, snot running into his mouth. Dan was dishevelled, and that said a lot about Dan, because he was always so immaculate. At the quarry he was now known as the Gentleman. Tonight, his face was pale and lined and his eyes were lit with an unholy light. They stood there for a long time until Zeb became aware of practicalities and lit the already laid fire and filled the kettle. They waited for it to boil, trying to understand what had happened.

Jim was not that badly hurt, and Dr McKenna was able to send him home with cuts and bruises. He was minus bits of skin on his face and hands, but since he had been wearing thick clothes against the wet weather, and hat, scarf and gloves, his raiment had taken the impact, so Dr McKenna had said. Pat was there when Mrs Pennyworth came for her son. She looked accusingly at him, as though this had been his fault, and Pat felt keenly that it was. He found it difficult to look back at her with any politeness.

Dr McKenna told her that her lad was fine and would be fit in a few days. He had landed on the grass and not on his head, he said cheerfully. She said she could not imagine what on earth had been going on, but Dr McKenna assured her that accidents happened all the time and that Jim was a lucky and plucky lad. He was shocked and she should make him rest and have a few days off work, but the doctor was sure that Mrs March would want it so.

The doctor's housekeeper plied Pat with tea, but he kept spilling the hot liquid on his hands. When Jim and his mother had gone, the doctor took Pat through to see Shirley, and there she was, lying on the doctor's couch. The doctor said how sorry he was, and asked if Pat wanted a little time with her.

'Are you sure she's dead?' Pat said, as though there might be even a slight possibility that Shirley would wake up and say that everything was all right and how wonderful it was that they would have a new house, and she knew the little boy would be fine with Daniel and Zeb and Alice, and she would go back to the house with him and his parents and her girls and everything would be all right. Slowly the realization took hold that nothing would ever be all right again.

'If it hadn't been for me . . .' he began, and the doctor sighed and sat him down on a big chair beside where Shirley was lying.

'Oh Pat, don't take on so much. There isn't enough guilt in all the world for what happens to people, and nobody can help things sometimes. We go crashing about doing our best and making such a mess of everything.'

'She grieved over the lad.'

'Aye, she would do. Why don't I take you home?'

'Shirley?'

'Shirley will be fine here. I will sort things out.' He ushered Pat from the room where Pat felt as though his life had ended, and the doctor's own groom had made ready the horse and trap, and Pat got into it and they made their way through the village and up Crawleyside Bank. There the doctor put him down at the end of the terrace where he lived.

Pat felt old, so very old – older even than his parents. They had not had to confront this. They'd had to confront things just as hard: trying to get out of Ireland; crossing the sea to here instead of starving; his father taking on work that was beneath him. His father had been learned and respected, but he had to take on labouring work just so that they could eat, and Tow Law was a rough town then, with fighting in the streets at night and women screaming over the road at one another, children crying in unmade back lanes and netties stinking with shit when they were not emptied. He remembered lying in his bed and huddling beneath the covers for fear somebody should come and get him, but they never had.

He was no worse off than anybody else, but his wife was dead and he had to face his children and parents and try to go on without her. He couldn't imagine it. He would rather have had her there, silent and against him as she had been for so long.

He made his way in quietly, hoping that they were sleeping, but no such luck. His mother appeared like a shrivelled shadow.

'What on earth is going on?' she said. 'Why have you been so long? Your father wandered outside twice because I didn't like to lock the door. I kept thinking you and Shirley would be back any minute. The girls cried for so long when they went to bed. What a day.'

He looked at her thin, lined face and how it dropped; and her grey and white hair and how she kept it clipped up so that no one should see how sparse it was. He could see the pink of her scabby scalp beneath it. Her eyes were watery so that nobody could see the colour, and she looked beyond him with that awful look on her face that she had always given Shirley, as though Shirley had no right to her boy. Well, it looked as though her wishes had come true.

He tried to do it softly.

'There was an accident,' he said. 'Shirley was hurt.'

His mother didn't comprehend, or perhaps didn't choose to. 'What was she doing?' she enquired, with a sharp nip in her voice. 'What on earth did she think she was doing, running off like that and leaving me with everything to do? I always wished you hadn't married her. There were a dozen and more lovely girls who would have had you, but no, you had to settle for somebody like her. So where on earth is she?' His mother looked around him for evidence of the runaway.

'There was an accident. Shirley was hurt,' was all he could say, and he heard his mother take in her breath and then let it go.

'An accident? What happened? Whatever was she thinking?'

'She heard the pony cart when Daniel Wearmouth was taking his son to the sweet shop for the weekend.'

'She couldn't have heard it from here,' his mother objected. 'She couldn't possibly have heard it from here. I didn't hear it, the children didn't. She shouldn't have run out like that. I did tell her not to. I did try to stop her. Is she badly hurt? Is she with the doctor? Will she have to stay there? How will I manage all alone with everything to do? And for how long?' His mother paused there, putting up both skinny mottled hands to her face as though she could keep out the grief of Shirley's stupidity. 'She ran out. I couldn't stop her.'

'You weren't to blame,' Pat said, as the doctor would have done. There was no point in his mother worrying about such things.

'No. No, I wasn't. I looked after everything. I saw to the children and to your father. When is she coming home?'

'She isn't coming home,' he said, as gently as he could. 'She died.'

His mother began to wail, so he took her to bed and watched her cry herself stupid until she breathed easily and slept.

The little girls were restless but not quite awake. He lay down with one at either side of him, and kept still until they snuggled in against him. He would tell them in the morning. He would say that their mother was in heaven. What else could he possibly say?

Fifty-Four

The publication party for Cuthbert Ironside's book was cancelled. Mr Bailey was relieved. He felt awful that such a thing had happened to the village, and yet it meant that he did not have to attend this event that he had been dreading. When Mr Vernon announced, the day after Shirley's death, that the publication party must be postponed, perhaps until the summer, Mr Bailey could tell that Cuthbert Ironside was upset.

'Nobody would come,' Mr Vernon said gently, 'and it would be disrespectful in the circumstances. This is a very small community. We ought to leave it until much later. For many of us, this Easter will not be a time of joy.'

'I didn't know the woman,' Cuthbert said shortly, and Mr Bailey could see what a huge disappointment it was for him, and that he had no sense of community here because he had been away for years. Also, he had been enjoying his celebrity and in some ways Shirley had taken the shine off it. She had usurped his place as the object of interest. Mr Bailey tried not to judge the man and failed.

'And what about the wedding? Am I supposed to have that taken from me too?'

Mr Bailey was surprised and rather amused that Cuthbert cared so much about his marriage. Usually it was women who attached such importance to these things.

They were in the sitting room at the Vernon household, all five of them in a circle before the fire. It was a horrible night. Everybody thought that Easter would be fine, and it never was, Mr Bailey thought.

And yet he loved this time best. Perhaps Christmas should have been dearer to him, but since he had come home to the dale and lovely Alice Lee and his now married son, he was prepared to enjoy Easter Sunday and the risen Christ as he had when Zeb was a little boy, when he had been truly happy, as perhaps only the young in their inexperience are.

The coming marriage of Miss Emily and Cuthbert Ironside had ruined all hope of such things for Mr Bailey. He had known that he would be obliged to sit through the publication evening and attend the wedding of the lovely lady he cared for so much, as she married a man he tried not to hate but disliked with fervour and anger.

Mr Vernon turned to his sister.

'That must be up to Emily, ' he said.

Mr Bailey was not usually a good reader of minds, but he could see that Emily was struggling with the respect that she ought to show at such a time and the way that she really wanted to marry this man.

To her, he was young and rich and attractive. He had been right, he thought, when he had told Zeb that Emily was entranced. She looked at Cuthbert as though he was the best Easter present, the biggest prize. If she let go of him she might not have another chance. He might change his mind, go for a woman who was more easily won. Mr Bailey could not let that happen.

Selfish as he knew he was, when the silence went on and on, he ventured to say, and it was one of the hardest things he had ever done, 'If the wedding were private and the vicar would agree, and if it were just you and Mr Ironside's parents and you came back here and made no fuss, surely you could not be faulted for lack of feeling?'

Mr Bailey wasn't given to calling himself names, but in the moments that followed he knew himself for blockhead, clown, idiot, and knew that he had condemned himself not just to a solitary life, such as he had had before he had fallen in love with her, but a bleak future. His wife was dead and Miss Emily was not to be his.

Although he knew Cuthbert Ironside to be self-absorbed, selfish and boring, he did seem to care for her. Mr Bailey could see it by the look in his eyes. There was no way in which he, John Bailey, would cause Miss Emily to lose the love of her life, the one man she thought would make her happy.

Cuthbert looked gratefully at him and tears filled Miss Emily's eyes and Mr Bailey said, 'If you like, I could have a soft word with the vicar and you could go ahead. It would take just a short time for the wedding and then back here for a meal and then whatever the newlyweds wanted. The church is already booked, so why not?'

'Oh Mr Bailey, how very kind of you,' Miss Vernon said.

'Not at all.' Mr Bailey looked straight at her brother, and he saw that Mr Vernon thought he was right.

The two sisters rushed out as though tea at that point was imperative, and Cuthbert Ironside came across and took Mr Bailey's hand in both of his and thanked him so profusely that Mr Bailey tried not to dislike him any more. He failed in this, but he had tried.

It was at that point that Mr Bailey decided he would ask Zeb and Alice if he could move back in. He would sleep on the couch in the back room if he had to. He could no longer stay in the Vernon household where his heart was breaking and he wanted to break heads because of it.

Fifty-Five

When Daniel Wearmouth presented himself in Holyhead Hall on the Saturday morning, he did not know if what he was doing was right, but somebody had to do it. It was quite early. He had been, unsurprisingly, unable to sleep after what had happened. He was not feeling very well. He didn't so much mind the cuts and bruises, or the aching of his body – he knew that he was lucky to be alive – it was the shaking of his hands that bothered him most of all, and the way that his mind played over and over the images of what had happened.

He hadn't wanted to come, and was half hoping that somebody had already relayed the news to Mrs March, but it had to be officially told so here he was, standing in her drawing room, hoping that he did not have to first explain to Sawrey March, or his weird sister, the news of the accident. And so he felt relief when she came in alone, and dreaded that she so clearly didn't know what had happened. But, like many older people, she had been through a great deal by now and read his face immediately.

'Daniel,' was all she said, and then of course her thoughts went to the child. 'Is Frederick ill?'

At least he could say something positive on that score. 'No, no,' he said, 'not ill. No.' The boy was silent, shocked from the accident. It had been a long time since he had seen Shirley, and it was possible he would not take on the gravity of the event, the horror of it all.

Dan faltered. He had rehearsed his words several times on the way here, and now he couldn't think how to put it. No matter what he said, the blow could not fall softly.

'I wasn't sure whether you might already know. There was an accident on Crawleyside Bank last night after I picked up Frederick.' He waited for her to say yes, she had heard, but it was obvious by her face that she did not. 'Pat's wife, Shirley, ran out in front of the pony cart.'

Mrs March sat down abruptly on the nearest chair, which was a large sofa. 'What happened?'

He explained as briefly as he could, and if her face could have paled any further, which he doubted, it would have. She seemed all of a sudden to be much older, as though her body sagged in recognition of disaster. He assured her that Frederick was fine and he told her that Shirley had died.

He knew that she had met death before, but he did not think she had come close to the kind of death which you felt responsible for, even if indirectly. The guilt suffused her face, narrowed her lips and glazed her eyes. It was a long time before she spoke, and if Daniel could have thought of anything healing to say he would have said it.

'I wanted her to have him back,' she said faintly, after a small eon.

'Yes, I know.'

'Where he is now?'

And although she knew exactly where he was, she needed further reassurance that her grandchild, her only claim to the future, really was still with her.

'Zeb and Alice are looking after him. He was dazed and upset, but he slept.' Unlike everybody else, he thought. Daniel didn't think he had ever been as tired in his life. Really, God was most unfair, expecting people to make their way through life like they were drowning in thick treacle.

'You were giving them a new house,' she said. 'We talked about it? Did we talk about it? You were.'

'I showed Pat the house and he was going to tell Shirley.' Dan didn't say that Shirley had given up on her marriage and would have seen Pat in hell before following him to even a palace. The hardest hit in this was Pat. He would blame himself for it, but didn't they all?

Dan was playing over and over to himself all the awful things he had done. It was becoming such a dreary repetition, starting always with Arabella's death, his own incompetence and how he had run away. At least this time he had not run. He had wanted to. He had had to stop himself from gathering Frederick close in his arms and running away. He thought he might run to where Mary had gone, she had always been so kind to him, or followed Cate and left it all behind. God was testing him truly this time. He knew he must not run, he must stay here and take the responsibility and try to live with the awful person that he was.

He and Mrs March between them had taken the child from Shirley, and it had killed her. Frederick should never have been taken away, and they had all reaped the horror of what they had done.

Fifty-Six

Pat alone followed his wife's coffin down the aisle and into the church. He had asked nobody to go with him. The children had cried for days. His father didn't know what was going on and didn't even ask for Shirley, and his mother went about tight-lipped. In some awful ways, it was very much as it had been for months.

He could not believe that Shirley's body lay in the coffin, but he had been without her now for several nights. He had not spent a night alone since they had been married, and was reluctant even to go into the room, it had become so huge and so empty. It was like Shirley had disappeared into him and broken his heart. He felt so heavily weighed down with guilt that he could not think of anything else. He knew that he would have to deal with this for the rest of his life.

He was aware of Zeb, Dan and Alice sitting just behind him with the little boy, and he was grateful for the show of solidarity, but he couldn't speak. He just sat there and let the service wash over him. He had been born a Catholic but there were no Catholic churches here. He had not thought about it for so long. How much he wanted to go to a Catholic church now and be forgiven the sins that sat on him so hugely.

He was also aware of Mrs March, her husband and his sister sitting at the other side of the aisle. He wondered how Nell March felt, and how much she thought the responsibility for this was hers. Dan must feel the same.

Pat didn't even want to see the boy; he could not stand any more. All the way through the service he listened in case the child cried, but there was no noise from behind him except Alice stumbling through the service, obviously upset. Pat wished she had been sitting with him. She had caused Shirley to have the child, to love the child, and the child lived because of her. He did hope Alice didn't remember this and feel bad about it, but so many people felt guilty and responsible. The two men seemed silent. He could hear no song, no hymn, no prayer.

Pat, following the coffin, had wanted to be aware of nobody but his dead wife, but the trouble was that he took in the people in their pews and by the time he got to the front he could have named everyone who was there. He was grateful to them all.

The workmen who had helped at the accident were sitting further back, and Jim Pennyworth, limping and with his arm in a sling, was with both his parents. All the quarrymen and most of their wives were also present, and Dr McKenna and a lot of people who went to Alice's shop were there too, so the church was full.

Susan Wilson came in at the last minute, just before the coffin set off, and slid into the pew next to Dan. He smiled apologetically at her and was rewarded with the ghost of an almost smile. The shopkeepers had come, which meant everything must be closed, Pat thought, and all for Shirley's sake. He was glad of that. Even Mr Calland, the solicitor, and his wife were there. The farmers and their families came also. Many of them had not known Shirley, but they had all heard about the accident, and even if it was just blatant curiosity, it was mixed with sadness and a feeling that it was the kind of thing that could have happened to any of them. They were showing their solidarity, and why not?

Pat could tell how awful Nell March felt by the way that she didn't look up. He could see the top of her elegant black hat, and he thought the poor woman must feel she would be in mourning for the rest of her life. She looked as though she would have given a great deal not to be there.

Pat could not remember ever having seen Augusta March before today. It was said that she was mad and went nowhere, but she seemed perfectly normal to him and wore black like everyone else. The only evidence that she was different was that she stood between her brother and his wife, as though she needed their support. He thought it was brave of all of them to be there.

Zeb had volunteered Mrs Garnet to see to Pat's mother and father, and Mrs March had sent her maid along with the nanny who had not yet been dismissed. Pat felt the irony of it. Now that Shirley was dead he had three women to see to his household, whereas Shirley had been a shadow from the effort of how much there was to do. He wished he had done something to aid her sooner, since he had been making more money. Guilt, guilt, guilt. Would he ever feel anything else? Would he ever stop this self-loathing?

The burial was even worse than the service. Pat could not believe that his young wife was in the ground, buried, never to be seen again. How would she breathe? How would he breathe without her? How would he live? How would anything ever go forward from here? He wanted to go back and have things happen again, and better. He wanted the new house for Shirley, and help, and to have Dan and Zeb and Alice there with them in the garden for an outside meal on a lovely summer's day, sharing the boy between them, coming together such as they never had and now never would.

There was a tea afterwards in the church hall. Pat was stunned. His wife was now underground and it was as though everything was normal. He stood just inside the door, not knowing what to do. Did you learn what to do when your wife died? Was there some kind of etiquette, if that was the term, for such things? How would anybody learn it? Who would want to? Who could bear it?

People had brought flowers – daffodils, narcissi and crocuses. The flowers were all white and yellow. How could Shirley die when everything else was being born?

People kept coming up to him and holding his hands until he badly wanted to put them in his pockets or behind his back, but it would have looked so awful, and this was all about looks, he could tell.

There was the clatter of crockery as women did as women do on such occasions, and boiled kettles and made tea and handed round cups and saucers, fussing gently and joshing one another and even attempting humour. He thought how kind it was of them. Was there ever such a ceremony as tea drinking? How many hearts were warmed by the very doing of it?

There was a big table of food, though he felt he would never eat again. The noise grew as the church hall filled, and he shook and shivered and wished he could be somewhere else, somebody else, away from here and know none of it any more. He wanted to be up Crawleyside Bank and have his Shirley there with him, without the little boy who had caused all this grief. That was sad and bad, he knew. A little boy.

He must have spoken to everyone. He saw how he smiled politely at them and heard himself thank them and say they were good to be there.

Easter would never hold joy for him again, he knew it now. How many people lost those they loved during festivals of joy? Though when was a good time to lose a loved one? Was it best in spring, when everything awoke and renewed? Was it good in summer, when the cattle stood under the trees, knee deep in grass, and buttercups swayed in the meadows. Was it better when the orange leaves fell from the trees and everything died? Yes, perhaps in autumn you could bear it. Everything else was dying and yet it would be renewed so that was no good either. And in winter, when the fields were white and the sheep huddled by the hedges and the pheasant croaked so loudly in the afternoons, who could bear it then?

His Shirley was gone. He would never see her, speak to

her or hold her again, and it had been because of what he had done and not done, and he would never forgive himself.

Nell badly wanted to get away without speaking to anyone, but she did not want to cause offence. Pat did not talk to her or even look at her, and she had no idea what to say to him. She hated the way he had walked into the church on his own, but she dared not go anywhere near him. He had lost his wife because she had wanted the child.

The only thing she was pleased about that day was that Sawrey and Augusta had gone with her. She had never imagined Augusta going to anything. The doctor was coming from Newcastle every week to see her, and she was making rapid progress.

She now came downstairs every day and sometimes even ventured outside, but for her to come to a funeral . . . Nell had not expected it, and when Sawrey told her that both he and his sister would go with her, it had done nothing but make Nell cry. She found Augusta a black dress from her ready supply. Nell was beginning to think that she would wear black for the rest of her life. Right up to the moment when they left, Nell driving a new trap and with a different horse (they had caught the other and it was going to be well, but it shivered and no doubt remembered), she expected to go alone. But as she left the house, they followed her, and she was glad of them there.

*

The little boy had slept all the way through the service. Alice was glad of that. Mrs Garnet had offered to take him while they were there, and Alice knew that people did not approve of children at funerals, but she thought that perhaps they should make an exception in this case. Mrs Garnet had gone off to help Pat's family, so in the end she had had to take him with her. She willed him not to cry, and thankfully he didn't.

He was exhausted by everything that had happened to him, she thought, and must be thoroughly confused. She had had him in her house ever since the day of Shirley's death. She didn't know whether to be glad he was there, or sorry that Shirley had died before a decision was made, a decision that Alice knew now would have meant the little boy going back to Shirley and his real home.

Dan seemed to expect her to have the child with her, and since Mrs Garnet was there all day it should have been no problem, but the fact was that she spent all her days in her shop now and Mrs Garnet had gone to Pat's house. The child needed to be with Shirley in his own home, not with her and not with his grandmother. The only mother he had known had died, and they had all played a part in it.

She wanted to be back in her sweet shop, not here with a child that wasn't hers. She had so badly wanted her own child, and whilst she knew that Frederick had helped her get well, it didn't feel right. After the funeral, she would have to make the men understand that she would not take this child for hers, that they would have to make other arrangements, but for today she smiled and was polite and helped as much as she could because of what Pat had been through and would go through.

When they came out of the church hall, neither of them said anything, but Dan was aware of Susan having put her hand through his arm, as though she needed comfort or needed to give it. It felt strange to him, but then everything felt strange.

'I'm so sorry for what happened, Daniel,' she said.

'I'm sorry too,' he said, and he didn't think that either of them was thinking about Shirley necessarily. 'Will you come back to the sweet shop with us?'

'No, I don't think so, but it was nice to be asked.'

She stopped there because the solicitor's office was just across the street.

'I have been asking Mr Calland about the fact that our marriage hasn't – hasn't worked out. I think we would both agree on that. I asked him whether it would be possible that we could be free, but it is a very complicated process. I don't feel married to you and I'm sure you don't feel married to me. If you ever find somebody new you must let me know and we shall do what we can.'

Dan was grateful that she should even talk about something that he had got so wrong, not just once but twice. For some reason it made him smile.

'It's funny?' she said.

'No, I was just remembering. I don't think I shall want to get married again, I'm so very bad at it.'

That made her smile.

'I did love you very much,' she said.

'I know you did and I loved you.' And he leaned forward and kissed her cheek, and then he watched her walk across the road. She looked so elegant, but better than that she looked confident, and there was something of contentment about her gait.

Marry again? Would he crash into other women's lives and cause mayhem? He didn't think so. He was just glad to have some place to go where he had people who cared about him. He didn't think Susan had that. Or had she just rejected it?

He went back to the sweet shop, where Alice had already put the kettle on. They would comfortingly drink tea for the umpteenth time that day. Thank God for it.

There wasn't much to say. The little boy went to sleep in his arms by the fire, and Zeb and Alice sat close and talked, as only couples do talk, he thought in small envy, of who had been there, of who hadn't, of how people had looked and how Pat would manage now. Zeb said that later he would get Pat to go to the Grey Bull. He would have little peace at home with his father so ill and his mother so bitter and two little motherless girls.

'A couple of pints might help,' Zeb said, and he turned to Dan and he said, 'You must come too.'

'That's not fair,' Dan said.

Zeb stared at him.

Dan nodded at Alice. 'There's no reason why Alice should stay here with the child.'

Zeb looked at her. 'Do you want to come to the pub, Alice?'

She pretended to smack him on the arm, and he put his arms around her in affection.

'No, but I don't want to be dumped with the little boy either. He's not mine.'

It was brave, Dan thought, and she was right. He was not her child. Perhaps she was facing the fact that she would have no child. She had her husband and her shop.

'You're right,' Zeb said. 'I'm sorry. Why don't we ask Pat if he wants to come to tea and bring the little girls?'

'We need to help him to find somebody to look after them,' Alice said.

And, Dan thought, he needed somebody to see to his boy, and he needed a new house and to build a new life for the two of them. In time, the boy would inherit the quarry or whatever was working for them at the time. He thought of what it would be like to take his son to work as his father had taken him.

Fifty-Seven

Miss Emily and Cuthbert Ironside were to be married on the Saturday after Easter. It had been booked at the church for some time, and when Mr Bailey spoke to the vicar and told him how small it would be, without fuss, and that both participants wished it, the vicar had been lovely and said that of course he would perform the ceremony.

The vicar was having a very busy Easter week, Mr Bailey thought.

So, relieved of his responsibilities and saying haltingly that he would like to go and stay at the sweet shop for just a few days, Mr Bailey found himself welcomed by all there. Daniel assured him that Frederick slept through the night, and there was enough room since the boy slept on a small bed they had found for him. When Mr Bailey said that he snored, Daniel said he really didn't care.

After Shirley's funeral, all Mr Bailey wanted was to go back to the sweet shop and pretend that nothing had happened. He was so tired.

On Easter morning they went to chapel. The place was full, as Mr Bailey had imagined the church would be, and nobody was in a good mood, but they had to sing hymns and it made him feel better. They returned to the sweet shop and there were good smells from the joint of lamb with rosemary that Alice had earlier put into the oven.

Dan had invited Susan to dinner and nobody minded. They sat down to lamb glazed with honey. They didn't say much; they were just glad to be alive. They thought of Pat and what his Easter Day might be like. At least he had women there to help it along.

Alice took herself to bed after they had eaten, telling them they had to wash up. The little boy was lively, so they coped as best they could, but night fell early and none of them was sorry to see it. They sat by the fire and didn't talk much, but they drank rather a lot of whisky. When Alice came down at teatime they gave her cake and she had whisky too, just a little in her tea, and later rather more in a glass.

It snowed. Why would it not? Everything else had gone wrong and so it snowed and snowed and bloody snowed. It was quite usual there at this time of year. Lambing storms, the farmers called it. The lambs were born and dried off and then down it came, and they would spend days trying to dig the poor sheep and their offspring from the snow, which fell not just in the hills but even by the river on the lowest farms.

They were soon up to their knees in the stuff. Was God trying to distract them from bigger problems? They had to shovel their way out, and Mr Bailey was hardly surprised when three days later Miss Vernon, Florence, came to him in the street where he was shovelling.

'Mr Bailey, I don't like to ask you, but we would like you to come to the wedding.'

Mr Bailey could have thought of a great many things he would rather do, but she carried on speaking before he had the chance to say anything.

'Mr Ironside's parents are snowed up in Wolsingham.'

He wanted to ask how the hell he was supposed to be at the wedding where the woman he loved was to be married to another man.

Miss Vernon was so earnest. She said that there would be but her brother and herself, and she would be so glad if he could be there. He could think of no reason why he should not be, and so he agreed that he would.

As he thought over it later, he called himself a lot of names. He was beginning to think he was the stupidest person on earth. Why would he go and watch them being married when he didn't want to? They could not expect it, and in an awful way Shirley's death was the perfect excuse. Just as he was about to swear out loud, Zeb came in.

Mr Bailey had gone upstairs; it was all the refuge any of them had. Now that four of them and the boy were living together, there was not a lot of privacy or opportunity to think. Indeed, he thought that Alice was given to not saying a great deal while feeling a lot, and tired of them quickly. He didn't blame her.

Zeb pushed open the bedroom door. 'Can I help?'

Mr Bailey shook his head. 'Miss Vernon wants me to go to the wedding.'

Zeb was vociferous in his disclaiming of this. 'Why should you go?'

And then Mr Bailey, loving his son for his concern, explained that nobody would be there and it was not right. 'I must go,' he said.

So the following day, at the appointed time in the late morning, Mr Bailey set off for the church, and with him were his son and his son's wife and his son's friend and Frederick Almond, who was heir to the quarry and demanded to be down so that he could walk with everybody else.

They let him down and he took hold of his father by the hand. They walked up the street the short distance to the church to celebrate Miss Emily marrying Mr Cuthbert Ironside, and if they wished that things had been otherwise, at least they had sufficient sense not to say anything.

No bells rang. The streets were white and empty, but the snow had receded to the sides of the houses and the edges of the fields and the backs of gardens. Mr Bailey kept thinking of how it would not take long and then he could go back and sit by the fire and try not to think of how things might have been. There was no point in it. What might have been was only for dreamers.

Miss Emily wore a blue dress. Mr Bailey could not remember having seen such a beautiful bride before now. Alice put her hand through his arm in comfort. Earlier she had shouted at Zeb about going to the wedding. Mr Bailey could not remember such a thing happening before. His daughter-in-law was such a wonderful, perfect woman, so he had been shocked and just a little pleased to hear her downstairs telling Zeb that she was damned well not going and she was sick and tired and fed up of other people.

Mr Bailey had heard the door slam and then the silence between the two men. He had gone downstairs and past them, and had followed her outside into the small space which did as yard and garden. She was crying. He took her into his arms as he had never done before and she wept into his shoulder.

'Why did Shirley have to die?' she sobbed.

'Maybe God loves her.'

'He can't have needed her as much as Pat does. I don't think God loves any of us.' And she tore away, but the fight was almost gone from her, Mr Bailey could see.

'Do you know there is a creature which exists only to worm through children's eyes and blind them?'

Alice, face pink with tears, turned to him, astonished. 'And God made that?'

'Oh Alice. All he can do is pick us up and carry us.'

Alice didn't reply. She reached towards him and kissed his cheek.

As they walked back from the wedding, snow began to fall again in great square flakes. It came down silently, softly and wrapped the village in white.

Zeb stoked up the fire and the little boy sat on Mr Bailey's knee as he told him a story.

'Once upon a time,' he said, 'there was an enormous turnip. The grandfather of the family grew this turnip, and it was so big that he couldn't pull it out of the ground.'

Frederick closed his eyes as Mr Bailey went on with the story, of the grandmother helping and then the children and the family dog and the family cat, and in the end, of course, it was only when the smallest and weakest member of the family, the mouse, who of course was called Frederick, came and helped, that the enormous turnip came out of the ground. Then they chopped it up and invited the whole village, including all the animals, to eat with them, and they cooked it in a hundred pans and when it was soft they mashed it with lots of butter and salt and pepper and then they ate it with their Easter dinner.

The little boy looked up when the end of the story arrived. 'Are we having turnip?' he said.

And Alice assured him that they were, and that if he came and helped her they would mash it up together and put lots of butter in it. And salt. And pepper.

Fifty-Eight

'Harry has had his birthday,' Mary wrote. As though I would have forgotten it, Cate thought. She looked up from her desk and out across her domain, and to her surprise she found that she was happy. It was true she missed her son every day, but she could see the big gardens from where she sat in her library and she was learning to love this place now that she had made it hers.

Her parents had not exactly ceased to exist, but she had ceased to love them. They lived in the same house, but it was hers. Her mother never contradicted the orders she gave, and Cate thought she was glad that she didn't have to do anything. She would go out to tea with friends and fuss in the garden and make desultory conversation about the people she met and the things she did.

Cate had become too kind to snub her and would listen patiently about other people's married daughters and other people's grandchildren. Her mother never mentioned Harry; her parents had accepted easily that he was dead and she did not deceive herself. Her child had been born out of wedlock and they would not cease to be ashamed of her and of him.

In a sense they might have been pleased or at least relieved that the child had died.

In fact, the child was now on his feet. Mary sent an account of him pulling himself up on the nearest piece of furniture, which had been a stout dining room chair, and of how he was into everything and would spend hours with the nursery nurse holding both his hands as he took solid steps across the floors.

It was a source of amusement to Cate that Mary had acquired servants and seemed happy with them. Having been a servant before, she was no doubt aware of what their lives were like and hopefully treated them better because of it.

Cate lived vicariously through Mary, and treasured every detail of the life that she and Mary were able to give her precious son. She did not dream of the day when he might come home. She was glad to give them freedom and a new world, and hoped that he might prosper there. She was envious of Mary, it was true, but she liked Mary so much that she could not feel like that for long. She would always owe her life and that of her child to the dearest friend that she had ever known.

Mary told Cate how she read the child to sleep every night and how he looked like both his parents. Mary must know that Cate had loved Henry, she could not help herself, so she was glad that her boy looked like him, but also that he was like her in so many ways.

She didn't long to marry and have other children. She was enjoying her power too much, and she feared that men would try to take her freedom. She would not let them do that now.

Neither did Mary ever talk about marriage, and as an apparently rich widow with a child she must be eligible. Cate thought that her father and the disgusting Ned King had put her off. Perhaps in the future things would be different. Or would she always shy away from contact, having been so very badly burned?

Cate looked up as she heard a noise, and there was Charles, smiling at her as he came to the library door. He was always admitted readily since they were now friends. She did not feel he threatened her any more. She still wished that he would marry, but that too seemed less and less likely. She hadn't seen him in several weeks.

'Why don't we take the horses to the river?' he suggested.

'I'm busy, Charles.'

'You're always busy. Come on. It's a mild day – we don't get many of those. It's bound to rain tomorrow. Just a couple of hours.'

He was right, she thought. He had learned to stay at the distance he had been put, but now and again he made a simple request. Since they ran estates and she thought he had a good head on him and was sensible, she could ask him anything. He would ask her about various problems and she had grown to appreciate the things they had in common. She was prepared to settle for that, as was he, she thought.

She put down the letter from Mary. She had read it three times and by the end of the week would know off by heart what was happening in Halifax, from the friends Mary was making to how the garden was and how the summer would be. Mary was settled there and Cate envisaged the little boy happy and on his feet in that land that was so far away from her. She went out to the stables, chatting with Charles as they walked.

Fifty-Nine

Nell didn't know what to do. She couldn't settle to anything. Dan had not offered to bring the child to see her, whether from tact or because he didn't want the boy there she didn't know. Half of her was glad of it and half of her felt guilty, and another half of her was sad and that was too many halves, she thought, sighing hugely.

The weather was so fair that she resented it. She felt as though it would improve her mood if it rained, but it was stubbornly beautiful every morning when she looked out of her window. That Shirley McFadden was dead was her first thought each day. She had caused Shirley to die and there was no getting away from it.

She missed the little boy, in a way, but she did not miss how he so obviously disliked her, or how he had howled and cried and screamed for Shirley. How she wished that she had let him go.

There was an enormous hollow where day-to-day living had been. She had thought she had been getting a grip on normalcy, with her new husband, a new home and hopefully some kind of interesting future, but now all that seemed stupid and unimportant. She wanted to go to Pat McFadden and apologize, but she couldn't think what she might say once she got there. Shirley would not be there, and she didn't know where the little boy was. She couldn't bear the thought.

She thought that Pat must hate her, and possibly himself, too, for taking the child from Shirley. The boy had obviously been better with her than away, but it had not been obvious at the time.

She tried to go about her daily tasks and found each one impossible to achieve. She was so tired that she thought she might never be pleased or excited about anything again.

At first, Sawrey and Augusta went on as usual, and she didn't really notice any difference until one morning about three weeks after Shirley's death, when she found Augusta setting tea down beside where Nell had fallen asleep from sheer exhaustion some time earlier. She was on the sofa. She didn't sleep any more, what with the horrible guilt and despair, and so she didn't think about it for a second when the cup and saucer arrived quite smoothly on the table beside the sofa.

She gazed at Augusta as though she had never seen her before. Augusta sat down beside her and stroked her face, just as she might have done with a kitten. 'Poor you. How are you feeling?' she said, as though Nell had been ill.

'I'm – I'm fine,' Nell stuttered, sitting up, and then Augusta put the cup and saucer into Nell's hands.

'Sawrey and I are worried about you. You did the best you could.'

Nell was astonished. Augusta had never in her life understood anyone else's problems. Nell had assumed she was just not up to it, and that she would go on and on in the self-absorbed way she had, but Augusta was changing.

'I didn't understand,' Nell said. 'I made a mess of it.'

Augusta smiled now sympathetically. 'But there are lots of things you got right. You can't get everything right. Sawrey has bought you a present.'

Nell was astonished again. Sawrey had bought nothing in all the time they had been married, though Nell had said to him any number of times that he was free to do so. The bills came to her and she paid them, but it was his money too. He never bought so much as an ounce of sweets.

'It's outside,' Augusta said, and got up.

Nell swallowed a mouthful of tea and found it was just as she liked it. Then she followed Augusta outside to where the stables had been built. There was nothing in them other than the two horses that pulled the pony cart. Nell didn't want to think about that, but they went further on and found Sawrey standing outside a stable. He gestured and Nell gazed inside to see that there was a new horse.

'It's a dales pony,' he said, 'just about the right size for you, you being so little.'

'But – but I don't know how to ride and – and I'm old.'

'This pony is very good. I bought it specially so you could learn to ride. And I bought a horse for me, he's across the yard, and I'm going to teach you. I thought you might let Augusta try too, because if she likes it – and she was a very good rider as a little girl, you know – we could buy another and we could all go out together. There's nothing in the world quite as good as riding a pony.'

'Shall I tell you what the pony is called?' Augusta said, materializing beside them. 'She's called Peggy Sue.'

Nell gazed at the animal, awestruck and somehow pleased. 'It's a very good name,' she said.

'Would you like to try her?' Sawrey said.

Nell wanted to refuse, to tell him that she was too tired, too grieved, too old, too cowardly, but somehow she couldn't. And so she was shortly on a horse for the first time in her life. It seemed such a long way down. Sawrey stood by the horse's head and led her down the lane, and Augusta went with them.

It had not occurred to Nell that seeing the land from a pony was quite different. It looked new and fresh and it was a lovely day. Peggy Sue moved so rhythmically, and she smelled of warmth and of hay. They went all the way down the track that led to the main road before turning back. When she came to get down, her legs ached and so Sawrey lifted her down into his arms. As she got level with his face he kissed her.

'Now come on, Nell,' he said. 'We're going to get into the pony cart and go to the village.'

Nell wanted to say that she couldn't, that she might never do such a thing again, but she didn't. She and Sawrey got into the trap and he drove the pony down the hill where Shirley had died, into the village and from there towards Frosterley. Nothing happened, nobody got hurt, nobody in the village stopped and stared and said, 'That woman killed Shirley McFadden.' Nell felt as though she had survived something awful. She had survived it, and now she would have to learn to live with it.

When they got home, the groom took the pony and trap and Sawrey urged Nell in for lunch.

'Do you remember when you first came here and you were so kind to Gussie and me?' he said. 'Well, we are going to be kind to you now, because you've given us a good life.' And he tucked her hand through his arm and took her inside.

Whatever else she had done, whatever she had made a mess of in her life – and she did not acquit herself easily – this was something she had achieved. She had enriched the lives of these two people she had come to love, and they had banished loneliness from hers.

People who had never lived by themselves had no idea what silence was really like. Nobody should have to live alone; it was too hard. Now she had a family and some kind of a future, and for a woman who had been through so much, that was a great deal. Loneliness was gone and she had finally come home.

The Quarryman's Wife

Elizabeth Gill

Torn between love and duty . . .

When Vinia walked down the aisle she knew it was a marriage of practicality: as the owner of the local pit, Joe could provide her with a life of status. But her heart lies with another . . .

With gypsy blood in his veins and an intense passion in his soul, Dryden has always held a torch for Vinia. And with the death of his wife, he vows to make good on the lost years when they were apart.

Will Vinia find a new chance of happiness or be forever destined to a loveless marriage?

Quercus

Orphan Boy

Elizabeth Gill

He has no home to call his own.

Born to a mother who died in childbirth, and to a father who could never truly love him, Niall McAndrew grows up a solitary child, without a home to call his own. His only friend is Bridget, a young girl forced prematurely into womanhood. Niall has brains, spirit and ambition, as well as devastating good looks. He soon begins to make his own way in business, and becomes famous throughout the Newcastle area by befriending the wealthy and powerful mine-owner Aulay Redpath and his beautiful daughter Caitlin.

But Niall's loveless childhood has left its mark. Can he ever find the personal happiness he yearns for?

Quercus